"The drama [is] so harrowing you'll be looking for a life vest before the last wave drenches you . . . [A] smashing maritime adventure."

—*Mystery Scene*

"Stabenow's descriptions of the ensuing duel at sea . . . make for edge-of-seat stuff . . . And the creepy, authentic-sounding terrorist scenario will make readers sit up and take notice of a state that some Americans forget is actually there."

—*Booklist*

"Excellent."

—*Publishers Weekly* (starred review)

"*Blindfold Game,* like its predecessors, can be read on two levels—as a cleverly executed thriller with an intriguing protagonist, or as a fascinating exploration of an exotic society with its own unique culture. Either way, you can't lose."

—*San Diego Union-Tribune*

. . . AND MORE PRAISE FOR
New York Times BESTSELLING AUTHOR
DANA STABENOW

"Stabenow's . . . books are always welcome for their Alaskan scenes and their true-to-life characters."

—*Rocky Mountain News*

"Dana Stabenow excels at evoking the bleakness and beauty of the far north."

—*Seattle Times/Post Intelligencer*

MORE . . .

A GRAVE DENIED

"Stabenow is a fine storyteller, but it is her passion for the Alaskan landscape and the iconoclastic people who inhabit it that fires this series and lifts this latest entry to its pinnacle."

—*Publishers Weekly* (starred review)

"The skillful Ms. Stabenow has created a believable, well-defined character in Kate and placed her in a setting so beautiful that the crimes she investigates seems almost sacrilegious ... this is Ms. Stabenow's 13th Kate Shugak novel, and they just get better and better."

—*Dallas Morning News*

"A gifted few are able to employ the setting as something more, an ingredient that adds texture and tone and lifts the story out of the commonplace and into the rare ... to these, add Dana Stabenow ... [a] splendid evocation of the Alaskan landscape."

—*San Diego Union-Tribune*

"The characters literally come alive to bring you into this fast-paced thriller, which will keep you turning the pages of this high-voltage mystery."

—*Rendezvous*

A FINE AND BITTER SNOW

"Among the series' best."

—*Booklist*

"Rich with details about life in this snowbound culture, the story moves at a steady pace to a classic ending."

—*Publishers Weekly* (starred review)

"Stabenow uses the merciless magnificence of her state to create a stunning backdrop for her intense and intelligent mysteries."

—*St. Petersburg Times*

BLINDFOLD
GAME
Dana Stabenow

St. Martin's Paperbacks

BLINDFOLD GAME

Copyright © 2006 by Dana Stabenow.
Excerpt from *A Deeper Sleep* © 2006 by Dana Stabenow.

Cover photo of water © Lowell Georgia/Corbis. Photo of radar signal © Sanford/Agliolo/Corbis.

Library of Congress Catalog Card Number: 2005049775

ISBN: 0-312-93755-5
EAN: 9780312-93755-3

Printed in the United States of America

St. Martin's Press hardcover edition / January 2006
St. Martin's Paperbacks edition / December 2006

St. Martin's Paperbacks are published by St. Martin's Press, 175 Fifth Avenue, New York, NY 10010.

10 9 8 7 6 5 4 3 2 1

For Catherine Ann Stevens
(she knows why)
(oh, all right, maybe a little for Ted, too)

Offshore where sea and skyline blend
  In rain, the daylight dies;
The sullen, shouldering swells attend
  Night and our sacrifice.
Adown the stricken capes no flare—
  No mark on spit or bar,—
Girdled and desperate we dare
  The blindfold game of war.

—RUDYARD KIPLING, "THE DESTROYERS"

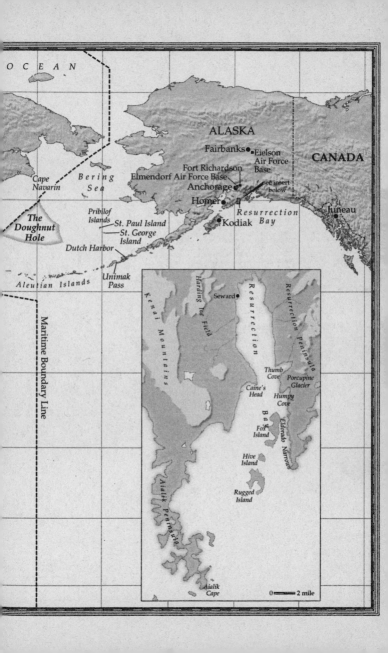

1

october 5, 2004
pattaya beach, thailand

MUCH LATER, WHEN THE glass had stopped flying and the screams of pain and fear had died to moans and whimpers and the hoarse rattles of death, when the bodies had been taken to the morgue and the injured to the hospitals, when the television cameras had gone and workers had begun to clear the rubble and business along Central Street began to return to a shaken sort of normal, very few people remembered the two men who had been standing on the corner of Soi Cowboy when the bomb went off.

They were definitely Asian, or so said a vigorous, middle-aged woman who owned a pornographic comic book store nearby. Slim, short, narrow eyes, sallow skin, neatly clipped straight black hair, she remembered them clad in identical short-sleeved shirts and light cotton slacks in nondescript colors. A hundred like them sidled into her tiny shop every day to thumb through her merchandise, avoiding eye contact as they made their purchases.

A young man, the proud owner of his own car who specialized in delivering takeout to the pleasure palaces on Soi Cowboy and whose car had been parked twenty feet from the Fun House when the explosion occurred, had been blown backward the entire length of the block. He had landed hard on his back at the feet of the two Asian men, splattered with nine orders of pad thai and the brains of a twenty-year-old American marine on leave from Camp Butler on Okinawa. As he looked up at them, a man's leg hit the side of the Pattaya Inn just above their heads, and what the delivery man found most odd was that the two men hadn't looked at the leg, or even at him, instead focusing their attention on the chaos that followed the blast.

An elderly Japanese tourist, seeking relief from his shrew of a wife in Nagasaki in the fleshpots of a resort known for its willingness to provide pretty much anything animal, vegetable, or mineral in the way of entertainment, was sure the two men he had hobbled hurriedly by were Korean, because he'd killed his share in World War II and he ought to know.

At the end of the day the body count had climbed to one hundred and fourteen dead and another two hundred injured. At least half of these were Thai nationals, many of them dancers and prostitutes, sex shop owners, and bartenders. They merited little beyond the standard obligatory protestations of outrage and vows of retaliation from the nation's capital, quickly spoken and as quickly forgotten.

The other half was another matter. Seventeen American servicemen were dead, twenty-two more injured. Eleven Australians, four New Zealanders, nine Germans, and one Frenchman would never see home again. It was the Japanese tourists who were hit hardest, although it would take a month before all the body parts had been assembled, DNA matches made. The count would stop at thirty-one.

In the following days the world waited for someone to take responsibility for the bomb. After all, that's why these things happened, one man's terrorist or another man's revolutionary set off a bomb on a bus in Jerusalem or on a U.S. destroyer in Aden or outside a federal building in Oklahoma City because he wanted attention, the bright lights of the television camera aimed squarely at his cause. Yasir Arafat would have been just another old man in a galabia spouting anti-Israeli rhetoric without the photogenic properties of the suicide bombers and their residue in Gaza and on the West Bank. So the world waited, for al-Qaida or Hizballah or the IRA or FARC or the Basque Fatherland to step up and declare another victory in the war against first world aggression, Western decadence, and the free-market economy. Or perhaps the hostility was directed against the insidious creep of the Big Mac or the pervasiveness of Steven Seagal movies, either of which a lot of Westerners would have found more logical than the first three as a cause worthy of riot in the streets.

None of these organizations had set the bomb, however, or at least none of them took credit for it. A guy did go into Roy's Bar in Wallace, Idaho, ten days after the event and started bragging about how he'd just come back from putting a bunch of gooks into body bags. It turned out that he was the founder of White World, which couldn't exactly be called a white supremacist group as he was the sole member, and the closest he'd ever been to Thailand was the International District bus stop in Seattle on his way to an Aryan Nations meeting in Aurora. The bar patrons hadn't left a lot for the police to scrape up off the floor anyway. Not that they'd hurried to the scene when they got the call.

But in Pattaya, the comic shop woman and the delivery boy and the Japanese tourist remembered the two men standing so calmly in the middle of so much death and destruction, and wondered.

They would have wondered even more if they'd seen the two men turn and walk away, down Central Street, maintaining an even, unhurried pace, ignoring the wailing sirens and the flashing lights streaking past them toward the steadily mounting rumble of disbelief and horror.

A middle-aged woman, plump and improbably blond, did see them go. She wiped at the trickle of blood on her forehead where a piece of the left taillight from the delivery boy's car had sliced open her skin, replaced her digital camera in a capacious shoulder bag, and steadied her shaking legs to follow.

The two men walked a little over half a mile and turned down a lane that led to the beach. Here all was peace and order, no storefronts destroyed, no blood pooling in the street, no ambulance doors slamming on the dead and the dying. A causeway led to an outdoor cafe on a platform on pilings over the beach and a table in the shade of a large marquee. They ordered chai tea in North American English, but the waiter, an elderly French expatriate who had fled to Thailand after the fall of Saigon, didn't think they were American or Canadian. They looked too much at home, unlike the average Western tourist, who was apt to stare around incredulously as if he'd never seen a third-world country before. These men drank their chai tea without first scrutinizing the rim of the glass for germs. If they hadn't spoken such good English he would have thought they were Korean, the height and broadness of the cheekbones, perhaps. He also thought they might be brothers, but when questioned later he couldn't say why. Did they look alike? Not particularly. One seemed a little older than the other. It was just a feeling he had. One developed certain instincts after thirty years of serving patrons in a Pattaya bar, where sooner or later all the world came to drink.

"A terrible thing, this bombing," he told the two men in a placid voice as he set their drinks on the table. "One lives and works one's whole life expecting these things to happen elsewhere, and then—" He shrugged. "No place is safe nowadays, what with all these terrorists fleeing the American invasion of the Middle East to set their bombs in poor countries like Thailand."

"A terrible thing," the older man said without inflection.

The waiter looked up to see a woman hovering in the doorway with a smear of blood on her forehead, and he bustled forward solicitously. Her weight alone was indication enough of her nationality, and when she ordered a Budweiser it was confirmed beyond all reasonable doubt, but her voice was low and pleasant, a relief. He seated her a table away from the two men, or no, the two had been joined by a third. He would have returned to take the third man's order, but a group of German tourists chose that moment to arrive and push all the tables into one corner together so they wouldn't have to suffer the horror of sitting separately. They chattered excitedly about the bomb, exclaiming how lucky they'd been to have escaped, and peppered the waiter with questions about who could have done such a thing and was Thailand plagued with terrorists, too, and the waiter took innumerable orders for Oolong-Tea-nis and Monkey Faces. Nobody ordered scotch anymore.

By the time he finished serving the Germans, the three men had been joined by a fourth, and he squared Gallic shoulders and marched back to take their orders. His murmured apology for the wait was waved away with a magnanimous hand by one of the newcomers, a younger man clearly of mixed Eastern and Western blood who carried himself with the assurance of one who had been born free in an Asian nation, which meant either Singapore or Hong Kong before the handover. There was some Norwegian or possibly some German mixed into his genetic pot, too. Something Teutonic, at any rate. He wore very good clothes, a loose-weave jacket over a T-shirt and casual slacks. The huaraches were hand-stitched leather and the bright red handkerchief peeping out of his jacket pocket was raw silk, probably also hand-stitched. The man smiled at him, a charming, slightly crooked smile, reminding the waiter of a photograph he had seen of a young Elvis Presley. He sighed a little.

The fourth man was Chinese, older, and there was nothing to sigh over about him. His skin was burned a dark reddish brown from years in the sun, his narrow eyes made narrower by folds of enveloping wrinkles, his hands calloused and hard, his arms roped with muscle. He looked like a street fighter, an impression underlined by the scar that bisected his left eyebrow and a nose that had been either so thoroughly or so repeatedly broken that its bridge was almost flat against his cheekbones. A puckered scar showed briefly beneath the short sleeve of his shirt. A puncture wound of some kind, a knife perhaps? A bullet, more likely.

The Chinese saw the waiter looking and returned a flat, unblinking stare. There was something reptilian in that stare, without fear or feeling. For all his experience and sangfroid, the waiter had to make a conscious effort not to take a step back. He had to clear his throat before he could summon enough voice to ask them what they wanted. The younger man ordered Tiger Beer. The Chinese ordered green tea. The waiter left, more quickly than he had arrived, and regained his manhood by bullying a British couple into a table in a high-traffic area right next to the bar, and forcing them to order the bamboo martinis instead of the lager they had come in for.

The Singaporean pulled out a cell phone and placed it in the center of the table. The Chinese lit a cigarette from the end of the one he already had going.

The phone rang. The older Korean picked it up.

A pleasant voice speaking fluent English with a thick East European accent said, "Mr. Smith?"

"Yes."

"Your Chinese guest is Mr. Fang. He holds a master's certificate, has thirty years' experience at sea, and will be responsible for putting together the crew and acquiring and operating the vessel. We have the highest confidence in his abilities."

"Yes," Mr. Smith said.

"The Singaporean is Mr. Noortman. In your initial contact with us, you stressed the need for someone who specialized in cargo."

"Yes."

"Mr. Noortman is, quite simply, a genius with international maritime shipping. He is also a full partner in Mr. Fang's concern."

"Yes."

"Your fee was posted to our account in Geneva this morning. I believe this concludes our transaction. It has been a pleasure doing business with you. If you need help in finding the appropriate personnel for future ventures, please don't hesitate to contact us."

"Thank you." The older Korean disconnected and put the phone in his pocket. "English?" he said, looking at Fang.

Fang inclined his head, as did Noortman.

The older Korean's smile was noticeably lacking in either friendliness or humor. "My name is Smith." He indicated the younger Korean. "This is Jones."

Fang said, "I am told you need a ship."

"Yes," Smith said. "A ship of a specific kind."

Fang suppressed a yawn. "How big?"

Smith slid a piece of paper across the table.

Fang read it and looked less bored. "This is . . . an unusual request."

Smith said nothing.

Fang passed the slip of paper to Noortman. Noortman's eyebrows went up and he exchanged a glance with Fang. Fang said, "Did you have a particular port in mind?"

"Petropavlovsk-Kamchatsky."

Fang was impressed, and not favorably. "It will be expensive," he said at last.

"The monies were deposited to your account this morning."

"You seem to be extraordinarily well funded."

Smith smiled again. "There is always money available to pursue the cause of righteousness."

Fang meditated on this for a moment. The money was already in their account. And it was a large sum, enough, he decided, to quash his misgivings. "A crew of fifteen should be adequate."

"We will not be boarding in the usual fashion. A crew of five, enough to operate the ship, will do. I and my men will provide any additional help that will be required."

Fang shoved his glass to one side and leaned forward. "I don't work with amateurs."

A siren wailed in the distance and set the German table buzzing again with exclamations and murmurs. The plump woman produced a tiny digital camera from her handbag and asked the waiter to take her photograph, and then several more, just to be sure. With an air of infinite patience he complied and then at her request brought her another Budweiser.

"We're not amateurs," Jones said, speaking for the first time.

Fang's lips tightened. "How are we boarding?"

Smith looked at Noortman. "I'm told you're a genius in international maritime shipping."

Noortman displayed no false modesty. "Yes."

"You'll need to be." Smith told him why.

Beyond a slight widening of the eyes Noortman did not seem overly intimidated. Fang looked as if he wanted to leave the table, but he thought of the deposit and stayed where he was. "How long will we have to be inside?"

"That depends on how good your colleague really is."

"And after your cargo has been delivered?" Fang said, hesitating only slightly between the last two words.

"Provision has been made for the crew to leave the scene in a safe and timely fashion." Smith's smile was brief and thin. "The plans will of course be ready for you to preview prior to our departure."

Noortman, if anything, might have been excited by the challenge presented to him. "I will find you a ship that best suits your purposes, Mr. Smith, and determine how and where it stows its cargo. There is also the port. I'll need to study ship traffic and to monitor cargo movement onshore and off." He paused. "If all goes well, I should have a candidate and a plan of action for you to approve in two or three months. Possibly less. Possibly more. One must always allow for weather."

"Three months," Smith said. His face was so expressionless that it was difficult to tell if he was happy with Noortman's estimate.

"And," Noortman said, "it will, as Mr. Fang has told you, be very expensive indeed."

"But it can be done."

Noortman smiled widely. A gold tooth flashed from

the right side of his mouth, and it was altogether a very different smile than Smith's. "If you have enough money there is nothing and nowhere I can't ship any cargo you care to name."

Smith nodded. "I see. Very well. We are agreed. Mr. Jones and I have an appointment elsewhere." He rose to his feet, Jones rising with him.

"Did you have a date of departure in mind?" Fang said.

Smith's stare reproved Fang's sarcasm. "Proceed with your preparations immediately. I wish to be operational by the fifteenth of January."

"You're not giving us a lot of time," Fang said.

"But we are paying you a great deal of money," Smith said gently. He saw no need to explain that the longer it took to put an action like this one in motion, the more susceptible it was of discovery by the authorities. Even the most inept government agent was liable to stumble across one of the many threads that would go into making the rope by which Smith meant to hang his target out to dry.

Fang looked at Noortman, whose dark eyes were snapping with excitement. "All right," Fang said at last. "We're in."

"I will need a contact number," Noortman said.

"We will call you," Smith said.

Noortman spread his hands. "If there are difficulties—"

"Solve them," Smith said.

Noortman inclined his head. "As you wish."

OUTSIDE THE CAFE SMITH slammed the cell phone against a cement wall and tossed the resulting pieces into a series of trash cans they passed on their way to the street. They hailed a motorcycle taxi, whose driver chattered enthusiastically about the bombing and offered to drive them right up to the front of the Fun House, or what was left of it. Smith and Jones declined. Aggrieved but resigned at this lack of interest, the driver picked a slow but steady path through the emergency vehicles and the rubble and delivered them to the Pattaya AirCon Bus Station on North Pattaya Road.

The bus to Bangkok took three hours. In Bangkok, they bought round-trip coach tickets on a British Airways flight for London that left at twenty minutes past midnight, from a small travel agent on a side street using credit cards under the names of Smith and Jones. The agent was grateful for the revenue and took no notice of the shiny new cards or the incongruous names.

In a department store large enough to provide anonymity they purchased a small suitcase for each of them with cash, and filled the suitcases with a few garments from a different store and toiletries from a drugstore two blocks away, because people traveling with no luggage aroused suspicion in this untrusting age. They checked in, correctly for an international flight, three hours before departure, attired in neat suits and ties and shoes polished to a high gleam, and suffered through the minor indignities inflicted upon them by the security and customs personnel. They were passed through without incident.

The plane departed the gate precisely on schedule. As they lifted off the end of the runway, Jones turned to Smith and said, "Why?"

"Because we were there," Smith said. "And because we could."

2

heathrow
october 6, 2004

SMITH AND JONES ARRIVED in London at
6:30 A.M. Greenwich time, ten minutes ahead of
schedule and seven hours before their next flight,
time enough for a proper breakfast and to read the ac-
counts of the bombing in the London newspapers. One of
the stories had the Tamil separatist movement claiming
responsibility, but general editorial feeling was that this
was mere braggadocio. The *Times* deplored the exporta-
tion of terror to tourist communities, beginning with the
attack on the *Achille Lauro,* continuing with the bombing
of the bar in Bali, and now this outrage. They were careful to call the target a nightclub and not a whorehouse.
The *Guardian* had discovered a minor Welsh poet among
the dead and had devoted quite half of their obituary page
to him, paying graceful homage to a body of work they
had not deigned to recognize during the author's lifetime.
On its front page the *Mirror* had a photograph of the head
of a bar girl lying six feet from its body. Her lipstick
wasn't even smudged.

They boarded a plane for Moscow at thirty-five minutes past one, which was where the plump blond woman from the cafe in Pattaya Beach lost them. They arrived at Sheremetyevo Airport at half past eight in the evening. They checked into a hotel for the night, slept soundly, and boarded yet another airplane the following morning for Odessa. The taxi driver, a thin adolescent with a chin that was trying hard for the unshaven look and blond hair that looked as if it had been shorn, shredded, and glued back, heard the address he was given with a professionally bored look and delivered Smith and Jones to a nondescript office building near the top of the Potemkin Steps. They took a very slow elevator to the seventh floor, where they were met by a young, beautiful, and exquisitely dressed brunette who escorted them into a small but luxuriously appointed meeting room with windows giving a sweeping view of the port of Odessa and the Black Sea. The docks were crowded with oil tankers, bulk carriers, containerships, and tramp freighters of every make and tonnage, flying flags from all nations, although it was sometimes difficult to see those flags through the forest of cranes working to load and unload cargo.

They were asked what they wished for in the way of refreshment. Tea, please, they said. Smith went to the window while it was being fetched. Jones joined him. They stood, contemplating the vista spread out before them.

"For the first time, I think perhaps it might be done," Jones said.

"It will be done," Smith said.

The door opened and a tall, big-bellied man with a baby face and pale, thinning hair cut so close to the scalp he looked fashionably bald came into the room. His gray wool suit was exquisitely tailored. Beneath it he was lavishly scented. A watch and rings shone from wrist and fingers, discreetly, it must be said, but with the gleam of true gold and the flash of real diamonds none-theless.

He walked forward with a bouncy step and clasped Smith's hand between both of his. "My friend, my friend, it has been so long since we has met. Come, sit, eat, drink." He waved forward another man carrying a tray, dismissed him, and proceeded to fill the cups himself. "A little sugar, eh? Ah, you see, I remembers! Peter his friends forget never!" He handed out cups.

They were made of fine, thin china decorated with delicate sprays of pink flowers. Smith and Jones held them awkwardly while the Russian emptied his with noisy enjoyment. "There!" he said, banging his cup down in its saucer with a movement that should have shattered it. "You may has your coffee, pah, a harsh drink accurate for peasants and Americans. For gentlemen only the tea is." He bent a shrewd gaze on Smith. "The last shipment is pleasant?"

Peter was fearless in his use of the English language, if not quite as fluent as he thought he was, but Smith knew what he meant. "Perfectly," Smith said.

"Again and yet here are you. This time what for you I do, my friend, my very old friend? What has the inventory of Peter which can excite a customer so nice in his testes?"

Smith told him.

Peter shrugged. "Easily available. I have associations in Russia, in Libya, in Afghanistan—"

"I would prefer North Korea."

Peter made a face. "That will be the more tricky, yes?"

"And the more expensive?" Smith said. "It does not matter."

However odd Peter thought this request, he didn't earn his fees by letting it show on his face. He made an odd little bow and spoke in a hollow, echoing lisp. "By your command." Peter, unfortunately, was a devotee of *Battlestar Galactica.* He had all the episodes on a set of bootleg VHS tapes, with which he had bored a series of nubile companions who were intelligent enough to pretend an interest in Cylon tyranny for as long as they enjoyed Peter's support.

Peter laughed heartily at his own joke until he saw that Smith and Jones did not share in his amusement. "Ah well," he said philosophically, and with a flourish worthy of a professional magician produced a gold-monogrammed handkerchief to mop a sweaty brow. "A telephone call, minutely. I know a general—ah, ah!" He wagged a mischievous finger back and forth. "I must not to reveal my sources, even to such an old friend as you, or there will be no need for Peter's services!" He laughed again.

He stopped laughing when Smith told him what else he wanted. "My friend, my old friend," Peter said, looking very grave and shaking his head. He even paused to get his grammar in order. "This thing will be very difficult and very dangerous to aspire, and even more bad to transport. Such things are guards by incomplete companies of soldiers. A nations of them, almost." He cocked his head. "And even for me, Peter the Wolf, it will be expansive. Very, very expansive indeed."

"Call your bank," Smith said.

Peter's eyebrows shot up in less than genuine surprise. He produced a cell phone and dialed a number. A voice answered. He asked a question, waited for a reply, and disconnected. He looked across at Jones and said, "Do you know who besides you sits, young man? A sorcerer! He makes numbers in my account doubles overnight!" He turned again to Smith. "Where?"

Smith told him.

Peter stroked his chin. "Hmm. Yes, I supposed it could be done. But—"

"It will be expensive," Smith said. "I know. Will the amount cover it?"

"When?" Peter said.

Smith gave him the same answer he had given Fang. "I wish to be operational by January fifteenth."

"Where please to ship?"

"Petropavlovsk."

Peter spread his hands. "I see no problems."

"Then let us proceed," Smith said.

"By your command," said Peter again, rising to his feet and bowing. "It is, as always, a pleasure giving you the business, my old friend. Dmitri! Call the guests for our car." He looked back at Smith. "Will you to stay the night?"

Smith shook his head. "Thank you, but no. We have another appointment elsewhere."

Peter sighed, spread his hands in eloquent dismay, and said to Dmitri, "And take them to the airport."

The door closed behind them and Peter's smile vanished. He pulled out his phone again and dialed a number. A recorded message played, and he punched in a code. A voice said, "Yes?"

Without identifying himself he said, "I have had an unusual order."

"Four o'clock." The voice hung up.

Peter disconnected, and regarded the phone thoughtfully. Even if the call had been traced, the conversation had been so brief and so cryptic that nothing could be made of it.

Still. Better men than he had been tripped up by hanging on to the same cell phone for too long. Those Americans and their damned satellite technology. Their ingenuity was admirable but their nosiness was not. It was getting harder by the day to make an honest living.

He went to the window, opened it, and let the cell phone fall seven stories to the alley below where it shattered into a thousand pieces. "Masha, my little dove!" he said, raising his voice.

The door opened and the beautiful young brunette looked in. "Yes, Peter?"

"Get our coats. We are going out."

AT FOUR O'CLOCK PETER was at the railway station, guidebook in hand, face raised to admire the dome and point out its highlights to the young brunette who hung on his arm and his every word.

"Truly magnificent," a voice said at his elbow. It was the voice from the phone, only this time it was speaking a flawless and idiomatic Russian with the barest hint of Romanov in it. Peter turned to greet him, beaming.

"But yes, magnificent," Peter said enthusiastically in the same language. "An architectural marvel, and yet a working building in the heart of our beautiful city!"

"The archways over the stairs have always reminded me of a Moorish castle."

Peter beamed at his new friend. "But yes, how clever of you to notice!" There followed an exchange on the Islamic influence on that part of the world. Suleyman the Magnificent was mentioned, as were his mosques, his contemporary Leonardo da Vinci, and his wife Roxelana, the latter with some eloquent eye rolling. At last Peter said, "But this is dry work. Masha, my sweet, could you find us some coffee?" He turned to the man. "And for you as well, sir?"

"I couldn't possibly trespass on your hospitality, sir."

"Nonsense! Coffee for three, Masha, my little dove."

The girl moved off, clutching the wad of cash Peter had handed her—from which Peter would expect no change, a constant feature of the openhanded generosity which had so endeared him to successive companions—and the two men resumed their adoration of the architecture. They consulted the guidebook frequently, pointing from various passages on the pages to the relevant crown molding, and entered into what anyone listening would have heard as an enthusiastic debate on the relative merits of Doric columns versus Corinthian.

"I see what you mean," the man said. "Oh, thank you, thank you very much, my dear. You are too kind." He accepted the cup from Masha, contriving to capture her hand and press a clumsy kiss to the back of it.

Masha's eyes fluttered, and if she didn't actually blush she did manage an up-from-under look through her eyelashes that caused the other gentleman to spill coffee down the front of his coat. He drank what was left, exchanged a few more pleasantries with Peter, kissed Masha's hand a second time with only slightly more panache, and took himself off.

"You are a vamp, my little Masha," Peter said, laughing. "Your flirting frightened the gentleman."

The girl opened her eyes very wide. "But no, Peter, I was not flirting with him! I was merely being polite!"

He hugged her and kissed her, and then kissed her again. "I adore you, my Masha! Shall we go home?"

Masha, who had been standing on a marble floor in four-inch heels for over an hour, agreed, even if it did mean another interminable evening with Apollo and Starbuck. At least in Peter's apartment the vodka was Stoli, the caviar was beluga, and the bed, when Peter eventually let one sleep, was a Verlo Heritage Limited, specially imported.

3

HUGH'S TEMPER WAS NOT improved by the sight of his overflowing mailbox or by the stack of message slips held down on his desk by the soapstone bear paperweight. The bear had been a gift from Sara the last Christmas they were in high school together. He wanted to pick it up and heave it through the window.

He didn't, of course, but sitting on the impulse just pissed him off more.

There had, in fact, been no moment during which he had not been thoroughly pissed off since he woke up alone in his Anchorage hotel room yesterday morning. His admin assistant had taken one look at his face as he came in the door this morning and speech had withered on her tongue. He took a deep breath and let it out, uncapped his vente quadruple shot americano, took a big swallow to get his heart started, and began wading through the mess.

There was the usual assortment of pleas for help from agents and informers in the field, from Tokyo to Taiwan to Ho Chi Minh City to Shanghai to Bangkok to Singapore to Calcutta. They wanted to pay off a source, they needed to verify intelligence, they had had to bribe a local official for a satellite uplink. The official had discovered who he was really dealing with and had doubled the already astronomical price. Hugh was in no mood to be generous with the hard-earned tax dollars of the American citizen this morning, and he rejected all but one request out of hand.

A high-ranking Pakistani military officer had made an oblique approach to a junior officer of the American embassy at a cocktail party in Karachi, and the consul had handed the contact off to the case officer in Delhi, who had confirmed the identity of the officer in question and was recommending the agency make the officer an offer for his services. A walk-in snitch, Hugh's favorite kind, and he e-mailed the case officer to proceed. There was too damn little in the way of human source intelligence available to the Directorate of Intelligence these days and he was willing to investigate every possible source no matter how unlikely, as these social first contacts too often proved to be. There were a dozen open cases that needed monitoring, some that needed orders issued for further action, and one that needed closing because the source had disappeared, which meant he had probably been discovered, which meant that he was either dead or in the wind. The intel the source had produced had bordered on hearsay and speculation, but he'd been on the payroll for six years, during which time he'd come up with maybe three really useful pieces of information, one concerning the sale of CBRN weapons components to North Korea, and the case officer in Shanghai had thought they ought to do something for the family. Hugh almost rejected this request, too, until he realized he was in no frame of mind to be making this kind of decision. He e-mailed the man in

Shanghai and told him to do what he thought appropriate within budgetary constraints.

The phone rang. He snatched it up. "What?"

The voice on the other end said, "Sadly, that does not sound like the voice of someone who just got laid."

Hugh's grip tightened on the receiver. "I'm busy, Kyle. What do you want?"

There was a brief silence. "Okay, let's start over. This is Kyle Chase, your oldest, bestest friend from when you were in diapers. Lilah and the kids are fine, thanks."

No way was Hugh going to let Kyle lay any guilt on him. "I know that, I played horse with Eli and crazy eights with Gloria this weekend, not to mention ate large of Lilah's pot roast."

"It was my pot roast, actually. Lilah can't cook worth a damn. Only bad thing I can say about her."

Hugh didn't say anything.

Kyle sighed. "So, did you miss her? I didn't think her trial had finished up when I sent you over there."

"It hadn't. She was finishing up her testimony when I walked in."

Kyle's voice brightened. "So you did see her?"

Hugh hesitated.

"I knew it, I knew all you had to do was see each other and you'd both be toast. So tell me all about it and, please, don't omit one shocking or salacious detail. I'm here for you, buddy. Go ahead. Share."

Some of the tension went out of Hugh's shoulders at Kyle's determinedly sophomoric banter, and he swiveled to put his feet up on the desk and stare out the window at the aspens crowding the edge of the perfectly manicured lawn. "She had a room. We went back there. I spent the night. Next morning when I woke up, she was déjà vu." The sheets hadn't even been warm next to him.

A long silence, and then a respectful whistle. "Man. I gotta hand it to her, that's really cold."

Hugh half smiled. "You don't have to sound so admiring."

"Yeah, but it's got style, you know? Can't fault our Sara for not making an impact."

"Tell me about it." Hugh paused. "She was happy to see me. She was at first, anyway. I don't know what she was feeling when she woke up."

It sounded like Kyle was rubbing his hand over his face. "How long you been married now, buddy?"

"Ten years. Like you weren't there."

"And how many of those years have you and Sara spent in the same town?"

"Cumulatively? About a year, total."

"How many times you actually answered the same phone when you were home?"

This was cutting to the heart of things with a vengeance. "Twice."

"And that probably includes that sleazy little motel down the road from the academy. Or do I mean that skanky town house in Alexandria when you were going for your doctorate and she was at Georgetown going for her master's? The one where the roaches were bigger than the rats?"

Hugh was counting on his fingers. "No, wait, there was that apartment in D.C. Three times."

A pause, then a sigh. "What I'm saying. You want things to change, start there."

"What about my job?" Hugh said.

"What about hers?" Kyle said. "She always wanted the Coast Guard, ever since we were kids. Hell, she bucked both parents to get into the academy, and you followed right along, even got into Harvard so you'd be in driving distance while you were both in school. Time was you admired her guts and her determination."

"Time was I wasn't married to her."

"And," Kyle said, unheeding, "she was never going to be satisfied with shore duty. You knew going in she was going for her own ship as fast as she could, and you barely got through graduation before you married her anyway."

The silence stretched out. "Hugh?"

Hugh sighed and rubbed his eyes. "Yeah. I knew."

"Besides, it's not like you aren't a fart in a skillet your own damn self, always going three different directions at once in your job."

"Yeah, Kyle, I think I'm going to let you go as my marriage counselor, you're not exactly inspiring me with hope here."

Kyle said simply, "Who else you got?"

Kyle Chase and Hugh Rincon had been two of a trio of friends born in a coastal village in south-central Alaska. The third was Sara Lange. All three of them were children of successful fishermen, and all three of them had been expected to follow in their fathers' footsteps on the decks of their respective family vessels. All three sets of parents had been vastly disappointed, and if a childhood of getting into as much trouble as humanly possible hadn't formed an unbreakable bond, then the joint sufferance of massive parental disapproval certainly had. Hugh laughed shortly. "No one. Apparently."

"Not true. You've got me, and you've got Sara. You'll always have me. Question is, will you always have Sara?"

"I'm not sure I've got her now."

"Be good to find out."

Hugh looked at his desk, piled high. "I've got to get back to work, Kyle."

"Yeah. You might want to think some about that, too."

"Tell Lilah and the kids hi."

"Will do. And Hugh? All you have to do is figure what's more important. Sara? Or your job?"

Kyle hung up, which was all right, because Hugh didn't have an answer for him. His assistant, plump, perky, bright-eyed Marie, stuck her head in the door. "We ordering out for lunch, boss?"

He looked at the clock to discover that four hours had passed. "Oh. I guess."

"The usual?" When he clearly couldn't remember what the usual was she elaborated. "Turkey and cranberry sauce on sourdough, side salad with blue cheese, chips, and a bottle of water."

"Sure."

"Okay." But Marie lingered.

He looked up. "What?"

Marie's look admonished him for his abrupt tone. "Are you going to see her or not? She's been waiting all morning."

"Who's been waiting all morning?"

"Arlene Harte."

Hugh sat up straight. "Arlene's here?"

Marie huffed out an impatient breath. "I left you a note."

Hugh picked up the soapstone bear. The note, stained with coffee, was stuck to the bottom. *Arlene Harte here requesting an audience with His Nibs.* Marie's neat handwriting had even made a note of the date and time, that morning, 7:55 A.M.

"Shit," he said, and got to his feet.

Arlene was sitting in an anonymous anteroom just off of one of Langley's equally anonymous hallways. Hugh had long thought that the idea behind the decor or lack thereof was that if the barbarians ever got inside the gates they would be incapable of finding their way through this much bland to any worthwhile target.

"I'm sorry as hell, Arlene," he said. "I missed seeing your note until now."

She smiled and stood up. "No problem. Finished the Sunday *New York Times* crossword while I was waiting."

He took it from her. "So you did, and in ink at that, you slimeball." They shook hands warmly. "Come on in. Coffee? Tea? Wait a minute." He stuck his head back out the door. "Marie, make that lunch for two."

"Gotcha, boss."

Arlene settled herself in the chair across from his desk. "Thanks for seeing me without an appointment."

"Anytime, Arlene, you know that." He smiled at her. Bad mood or not, he was always very nice to Arlene. A comfortably sized blond in jeans and blazer over a white turtleneck, she looked like someone's youthful grandmother. In truth she was anything but. Retired from the Associated Press after a thirty-year career reporting every global conflict from Vietnam on, she was spending what was commonly referred to as her golden years as a monthly columnist for *Travel + Leisure*. She was unmarried, without children, made her home in a one-bedroom walk-up in Georgetown, and seemed comfortable with the choices she had made in her life. She spoke French to the Paris-born and was famous for never missing three square meals a day in any war zone. It wasn't a bad résumé in the spy biz. "How's the job?"

"They pay me to travel around the world and write about it. What's not to like?"

He laughed. "I want to be you when I grow up."

"So do I."

"What brings you home, Arlene?"

She let her smile fade. "You know I was in Pattaya Beach the day of the bombing, right?"

Hugh looked at her. "Really," he said. "I didn't know, as it happens."

Her mouth tightened. "I was afraid of that. I sent my report in by way of the American embassy in Bangkok. I knew when I didn't hear from you that you'd probably never gotten it. Diplomats." The word was an epithet.

"Squared," Hugh said with feeling.

"That's why I came in when I got back." Without hurrying, Arlene unwedged an envelope from a battered leather bag on a short strap designed to hug her shoulder. Hugh had never seen her without it. He had been curious enough one day to rifle through it when she was out of the room and had excavated a reporter's notebook, her passport, a lone Visa card, a fistful of *Travel + Leisure* business cards imprinted with her name, her office phone number, her cell phone number, her fax number, Marie's phone number, Hugh's phone number, and a Hotmail e-mail address to which Hugh had an icon on his desktop with the password already programmed in. He had just excavated a twelve-pack of Uniball gel pens with medium points when she came back into the room.

"Where's your computer?" he had asked, and she had laughed and told him she had accounts in cybercafes from Bakwanga, Zaire, to Galahad, Alberta. "Cheaper than trying to find a tech when your computer freezes up."

"And a lot harder to trace," Hugh had said. "Why so many pens?"

"Two reasons. One, you can use pens for currency in a lot of third-world countries."

"And?"

"And I might run out of ink."

Marie brought in the sandwiches and drinks. Arlene waited for the door to close behind her before laying out a row of photographs across Hugh's desk. They ranged from clear to indistinct, and once Hugh mentally filtered out the background noise in the way of waiters and drinkers and diners and Arlene, smiling at the camera with her curly hair frizzed into steel wool from what appeared to be a high level of humidity, they featured four men sitting at a table in front of a white sand beach with a strip of blue ocean beyond. He fished a magnifying glass out of a drawer and ran it over their faces. Two of them in particular drew his attention. "Hey?" he said, with a gathering sense of incredulity.

"Which one?" she said.

"The skinny one on the right." He punched up a file on the computer and typed in a name. A mug shot flashed on screen. "Noortman, Jaap Junior."

Arlene gave a satisfied nod. "Our friendly neighborhood international pirate."

"Is—" His voice failed him. Arlene waited, her expression somewhere between expectant and joyous. "Arlene, is Fang the guy sitting on his left?"

She nodded, a grin breaking out. "I wasn't close enough to catch the whole conversation, but I definitely heard Noortman call him Fang."

Hugh dropped the magnifying glass and stared at her with something approaching awe. "Holy shit, Arlene. I don't think we've got a photo of Fang. And we sure as hell don't have one of the two of them together."

"You do now."

Hugh didn't grudge her the satisfaction he heard in her voice. As far as she was concerned she could have retired at full pay on this one photograph alone. He took a self-indulgent moment of his own to congratulate himself once again on being smart enough to hire her.

They'd met three years ago, when Hugh had been seated at Arlene's table at a mandatory second-banana appearance to support the director when he spoke to the National Press Club. From the subsequent conversation Hugh had deduced that writing a travel column wasn't going to keep Arlene interested for very long. He'd asked for her card and called the next day to invite her to lunch at a small Indian restaurant, where she ordered the hottest curry on the menu. Her eyes hadn't even teared up. Hugh had recruited her on the spot. She was one of three in his private stable of informants, all personally recruited and trained and all of whom reported directly to him.

The new big thing in the intelligence community was satellite surveillance, and much was made of the ability to read the license plate of a truck from low earth orbit. Hugh relied upon it himself every day on the job, but when it came right down to it, there simply was no substitute for the human eye, informed, trained for detail, and on the scene. He had chosen his operatives because they were multilingual and already widely traveled, with an inborn predisposition to head straight for trouble and an equally inborn lucky streak that enabled them to get out of it again with minimal damage, to themselves or their nation.

At which time they would call Hugh, or e-mail him, or show up in his waiting room, and his files on the pace of construction of nuclear weapons facilities in Iran or what Russian arms dealer was selling off surplus AK-47s in Bryansk or which Pakistani general was plotting an attack across the Pakistan-Indian border increased by another piece of information. It was almost never a vital piece in and of itself, but each piece fit into a larger puzzle whose growing picture helped him see what was going on in the world beneath the headlines on CNN. In his job he needed to know what was going to happen, not what already had. He was an analyst, a synthesizer, a spider sitting at the center of a web, recording each distant vibration of silk in an effort to predict from what direction the next threat was going to creep.

He laughed at this flight of fancy.

"What?" Arlene said, startled.

"Nothing. Sorry." Fang and Noortman having drinks on a Thai beach with two unidentified Asians was definitely something he needed to know more about. "Go ahead," he said with an encouraging wave. "Tell me the tale."

Arlene folded her hands neatly in her lap and reached back for the memory of that terrible day.

She'd been in Pattaya Beach to write a column on single destination resorts going up in the area and had been wandering around in search of local color. She'd been a little over a block away from ground zero when the balloon went up. Her voice remained even and matter-of-fact, but it was clearly an upsetting memory.

Hugh made a comforting noise and nodded encouragingly.

"There were these two guys." She pointed at the photos. "Asian for sure, Korean I'm thinking. Everyone else is screaming and feeling for where their eyes or their balls used to be, but not these two. They're standing there, not talking to each other, not helping anyone, just taking it all in. It—" She shrugged. "They looked, I don't know, wrong. So I followed them to a bar on the beach. Pretty soon this guy shows up." She pointed at Fang. "Then Noortman appears, and I remembered that day we spent going through your bulletins."

Hugh nodded again. One of the many reasons he had recruited Arlene was the fact that she literally never forgot a face, whether she saw it in person or posted on the wall of a post office.

"So, I got out my camera and told the waiter I wanted to take some pictures to send home to my grandkids. I talked to him in French and even though he informed me that my accent was *odieux* and my grammar *horrible, hein,* what could one expect of *les américains* after all and *du moins* I was trying, so he agreed to pose for a few pictures of himself so that I'd have a memento of that day on the beach at Pattaya."

He looked at her purse. She grinned and opened it up to produce the tiniest digital camera he'd ever seen. "I've added to the armory."

"So I see, and lucky for us." He looked back at the photos. "Did you follow Fang?"

She shook her head. "That meeting looked a lot like somebody was hiring somebody else. I figured it'd be better to follow the boss. Looked to me like the boss was those two, so I followed them to Bangkok, and from there to London. They stopped in Bangkok long enough to acquire clothing and one piece of luggage each," she added. "And before you ask, they bought their tickets through a travel agent that day, on a credit card that is paid off out of a numbered account in Riyadh. I went back and checked."

"Yeah?" He looked again at the photographs, and at the two men with Fang and Noortman. Something nudged at his memory and he chased it down, a report in from another field agent a week, ten days before. He looked up at Arlene. "What were they doing in London?"

"Passing through."

"Where were they headed?"

She looked a little embarrassed. "I lost them at Heathrow."

"Come on."

"It wasn't my fault."

"How do you mean?"

She pulled out a Visa card and held it out. "My company card was refused at the ticket counter."

He took it automatically. "You're kidding me."

She shook her head.

He could feel his face getting red, the curse of his mother's Scandinavian ancestry. He hit the intercom button with unnecessary force. "Marie? Get Arlene a new Visa card, will you? Ready for her by the time she leaves. No credit limit and no expiration date. My authorization, priority one. If you have any trouble with accounting, route it through miscellaneous operating expenses, Asian desk."

Marie kept the books for his office and knew as well as he did that his operating expenses were maxed out, but she didn't even consider arguing. "Okay, boss."

"Thanks," Arlene said. "I was able to see where they were going."

"The Koreans? Where?"

"Moscow."

"Moscow?" Hugh said. "Moscow, Russia?"

"It wasn't Moscow, Idaho."

"And this was in— What day was the bombing?"

"October fifth. Why?"

"No reason," he said, and added with real feeling, "Dammitall, anyway."

She knew what he meant. "Yeah. I tried to bribe their names out of the ticket agent, but I must not have had enough money. She called them Smith and Jones."

"Ha-ha," Hugh said.

"Yeah." She tapped the photos. "I don't have anything to back me up here, Hugh, but I've got a nasty feeling about these two guys. I think they did it."

"What?" Hugh said, but he already knew.

"I think they're the ones who set the bomb on Soi Cowboy."

4

langley, virginia
october 20, 2004

HUGH ARRANGED FOR ARLENE to dictate her report in full, had it transcribed, and the next morning presented himself at the office of the director. He was shown in almost immediately.

The director of the Central Intelligence Agency served at the pleasure of the president of the United States. Appointees in the past had run the gamut of ability from intelligent, experienced bureaucrat with time served either in one of the services or the agency itself to clueless sycophant with deep pockets, the better to give large campaign donations.

The current occupant of the big office had some pretence to experience, having been deputy director during the last Republican administration, but he was also a very rich man who had contributed heavily to the reelection of the current resident of 1600 Pennsylvania Avenue, and he tended to trim the sails of his agency to a course somewhere between political expediency and effective operations. His employees made ruthless use of his ready access to the Oval Office and largely ignored him the rest of the time. He was perfectly aware of this, and so long as they made him look good he was willing to tolerate it, generating an atmosphere of mutually assured disdain.

Hugh's view was more cautious. This was a man who had survived the fallout of 9/11, which had rained down a great deal of grief on the intelligence community in the form of departmental inquiries, internal investigations, and congressional hearings, not to mention the scrutiny of the press and the wrath of the public. The director had the ear of a president who to all appearances was about to be reelected by a respectable majority. Further, he had served four terms in the House of Representatives in administrations both red and blue, during which he had made connections he maintained to the present day over a series of breakfast meetings. At these breakfasts he presided over a judicious distribution of titillating tidbits of information concerning the personal peccadilloes of various heads of state. If that wasn't enough, he played tennis with the chair of the Senate Armed Services Committee twice a week when they were both in town.

No, what the director lacked in experience and ability he more than made up for in moxie. Hugh treated him with a deference he kept sincere enough to allay any suspicions the director might have that Hugh was actually more in charge of his section of the agency than the director was. In his turn the director appreciated Hugh's intelligence, ability, and tact. They both got a lot more done that way.

"Hugh," the director said as Hugh came in, and stepped around his desk to give Hugh a warm handshake and a hearty slap on the shoulder. "I haven't seen you since you got back. I read your report, of course. Well done, well done, indeed."

In truth it had been a nightmare of a trip, thirty briefings in FBI field offices around the nation in fourteen days, the last of which had been Anchorage. He'd written the report on the plane home, so it was nice to know it was coherent. "A series of briefings on the Asian political scene to other agencies merely, sir," Hugh said.

"A dispensing of information, rather than a gathering of it?" the director said with an avuncular twinkle. Hugh agreed to this without wincing, and they disposed themselves respectively in an overstuffed couch and a matching easy chair, both in soft brown leather that was as comfortable as it had been costly, and chatted about various matters while they waited for the coffee to be brought. When it arrived the director poured, not forgetting to add cream and sugar to Hugh's cup. No small measure of his success was due to his capacity for remembering details.

"Well, what can I do for you today, Hugh, my boy?"

No one called Hugh "my boy," not even his own parents. Especially not his own parents. "I've just had a report, sir, from one of our operatives. It concerns the October bombing in Pattaya Beach."

The paternal attentiveness on the director's face didn't change. "Tell me all about it, my boy."

Hugh did, beginning with a recap of the experts' best reconstruction of the bomb itself, going on to the death and destruction of which it had been the direct and proximate cause, the body count, with American casualties a separate category, and ended with Arlene's sighting of the four men in the beach-side cafe.

"Arlene Harte?" the director said. "The Associated Press reporter?" The director kept close tabs on the Washington press corps.

"Retired," Hugh said.

"She's still a reporter."

"A column for an international travel magazine," Hugh said. "Reporters are by definition trained observers, sir. This wouldn't be the first time the agency has made use of their skills, and I have every confidence in Harte. We've had her on the payroll for some time now, freelance, and she has brought us a great deal of quality product."

He hated using the word "product," but it was the current director's determination to scrub the intelligence vocabulary clean of anything that might give off the even slightest aroma of actual spying. Hugh supposed it was marginally better than HUMINT, agency speak for human source intelligence.

"Still, my boy, a reporter," the director said, a little reprovingly.

Hugh inclined his head, acknowledging the indisputable fact of Arlene's chosen profession, and moved on. "Harte tailed the two Koreans she observed meeting with Fang and Noortman to London, where she further observed them boarding a plane for Moscow."

"And did they stay in Moscow?"

"She was unable to follow them beyond London, unfortunately. But I think they went to Odessa."

"Really. And why do you think that, my boy?"

Hugh opened a folder and extracted a file. "I have also received a report from Bob Dunno, our operative at the American consulate in Odessa. As you know, third-world nations are being flooded with surplus arms from the former Soviet states. It's about the only way the former states have of raising cash, and it's a buyer's market. Odessa is home to several high-profile arms dealers, including Pyotr Volk, a.k.a. Peter the Wolf." He saw the director's look, and nodded. "Peter's little joke, he's a Prokofiev fan."

"Not his real name?"

Hugh didn't dignify that question with an answer. "Over the past five years Peter has used the cash flow generated from selling Russian arms in bulk quantities to expand his inventory, which now includes weapons and matériel from every nation that manufactures them, including our own. This of course has led to a certain amount of, well, friction with our security services."

The director gave his rich chuckle. "I would certainly hope so."

"Bob Dunno met him at an embassy party they both attended in Moscow."

"What was the party for?"

Hugh was thrown off his stride. "I, uh, don't know, sir."

The director gave a reproving shake of his head. "You know how I savor the details, Hugh."

"Yes, sir." Recovering his momentum, Hugh continued his briefing. "Peter has a well-developed sense of self-preservation for an international arms dealer. This occasionally leads him to sell us the odd tidbit of information. He deduced, and rightly, that we'd be more inclined to look away from his activities if he cooperated with us now and then."

"And he's hoping we'll take out his competition with the information he gives us," the director said.

Hugh smiled because it was expected of him. "And leave him in place, yes, sir. At any rate, Peter contacted Bob on October sixth and passed on the news that two young Asian men who fit the description of the two men Arlene followed had come to Odessa and placed an order." Hugh passed the director a sheet of paper.

The director read down the list. "What's cesium?"

"Cesium-137 is one of twenty radioactive isotopes artificially derived from the naturally occurring element cesium." At the director's request, Hugh spelled it. "It is used in radiology for medical and industrial purposes."

"Like X rays?"

"It is used in radiotherapy machines, sir, for the treatment of cancer."

The director meditated on this for a moment. "My aunt had breast cancer. She had surgery, followed by chemotherapy, followed by radiation therapy. That what we're talking about here?"

"Yes, sir."

"It actually burned her skin," the director said. "She looked like a molting lizard for a while there."

"Yes, sir."

"What's it look like? This cesium-137?"

"Not much different from talcum powder."

"Does it glow in the dark?"

"A luminescent blue, sir," Hugh said.

The director looked up. The question had been asked in a jocular tone and Hugh's answer had been dead serious. "I see. And Peter's report of this purchase of this substance upsets you why?"

"Cesium-137 is one of many substances that would be most effective in the manufacture of a dirty bomb."

The director sat back. "What kind of damage are we talking about here?"

"Use enough TNT to explode a couple of ounces of cesium, sir, and the fallout would spread a minimum of sixty square blocks. In a city of any size, Los Angeles, say, or New York, or Washington, D.C., such an event could render hundreds of buildings uninhabitable and put hundreds of thousands of people in the hospital with radiation sickness. It would take years and very probably billions of dollars to clean up the mess. The medical and emergency infrastructure of the nation would be overwhelmed. There would be a severe impact on essential services."

"I imagine someone has done some sort of test scenario."

"Unnecessary, even if true, sir."

"What do you mean?"

"In 1987 in Brazil a private medical clinic went belly up and the three doctors who owned it walked away, leaving the building to deteriorate and eventually be looted. It was a cancer clinic. It had a radiotherapy machine which contained a lead canister containing approximately fourteen hundred curies of cesium-137."

The director gave him a long, level look.

Hugh elaborated. "Enough that when the looters opened the canister, adults and children both could rub the powder on their bodies so that they would, as you say, glow in the dark."

"Why on earth would they do that?"

"They thought it was pretty. Later, the powder transferred from their hands to their food, which was of course toxic when ingested. It was a week before a health care worker who'd had some training diagnosed what four people had already died from and what two hundred forty-four people had been contaminated with on a first-contact basis. The authorities ran a Geiger counter over the people they considered the most likely to have been contaminated, but unfortunately they didn't take the procedure seriously enough to put their techs into protective gear. They didn't decontaminate the ambulances used to carry the victims. Homes, businesses, soil—" Hugh shook his head. "Goiania has a population of seven hundred thousand. They ran the Geiger counters over thirty-four thousand people, about all they could fit into the soccer stadium, but . . . well. It's got a half-life of thirty years."

"The people who died. What did they die from, exactly?"

"Radiation destroys human cells, most rapidly those of the skin, hair, gastrointestinal tract, and bone marrow. They died of pneumonia, blood poisoning, and hemorrhaging."

Hugh used the following silence to tidy up his paperwork.

"A nasty kind of talcum powder," the director said finally.

"Yes, sir."

"Is Peter willing and able to give us any further information?"

Hugh hesitated. "I don't know, sir."

The director raised an eyebrow.

"This was the last time we heard from him. His office blew up later that same evening."

"Our Korean friends?"

"We don't know. It seems likely. They had motive, in wanting to hide their business with him. They certainly had means if they are the people behind the Pattaya bombing. And they had opportunity, being the only business meeting Peter had that day, according to the security guard at the entrance."

"Is Peter dead?"

"We don't know, sir. His body wasn't found, but then there wasn't a lot left from which to make an identification. The explosion took place after midnight when the building was closed, so he could well have left for the evening. On the other hand, I don't think Peter keeps banker's hours." Hugh raised his shoulders. "If he's alive, he hasn't surfaced. Bob Dunno talked to the girlfriend, who knows less than nothing, naturally." Hugh was sure there was plenty Bob wasn't telling him about the girlfriend but he refrained from saying so. "I have instructed informants to keep watch in all the likely places. He could be dead, or he could be anywhere."

"Switzerland?" the director said.

"More likely Nassau, or Brazil, or Seattle."

The director was startled. "Seattle?"

"He hasn't broken any American laws, at least not yet, and he has a distant relative in the Russian émigré population there."

"Mmmm." The director meditated upon the photographs. "These two young men appear to have no appreciable money problems."

"Peter was given a phone number in Switzerland. An electronic transfer. I've got a source ferreting around, but you know the Swiss."

There was a brief silence. The director stirred. "Odessa," he said ruminatively. "Odessa. So that's where we put Bob Dunno out to pasture."

Hugh said stiffly, "Hardly out to pasture, sir. At last count there are over fifty sites in what was the Soviet Union housing enough weapons-grade fissile materials to make as many as seventy thousand nuclear bombs, most of it unsecured. I believe Bob was stationed in Odessa because of his knowledge of Soviet weaponry and his contacts there. Not to mention his fluency in Russian."

"Hugh, my boy, everyone who reads the front page of the *Washington Post* knows all about how familiar Bob Dunno is with his contacts." The director leaned forward. "Do you think it's true? Was he really sleeping with the premier's daughter?"

Doggedly, Hugh kept to the point. "When Harte lost the two men in London, she returned to Pattaya Beach and made further inquiries. During the course of those inquiries she found three witnesses who saw two young Asian men fitting the descriptions of the two men she saw meeting with Fang and Noortman. These witnesses noticed these young men in particular because, unlike everyone else in the area immediately following the blast, they were so calm of manner. One of the witnesses said they seemed almost to be observing."

The director shrugged. "Not conclusive in and of itself."

"But interesting nonetheless, sir." Hugh put the file back together. "I think these two men should be red-flagged, sir. I think we ought to have mug shots from the pictures that Harte brought us and circulate them to all desks and field agents in the Far East, and possibly the entire network. Further, I think we should alert the FBI and the other agencies, including the Coast Guard."

"The Coast Guard?" The director chuckled.

"I would point out, sir," Hugh said, and this time he was unable to keep the edge from his voice, "that these two men were observed in the company of the Chinese pirate, Fang, and his longtime confederate, the Singaporean Noortman. Fang and Noortman we know to be responsible for the high seas piracy of as many as twenty-three freighters, at least a dozen of which held cargoes owned all or in part by American corporations. If Fang and Noortman are involved in whatever these two men are planning, it only makes sense that the planned attack is coming by sea. The Coast Guard will have to be involved, and sooner rather than later."

The director raised a quizzical eyebrow. "You haven't been talking this over with that wife of yours, have you, Hugh, my boy?"

Hugh set his teeth. "No, sir."

"I should hope not. There is no point in starting a panic with what is at this point pure speculation." The director settled back into the couch. "Do you have any independent confirmation of weapons sales such as you have described? Any satellite confirmation of weapons movement? The larger item certainly would be noticed, I would think."

"Admittedly, sir, our evidence to date is circumstantial, but if our agent is right and these two men are responsible for the Pattaya Beach bombing, the construction and detonation of that bomb implies a high level of experience, expertise, and commitment. Not to mention imagination. To my knowledge the Pattaya Beach bombing is the first terrorist attack employing a soccer ball."

The director inclined his head. "Point taken."

"It follows that they will be planning their next operation, and that it will include a similarly imaginative plan. The involvement of Fang and Noortman indicates that the attack will come from the sea. Their purchases from Peter Wolf suggest that—"

The director picked up one of the photographs. "Didn't I read somewhere in that file you gave me a while back that Noortman's a fag?"

Hugh blinked. "Sir?"

"Stands to reason Fang is, too, otherwise why they been together for— What was it you said? Nine years? Ten years?" The director tossed the picture back on the coffee table. "I'm glad you brought this to my attention, Hugh. I can see where there is cause for some concern. Let's alert the Far East staff to keep a watching brief for our four Asian friends, try to keep track of their actions."

"Yes, sir," Hugh said, "our staff and—"

"Let's not rile up the other agencies just yet."

"Sir—"

The director got to his feet. "I sure appreciate you coming in, Hugh, my boy. Keep up the good work."

And Hugh found himself on the other side of the director's door, his hand shook, his back patted, the recipient of a genial invitation for a game of tennis, which he did not play.

He steamed past the director's assistant without saying goodbye, which didn't matter because the head of the Middle Eastern desk was chatting her up in preparation for entry into the inner sanctum, a sheaf of reports in the crook of one elbow that undoubtedly included several items that would jack up the Homeland Security threat advisory to orange. "Harvey," Hugh said tightly.

Harvey Moskowitz, taking in the situation at a glance, said, not without sympathy, "Hey, Hugh." He stood up. "Talk to you for a minute?"

"The director's waiting for you, Mr. Moskowitz," the secretary said disapprovingly.

Moskowitz bestowed a ravishing smile upon her, beneath which she wilted visibly. "Tell him I'll be right in, will you, Georgia?"

The secretary murmured a dazed acquiescence as Moskowitz took Hugh by the elbow and steered him into the hall.

"Not for attribution, Hugh, I don't have any hard evidence, but a couple of my people have been hearing rumors about a large sale of some radioactive material."

Hugh's head came up. "I got the same rumor. Through Odessa?"

"My guy says Tiraspol."

Hugh closed his eyes to locate Tiraspol on an internal map. He opened his eyes again and Harvey said, "What?"

"Come with me," Hugh said. Harvey followed Hugh down the hall to a conference room with a bookshelf full of reference texts and pulled down an atlas. He flipped rapidly through the pages. "Here."

Harvey followed Hugh's finger. "Tiraspol, Moldova. So? Oh. I see. Right on the border."

"Not ninety miles from Odessa," Hugh said.

"Crap," Harvey said, inelegantly but accurately.

"Yeah."

"Is your info linked to al-Qaida?" Harvey said.

"God damn it, Harvey," Hugh said with enough anger to cause the other man's eyes to widen. "Does nothing other than al-Qaida register on anyone's radar around here?"

"Come on, Hugh. They found documents describing research into the construction of CBRN weapons in a house in Kabul, Afghanistan, and in the al-Qaida caves. It's not like they don't know how to make a chemical weapon, or a biological one, or a radioactive one, or even a nuclear one."

Hugh couldn't deny it.

"The nuclear one is the most expensive, so the thinking is they'll probably go with one of the other three," Harvey said. "Again, I ask the question. Is your info linked to al-Qaida?"

Hugh hesitated, and shook his head. "No. I think it might be connected to the same people who did the Pattaya Beach bombing."

Harvey relaxed a little. "And that was what, your standard black-market plastic explosive and a timer packed inside a—what was it?"

"Soccer ball."

"Right. Right." Harvey nodded. "Points for originality. You wouldn't look twice at someone sauntering down the street with a soccer ball tucked under one arm, unless you were in the U.S. And filled with nails and bolts. Instant shrapnel. Nasty." He meditated for a moment. "You got a real thing going on here, Hugh?"

Hugh's jaw tightened, and he had to work at it not to glance over his shoulder toward the director's office. "Nothing with enough evidence to warrant action."

"Ah," Harvey said. "Well, if I hear anything else."

"Yeah. Harvey?"

"Yeah?"

"Where did the rumor originate?"

"My guy heard about it in Hong Kong. Big operation, well funded, is what he heard."

Fang and Noortman operated out of Hong Kong. "Okay. Thanks again, Harvey."

Hugh strode down the hallway with a scowl so severe that the mail boy took an unintended detour through Records and got thoroughly lost in the wilds of the Castro files.

Marie looked up. "So, it went well."

He blew by her into his own office and tossed the envelope containing the Odessa report, Arlene's report, and the photographs on the desk. It skidded across the surface until it hit his in-basket, which was filled with six other reports of potential threats in the Far East, none of which were being taken anywhere near as seriously as Hugh knew they should be.

Hugh's problem was that the Far East just wasn't fashionable. No one seemed to take North Korea seriously, or not as seriously as they did Pickacountry, Middle East. Indonesia, maybe a little more so because of its large Muslim population, but there the terrorists were mostly blowing up Australians, and they'd taken as big a hit from the Christmas tsunami as everyone else so they weren't exactly at the top of their form. In Pattaya Beach, the casualties had been so evenly divided between East and West that the bull's-eye effect hadn't really registered with any one nation. India and Pakistan were sitting down like the lion with the lamb and actually talking to one another for the first time since World War II; in fact all the Indian Ocean nations were, another effect of the tsunami.

No, his nation's security and defense forces were focusing almost exclusively on the Middle East, and the hell of it was he couldn't say they were wrong. But, like Arlene Harte, he was uneasy. If she was right about the two Koreans setting the bomb in Pattaya Beach, they hadn't taken credit for it. Why not? By definition a terrorist's mission was to draw attention to his cause. Why, then, would these two men just walk away without so much as a phone call claiming credit for so many deaths, so much destruction, for the successful terrorizing of a heretofore peaceful resort, dedicated to the innocent pleasures of the leisure classes of many nations?

The only rational answer Hugh could find to that question was that these particular terrorists were practicing, warming up for the big event. He thought of the photographs taken at the scene of the bombing, of the lists of the dead, of the descriptions of the wounds of those who had survived. He thought of the soccer ball, which, from what the investigators could discover, had been drop-kicked onto the dance floor with some brand-new timing device they were still piecing together. The prospect of what the people who had thought up the soccer ball were dreaming up next gave him nightmares.

He hoped the director was right and that there was no need to panic. He hoped it, but he didn't believe it.

He rubbed his eyes and the first thing he focused on when he dropped his hands was the soapstone bear, a smooth, greenish brown image of a sitting bear playing with his own toes. He and Sara had gone out to the Alaska Native hospital in Anchorage that year, looking for gifts for their mothers. An old Yupik man was there with a cardboard box full of soapstone carvings. Hugh had fallen in love with this one on sight, and Sara had bought it for him behind his back and had given it to him that Christmas. It had sat on whatever desk was his from Harvard to Langley and all points in between.

He looked at the bear and he saw Sara, dark blond hair forever bundled into a ponytail, laughing blue eyes, tall enough to kiss without leaning over. They'd been born the same year in the same village, fought all the way through grade school, and fallen in love in high school, never to fall out of it again.

Or so it had seemed then. He wondered if there was anything that he had given her that she had turned into a talisman. He tried to remember the gifts he had given her over the years, and couldn't.

He could smell her on the clothes he'd been wearing in Anchorage two nights before. The clothes she had nearly ripped off him in that overheated little hotel room. Their meeting had been a gift of fate, her testifying in a court case, his delivering an intelligence briefing to Kyle's Joint Terrorism Task Force. Fate, and Kyle's propensity for matchmaking.

It gave him some small comfort that no matter how far apart they were geographically, or how many months it had been since they'd seen each other, or how far their marriage had drifted into harm's way, she had missed him every bit as much as he had missed her.

He heard Kyle's voice again, frighteningly matter-of-fact. *You'll always have me. Question is, will you always have Sara?*

He shook his head almost angrily and turned to his computer. He scanned in the photo of Fang, Noortman, and the two Koreans and sent it attached to e-mails to Bob Dunno in Odessa, as well as agents in the field in Switzerland, Brazil, and Bermuda to show to Pyotr Volk, alias Peter Wolf, if he ever surfaced, and ask him if these were his two customers. Since they were also two of the more likely suspects to have blown up his building, Hugh thought there was at least a fifty-fifty chance Peter might be willing to identify them.

After that he picked up the phone. When it was answered on the other end, he said, "Arlene? Hugh. How well do you know Hong Kong?"

5

october 22, 2004
slime banks, north of the alaska peninsula
on board the uscg cutter *sojourner truth*

I SAY WE USE him to troll for orcas."

"That's a little harsh, Petty Officer, don't you think?" Sara said, trying not to laugh.

"Already tasked anyway," Chief Mark Edelen said from the conn.

"Tasked how?" PO Barnette said, raising one skeptical eyebrow. Or so Sara assumed, as it was 11:00 P.M. of a Bering Sea winter's night and there was nothing blacker this side of hell. The bridge had red filters taped over the navigation and radar and fathometer screens, dimming their readouts and allowing everyone's eyes to adjust to see out the windows. Except for Orion looming large on their starboard bow, there wasn't a lot to see, and wouldn't have been much beyond an endless green ocean even if it were daylight.

But even in the dark Barnette sounded skeptical, and also thwarted. Seaman Rosenberg, an eighteen-year-old typically twirpish adolescent fresh out of boot camp, had managed in only fifteen days underway to step all over the senior crewman's toes.

There was a smile in the chief's voice when he replied. "They duct-taped his bunk shut, poked a hole in it, and sprayed it full of Right Guard."

"Ouch," Sara said. "Why?"

"Because he hasn't had a shower since he got on board," PO Barnette said, "and when you're sleeping forty-two to a room it can get kind of rank. Plus he's been puking his guts up ever since we left the dock. You can smell him coming a deck away." A brief pause. "Ma'am."

The smile in the chief's voice was wider this time. "They also stuffed all his clothes into his duffle and filled it with Scrubbing Bubbles Basin Tub and Tile Cleaner."

"You're kidding."

"Nope. Well, you know."

"No. What?"

"It's a disinfectant."

Sara couldn't help it, she let loose of the laugh that had been building inside for the last five minutes. She pulled herself together and cleared her throat. "I mean, this must stop, immediately."

They knew her, and they laughed. PO Barnette's ire was soothed, even if his hand had not been the one to mete out justice, and he returned to his brace at the conn, feet flat against the deck as if they'd been spot-welded there, hands clasped at the small of his back, leaning forward into the pitch of the ship. Salty, that was PO Barnette, eighteen years in. He never lost his balance, not even in the heaviest seas, as opposed to Sara, who had long ago perfected a complicated polka slash tango with the ship on any seas over three feet. It was effective; it had been years since the sudden lurch of a hull had tossed her into a bulkhead, but still she envied PO Barnette's tranquil stolidity.

The bosun's mate, Thomasina Penn, went back to the plot table to continue work on their route, but it was perfunctory as they were running box ops, hiding from a hurricane-force low in the lee of St. Paul Island in the Pribilofs. Running box ops meant steering a course confined within a box drawn on the radar screen that out of sheer boredom on occasion resembled the initials of the officer on watch. The S for Sara was fun, the L in Lange less so.

Mark Edelen's initials were more challenging, resulting in a call to the bridge earlier that evening from the captain requesting the conn to straighten out their course so his dominoes wouldn't keep sliding off the wardroom table. It was the threat of being drafted into playing dominoes that had caused Sara to retreat to the bridge in the first place.

As executive officer, she was exempt from watch rotation, but truth to tell, she missed it. She missed the heave and roll of the sea at night, more pronounced on the bridge thirty-six feet up from the waterline than it was in her stateroom two decks below. She missed the occasional glimpses of white as the bow sliced through the ocean. On clear nights it was horizon to horizon stars, crowding one another in three hundred and sixty degrees of sheer glory.

Nights like tonight. On nights like tonight, it was as if they were sailing straight off the edge of the earth and into the cosmos. Nights when the moon came up or the aurora came out verged on the paranormal.

On the night watch voices were muted, lights were softer to the eye, and the seas seemed somehow less severe no matter the height of the wave or the length between swells. At night, things were a little less formal and a little more friendly. Sara loved her job and she loved the Coast Guard, but executive officer was just another description for captain's hatchet man. It could get pretty lonely, especially since she was the only female officer. Being one of only eleven women in a crew of a hundred didn't help.

Promotion to executive officer was not anything an ambitious officer in the United States Coast Guard refused, not if she were in her right mind, but as XO her days with filled with administrative minutiae and a lamentable lack of action. Logistics made the boat go, she understood that, but instead of driving the boat—or standing watch—her days were spent in two-hour meetings over ways to dispose of the trash accumulated during a fifty-one-day patrol on a ship with ten officers and ninety enlisted men and women on board. It wasn't that she wanted to be an ensign again, but she wished, not for the first time, that she were on a smaller ship with fewer officers, where once in a while she might get to lead a boarding.

And where she didn't have so many memories eight hundred miles off their starboard bow. She pulled her hat down to hide her expression, forgetting that it was black as the pit on the bridge, raised one foot to the ledge that ran around the radar console, and wedged herself in the narrow space between it and the control console. She put an elbow on her raised knee and her chin in her hand.

"Can't sleep?" the chief said in a low voice.

"Dominoes," Sara said.

He laughed. He had a marvelous laugh, which pretty much matched the rest of him. He was smart, funny, and good at his job, and if that wasn't enough, he was handsome, too, with the most beautiful brown eyes Sara had ever seen. That wasn't all that was beautiful about him, either. Their first full day underway she'd gone below to work out in the ship's gym and found the chief there before her, dressed in T-shirt and shorts, far less clothing than she was accustomed to seeing him in. She'd been unable to meet his eyes for a good twenty-four hours afterward for fear that he would know exactly what she was thinking. Aside from the fact that she was an officer and he was an enlisted man, that they were underway on two hundred and eight-two feet of ship that seemed to shrink with every day of patrol that passed, and that the last thing the crew needed was to have its nose rubbed in what the Coast Guard officially referred to as an "inappropriate romantic relationship," they were both married to other people.

Even if Sara was feeling less and less married as time went on. "Got any plans for Dutch?" she said at random. She didn't need to be thinking about Hugh.

They were headed for Dutch Harbor the next day, their first port call of the patrol. "Seafood buffet at the Grand Aleutian," Mark said. "Hike up the mountain beforehand to earn it."

"No joy ride on the helo?"

The helicopter pilots took crew members for rides in port, racking up hours in the air and making friends with the crew as a bonus. "Nah," Mark said, with the disdain only a career sailor could display toward an aviator. "I've been. Figured I'd let some of the newbies have a shot. You?"

"District is flying in for a briefing."

Mark's teeth flashed. "Oh yeah, I remember you and the captain talking about that the other day. What was it Winston Churchill said? Something about democracy being the worst system of government ever invented, except for all the others? Didn't mention bureaucracy, did he."

And he could read. Sara hardened her heart to this suddenly even more attractive man and did not reply. Instead, she thought about what she always thought about, her next duty assignment, and if she could finagle another tour in Alaska, or at the very least on the West Coast. She

was terrified that she would be assigned to command in
D.C. again, and was equally determined to foil, thwart, or
otherwise avert that misguided effort on the part of her
commanding officers if at all possible.

She'd been amazing lucky so far. The *Sojourner Truth*
was her fifth boat in ten years, if you counted her summer
on the *Eagle,* the Coast Guard's tall ship, and she did. She
would have her cutterman's pin before the year was out,
denoting seven years' sea duty, which included two years'
command of a one-ten white hull out of Eureka, California. The time in D.C. had probably been essential in getting her the one-ten, she admitted, if only reluctantly and
if only to herself, but shore duty was not what she had
signed on for with the U.S. Coast Guard, and she made
sure that every commanding officer she served under
knew it. She'd been lucky in them, too, but then she
worked hard at fostering the good opinion of her COs.
When she had gotten the *Sojourner Truth,* she had
showed up for duty a week early and spent that time
learning every nook and cranny of the ex-navy salvage
tug from bilge to crow's nest and pestering the then first
officer for every detail of his two years on board. When
she had drained him dry, she started in on the engineer
officer.

Blond hair, blue eyes, and long legs tended to engender
thoughts other than her competency as a serving officer in
the "always ready" service, but it helped that she deliberately desexed herself for each patrol, wearing her uniform
a size too large, with a T-shirt and leggings beneath, no
makeup, no jewelry, no perfume, no scented soaps or
body lotions. Her hair she kept just long enough to wear
in a ponytail, drawn through the band of the uniform base-
ball cap, which never left her head except at flight quarters, meals, and asleep in her bunk. She showered, she
washed her clothes regularly, she was clean and neat—if

only to keep herself from the unfortunate Seaman Rosenberg's fate—but that was the most effort she made for her personal appearance under way.

"For crissake, Sara," Hugh had said the first time he'd seen her in what she called her underway ensemble, "where are your breasts?" He'd pulled out the neck of the dark blue polar fleece jacket to check that they were still there, and that had been the end of that conversation.

She drew in a sharp breath. It had been a while since Hugh Rincon had managed to creep into her thoughts unawares, and now there he was again, the second time in five minutes. She wondered how he was, what he was doing, whether he was still in Anchorage or back at his desk in Langley, gathering gossip in the service of his country.

It was with heartfelt relief that she heard the marine band crackle into life. The voice was male and on the ragged edge of panic. "Coast Guard, Coast Guard, this is the fishing vessel *Arctic Wind,* emergency, emergency, Coast Guard, Coast Guard, this is the fishing vessel *Arctic Wind,* over."

In a photo finish Sara beat both Mark and Tommy to the microphone mounted over the plot table. "Fishing vessel *Arctic Wind,* this is the Coast Guard cutter *Sojourner Truth,* go up to two-two-alpha."

"Up to two-two-alpha, roger."

She reached up and clicked the frequency knob on the radio to twenty-two-alpha, aware of an attentiveness on the bridge that had not been there a moment before. "*Arctic Wind,* this is cutter *Sojourner Truth,* how copy?"

The voice came back with distinct relief. "Five-by, *Sojourner,* good to know you guys are out there."

"Good to hear, *Arctic Wind,* what's the problem?"

"*Sojourner,* I've got a deckhand with three-inch J-hook in his eye."

"Chief, call the captain," Sara said to Mark. "Tommy, pipe Doc and the aviators to the bridge." She keyed the mike. "*Arctic Wind,* roger that, you've got a deckhand with a three-inch J-hook in his eye. Is he conscious?"

"He's conscious and he's mobile, *Sojourner.* It's still got the bale attached. I've got the hook stabilized with a bunch of tape and gauze, but I don't know where the barb is. I don't want to mess with it any more than that."

"Don't touch it!" Tommy said involuntarily. Sara keyed the mike and said, "Roger that, *Arctic Wind,* what's your lat and long?"

She turned to watch Tommy punch the numbers into the radar as the longliner skipper read them off. The screen readjusted itself and the bosun's mate ran the cursor over a small glowing green X on the screen. "A little over forty miles north-northeast of our present position, XO."

"Come about to zero-three-zero, all ahead full," she told the helmsman.

"Zero-three-zero all ahead full, aye," Seaman Eugene Razo replied. A moment later she felt the vibration in the deck increase as the cutter leaped forward in pursuit of her top speed, fifteen-point-four knots.

"*Arctic Wind,* this is the *Sojourner Truth.* We're on our way. We'll either be sending a boat over or doing a hoist with our helicopter. We'll let you know which so you can make ready."

She waited. They all waited. At last the *Arctic Wind* came back on, her skipper sounding very tightly wound. "*Sojourner,* I'm not set up for a hoist by helicopter. I've got wires and crap all over the deck."

She heard the door open behind her and heard Mark say, "Captain on the bridge."

"Understood, *Arctic Wind,* stand by," Sara said, and turned.

USCG Captain David Josephus Lowe was a short, stern-faced man who made up for his lack of height with a determinedly erect carriage. A strict, by-the-book disciplinarian redeemed by an equally rigid sense of fairness and an elusive sense of humor, his command was nothing if not restful. So long as the crew did their jobs when and where he told them to and did them well while they were at it he had no complaint. If they didn't, he had no difficulty in saying so and, if the problem proved to be repetitive, in meting out swift and sure punishment at mast. There was comfort in knowing always exactly and precisely what was expected of you, and security in knowing the rest of the crew knew it, too. Sara had served in far worse commands.

"XO," Captain Lowe said, settling into the armchair bolted to a metal pole to the right of the bridge console. He always sat a little forward, the crew speculated, so his legs wouldn't stick straight out like a little kid's in a high chair.

"Captain," she said, facing him and going unconsciously into a brace that mimicked PO Barnette's, shoulders squared, feet spread for balance, hands clasped at the small of her back. "We've got a longliner fishing pacific cod approximately forty miles north-northeast of our present location."

The door to the bridge opened and she looked over the captain's shoulder to see Doc Jewell enter the bridge. She waited until he was standing next to her to continue. "They've got a crew member with a three-inch J-hook in his eye. Their skipper says he's got the hook stabilized with gauze and tape."

"Is he conscious?" Doc said.

"Yes, and his skipper says he's mobile, which I guess means he can walk."

"Can he climb into a basket?"

"The skipper also says he's not set up for a hoist by helo."

"Why not?"

"He says he's got wires and . . . stuff all over the deck."

The captain looked at Doc. "You feel comfortable taking an EMT over in a small boat and bringing the guy back here?"

Even in the dim light of the bridge Sara could see that Doc was less than thrilled at the prospect. "Even with the hook stabilized, Captain, we'd have to get him down the side of his ship and up the side of ours. And then the action in the boat coming over. A hook in the eye . . ." Doc shook his head. "I don't like the odds of getting him on board without doing more damage."

"How long is the longliner?" a new voice said, and Sara turned to see the two aviators standing behind her.

"A hundred and seventy feet," she replied.

The aviators exchanged a look. "In a hundred and seventy feet," Lieutenant Laird said, "we can hoist from somewhere."

Lieutenant Sams nodded.

The longliner skipper was not happy. "I'm not set up for a hoist," he repeated, his apprehension coming through loud and clear. "I've got two masts and a guy wire running from the bow to both masts to the stern, and trash and crap all over the deck."

"How long will it take us to get into range for the small boat?" the captain said.

"Two and a half hours, sir," Tommy said.

"Devil's advocate, Captain?" Sara said. "If we slow down to come onto a flight course to launch the helo and they can't get the guy off, it'll take that much longer for us to go get him by small boat."

Harry Sams's lower lip pushed out into something perilously close to a pout, and Roger Laird opened his mouth, but before either aviator could start whining the captain called it. "Let's try it by helo first, night-vision goggles."

Doc looked immensely relieved. "Agreed," he said.

"Aye aye, Captain," the aviators said in unison and then left the bridge in a hurry, like they were afraid the captain might change his mind.

The operations officer showed up, in gym shorts, sweaty and out of breath. "I'm sorry, Captain, I was working out, I didn't hear the pipe."

The captain jerked his chin at Sara, who said, "We've got a hundred-and-seventy-foot longliner forty miles off our starboard bow. He's got a deckhand with a three-inch J-hook in his eye."

Ops, Clifford Skulstad, a slim, intense lieutenant in his late twenties, whistled. "That's gotta smart," he said. "The aviators tell me we're trying an NVG hoist?"

"Roger that," Sara said, and Ops went to the nav station to coax the sat phone into operation, which he alone on board seemed to be able to do.

"Flight quarters," the captain said, and everyone on what was now a very crowded bridge pulled off their caps and stuffed them into their belts or hung them on bulkheads or wedged them behind handrails. Ensign Hank Ryan, the helo communications officer, donned mike and earphones and started turning things on. As the closed-circuit television overhead warmed up, they saw the hangar telescoping back and the helmeted and vested hangar deck crew scurrying around. On the sat phone Ops called Anchorage to arrange a Life Flight to meet the helo in Dutch Harbor, and then got the name of the ship's agent and called her, too.

"I relieve you, Chief," Sara told Mark.

"XO's got the conn," he said, followed by a chorus of ayes acknowledging the handover.

"Helm, steer three-four-zero, all ahead full," Sara said.

"Three-four-zero, all ahead, aye," Charlie said.

Sara took up station in front of the control console and watched the bow pull to port. The *Sojourner Truth* was a joy to handle, quick to respond, a Cadillac of a ride. There wasn't five knots of a prevailing breeze, and most of the wind now coming across the port bow was created by their own forward motion. There was no pitch and no roll to speak of. Conditions could not be better for a helo launch. If it was daylight, they would, in Coastie vernacular, be riding the seagull's ass. "Maintain course and speed," she said.

"Maintaining course and speed, aye," the helm responded, and everyone turned to watch the television screen as the helo was rolled out onto the hangar deck, its rotors unfolded, and the flight crew climbed in. The rotors began to turn, slowly at first, accelerating into a blur.

"Black out the ship," the captain said, and everything except for the nav screens was turned off, including the running lights, because any light no matter how small could white out the night-vision goggles. It wasn't exactly legal, but it was an acceptable alternative to crashing the helo.

"Go for launch, Captain?" Ryan said.

"Go," the captain said. Ryan spoke into the microphone and almost instantaneously the whine of the helo ratcheted up to where it drowned out the *Sojourner*'s engines. A dark shape rose into the air off their stern, nosed into the wind, and roared past their port bow.

"Secure from flight quarters," the captain said, and everyone put their caps back on.

"Resume course zero-three-zero, all ahead full," Sara said.

"Zero-three-zero, all ahead full," the helm replied.

Everyone strained their eyes at the distant masthead light on the northeastern horizon. Sara couldn't get the image of the fisherman with the three-inch J-hook in his eye out of her mind, and she knew she wasn't alone.

Five minutes later Laird's voice crackled over the radio. "Longliner *Arctic Wind,* this is Coast Guard Rescue six five two seven."

"Coast Guard, *Arctic Wind,* go ahead." The skipper sounded unenthusiastic but resigned.

"Yeah, *Arctic Wind,* Coast Guard, could we get you to turn out some of your lights? We're operating with night-vision goggles and light kinda gets in the way."

"Roger that, Coast Guard." There was about five more very long minutes' worth of conversation as the helo and the longliner identified which lights should be turned out.

"Yeah, *Arctic Wind,* Coast Guard, that'll do it. We'd like to hoist from the portside stern area, I say again, portside stern. Can you get your guy out there?"

"Roger that, Coast Guard."

Sara peered through the forward windows, trying by divine telepathy to follow what was going on on board the longliner. After a moment a smaller light came on next to the brighter masthead light off their starboard bow and lifted up and away. "They're off," she said.

Laird's voice came over the radio. "Cutter *Sojourner Truth,* Coast Guard helo six five two seven, we're off and en route for St. Paul. Our compliments to the deck crew, they were flawless."

"Roger that, six five two seven," Ops said. "Cutter out."

"Helo out. See you tomorrow morning."

No one cheered out loud but there was a communal exhalation of breath. Ensign Robert Ostlund, the landing signals officer, entered the bridge. "Everything by the book and then some, Captain. The deck crew performed just about perfect."

"Coast Guard cutter *Sojourner Truth,* longliner *Arctic Wind.*" If the guy had been anything but a Bering Sea fisherman he might have been crying, he sounded so relieved. "Thank you. That was amazing, I didn't know you guys could do that."

"All part of the service, *Arctic Wind,*" Ops said. "Cutter *Sojourner Truth* out." He clicked the marine radio back up to channel 16 and said over his shoulder, "Let's see if he remembers that the next time we board him."

"Well done, all," the captain said. "XO, pipe the news to the crew. Wait, belay that last," he added. "Let them sleep. And holiday routine tomorrow until noon."

"Aye aye, Captain," Sara said. She'd have to revise the plan of the day, but the flight deck crew, some of whom were also boarding team and fire team members, would work better with the extra rest.

Within sixty seconds the bridge was empty of everyone except Sara, Chief Edelen, PO Barnette, Tommy Penn, and Seaman Razo. In all, the SAR case had taken about ninety minutes from the time the first call came in from the *Arctic Wind* to the last communication from the helo.

Mark grinned at Sara. "Coast Guard," he said.

"Jobs that matter," she replied, and everyone laughed.

Yeah, she might be what the Coast Guard called a geographic bachelor, estranged from a husband she hadn't seen in over a year, if you didn't count last week's quickie in Anchorage, and she was determined not to. She might, at present, be in a job where she told other people what to do with the big toys rather than get to play with them herself.

But one thing for sure.

She really liked the night watch.

6

november, 2004
hong kong

NOORTMAN CHOSE HONG KONG as his base of operations for the new commission, partly for its location and partly because anything could be had there for a price. Also, he was a little lazy and he liked the idea of working from home.

Maritime freight was his specialty: his vocation and his avocation. He'd spent much of his childhood on the docks and the marinas of Singapore, watching as the cargoes of the world's nations were off-loaded from the gigantic maw of one ship's hold to be freighted to another dock and deposited in the hold of a different ship bound for another port. Fruit from New Zealand. Vegetables from Chile. Beef from Argentina and lamb from Australia. Computer chips from Japan, waybills beautifully inscribed with Japanese characters that looked more like art than a cargo manifest. From Thailand, beds and dressers and tables and chairs made of teak, from the United States entire ships full of Ford Escorts, from Canada wood products from raw timber to wood pulp to newsprint. From China textiles and toys, from Jamaica sugar, from Sierra Leone cocoa.

He would scribble down the cargoes he saw each day on a notepad and at home look up the countries of origin and destination in his father's atlas, a tome so large that as a boy he was barely able to lift it down from its shelf. Its pages were filled with colorful illustrations of the world's great mountains and canyons and rivers and deserts, and maps topographical, agricultural, and political. He mooned over the oceans and the coastlines of continents and fell headlong in love with the perfect natural harbors created by islets and inlets and peninsulas, places like Sydney and San Francisco and Seattle.

Not so surprising, certainly not from a boy born to a nation made up of fifty-nine islands, with only two percent of its land arable and a less than amicable neighbor across its only border. It followed that the lifeblood of that nation would be carried by ships, and that much of that nation's industry would be concerned with ships and the sea.

Apart from inclination and familiarity, there were personal reasons as well. He was following in his father's footsteps, a respected man on the Singaporean waterfront. The elder Noortman was a Netherlander who had gone to sea when he was sixteen and fetched up on the shore of the South China Sea, there to meet and marry a less than beautiful but very well connected Singaporean woman whose father had retired from twenty years at sea to a post with the Board of Customs in Singapore, and who brought his new son-in-law into what he regarded as the family firm almost immediately, which would have been impossible otherwise for a white man with no connections.

Noortman's father rose slowly but steadily in rank, achieving a local reputation for ability and an international reputation for probity, by which was meant that he stole no more than what was generally recognized as a reasonable percentage of the worth of the goods that passed beneath his mark. Neither did he flaunt his extracurricular earnings in a vulgar display of wealth, which he well knew would provoke envy and suspicion, because he was already laboring under the handicap of his white skin. He maintained a modest if well-appointed home in the Orchard suburb for his wife, son, and two daughters, who were sent to public school, and the son on to the National University of Singapore.

Young Noortman graduated in the middle of his class, although he could have achieved high honors were it not for the admonishments of his father, whose own credo was never to draw any more attention to oneself than absolutely necessary. The younger Noortman's degree was in business administration, but his real education took place on the docks, working nights and weekends for the Board of Customs, learning the arcane language of international shipping, no little facilitated by his flair for languages. This polyglot state had been inculcated almost from birth, as his father decreed that the family would speak Chinese on Mondays and Tuesdays, Dutch on Wednesdays and Thursdays, and English on Fridays, Saturdays, and Sundays. Noortman expanded his international vocabulary in school, studying French first, which introduced him to the Romance languages, and then Russian and Japanese, to the point that one day an instructor wondered out loud why he was majoring in business instead of in languages. He invited the young man out for dinner at a first-class restaurant run by an expatriate Filipino chef. There followed further discussion of Noortman's tendency toward the multilingual, what he might do professionally with such an agile tongue, and seduction. Noortman thoroughly enjoyed both the chicken adobo and the sex.

From his instructor, an Israeli who had found the con-

tinual state of war on his nation's borders to be aestheti-
cally distasteful and had emigrated the day after he was
of age, Noortman gained, among other things, a working
knowledge of two more languages, Hebrew and Arabic.
The instructor was moved to say, "There is a real future in
government for a young man with your talents."

Noortman, to whom double-entry bookkeeping did not
come naturally, reported this to his father that evening—
his father had decreed that he would pursue his studies
from home, not from a room in a dormitory on campus—
with the admittedly faint hope that he might be allowed to
take his future into his own hands. The elder Noortman
had replied calmly, "There is a real future in the customs
service as well."

Resentfully, Noortman went back to school and continued to wrestle with interest rates and amortization and
debentures. When he graduated he made a second bid for
freedom, requesting permission to pursue a master's degree in languages. This, too, was denied, and his resent-
ment, festering beneath a dutiful facade, grew into a bitter
anger. Still dependent on his father's largesse, he accepted an offer of employment in the customs service. If
he was not quite under the direct supervision of the elder
Noortman, then he was close enough for his father to cri-
tique his job performance every evening after dinner.
Which he did, with a devastating eye for every tiny error
and a dispassionate manner of speaking that was wither-
ing in the extreme. The younger Noortman endured these
critiques with outward calm, but he was already looking
for a way out.

By this time his clothes occupied half the closet and
drawer space in the Israeli instructor's home. He told his
father the instructor was continuing to tutor him in languages, which was technically the truth. The elder Noort-

man, in the magisterial way that his son had come to detest, decided this was acceptable. Freighters, containerships, bulk carriers, tankers, military vessels of every size
and shape, cruise ships, they all docked at Singapore, and
they carried multinational crews. Many languages could
greatly enhance one's future in the customs service.

One day, a year into full-time employment in the family business, he was told by his father that he had located
a suitable bride for his son, a well-connected young
woman whose father was a relation of the Goh family, a
scion of which currently occupied the prime minister's
office. The Goh family's reservations over allying themselves with a half-breed had been overcome by the general respect with which the elder Noortman was regarded
by people who mattered. The matter was fully explained
to the younger Noortman, who walked out of his father's
study that evening with the sound of a cell door slamming
in his ears.

The following week, a wiry Chinese man in his late
thirties had appeared in the customs office. He asked for
Noortman in Mandarin.

"I am Noortman," the young man replied, in that same
language.

The Chinese looked at him with an indifferent gaze.
"Not you."

At that moment his father appeared and shepherded
the Chinese into his office and closed the door behind
them. They were in there for quite some time, and when
the Chinese left the elder Noortman escorted him to the
door and all the way out to his car, an honor usually ac-
corded only to high government officials on fact-finding
missions.

"Who is the Chinese man you spoke to today?" Noortman asked his father over dinner that evening.

His father returned an impassive stare. "He is nothing and no one to you. Do not speak of him again."

The next day the younger Noortman noticed a great deal of activity on and around a freighter moored three docks down from the office. When he went to take a closer look, he was waved off by a man with an automatic rifle slung over his shoulder and no uniform.

He sat on a crate just outside the perimeter created by perhaps a dozen such men, the majority of them Indonesian and Filipino, he thought, all with the same flat, steady regard. This regard was trained outward, away from the ship they ringed, ignoring the cranes and trucks moving around them as container after unmarked container was unloaded, settled onto the back of a flatbed, and moved off the dock. The men were rough-edged and muscular. They continued to ignore him so long as he did not breach their perimeter, but when he appeared the next day the Chinese man he had seen in his father's office came down the gangway of the freighter and walked up to him. "What do you want?"

Noortman rose to his feet without undue haste, a nice blend of deference to elders and a display of self-confidence. "I am the son of Noortman, the customs agent."

"I know," the Chinese said. "What do you want?"

"I have been watching you. Over the last thirty-six hours, you have off-loaded almost one hundred containers of freight and reloaded them on a freighter bound for the port of Tokyo."

The Chinese did not change expression.

"I notice that my father passed all of the containers from your ship through customs, even when he had to work overtime to do so."

"And?"

"My father is a creature of habit. He goes home to sit down to dinner with his family at six P.M. every day of his life."

The Chinese watched him with a menacing gaze meant to intimidate, very similar to those of the guards posted round his ship.

The younger Noortman continued to speak. His father would have been proud of his careful, detached manner. He hoped he didn't look as frightened as he felt, but he could either wait for his doom to be pronounced or he could try to build a future of his own. Desperation was a highly motivating force. "I notice that the identification numbers on the containers have been very recently renewed. I notice also that they have been reinforced to carry heavier loads."

"You're a very noticing fellow," the Chinese said.

It was not a compliment. "Very," Noortman agreed, not without an increase in heart rate. There was something very initimidating—and not a little exciting—about the Chinese's cold eyes. "And then I remembered reading in the newspaper one month ago of the taking of a ship loaded with aluminum ingots in the Makassar Strait. Pirates boarded her at four in the morning, shot the captain and crew, and tossed their bodies overboard, and vanished into the night." Noortman paused. "One of the crew survived. He was pulled out of the water by a fisherman the next day, and he lived long enough to tell the authorities that the head pirate was a Chinese man in his thirties or forties, wiry, with a very dark tan and black hair cut very short, like American soldiers in the movies."

He paused, and let his eyes wander over the Chinese's brush cut. "The ship has not been found. Neither has its ten-million-dollar cargo."

The Chinese said nothing, calloused hands remaining loose at his side, but there was an alert set to his head and a thoughtful expression in his eyes that had not been there before.

"It was an interesting story, and I looked for more, but there was nothing. The ship and its cargo simply disappeared." He stopped to consider, and added, not without admiration, "It must have been very carefully planned, to be able to make a ship of that size disappear. Not to mention, Mr. Fang, seventy metric tons of aluminum ingots."

Fang's expression did not change. "Supposing I was this Chinese pirate," he said. "According to the story you read, I made a ship disappear, and I made its crew disappear, and I made seventy metric tons of aluminum ingots disappear. How hard would it be to make you disappear as well?"

"True," the younger Noortman said, nodding. It required an effort to keep his expression as bland as his voice, but he thought he succeeded quite well. "Very true. But I was able to figure out who you were and what you were doing here the first time I saw you and your ship. If I could do so, so, too, could others." He let Fang think this over.

Fang did, and gave a slight nod. Possibly he was reluctant to kill his pet customs agent's son. Possibly he was intrigued by the younger Noortman's self-assurance. At any rate, he stayed his hand, for the moment.

"Had I been in charge of—disbursing, shall we say?— the cargo in question," Noortman said, almost dreamily, "I would, first, have done a better job of replacing the identification numbers on the containers. I know, I know"—he raised a hand, palm outward, although the Chinese had yet to say anything—"given the amount of freight traveling the oceans these days, it is very hard to track down any one container. But, as I said, if I could figure out what is going on, so could someone else, so why take the risk when a decently faked registry, a good stencil, and a steady hand is all that is required to ensure disinterest on the part of the world's customs services?"

He didn't wait for an answer this time. "Secondly, I would have made sure that no one customs agent in any port had total authority over the cargo. Thirdly, I would have made arrangements to off-load the cargo in more than one port, and possibly even to transfer the cargo to another ship between ports." He paused to consider this. "Possibly. It is unwise to put one's trust in any one agent in any one port, and it is unnecessary, especially if a good forger provides a believable provenance for the cargo."

The Chinese regarded him meditatively. The moments ticked by. Noortman didn't squirm. Eventually, the Chinese man said, "How did you know my name?"

Noortman smiled. It was a charming smile, attractive, infectious, disarming (the gold tooth would come later), and he knew it and employed it selectively. "I heard one of your men call you by name yesterday."

Fang's lips tightened. "Which one?"

Noortman's smile faltered. "I don't know. One of the guards you have stationed round your ship. I think the guard in charge."

Without turning his head, Fang said sharply, "Win!"

A guard trotted over. "Go to the bridge and wait there until I come."

The guard, a young man, impassive as his boss, gave a nod and trotted to the gangway.

Noortman never saw him again. Fang was not a forgiving employer. It was the first lesson Noortman learned in association with the sometime master mariner and full-time pirate, and it wouldn't be the last, but it was by far the most important.

Noortman resigned his position that evening after dinner, in his father's study. The elder Noortman was at first disbelieving and then angry. He came out from behind his desk like the wrath of God and hit Noortman hard enough to loosen three teeth. Noortman got back on his feet and picked up a thick book his fall had knocked from the shelves. The next thing he knew his mother and sisters were pulling him from his father's body, supine on the floor with his face unrecognizable beneath a wash of blood. He couldn't see that shade of red today without re-membering a flood of pure joy.

That had been nine years before. Noortman was now thirty-four, with a growing reputation in the international maritime freight business, a slightly less admirable but no less respectful one with Interpol, and healthy bank ac-counts in Hong Kong, Zurich, and Nassau. Over the years, Noortman had become a master of the shell game of international maritime freight, moving containers and ships as if conducting a game on a chessboard. It was challenging, exciting work, not least because he knew very well that if caught practicing this commodities sleight of hand the ocean-view apartment in the Hong Kong high-rise would be replaced by a cot in a twelve-by-twelve cell. And that was only if he were arrested by Western authorities. He shuddered to think of the conse-quences of being arrested in his native Singapore.

He avoided targeting U.S. and Russian-owned ships as they were known to carry small arms, and added British ships to the no list when they began hiring ex-Gurkha sol-diers for on-board security. He took pride in the fact that he had done his work so well that in nine years Fang had faced serious opposition from only three crews. None of them survived the experience, of course. Fang was insis-tent on leaving no witnesses behind, and he especially hated cameras of any kind. The new cell phones, with their photograph-taking capabilities, were a target of par-ticular abhorrence, and Fang insisted on being the only member of any of his crews who carried a phone. If anyone protested on shore, their services were declined. If anyone protested at sea, they joined the crew of the captured vessel as shark food.

From the small bits that Fang let fall during their association, Noortman knew that Fang had been raised in a hard school. Son of a Shanghai prostitute, father unknown, he took to the sea as a boy and grew up smuggling goods between Taiwan and China. He said he had a master's license, but Noortman had never seen it. He knew how to handle a ship, and more important for their business, he was extremely efficient at hijacking them. Noortman regarded himself as the brain of their operation and Fang as the brawn, but he never made the mistake of saying that to Fang.

Fang knew it anyway, but his bottom line had trebled and quadrupled since he'd brought the young Singaporean on board, so he let it slide. He'd never given a lot of consideration to retiring before this, but Noortman's genius was such that Fang was beginning to entertain thoughts of a positively middle-class nature, involving a luxury apartment in Shanghai, a plump, placid wife, and perhaps even sons to carry on his name. No, he had no intention—no immediate intention—of teaching the younger Noortman a sense of humility.

Having identified a likely target, Noortman would plot its course, consider and discard and eventually find the ideal point of interception (he enjoyed inventing business euphemisms for what was essentially high seas piracy), after which he turned this information over to Fang. After that it was simply a matter of placing the stolen cargo with the appropriate customer for the maximum profit, snapping his fingers at the law enforcement agencies of literally dozens of countries as he did so.

All this had seemed the height of adventure when he was twenty-five. Not to mention profoundly satisfying when he, dutiful son that he was, went home once a month to spend a weekend with his parents and indulged in a good, long inner chuckle when he sat down across the dinner table from his father, blind in one eye and deaf in one ear from the beating his son had given him. The elder Noortman might have been blind in both eyes for all the notice he gave his son on his irregular visits.

The younger Noortman also very much enjoyed bringing back black pearls from Tahiti, diamonds from South Africa, and emeralds from Colombia and laying them, metaphorically speaking, at his mother's feet. That good, silent woman was appreciative if somewhat bewildered. She never did work up the courage to ask him where it all came from, and she never ceased to produce an endless line of eligible young women for his inspection and approval.

Even these trophy visits home were beginning to pall, though. So when Smith and Jones presented Noortman with this new, much more difficult, and altogether more dangerous challenge, he had embraced it with enthusiasm. First he looked at the area in question, working the phones and the Internet, monitoring ships and cargo moving in and out of the various ports. Many of the ports were so obliging as to have multiple remote cameras mounted over their docks, and it cost only a small portion of the sum set aside for operating expenses to hire a computer technician from a small, anonymous firm in Calcutta that specialized in such things to hack into the various operators' computer systems to access them and feed the displays to Noortman's computer.

He watched the traffic in and out of these ports for a month, looking up each ship's AIS and searching their most recent ports of call, working up a history of each going back five years.

The automatic identification system was a praiseworthy attempt by the International Maritime Organization to have every ship on the seven seas broadcast an identification number to be picked up and monitored by satellite. This was a good idea for shippers, who could track their cargos around the world, and a great idea for pirates, because anyone with a fifty-dollar receiver from Radio Shack could also monitor them and identify the most lucrative targets.

He followed their current voyages via their AIS numbers through a satellite tracking firm that had proved reliable in the past. Most of this information would be discarded as he whittled down the list, but Noortman was nothing if not thorough.

In the end, he had ten prospects, of which he eliminated seven on the grounds that their owners were too easily identifiable, if only to him. Of the three remaining, one ship looked very promising, registered out of Niue, an island nation in the South Pacific, one of whose very few viable industries was registering offshore firms wishing to avoid filing financial statements and paying taxes, owned through a Panamanian company with headquarters in Liberia and a parent company incorporated in the Bahamas controlled from Amsterdam and bankrolled out of Switzerland, where the trail ended abruptly in a Byzantine layer of partnerships and limited-liability corporations. He was so delighted with the artistry inherent in this industrial-strength obfuscation of lawful accountability that he promised himself he would trace the ship's owner to the top of the food chain after the job was done.

It was at present leased to a Russian corporation. One of the attractions of this particular ship was that it was scheduled for maintenance next month in its home port.

Since the Wall came down in 1989, pretty much everything in Russia could be had for the asking in exchange for currency of any solvent Western nation. Noortman chose a dock, contacted a local expediter, and bought a local customs agent. In all it took about an hour, and the total cost would be the lowest expense on this operation's balance sheet.

The deck-top cargo took a little longer and cost a great deal more, but it would be loaded out of the same port. Pitiful, really, and no challenge at all for a man of his skill and experience.

The cargo from China required a little more finesse, although with the precipitous drop in the price of Chinese steel over the past two years he was able to negotiate a price that would not only give them enough ballast for a reasonably smooth ride but also ensure a more than reasonable profit on the other end.

Always assuming Mr. Smith and Mr. Jones had any interest in selling. Which he was fairly confident they did not. He arranged for lading and customs in Shanghai and then went to the market to buy fresh fish for the sashimi he would make that evening for the handsome young lawyer he hoped would become his next lover.

Seven weeks after they had met with the Koreans in Thailand, he called Fang and reported in.

There was a long silence. "What?" he said.

"I'm worried about this one," Fang said.

"Why?"

"Perhaps it is our customer."

Noortman was no fool, and he gave Fang's concern due consideration. "They don't leave witnesses, do you mean?"

"No, not that—less refuse for me to dispose of. No, what bothers me is that they are fanatics."

Noortman shrugged. "They are customers. They pay us, we provide a service."

"I don't trust people with causes. They are not rational, and therefore they are dangerously unpredictable."

"They have given us a very large sum of money. Without haggling over the price. This argues a very strong commitment."

"That may be what worries me most," Fang said.

Noortman laughed. Fang didn't. "What?" Noortman said.

"How do we get off?"

"Mr. Smith said he has made arrangements."

"You are very confident for someone who won't be along for the ride. I'd like a few more details."

"Mr. Smith seems to be very security conscious."

"He certainly does," Fang said.

When Noortman's phone rang next it was Smith. Noortman, mindful of the respect due an employer with a bankroll the size of Smith's, sat up straight and gave a sober précis of his progress to date.

"That is acceptable," Smith said. He stayed on the line.

"There was something else?" Noortman said cautiously.

"Yes. I have another task for you. You alone."

Translated, this meant Fang was not to be told. After a moment, Noortman said, "What is this task?"

When Smith finished speaking, Noortman was silent.

"Well?" Smith said. "Are we agreed?"

Fang would show no mercy if he knew that Noortman was cutting deals behind his back. Still, Noortman wasn't a fool, he knew that Fang was thinking of retiring. Even if Fang survived this trip, doubtful now that he knew of this second of Smith's requirements, Noortman would very probably be looking for employment elsewhere.

But perhaps it was time for Noortman to step out on his own, to prove his own abilities to future associates. He made up his mind and, conscious of the acceleration of his heartbeat, said, "It will be very expensive."

"It always is," Smith said.

When they completed their business, Noortman hung up the phone and looked at his palm. It was damp.

One thing Fang was right about. Fanatics were dangerously unpredictable.

7

december 2004
wonson, north korea

"IS SPIRIT WILL WANDER," Jones said.

"Why, because we weren't here when he died?" Smith said, and snorted. "Superstitious nonsense."

They stood at the foot of the grave. It was mounded in traditional fashion to prevent water seepage, but there was no headstone. The caretaker had had to give them directions to their father's grave.

"What did he die of?" Jones said.

Smith shrugged. "An infection that could have been cured by a nonprescription drug available over the counter in any Western pharmacy." His hands tightened into fists. When he became aware of it, he loosened them, deliberately relaxing one finger at a time. He breathed in and out again. "We will change this."

Jones was less certain. "Will we?"

Smith had no doubts. "We will," he said firmly.

"Will the Americans even pay attention?"

Smith gave a thin smile. "They will have no choice."

Jones wasn't so sure, but he didn't want to start a fight, at least not one on a less than international scale. They stood side by side at the foot of the grave, staring at the mound of dirt. "Perhaps we'll be back in time for *sosang.*"

"Perhaps," Jones replied, but neither of them believed it. By the first anniversary of their father's death his two sons would be dead or imprisoned in a land far away from this cemetery, and they both knew it. He turned. "Come. Uncle has a bed for us."

THERE WASN'T A BED but there was a roof. It was chilly because there was no heat, and dark because the local electric utility had run out of fuel and had no money to buy more, but cold water still ran from the one tap and their uncle had managed to beg, borrow, or steal a few ounces of real beef, which he offered boiled in grass soup. Afterward he served them a traditional Korean tea, pouring boiling water from a tin saucepan dented almost but not quite past the point of function into a heated clay teapot. He poured more boiling water over the outside of the teapot as the tea brewed. He poured out the first two brews in ceremonial fashion, and everyone pretended not to notice that there were no tea leaves in either.

To the third brew he added the leaves, although so few the resulting liquid was still mostly water. It was hot, though, and warmed them as it went down. They drank it slowly, conversing in quiet tones, also from tradition but also because they didn't want their uncle's neighbors to learn that he had company and turn him in for harboring fugitives in exchange for a handful of rice.

Uncle had shrunk in the two years since they had seen him last, a boy's body with an old man's face. His skin and hair was colorless from malnutrition, and the sore on his left nostril where the border guards had pierced a hole to string him to the other captured escapees had never completely healed. He wore tattered trousers beneath a patched and faded jacket. The rags wrapped neatly around his feet in lieu of shoes he had somehow managed to keep mostly clean.

He spoke a few words, all his energy having gone into the welcome he had prepared for his nephews. He didn't know how their father had died, but he praised the Morning Star for bringing him home and allowing him to be buried next to his wife, who had starved to death, his third son, a soldier who had been shot by his commanding officer when he refused to rob a peasant's home to feed his troop, and his two daughters, who had died of exposure following their mother's death.

When the tea was done, the three of them curled into threadbare blankets on a thin cot placed as close to the tiny stove as possible without setting the cot on fire. The brothers lay on either side of their uncle, and it was probably his warmest night since his wife had been sent away to a camp for daring to cross into China and ask for rice, a capital offense against the North Korean ideology of Juche, or self-reliance.

In a nation so self-absorbed that its modern history began in 1912, the year Kim Il Sung was born, Juche was only one more example of political solipsism that, however much it defied reality, guided the lives of its citizens from cradle to increasingly early grave. It was why the uncle of Ja Yong-bae, alias Smith, and Ja Bae-ho, alias Jones, believed that Kim Jong Il, known to his people by many names, including "the Morning Star," had personally interceded to bring his brother's body home.

His sons had escaped this philosophical inculcation when their mother had shoved them across the Chinese border ahead of her, and had turned to offer the guards pursuing them the rings from her fingers and the bodies of her daughters in exchange for her sons' freedom.

THE BROTHERS SET OUT the next morning to walk from their uncle's house to the nearest town, some twenty miles distant. From there they hitched a ride to Pyongyang. They contacted a local smuggler with whom they had had dealings in the past. He put them on a fishing boat that managed to slip past the defenses of two nations to put them ashore on a deserted stretch of coastline south of the DMZ. Under cover of night and a fortuitous fog they walked to Inchon and took a train to Seoul.

They arrived at the Great East Gate Market by midnight. The streets were mobbed with Koreans selling everything from New England Patriots jerseys to knockoffs of Halston dresses and Levi's jeans. Down an alley they found a merchant selling Brooks Brothers suits, or what looked very much like them. Smith exchanged a few words with the merchant, who barely paused to acknowledge them before jerking a thumb toward the back of his stall. There they found two stools and a camp stove, and there they sat for three days, waiting. The merchant sold his Brooks Brothers merchandise steadily but not spectacularly.

At a little past 1:00 A.M. on the fourth day two tall young Russian women appeared, to greet the merchant with exuberant familiarity, to offer gifts of vodka and caviar, and to examine every single article of clothing he had in stock. Their Korean was competent if uninspired. A long, fierce negotiation followed that ended in the purchase of six men's topcoats, a dozen women's blazers, a dozen men's sport jackets, and various amounts of skirts, shirts, sweaters, and vests for both sexes. After extracting a twenty percent discount for paying in cash, one of the women counted out a large wad of money into the merchant's hand while the other muscled the clothing into an ungainly pile. Without looking up from the wad of currency the merchant snapped his fingers. Smith and Jones appeared with packs, to which the purchases were secured with rope. The women avoided looking at their faces and left soon after.

The brothers hauled the packs back to the coast, where they met the same smuggler, whose boat took them back across the border. From the coast they wended a tedious route north, on foot and sticking to heavily traveled roads, losing themselves in as much of a crowd as North Korea was at present capable of mustering. They crossed into Russia at Khasan, where the two Russian women welcomed them at the border, and rode in the back of a very cold step van with the cargo all the way to Khabarovsk. From Khabarovsk they took the Trans-Siberian Railway to Komsomolsk, again riding in the freight car with the Russians' payload. From Komsomolsk they were upgraded into a seat on the aging Tupolev into Moscow, where they took leave of the women, who paid them well and then tipped them, too, which made them both think they should have checked the pockets and the linings of the clothing to see what else they had been bringing into Mother Russia.

In Moscow they took an even older Tupolev to Petropavlovsk-Kamchatsky. Their forged passports, visas, and work permits went unchallenged. They found menial jobs as sweepers and loaders on the docks and a one-room apartment with light but no heat.

They settled in to wait, sinking with barely a trace into the general population, which unlike the citizenry of many Russian cities was fully occupied building ships for the Russian Pacific fleet, assembling Mig fighters for export, manning a steel mill to furnish material for the construction of both, and lading freight on and off the many ships coming into the port.

Within days, the others began to trickle into town in ones and twos.

Smith and Jones wielded shovels and picks and the occasional broom, and waited.

8

january 7
hong kong

HUGH LEFT BALTIMORE ONE evening at 8:30 P.M. and arrived in Hong Kong the next day at 1:05 P.M. He didn't sleep well on jets, spending most of his time holding them in the air by the armrests, and he was feeling distinctly travel worn when he came through customs.

He was also weighed down by the possibility that he was going to be fired for any number of reasons, among them disobeying a direct order and misuse of public funds, but he shoved that into the back of his mind and pushed through the crowd to the curb. A taxi pulled up and Arlene's voice said, "Get in."

He did and they pulled away with a lurch and a corresponding roar from a muffler that sounded as if it were hanging by a thread.

"How was your flight?"

"Give me a Super Cub anytime," he said. "What have you got?"

"No hello after I've spent two and a half months in the wilderness for you?"

"Hong Kong isn't exactly the wilderness, Arlene. Come on, give."

Arlene's smile was small and satisfied. "I found him."

"You told me that six weeks ago. What else?"

She pretended to pout. "I don't get to brag?"

"Later. Talk."

"I had a couple of local contacts, and one of them knows someone in Chinese customs. Turns out they've been interested in Fang and Noortman for some time. They've compiled quite the little dossier."

"You didn't manage to score a look at it?"

She smiled again.

"God, I'm so smart," Hugh said.

"For what?"

"For hiring you."

She laughed. "Naturally I agree."

"What was in the dossier?"

"Our boy's been busy." She recounted half a dozen of Noortman and Fang's jobs, including the most recent one. "They took a tramp freighter"—she closed her eyes for a moment—"the *Orion's Belt,* carrying a load of Chilean lumber from Valparaiso to Mumbai. Near as our friends can figure, Noortman, uh, rerouted the cargo to Sumatra and sold it on the black market. The Indonesians are desperate for construction materials after the tsunami, and they don't ask a lot of questions when a load of two-by-fours shows up at the dock."

"What did they do with the ship?"

"Sold it to shipbreakers in Alang." At his look she elaborated. "A beach on the west coast of India." She shrugged. "An efficient means of disposing of the evidence. I was writing a story on Mumbai a couple of years ago and I took a trip out there. Hell of an operation. The beach is six miles long and on any given day there can be as many as two hundred ships being scrapped at once. The ship would have been gone in as little as six months. Maybe a year. Like I said, efficient."

Sara would have hated the very idea of an operation like Alang's, Hugh thought. "Can our friends in Hong Kong prove any of this?"

Arlene snorted. "It was a French-owned, Liberian-flagged freighter carrying a Chilean cargo bound for India, with Indian officers and a Filipino crew, taken by pirates of multiple Asian nations in international waters. No one country even has jurisdiction over the crime scene, never mind any evidence that would stand up in court."

"Yeah," Hugh said. "So?"

"So, I've been watching Mr. Noortman."

"Have you? Any company?"

"Are our friends watching him, too, do you mean? They say not. I'd say yes, just not twenty-four seven. Noortman has done nothing to offend the local laws, which would be the smart thing to do if he wanted to stay here. Thou shalt not shit in thine own nest."

Hugh couldn't argue with that. "Where are we going?"

"To a restaurant with a conveniently placed front window. I've already reserved a table with a view of our boy's office building."

"Marry me," Hugh said.

She grinned. "You're too old for me."

"Noortman actually has a storefront?"

"Oh yeah, Hong Kong Fast Freight, Ltd., is very much on the up-and-up, licensed, bonded, registered, incorporated, files quarterly tax returns, contributes to enough local charities in small enough amounts to stay low on the local social radar screen. All perfectly aboveboard and squeaky clean." As an afterthought she said, "Of course, this is Hong Kong. Squeaky clean in Hong Kong isn't squeaky clean in, say, Seattle. Or for that matter Beirut."

"I thought everything tightened up after the Chinese took over."

Arlene gave him a look. "It's still Hong Kong."

Hugh, who wasn't about to admit that he'd learned most of what he knew about Hong Kong from the www .discoverhongkong.com Web site while he was sitting in the Baltimore airport waiting for his flight to board and the rest from James Clavell during the flight, gave a non-committal grunt.

"You've been here before, right? So I don't have to give you the tour?"

Half a dozen times to change planes, and once to meet in the British Airways lounge with a snotty little shit of a case officer who had started their conversation with a recitation of his family tree, which appeared to reach all the way back to the *Mayflower,* and reached forward to several members of Congress, a cabinet-level post in the current administration, and a Supreme Court justice. It had ended with the snotty little shit of a case officer white-faced and trembling, mumbling out his report of the nascent Islamic terrorist cell in Egypt he had stumbled across in his posting to the American embassy in Cairo. The report had been unexpectedly useful, but Hugh, who saved the rough side of his tongue especially for arrogant little pricks just starting out in the agency, didn't make the mistake of saying so. Said prick was now warming the most junior of junior chargé d'affaires seats in the American embassy in Zaire (or the Democratic Republic of the Congo or whatever the hell they were calling themselves nowadays), which gave Hugh the warm fuzzies all over whenever he thought of it, which wasn't often.

"I've been here before," Hugh said without elaboration. He was a desk man, not a field agent. He shook off his fatigue and watched the approaching skyline with interest. From a distance Hong Kong looked like a multitowered castle built on a tall green promontory, surrounded by the world's largest moat. The water was crowded with craft of every kind and size, from homemade junks to boxy ferries to sleek cruise ships.

As they entered the city proper, Hugh saw a lot of concrete, a lot of neon, and a shitload of people, many in cars. The traffic was bumper-to-bumper stop and go, and none of the drivers would have made it a hundred feet on an American street without being pulled over for felony tailgating. Everyone, pedestrian and driver alike, ignored the stoplights, and Hugh saw a black Mercedes roll through an intersection against a red and literally hit a woman in the crosswalk. The car was moving slowly enough that all it did was hoist her up on the hood. She slid down and yelled at the driver. The driver stuck his head out the window and yelled an uncomplimentary reply, and for a minute Hugh felt like he was in New York.

"Here we are," Arlene said, and leaned forward to tap the driver on the shoulder. They screeched to a halt, Arlene handed over an alarmingly thick wad of banknotes and they got out, elbowing for room on a street of storefronts thronged with people. "This way," Arlene said, and led Hugh through a glass door into a tiny anteroom with a podium barricading the rest of the establishment from just anyone who might wander in off the street. Arlene smiled at the hostess, who didn't smile back until the two hundred and fifty Hong Kong dollars Arlene tipped her disappeared down the front of her dress. She turned to lead them into the restaurant proper.

Arlene noticed Hugh's expression and said in a low voice, "Relax. It was only about thirty American, and that's cheap for a sit-down restaurant in Hong Kong."

"It's not that," Hugh said, looking over her shoulder.

"What is it, then?" Arlene followed his gaze, and her eyes widened. "Holy shit."

Noortman was sitting at the table in the window right next to the one the hostess was standing beside, menus in hand, watching them with an impatient look on her face.

For a moment Hugh was transfixed, and then he recovered his wits. "Smile and talk to me," he whispered to Arlene, and gave her a gentle shove forward.

"What if he recognizes me from Pattaya Beach?" Arlene hissed.

"He won't, he was too focused on his next big score," Hugh said, and prayed he was right.

It was a safe bet, as today Arlene was dressed in a deep blue suit, cream-colored silk shirt, heels, and pearls, and her hair had been moussed and blow-dried into a smooth knot at the nape of her neck. She looked nothing like the zaftig tourist in the Bermuda shorts the previous October.

Noortman, on the other hand, looked exactly as he had in the photographs Arlene took of him. His nose was aquiline but his eyes were Asian, and his teeth were square and white, with the exception of the gold-encased incisor that flashed when he smiled. His skin was sallow, his stylishly cut hair dark but not black. Like Arlene, he was dressed to suit his environment, in a charcoal striped suit with a dark red tie that matched the silk handkerchief peeping from his breast pocket. The watch on his wrist had the glint of Rolex gold. His shoes probably cost even more.

He was drinking tea as he scrolled down the screen of a laptop. The server brought a tray just then and made a distressed sound. Noortman looked up and smiled. Hugh was in the middle of being seated but it looked like a perfectly ordinary smile, no fangs showing, although it was a smile that seemed familiar, crooking up at one side in what could almost have been called a sneer. Otherwise,

Noortman looked like any other young and ambitious Hong Kong businessman.

Hugh became aware that Arlene was giving him a minatory look, and he realized their server had materialized. On impulse he told the server, "Tiger Beer." He smiled across at Arlene, and said in a voice just above a whisper, "You didn't think that because this restaurant was so close to his office that he never came in here? Even pirates have to eat."

Arlene hooked a thumb toward her sternum and mouthed words that Hugh couldn't understand. He shook his head. Arlene leaned forward. He met her halfway. "What?" he said.

"He's gay, right?" Arlene whispered.

"What? I don't— That's what it says in his files. So what?"

"After I leave, pick him up."

"What?" Noortman looked up at Hugh's unguarded exclamation and then went back to his braised abalone in oyster sauce.

"Pick him up," Arlene repeated. "You're a hunk, he's probably drooling into his plate over you right now." She reached into her bag.

He said the only thing he could. "I am not a hunk!"

She rolled her eyes. "Right. Robert Redford has nothing to worry about." She pulled her hand out of her bag.

"Arlene, I—"

"His apartment is close by his office. That's probably where he'll take you. I'll follow."

"Arlene, we don't even know if Noortman makes a habit out of picking up guys off the street, I can't just—"

"We don't know what kind of security he's got on his office or who else is keeping watch on it. Getting into his apartment is our best bet." Her bag vibrated. "I'm so sorry, please excuse me for a moment," she said to Hugh in a louder voice, in French, accompanied by a dazzling smile. She pulled out a cell phone and flipped it open. She listened for a moment and then let loose with more and very rapid French. "No, it's quite all right, Veronique, I'm only five minutes away. Offer him some tea, let him look over the closing papers, and tell him I'll be there immediately." She flipped the phone closed, shouldered her bag, and rose to her feet. She smiled down at Hugh, an infinitely kind smile, and, still in French, said in a soothing voice, "I'm so sorry our luncheon has been cut short, Mr. Reeve. As I was saying, I have several properties that I believe would interest you. Please call my assistant at this number"— Arlene handed Hugh a small square of stiff paper that later proved to be the business card of Arlene's accountant— "to schedule showings. *A bientôt.*"

With that, Arlene marched off, leaving Hugh seated at his table facing Noortman seated at his. Hugh's beer came and he downed half of it at one go. He looked up to see Noortman smiling at him. There was definitely something about the smile, but he still couldn't place it and he had other things to worry about.

Hugh could give a shit if men slept with each other so long as he wasn't one of them. He didn't care if they married and adopted seven kids and watched *The Birdcage* every night on the Bravo Channel. He himself was a flaming heterosexual. It wasn't that he thought Arlene's idea was bad, per se, it was just that he didn't have the first clue how to go about picking up a man.

Noortman was still smiling at him. What the hell. For starters, he smiled back. He even went so far as to salute Noortman with his beer.

The next thing he knew they were seated at the same table, his or Noortman's he could never remember, the hostess cooing at Noortman in Mandarin and Noortman kissing the back of her hand with his seductive sneer.

Then Noortman was speaking to him in flawless French and he was replying, and they were having a stimulating and informative discussion on Hong Kong real estate, which moved on to globalization and from there to the films of Pierce Brosnan, for whom Noortman appeared to harbor an inordinate fondness.

Noortman mentioned that he dabbled in Hong Kong properties himself off and on. What precisely was Hugh looking for? Hugh replied that he was interested in warehouse space along the waterfront for his import-export business. He was presently looking at various properties with a broker.

Really, said Noortman, how very interesting. He was in the import-export business himself and had extensive contacts with Hong Kong shipping firms. Now that he thought about it, he was convinced that just the other day someone had spoken of a very desirable property for sale, located conveniently near Central. He was sure he still had the listing. Would Hugh like to see it?

Of course Hugh would, who by this time was feeling much more relaxed. It turned out that picking up a guy wasn't all that different from picking up a girl. He managed not to flinch when Noortman smiled deeply into his eyes, and by a superhuman effort didn't jump when Noortman's knee rubbed against his beneath the table. By superimposing a woman's face over Noortman's features—it didn't matter that it was Sara's face he saw, he told himself—he was even able to put what he hoped was a little heat into his own expression.

It must have worked, because shortly thereafter Hugh found himself walking down the sidewalk, following Noortman as the other man wove a sinuous path between the moving mass of humanity that was Hong Kong. A horn honked, a jackhammer sounded, and people talked loudly in Mandarin and ten other languages, a few of which Hugh didn't recognize, which only added to his feeling of unreality.

Noortman turned down a side street, much quieter in volume and much tonier in appearance, with awnings out to the curb and uniformed doormen guarding brass-fitted doors. Noortman went into one, Hugh tagging along behind and doing his damnedest not to look around for Arlene.

An elevator whisked them up seventeen floors, and Noortman let them into a spacious apartment furnished with leather and teak and glass. There were intricate Afghan rugs scattered artfully across a maple floor waxed to a golden shine, and the crystal lined up over the bar looked fresh out of the vat at Baccarat.

"A drink?" Noortman said. "I have some very nice scotch."

"Sounds good," Hugh said.

While Noortman busied himself at the elegant wet bar, Hugh admired the sweeping view of the mainland, the Star Ferries working the sea between it and Hong Kong Island. Even at this distance the ferries looked ready to sink beneath the weight of rush-hour traffic, which Hugh had decided in Hong Kong was probably twenty-four hours a day. He wondered where the hell Arlene was. He wondered how long he could delay the inevitable before Noortman became suspicious. He wondered if this qualified as cheating on Sara. He wondered if the sweat pooling in his armpits was beginning to show.

He became aware of Noortman standing behind him. Deliberately relaxing his jaw, he turned.

"You're so tall," Noortman said in a soft voice. He reached a hand up to touch Hugh's hair. "Your hair is beautiful. Is it real?"

"Am I a natural blond?" Hugh said. He tried to laugh and had to abandon the attempt when his voice cracked. "Yes."

"And your eyes, so brown. It's such a wonderful contrast." Noortman took a sip of his drink. "People tell me I have a smile like— What is the name of that American singer? The one who shakes his hips?"

"Elvis!" Hugh said. "I knew you looked familiar."

Noortman smiled, satisfied. He took another sip and set the glass down. He took Hugh's glass and set it down, too. A foot shorter than Hugh, he let his hand slide up Hugh's lapel to his neck, and pulled his head down.

A moment later there was a knock at the door. Noortman pulled back, swearing under his breath. "I'll get rid of them. Don't move."

He went to the door, and Hugh, disobeying orders, followed behind on silent feet. Noortman opened the door and Arlene was there and already swinging her bag. It caught Noortman a hell of a thump on the left side of his head and he crumpled into Hugh's arms.

"Where the hell were you?" Hugh hissed at Arlene, dragging Noortman into the dining room and sitting him down in one of the chairs. "I actually had to kiss the guy, for crissake."

"Think of it as taking one for the team," Arlene told him, and hauled out a roll of duct tape.

"Notice my self-control," Hugh said. "You still live." He took the duct tape from Arlene and wrapped it around Noortman's torso and the chair back, Noortman's wrists and the arms of the chair, and Noortman's ankles and the legs of the chair.

"All right already," Arlene said. "The idea is to immobilize him, not shroud him."

"He's a spurned lover," Hugh said; "he's not going to

wake up happy." He added, "You tell anyone I kissed him and you'll never work on this planet again."

"It got the job done, didn't it? Stop being such a big baby."

Noortman groaned. After a moment his eyes opened and he stared at Hugh, at first bewildered, and then, as realization flooded back, hurt. Hugh felt ridiculously guilty.

"Mr. Noortman," Arlene said.

His gaze shifted to her. His brows came together and his voice came out a raspy husk of its former mellifluous self. Everyone was speaking French. "Who are you? What do you want?"

"We have some questions for you, sir," Arlene said formally. She reached into her bag and, before Hugh's disbelieving and slightly affronted eyes, produced a large claw hammer. The wood of the handle was worn smooth and the metal of the head was rusty and flaking. "We have no wish to resort to violence, Mr. Noortman, but we mean to have the answers to our questions before we leave."

After a moment Noortman got his jaw back into working order and said in a slightly shaky voice, "Questions? What questions? I demand that you release me at once. There has been some terrible mistake." He appealed to Hugh. "We were having such a good time. I don't understand what is happening here. Please let me go, and let us talk about this, get things straightened out."

"Jaap," Hugh said gently.

Noortman's eyes widened. "How do you know my given name? I didn't tell you. I—"

Hugh knelt down next to Noortman's chair and smiled. "Jaap Noortman, Junior. Born in Singapore in 1970, graduated from the University of Singapore in 1986. Worked a year for your father in the Department of Customs, until

you were recruited by the pirate Fang Ho to help him identify and move the cargoes he hijacks in the South China
Sea. How am I doing so far?"

Noortman swallowed. "I don't know what you're talking about. I was born in Singapore, yes, but I am a respectable businessman. I run a legitimate freight concern
here in Hong Kong, you can ask anyone. There has been
some mistake." He tried to smile, first at Hugh and then at
Arlene. The now familiar sneer was missing in action.
"Please, untie me, and I will verify my identity."

"We know who you are," Arlene said, and took the
hammer. "Gag him," she told Hugh.

Hugh hesitated, and then did as he was told. This man
had conspired in too many deaths for Hugh to feel com-
punction now. Arlene was right. The Koreans had been on
the loose too long, Fang and Noortman had been active in
their cause for too long, too much had been set into motion and too much was at risk. There was no time now for
subtle.

Hugh overlapped the duct tape at the back of Noortman's head and stepped back. Arlene raised the hammer.
Noortman's eyes bulged but Arlene didn't wait, she
brought the head of the hammer down as hard as she
could swing it on Noortman's right knee.

Her grunt of effort was drowned out by Noortman's
muffled scream. The duct tape strained as he tried to double over. Tears streamed from his eyes, mucus from his
nose. He made gagging sounds. Hugh kept his face impassive and reached out to rip the duct tape from Noortman's
face. He lost some hair as well as some skin. He screamed.

"Quiet," Arlene said, looking as bored as she sounded,
"or we'll have to gag you again."

"What do you want?" Noortman said, his breath coming in sobs. "It hurts, it hurts, it hurts!" The blood had
soaked through his pants and his knee was already be-

ginning to swell into a misshapen lump, straining his pants leg.

"I want to know where your partner is, Jaap."

Noortman shook his head, moaning. "I can't, I can't."

"Gag him again," Arlene said. Hugh, a little pale, stepped forward with the duct tape.

"No," Noortman screamed. "I can't tell you, I can't, he'll kill me!"

"Then answer," Hugh said.

"We know you're working for the two Koreans. What did they hire you to do? Where is Fang now?"

"I can't! He'll kill me, I tell you! He has killed others! He'll kill me, too!"

"I know," Arlene told him, "and I'm sorry about this, but I really am in a hurry." She nodded at Hugh. A little pale, he tore off a length of duct tape and stepped forward.

Frantically, Noortman tried to jerk his head out of the way. Arlene grabbed a handful of his hair and held him still while Hugh taped his mouth again. Noortman screamed behind the gag, and kept screaming as the hammer came down again on the same knee.

This time Noortman threw up behind the gag, and when Hugh ripped it free he had to step back quickly to avoid being hit by the braised abalone in oyster sauce he had just watched Noortman eat. Arlene grabbed Noortman's hair and yanked his head upright. "In October you met with two men from North Korea in a cafe in Pattaya Beach, Thailand. Who were they? What did they want?"

The bottom half of Noortman's right leg was canted at a hideously awkward angle. Blood ran into his fashionable leather shoe and stained its gold buckle. "I can't, I can't," he moaned.

Arlene raised the hammer, and this time she reversed it so that the claw side was down. Noortman saw it and screamed again.

• • •

AN HOUR LATER ARLENE and Hugh were in a cab on their way back to the airport. "Where the hell did you get that hammer?" Hugh said at random, trying not to think of the scene they had left behind in Noortman's apartment.

"There were a bunch of construction guys doing a re-model on a shop. There was an open toolbox with the hammer sitting right on top."

"Well done," Hugh said, but his heart wasn't in it.

"What's wrong?" she said, unruffled, matter-of-fact. "We got what we needed."

"Yeah," Hugh said. "We did that."

Her expression softened. "You're not in the field a lot, are you, Hugh?"

He tried to smile. "Once a desk man, always a desk man."

The things he had done in Noortman's apartment would haunt him for the rest of his life. Noortman had broken so quickly and so completely, he had given them everything they had asked for and more, but Hugh could find no cause in that for self-congratulation, and definitely none for humor.

"What next?"

Hugh thought about it. "Home," he said.

Arlene cleared her throat with delicacy. "Are you, ah, calling in first?"

"You mean the director?" Hugh thought about that for a while, too. He had a cell phone, but he always used a landline when he could. Cell phone signals were far too easy to tap into. "I'll call him from the airport."

"Will he believe you?"

Hugh took a deep breath and let it out. "Probably not. That's why I'm going home."

"Home," she said. "You don't mean D.C., do you."

He didn't answer. They rode for a few minutes in silence.

"Hugh, is this the smart thing to do?"

Hugh gave Arlene one incredulous look, and laughed out loud.

NOORTMAN LAY ON THE exquisite Afghan carpet where he had fallen from the chair when they'd cut him free of the duct tape. He didn't know how much time had passed. The bleeding had stopped, and so long as he remained absolutely motionless his leg didn't hurt.

Of course, if he so much as twitched, the pain was agonizing and all-encompassing, subsuming every other sense. At some point, he would have to crawl to the phone and call for help, which he planned to do as soon as he summoned up the necessary strength.

The color of blood was no longer pleasing to him. He would never again be able to tuck a red silk handkerchief into a pocket and think of his father. Instead he would think of himself, broken, bleeding, lying in his own filth, a victim of strangers who had invaded his own home.

The police, yes. He should call the police. As soon as he gathered a little more energy.

They would want to know what had happened. He had invited a stranger into his home and had been attacked, that was what he would say. Of course, his description of his assailant would be suitably vague. He wouldn't want Reeve interrogated, something that could cause untold complications. As a foreign national residing in Hong Kong, he had to be careful not to make a fuss. If he did, the notoriously parochial local police would find a way to invite him to leave.

He had never been a very good liar, so it was going to take some thinking out before he made the call, and he hurt very much and he was very tired.

And yet, and yet, he knew a tiny spark of triumph growing deep inside him.

He had told them, yes, told them enough for them to stop hurting him.

But not everything.

The fibers of the carpet pressing into his cheek, he smiled.

9

january 7
petropavlovsk

FANG WAS SWEATING IN spite of the below-zero temperatures and the brisk onshore wind that dropped the chill factor into the minus double digits. It didn't help that it was three o'clock on a January morning six thousand miles north of his usual area of operations.

The immense, untidy yard was a mass of rectangular containers imprinted with the names and logos of shipping firms from all over the world: Maersk Sealand, Cosco, Pan Ocean Shipping, Teco Ocean Shipping, even Czech Ocean Shipping and a host of other names of maritime freight firms too small or specialized to be immediately recognizable. The containers were lined up in rows forming aisles just wide enough for the tractors and lifts to maneuver between them.

The yard was brightly lit with halogen lamps mounted on fifty-foot poles, but the containers were stacked three high and cast deep, dark shadows, providing a wind tunnel effect to consolidate every passing breath of air into what felt to Fang like a gale-force draft. He shivered again, the nervous sweat congealing on his spine. The zip of his parka was already up as high as it would go, but he tugged at it anyway, and cursed involuntarily when the teeth caught at the flesh beneath his jaw.

Smith's head whipped around. He didn't say anything. He didn't have to. An unaccustomed flush flooded up into Fang's cheekbones. He set his teeth and looked down to fiddle unnecessarily with the chest strap of his pack. Like the parka, it was the very best U.S. military surplus issue.

They were crouched next to a twelve-foot chain-link fence topped with razor wire, just outside the reach of the lights, which were directed inward at the yard and the containers. Armed guards roamed the perimeter, but on a night like this they were spending more time in the guard shack down at the gate that faced the docks than they were on patrol. The shack was a hundred feet away, but every time the shack's door opened Fang could hear a burst of Russian music and loud laughter. Sons of bitches were probably knocking back the vodka with a fine and free hand. All the better for this operation.

They had gathered together in a group for the first time that afternoon, Smith and Jones and their twenty men, Fang and his ten. The building was a small warehouse with a loft holding up a hoist. There was a small area in back of the hoist where their equipment and supplies had been stacked in wooden crates stenciled with the logo of the United Nations and the notation PRINTED MATTER on the sides.

Another of Noortman's little jokes. If he'd called for the crates to be anything other than books, foodstuffs, say, or hand tools, no bribe would have been big enough to keep the Russian customs officials from helping themselves to a bonus and discovering the true contents of the crates. The UN logo, even Fang was pushed grudgingly to admit, was a mark of genius. Not only were they books, an observer would conclude, they were most likely tracts on crop rotation or home health care or English as a second language. Also, books were heavy, which would account for the weight.

They had pried open the crates and dressed in silence—fatigues, cold-weather gear, heavy lined boots with non-skid soles, headsets with microphones keyed to the same frequency. And of course weapons, pistols and rifles, the latest in automatic weapons, with enough ammunition to start a war.

Smith divided them into two parties, one with him, the other with Jones, and as soon as it was dark led them in small groups by various back alleys to the fence next to which they were currently huddled, blending into the winter landscape with white smocks enveloping them from hood to knee. And freezing to death in spite of the cold-weather gear.

The door to the guard shack opened with a brief blast of Elvis Presley singing about a party in the county jail, and a stray breeze wafted the smell of sausage to the huddled men a moment later. One of Fang's men stirred. Fang gave him a fierce look and the man subsided, but he was as unused to cold-weather work as his boss was. Fang only hoped they were all going to be able to walk when the time came.

Approaching footsteps crunched through the snow. Fang looked around and saw one of the guards approaching, a slight, slender man with a mismatched uniform carelessly buttoned, trailing a cloud of cigarette smoke. He moved his hand down the stock of his rifle and felt something touch his arm. It was Smith, who gave his head one small shake, warning Fang not to move.

The guard wandered down the fence. They caught the occasional snatch of song in slurred Russian.

The guard paused ten feet from where on the other side of the fence the last man in line crouched, and unzipped his fly. The urine steamed and hissed as it hit the snow. He shook, tucked himself back inside his pants, and zipped them up again. He lit another cigarette and blew out a luxurious cloud. He spoke a few words in Russian in a low voice.

Next to Fang, Smith replied.

"*Da*," said the guard, the only word in the entire conversation Fang understood, and strolled up to the corner of the fence, singing again as he went. It took a moment before Fang recognized the song as "Yesterday."

Smith signaled the man closest to the corner, who produced a pair of snips and went to work. Moments later he folded back a large section of the chain-link, stepped through to the other side, and held it as the rest of them moved silently through the hole and into the yard.

The guard watched, still singing, although he had moved on to "In My Room," giving a not bad impression of Brian Wilson. He seemed to go for mournful in his songs, but then he was Russian.

Once they were all inside the fence, Smith's man bent it back into place and fixed it there with unobtrusive bits of wire. The guard nodded at Smith and jerked his head.

He led them into the labyrinth of stacked containers, keeping to where the darkest shadows were cast, and after they turned the first two corners Fang was hopelessly lost. The yard was deserted, the late shift having knocked off at midnight, but the waterfront of a port city was never completely silent, no matter what season it was, and the wind carried the sounds of forklifts and hydraulic hoists and the subdued rumble of ship's engines, drowning out their footsteps in the snow, even if anyone had been around to hear them. It was almost too easy.

The guard led them to two containers toward the front of the yard, in the row closest to the large gate that fronted on the road that ran the length of the city's coastline. He stopped and turned to face Smith. He motioned, telling Smith without words to back up and take his men with him.

Smith looked at him without expression and did as the guard requested. The guard produced a ring of keys from a pocket and opened both the padlocks on both container doors. He did something else with a tool Fang couldn't make out in the shadowy light and the customs seals were also open.

The guard stepped rapidly back from the second door, still singing, this time a new song. Something about "son of a sailor," he thought, but his teeth had begun to chatter and he couldn't make out the words over the noise.

Another guard stepped from a row of containers, just out of reach for rushing, his rifle cradled in what looked to Fang like a competent grip. Fang, teeth still chattering, waited for the rest of the squad to materialize from the shadows and for him and his men to be arrested and escorted to prison, which would probably be warmer than standing around this yard.

The first guard stopped singing and said something to Smith. He snapped his fingers and pointed to the ground between them.

Smith looked at the first guard for a long moment.

The first guard snapped his fingers and pointed at the ground again. The second guard didn't move.

Smith reached inside his smock and brought out a fat envelope. He tossed it on the ground. The guard motioned for him to back up even farther, and Smith did so. The guard stooped to pick up the envelope and opened it, thumbing through the contents.

He looked up and nodded at Smith. The last of Fang's men, who had remained behind when they came through the fence, materialized out of the gloom behind the second guard. Steel flashed, dark fluid spewed across the snow, the guard fell heavily. Almost before he hit the ground Fang's man had recovered and pocketed the payoff.

Before the first guard could give the alarm, Fang was there, his knife sliding easily and expertly through the guard's uniform and his ribs, up and straight into the heart, stopping it in midbeat. The guard sucked in a great breath of air, shocked eyes staring into Fang's. He looked down at the knife, at Fang's hand on the hilt, as if he couldn't believe it, and then he, too, fell, the knife sliding free, the blade stained a dark purple in the lights of the yard.

Smith took a quick step forward and shoved Fang back. "What do you think you are doing?"

"No witnesses," Fang said without expression.

Jones shoved forward and he and Smith exchanged angry words in whispered Korean. It was obviously about Fang's action, and it was equally obvious that it was uncomplimentary.

"Enough." Fang nodded at one of his men. The Koreans watched as the bodies were arranged to look as if they had been fighting, as the guards' sidearms were fired into both their wounds, covering up the knife marks. The gunshots were masked by the roaring and clanking of heavy equipment operating nonstop all around them. In a town this size there wouldn't be a medical examiner or probably even an effective police force. The local cops would believe what was easiest for them to believe.

Smith, coldly furious, said, "If you are quite finished here, please explain to me who now is going to close and lock the doors behind us and reapply the seals?"

Fang nodded at the man who had taken out the first guard. "He is."

"And how, then, will he join us?"

"He won't. He stays behind. He stays behind," Fang repeated when Smith burst into another flood of Korean. He started toward the nearest container and after a tense moment Smith followed with ten of his men and five of Fang's. Jones and the rest went into the second container.

The door thudded shut behind them and Fang could hear the seals and padlocks clicking back into place. The dark descended like a suffocating blanket. Instantly Fang wanted to be back outside freezing his balls off. More nervous sweat rolled down his spine. He didn't like the dark, and he didn't like small enclosed spaces. He didn't like any of this at all, and the prospect of being stuck here for any length of time was not appealing. He wondered if he could advance the timetable and resolved to take up the topic with Smith at the earliest opportunity.

He wondered if Smith would listen to anything he had to say. He couldn't understand Smith's anger at the killing of the Russians. Anybody would think Smith wanted to get caught.

There was a snick and a light appeared. Smith had a flashlight. They were sandwiched between the doors and the cargo, equipment of some kind swathed in plastic and padding, most of it strapped to pallets. Smith motioned them to follow him as he edged his way between the front pallets and the walls of the container. This was ten times worse than just standing around in the dark. Fang's clothing and equipment caught on every protruding bolt, and several times he was afraid he was going to have to ask for help, but at last they were behind the first row of pallets.

Smith was already unhooking the second layer of strapping and was ripping into the crates stacked there. These crates were identified as being shipped to the Mattel Corporation. Fang examined the label more closely in the dim light cast by the flashlight and saw that the crates were supposed to be full of dolls. Instead they yielded hammocks and sleeping bags, chemical toilets, prepackaged foods, a two-burner camp stove, a set of cook pots, bowls and mugs and spoons, a satellite phone, a whole case of batteries for it, decks of cards, and a mah-jongg game.

The crates and boxes were disassembled and stuffed into the space between the cargo and the container. They attached hooks to the walls of the container and slung the hammocks. At Smith's direction, one of the men unfolded the stove and boiled water for tea and noodles. Fang slurped both down with gratitude, feeling the heat spread into his hands and feet.

Something flapped over his head and he ducked instinctively and looked up. The container had a canvas roof.

He looked at Smith. In a low voice Smith said, "We must be very quiet until we are under way."

Fang was more concerned about the loss of heat. He claimed one of the hammocks closest to the floor, unrolled a sleeping bag and climbed in without removing his boots. As he was pulling the bag to his chin he noticed a spray of blood extending from the back of his hand to the sleeve of his parka. The cold had already made it tacky to the touch, so he didn't have to worry about smearing it all over.

They were made aware of the arrival of morning by the increase in noise outside. Smith gave an order and the men secured everything that wasn't already tied down or tucked behind the cargo straps. A while later the container jolted as a tractor latched on, and the hammocks swung merrily as they moved out of the yard, down the shore road, and rumbled over the wood surface of what was probably a dock.

The sounds of chains jangling were heard, followed by an increase in the pull of gravity when they were hoisted into the air. Men bellowed and somewhere a crane clanked and groaned into action and the container began moving sideways. It stopped, swaying back and forth, and almost immediately began descending. They thudded into something and another voice bellowed. There were answering shouts from the other side of the container walls, and Fang and the rest of the men held themselves quiet and still. More shouting as the container was muscled into position. There was a loud clank as the hoist let go and a series of kachunks, when some kind of fastening kicked in. The voices and the sounds retreated, only to return not much later when the next container was loaded, and the next, and the next.

It continued for six hours. At one in the afternoon the ship shuddered into life, the engines starting with a rumbling roar. The deck vibrated, setting the hammocks to trembling. They got underway an hour later. Five minutes after that the first of Smith's men threw up.

By six that evening they were in the North Pacific, with seas Fang estimated as well as he could from inside the container running at least fifteen feet. The ship was rolling and pitching and corkscrewing, and it sounded like the screw was out of the water as often as it was in it. The ship's helmsman wasn't doing much to compensate, either. Fang foresaw an overhaul in the ship's engine room in the not too distant future.

By now all of Smith's men were puking, some of them just hanging their heads over the sides of their hammocks and others taking turns kneeling in front of the portable toilet. The miasma of vomit and sour sweat mingled with the smell of diesel exhaust creeping into the container. It was enough to make even Fang nauseated. He pulled his sleeping bag over his nose and thought again of that plump wife in Shanghai, with a sturdy son he could raise to be a real seaman, with his own shipping line bankrolled by his father.

This was going to be his last trip, he realized, and with the decision made, he felt almost lighthearted. One more trip, and home for good.

Fang curled more tightly into his sleeping bag and drifted off to the sleep of the righteous.

10

UNDER THE SURE HAND of Chief Edelen the *Sojourner Truth* sidled away from the dock at Dutch Harbor like a hooker caught by a cop in the act of propositioning a john, only with a lot more style. The sky was gray and so was the attitude of most of the crew.

This had not been the *Sojourner Truth*'s best port call. Two underage seamen had spent the better part of their first night in port at Tommy's Elbow Room and most of their second day and night confined to quarters, although most of that had been spent crouched over toilets in the head. Together they had been the proximate cause of three injuries bad enough for the victims to be taken to the hospital and damages to the Elbow Room and a passing pickup truck in excess of five thousand dollars.

It was one seaman's first offense and the other's second. Ensign Ryan had been the investigating officer. Still smarting from the harangue he had received from the owner of the hotel to which the two seamen had retreated, which harangue repeatedly featured the phrase "fucking

Coasties," his report on the incident had been tart and testy. Sara, still smarting from a lengthy conversation with the Dutch Harbor police chief, had signed off on the report without her usual diplomatic toning down of pejorative adjectives and passed it up to the captain.

The captain, still smarting from the two-hour delay in getting away from the dock, was disinclined toward forgiveness. He convened captain's mast before they were all the way out of Unalaska Bay in the hangar in front of all the crew not on watch, instead of in the relative privacy of the wardroom. The two seamen departed broken in rank with thirty days' restriction, thirty days' extra duty, their wages attached to pay for damages incurred, and with substantial portions of their asses missing. The captain vented the rest of his spleen on a pithy indictment of a dozen other crewmen who had had the bad timing to be present at the scene, including Petty Officer Barnette, all of whom he held accountable for not keeping their fellow crewmen from "steering into Stupidland." The crew didn't know who to be more pissed off at for that blanket condemnation, the captain or the offending crew members. PO Barnette, who had made an honest effort to break up the fight, was particularly stung.

It didn't help that the C-130 from Kodiak hadn't made it in with their last shipment of mail, and when they learned that District 17 had tasked them with patrolling the Maritime Boundary Line there was very nearly a mutiny. "There's nothing going on up there this time of year!" PO Barnette said when informed. "Ma'am," he added, a lot quicker than usual, when Sara glared at him.

To a man and a woman everyone on board hated patrolling the MBL. Basically they were there to show the flag. Most of the time the American side of the line was empty of vessels, all the fishing going on on the other side, in Russian territorial waters, which meant no boarding opportunities except for the occasional marine research vessel.

And it was fresh in everyone's memory that even when a foreign flag—say a Russian fishing vessel—did cross the MBL into U.S. territory, and even when a Coast Guard cutter—oh, say the *Sojourner Truth*—caught them half a mile the wrong side of the MBL with their nets in U.S. waters and those nets full of U.S. fish, when said fishing vessel hightailed itself back across the line into Russian territory the cutter was held on the U.S. side, fuming, waiting for District to give them permission to cross the line in hot pursuit.

Said permission, if and when it came, was always too late. Such had been the case the previous August, when District made them wait for the Russian Federal Border Service to show up and escort them across, thirty-six hours later. By then the illegal catch had been long since processed into unidentifiable filets packed deep in an endless line of refrigerated freight containers, the location data on the GPS altered or erased, and the taste of hot pursuit was cold ashes in Coastie mouths.

No, patrolling the Maritime Boundary Line was not an ingredient in any recipe for improving shipboard morale. Sara encouraged the training teams to pile on the fire and damage control drills and helo launches in the hope that it would keep the crew too tired to sulk. She and the senior chief had also organized a Trivial Pursuit championship for this leg of the trip, and the officers would be making pizza that Saturday in the galley, an event the crew always enjoyed, but they all knew it would take awhile before the goodwill kicked in.

She wondered how the miscreants were being treated by their fellow crew members below, but not for long and not with very much sympathy. She sat at her desk, brooding over the inevitable stack of reports, crew assignments, supply orders, and District communiqués.

She worked where she slept, in the forwardmost stateroom in officer country, a step and a stairway from another set of stairs leading to the comm deck and the captain's cabin, which was located directly beneath the bridge. XOs, mercifully, slept alone. She used the upper bunk in her room as a rotating library, but every privilege comes with a price. A stateroom to herself meant that under way there was no getting away from the job. There were two telephones in her stateroom, one of which was Velcroed to the head of her bunk.

As it should be, she told herself. Suck it up, Lange, and stop feeling sorry for yourself.

There was a knock at the door and she looked up. "Sparks? What's up?"

Sparks was the petty officer on duty in communications. He handed her an e-mail and made best speed in the other direction. She read it. "Sparks! Get back here!"

He returned, reluctantly. She read it again, letting him wait. She even read it a third time, hoping against hope that the letters would form new words. They didn't. "I am ordering you to tell me that this is a joke."

He looked as apologetic as his naturally mischievous face was capable of. "It's not a joke, XO. I confirmed, and you know how they are, they've already held a press conference from the bridge of their ship. I e-mailed my wife and had her check CNN. It's already aired. They're en route, all right. They may even beat us back to the line."

"You're fired," Sara said.

"Yes, ma'am," Sparks said, and added hopefully, "Maybe the Russians will sink 'em."

"I wish. Thanks, Sparks."

Correctly reading this statement as his dismissal, he returned to his duty station. Sara relieved her feelings with an uncharacteristic burst of profanity that earned an admiring glance from a passing seaman, and called the captain. "Captain, we've just received a heads-up from District. The Greenpeace vessel *Sunrise Warrior* is en route to the Maritime Boundary Line."

There followed a long silence. "What is their purpose on the MBL?" the captain said.

"According to Sparks, whose wife watched the press conference on CNN, they are protesting the overfishing of the North Pacific Ocean, which they say is causing the precipitous drop in the Steller's sea lion population in the Bering Sea, the sea otter population in the Aleutian Islands, and the salmon runs in Bristol Bay."

There was another long silence while they both thought about the last time they'd had dealings with the *Sunrise Warrior.* Six months before, Greenpeace had been protesting the taking of bowhead whales in the Arctic Ocean by the Inupiat people who lived there. Television footage had been involved, featuring bloodied whale carcasses being winched to shore and one memorable scene when one of the catch was revealed to be female and pregnant. Sara wasn't sure the sight of the dead baby whale rolling out of its dead mother's abdomen had faded from the public conciousness six months later. She knew for a fact that the footage of the *Sojourner Truth* getting in front of the *Sunrise Warrior* so the *Sunrise Warrior* couldn't get in between the whales and the exploding harpoon heads had not. They were still getting indignant letters from whale lovers all over the world.

At last the captain said, "Thanks, XO."

He was right. There wasn't much else to be said. At least this time nothing as beloved—or as photogenic—

as whales was involved. She hoped. "You're welcome, captain."

She hung up and sat staring at the screen of her computer, trying to summon up enough energy to move.

Truth was, she was tired. This was the *Sojourner Truth*'s second patrol in four months, the first one lasting fifty days and this one scheduled for fifty-one, with barely enough time in port between patrols for a crewman to father a child and then out to sea again. They were short two cutters on the Bering Sea, and the remaining fleet had to pick up the slack.

But she knew that it was as much loneliness and depression as it was fatigue. Her mind started backsliding toward that hotel room in Anchorage three months before. Just the memory made her breath come faster.

There wasn't anything she didn't love about sleeping with Hugh Rincon. They'd barely waited for the elevator doors to close before they were on each other, and she didn't know now if anyone had been waiting to get on when the doors opened again on his floor or if there had been maids or other hotel staff who had watched them stagger from wall to wall down the hall, see Sara climbing up Hugh's body and wrapping her legs around his waist. His tie was twisted around to the side and his shirt was missing two buttons by the time she got her key out, and by then he had his hand up her skirt and she had a very difficult time focusing on the lock.

And then they were inside the room and he had shoved her up against the door and gone down on his knees and his mouth was there and, oh, she couldn't get her legs open far enough, couldn't press his face to her hard enough, couldn't scream loud enough when she came. He got back to his feet and tossed her up into his arms for the three steps to the bed, threw her down, and fell on her before she had a chance to protest. Not that she tried. He didn't bother undressing, just moved his clothes enough out of the way before he was on her and in her, and that was when he stopped, bracing himself on his arms, looking down into her face with fierce eyes. "Sara," he said, his voice a husk of sound. "Sara."

"Move," she said, arching up, clawing frantically at his back, and he laughed, deep and low and triumphant.

He hadn't slept much that night, and hadn't let her sleep, either. He was proving to her how much she had missed him, and she knew it, and she didn't care. He wanted everything she had to give him and he took it without hesitation or apology, tender only when it suited him, rough and urgent when it did not.

She had reveled in it. She'd never understood other people talking about how the sex had become routine in their marriages. There couldn't be anything better than married sex, with each knowing exactly what button to push when, that one move that would—

"XO?"

Her eyes snapped open to see Ensign Hank Ryan looking in her open door with a quizzical expression on his face. By sheer willpower she forced the color from her face. "What's up, Hank?" she said.

"You look tired, XO," he said. "The cap'n still pissed?"

She sat up and said briskly, "Captain Lowe doesn't dwell, Ensign. It's done, it's over, and we're moving on. What's up?"

A member of that generation raised by baby boomers, he had no problem serving under a woman and moreover thought Sara was a damn fine officer, and if he also thought she was hotter than a stick of dynamite he was able to hide his admiration beneath a suitably professional veneer. He accepted the implied rebuke without flinching. He had some crew requests for training to discuss, and when he left she turned to her computer to check her e-mail. Hugh's name in the in-box was like a siren going off. She swore out loud, earning a quizzical look from BMOW Meridian, passing by on the bosun's mate of the watch's duty round.

She swore again, silently this time, resisting the urge to close the door to her cabin, and turned away from the computer and her in-box and the e-mail that seemed to glow in the dark.

That night in October was the first time they'd seen each other in over a year, since the big fight when she was offered the XO position on the *Sojourner Truth*. Hugh hadn't wanted her to take it, had wanted her to wait and try for another position closer to Washington, D.C., so they could be together.

But Sara hadn't been able to turn down the opportunity. "I've been working toward this for thirteen years," she told him, and cringed now to think how much it had sounded like begging. Why shouldn't she go where she wanted, where she was needed, where the opportunity was best for her career path?

"What about us?" he had demanded. "What the hell am I supposed to do while you're in Kodiak?"

"Other people do marriage long-distance. And it's not like it's the first time for us."

"Ain't that the truth," he said.

"What's your point?" she said.

"My point is maybe I don't want to do this anymore! Maybe I miss my wife! Maybe I'm ready for a real marriage!"

"It's not forever, Hugh. It's only two years—"

"Two years!" he said, and the fight was on.

It wasn't as if she didn't have her own store of ammunition. The only big fight they'd had after Hugh finished graduate school had concerned his decision to go to work for the Central Intelligence Agency, eight years before.

"The CIA!" she had said when he told her of his decision. "Are you out of your mind? How are you going to take any pride in working for an outfit that is never right, and even when by some miracle they are, nobody listens to them? You can't be serious about this, Hugh, you just can't be!"

But he was. There was enough left of the little boy who had read all of John Le Carré before he was twelve for his inner James Bond to thrill at the prospect of becoming a real live spy. His first paper in world history in high school had been on the history of espionage from Caleb to Christopher Marlowe. He'd majored in languages and elected communications as a minor, tailoring his education against a later fit into the intelligence community. He explained this to Sara, adding, "I can't believe you didn't notice."

"I thought you wanted to join the Peace Corps!"

He looked at her, still with that saintly patience that made her want to rip his head from his shoulders and hand it to him, and said, "Sure. Someday. When I'm older. When we're both older."

"When we're retired and too old to be of any use elsewhere," she freely translated.

They'd managed to battle their way back from that precipice to maintain an uneasy peace in a marriage that was conducted in at best rare and admittedly joyous fragments of time when they were both in the same town at the same time and at worst with long stretches of separation endured with at least the appearance of compliance.

Until she'd been offered the XO position on the *Sojourner Truth,* when it had been Hugh's turn to stage a meltdown. "We don't spend enough time apart already, now you've got to go to sea again?"

"You could move to Kodiak," she said, her turn to be patient, if not precisely saintlike.

"And what the hell am I supposed to do in goddamn Kodiak, Alaska, while I'm waiting for you to get back into port? Learn to speak grizzly?"

This time, the fight had ended with her packing her bags and moving into bachelor quarters on base until her orders came through. She hadn't called him before she left, either, maybe the one thing she felt guilty about.

Well. She shied away from thinking about how she'd crept out of that hotel room in Anchorage while Hugh was still asleep. Make that two things.

But still, it wasn't like Hugh didn't know whom he had married. They'd been friends since birth, coconspirators since they were five, and lovers since they were seventeen. During all that time she had never made a secret of her intention to follow a life at sea.

She tried to imagine that life without Hugh and couldn't, but truth be told, that was essentially the life she was living.

There were other maritime jobs, even other Coastie jobs she could have taken and been home for dinner every night, but none of them had either the sense of mission or the freedom of action she craved. With the advent of satellite communications it was true that much of the autonomy of a ship at sea had leached back to the District HQs, but she still dreamed of the day when she would command her own two-sixty-four. It was a dream she had had since her father sat her on his lap in the wheelhouse of the *Melanie L.* and placed her five-year-old hands on the wheel. Sara could have paid her way to the college of her choice with ease, but nothing but the Coast Guard Academy would do. She wanted ships, and in some atavistic throwback to a more barbaric time, she wanted an armed ship. She had been raised by a commercial fisherman in a commercial fishing town and there had never been any question what service she wanted.

She'd been lucky in being born American. She'd been lucky in that her father had had friends in the Coast Guard. She'd been even luckier to have been born smart enough and competitive enough and right-brained enough to merit a place in the academy.

She only wished she could apply those same qualities to her personal life.

For the first time she allowed herself to say the word out loud: "Divorce."

She hated the sound of it. For one thing, it signified failure. For Sara Lange, failure was not an option in any endeavor.

Even more important was the sense of being not quite complete without him in her life. With Hugh, she never had to explain herself. He always understood what she meant rather than what she said. He was the only person, come to think of it, who understood her relationship with her mother. She wasn't sure she understood it herself, but somehow Hugh got it.

Was it only geography that kept them from making it work? No. He worked for a government agency she despised in principle and in practice. She worked for a government service that replaced its personnel around the country and around the world in two- and three-year rotations.

She said the word out loud again. "Divorce."

It sounded just as bad as it had the first time, and she was therefore relieved when the quick rap sounded at her door. "XO?"

"Yes?" she said.

The phone rang at the same time Cliff Skulstad stuck his head in with something perilously close to a grin on his face. "We've got an incursion."

She unhooked the bungee cord that kept her chair from sliding away from her desk with the roll of the ship and was on her way to the bridge before the last word was out of his mouth, with not even a backward look at the screen of her computer and the unopened letter in her in-box.

THE BRIDGE WAS SILENT but for the whisper of static coming out of the radio and the sound of two hundred and eighty-four feet of metal hull slicing through a two-foot chop. There was a very slight long swell beneath the chop, not enough to slow them down and certainly not enough to cause more than the most imperceptible roll in a vessel with a fifty-foot beam and a three-thousand-ton displacement. The *Sojourner Truth* was a great ride, even in the Bering Sea, also known as the Birthplace of Winds, where boxcar lows beginning in Kamchatka regularly turned it into a roller coaster for every ship within five hundred miles.

A swift glance at the captain's expression told Sara that this was one of the times when he was going to compensate for his lack of height with a serious display of attitude. The helmsman, who looked as if he'd lied about his age to get into the Coast Guard, and not that long ago, either, appeared to be oblivious to the scowling visage glowering out of the captain's chair, but Sara noticed that his knuckles were white on the small brass wheel. She met his eyes briefly, and winked.

Seaman Eugene Razo eased off on his grip. He felt better with the XO on the bridge. They all did. It reflected no doubts about their commanding officer's abilities, it was just that Captain Lowe had a very low tolerance for ineptitude and while Seaman Razo was among the fortunate who had escaped the recent conflagration in Dutch Harbor, he had a lively sense of self-preservation and serious plans for his future that didn't include official reprimands in his personnel file. He had selected the Attu loran station as his first duty station so he'd have top priority for his next assignment, which meant he could select a ship out of his hometown of Kodiak with a fair chance of getting it. It was his firm intention to run through every black, orange, and white hull in the Kodiak fleet for the next sixteen years, until he retired at full pay to take over his father's halibut charter business in Larsen Bay. He was engaged to his high school sweetheart, at present studying for her teaching degree at the University of Alaska, Fairbanks. She would graduate this year and they would be married out of her father's house in Chiniak in June.

He stole a sideways glance at Lieutenant Commander Lange, standing with her shoulders squared, her hands clasped lightly in the small of her back, swaying slightly with the roll of the ship. She was taller than he was, he guessed right around five eight, with a lush figure that the baggy fleece uniform did absolutely nothing to hide. It was generally agreed among the enlisted men that Lange was the officer they'd most like to be marooned on a loran station with, but mostly they thought of her as a good officer, smart without being arrogant, friendly without playing favorites, and a good leader without descending into tyranny. She was also, they all knew, targeted for promotion. She'd have her own two-eighty sooner or later. Razo wouldn't mind serving under her when that happened, so long as her ship was stationed in Kodiak.

Sara, unaware of the Eugene Razo Seal of Approval she'd just been awarded, saw Razo's hands relax and faced forward again to watch the bow cleave white water against a gray sky. The old man was a good sailor, but he lacked anything approaching a recognizable social skill. Of course, that was why God made executive officers. She grinned to herself and bent a weather eye forward.

There was a ten-knot wind blowing out of the southeast, whipping the surface of the water into a froth of stiff white peaks. She raised binoculars to search the horizon. Still nothing. She consulted the display hanging from the overhead, with the *Sojourner Truth* in the middle of the screen and a series of dots in the upper-left-hand section of the screen moving in an elongated circular route the eastern edge of which defined the Maritime Boundary Line.

There were a lot of dots. She counted eleven, each of them representing a Russian seafood processor with one- and two-mile-long nets dragging the bottom of the ocean trailing behind, some of which played mother ship to smaller vessels with their own nets out.

One of the dots was way over the line, with another dot coming up fast behind her from the south.

"Where's our target, Tommy?" the captain said.

"They should be in sight at any moment, Captain," Tommy Penn replied.

"Good." The heavy beat of all four Caterpillar generators and both propellers pushed the *Sojourner Truth* along at fifteen-point-two knots, better than anything any of the rust buckets ahead of them could do. Sara had cause to know. It had become almost a habit to head out on patrol and arrive just in time to see the Russian fish processor *Pheodora* slide over the line from American waters to Russian.

It happened once and if you were charitable you might think it was a mistake, that the man on watch wasn't paying attention to his GPS, and okay, you'd let the incursion ride this time. It was not the Coast Guard's job to interfere with fishers going about the lawful business of making a living.

A second incursion, you could allow for wind and tide and swell and chop to shove the boat off course. Even a third time, you could make allowances for equipment breaking down. But crew carelessness, bad weather, and instrument failure did not explain five incursions. There wasn't any excuse, really; the Russians had established a 1.5-mile buffer zone on their side of the line in which no vessels were supposed to fish, specifically to limit the incursions that precipitated incidents like this one.

All five times the *Pheodora*'s skipper had been cagey enough to keep the ship within three hundred yards of the line, so that if a Coast Guard C-130 Hercules on patrol or a helo launched from a cutter appeared on the horizon, one kick to the rudder put the vessel's bow back over. Given the conservative nature of American interdiction on the MBL, that was enough to cause the Coast Guard to back off.

This, however, was the *Pheodora*'s sixth incursion in two patrols in one calendar year, and this time she'd been caught two miles into American territorial waters. Her gear was out, although the pilot of the Coast Guard Herc who had first spotted her had informed them that she was pulling it in fast. The *Sojourner Truth* had launched her helo immediately and the Herc had handed off hot pursuit and continued on its patrol.

Captain Lowe was a prudent man nearing retirement, not known as a cowboy, but it was obvious to all of them that he had had just about enough. The last time they'd threatened a boarding. This time, Sara was pretty sure, they would be boarding the *Pheodora,* arresting the crew, confiscating the catch, and taking command of the vessel to bring it into Dutch Harbor and turn it over to the federal authorities. Where, Sara very much hoped, it would be sold at auction to the highest bidder and the resulting monies invested in some worthy government agency, like, say, the U.S. Coast Guard.

"What the—" The captain was training a pair of binoculars on the horizon. "What's that?"

It was, of all things, a freighter.

The entire bridge crew stared. The chief put what they were all thinking into words. "What is she doing way the hell and gone up here? Especially at this time of year?"

She wouldn't have been such an odd sight if they'd spotted her four degrees south, where freighters and containerships hid from weather north of the Aleutians year round on the great circle route between Asia and North America, but here, crossing the Doughnut Hole, she was as exotic as a scarlet macaw in Kaktovik. She rode low in the water, indicating a full load. She had cargo containers strapped three high to her foredeck. Everything looked well secured, which made Sara think well of her master. The weather was clear enough to read the name lettered on her bow.

"Ops," the captain said.

"On it, Captain," Ops said, busy on the computer. A moment later he said, "Their IRCS checks out, captain. It's the *Star of Bali,* a tramp freighter. Panamanian-owned."

"Give them a call."

Ops reached for the mike. "U.S. Coast Guard cutter *Sojourner Truth* to freighter the *Star of Bali.*"

There was a momentary silence, then response. The voice was male, with an Indian accent that stumbled badly over the cutter's name. "Cutter *Sojourner Truth,* freighter the *Star of Bali.* We read you loud and clear, over."

"Yeah," Ops said into the mike, "freighter the *Star of Bali,* cutter *Sojourner Truth,* no problems here. Just wondering what you're doing so far north."

"Coast guard, *Star of Bali,* we running from weather, over."

"Any farther north and you won't have to worry about the weather, you'll have to worry about the ice," Ops said. He keyed the mike. "Yeah, *Star of Bali,* cutter *Sojourner Truth,* understood. What was your last port of call, what's your next port of call, and what cargo are you carrying?"

"Coast guard, *Star of Bali,* our last port of call was

Petropavlovsk, our next port Seward is. Our cargo is steel and drilling equipment."

Ops looked at the captain, who looked at Sara, who shrugged. "No reason to stop them, sir."

"No." The captain nodded at Ops.

"*Star of Bali,* cutter *Sojourner Truth,* good copy. Be advised, there is another storm headed out of the southeast, rated hurricane force."

"Cutter *Sojourner Truth, Star of Bali,* many thanks for the advisory. *Star of Bali* out."

"Safe journey, *Star of Bali, Sojourner Truth* out." Ops looked at Sara. "It takes all kinds."

"That it does," the captain said. "Back to business, people."

"Aye, Captain."

The radio erupted with an excited call from the lookout on watch above at the same time Chief Edelen said in a voice that was not quite a shout, "*Pheodora* in sight, sir!"

Everyone who had them raised binoculars.

The *Pheodora*'s rust-streaked hull was plowing along at full throttle, as evidenced by the wake boiling up from the stern, but the Russian processor's single-screw diesel was no match for the *Sojourner Truth*'s two, and they were closing fast. The helo, an orange flea to the *Pheodora*'s large bulk, was hovering on the starboard side of their bridge fifty feet off the water.

"Tell the helo," the captain said.

Ops reached for the mike on the radio with the secure operations channel. "Coast Guard helo six five two seven," Ops said, "this is the cutter *Sojourner Truth.* We have the target in sight, I say again, we have the *Pheodora* in sight."

"Two seven, *Sojourner Truth,* roger that. We have hailed them and requested that they heave to. They have not responded."

"Roger that," Ops said, and looked at the captain.

District, as fed up as the captain at the repeated incursions, had already given *Truth* the go-ahead. Captain Lowe nodded. Ops nodded back and said into the microphone, "Russian fishing vessel *Pheodora,* this is the United States Coast Guard cutter *Sojourner Truth.* You have intruded into American territorial waters and are in violation of the Maritime Boundary Line. Reduce speed and prepare to be boarded."

They waited. There was no noticeable reduction in the *Pheodora*'s speed. The captain's mouth thinned. Sara saw it and rejoiced inwardly. Ops was grinning openly, and the bridge exuded an air of taut expectation. Partly it was a desire to do good to wipe out the Dutch Harbor debacle, and partly it was delight at the unexpected gift handed to them by this patrol that none of them had wanted to go on.

It was also the John Wayne reflex, that intrinsically American instinct to chase after the bad guy, the chance to wear the white hat, the unmistakable thrill of the cops-and-robbers chase that came so seldom into the daily routine of their patrols. Sara bit the inside of her cheek to keep from grinning back at Ops.

Ops keyed the mike to repeat the message and at the same moment the secure channel erupted into life again. "*Sojourner Truth, Sojourner Truth,* this is Coast Guard Hercules aircraft one seven five two, come in."

Ops raised an eyebrow at Sara and said into the mike, "Go ahead, five two."

The Herc's aviator's voice was terse. "*Truth,* we've got another incursion about five miles south of your location."

The captain swung around in his chair and stared at Ops. "Herc five two, how far inside the line?"

"*Sojourner Truth,* five two, this one's a little over two miles inside."

"Son of a bitch," the captain said, frightening everyone within earshot. Captain David Josephus Lowe, officer, family man, and deacon of the Kodiak First Baptist Church, never, ever swore.

Sara, however, sympathized, and was thinking a lot worse than the captain was saying out loud. The Coast Guard had run into this before in the Bering, one or more Russian vessels making an incursion over the line at the same time, so that the one vessel being boarded occupied the attention of the lone cutter on patrol, while the other vessel pulled in their gear more or less at their leisure and moved back to their side of the Line. Bait and switch.

Ops said into the mike, "Herc five two, this is the *Sojourner Truth,* have you identified the vessel, I say again, what is the vessel?"

"*Sojourner Truth,* Herc five two, their IRCS number is about six inches high and on the front of the flying bridge."

Which meant that the foreign ship's four-letter international identification number had been deliberately painted too small for the Herc's crew to read from two hundred feet up going one hundred seventy knots, which meant the cutter couldn't input it into their onboard database.

"Five bucks says it's the *Agafia,*" Seaman Razo said.

Chief Edelen snorted. "No bet."

The *Pheodora* and the *Agafia* were both leased by the same Russian fish processor. In the litter of three-hundred-foot vessels maintaining a year-round presence in the Bering Sea next to the Maritime Boundary Line each year, the two could always be found near each other, and all too often a little too close to the line for comfort. This put them both in the HIV or High Interest Vessel category.

The captain said nothing. Sara wanted to scream with impatience. Instead she said to Ops, "Ask the Herc about fuel."

"Coast Guard Hercules aircraft one seven five two, Sojourner Truth, how much fuel do you have?"

There was a brief pause. "*Sojourner Truth,* Herc five
two, we've got maybe four hours before the point of no
return."

"Raise Kodiak and tell them to dispatch another Herc,"
the captain said. "Then get the helo back here to refuel.
Tell the Herc on the scene to maintain contact until they
can hand off hot pursuit to our helo."

Kodiak came on the air and confirmed the dispatch of
the second Herc with so little questioning that Sara knew
they'd been monitoring the channel from the beginning of
the incident and had been standing by for just this request.

Maintaining hot pursuit was critical in making a legal
case in a federal court against a substantial piece of property owned by a foreign corporation. The Russians'
lawyers were usually American and the best that money
could buy, and the first thing any decent attorney said in
this kind of case was that the pursued vessel hadn't heard
the order to give way.

As if she had spoken out loud, Ops keyed the mike and
said, "Russian fishing vessel *Pheodora,* Russian fishing
vessel *Pheodora,* this is the United States Coast Guard
cutter *Sojourner Truth.* You are trespassing in American
territorial waters, I say again, you are trespassing in
American territorial waters. Reduce speed and stand by
to be boarded."

"Any answer?" the captain said, formally and unnecessarily.

"No answer, Captain," Ops replied, equally formally.

There was a long moment of silence. "Break out the
fifty caliber."

"Sir?" Sara said.

The captain chose to overlook her involuntary exclamation. "Muster the gun crew and mount it forward to starboard."

Sara pulled herself together. "Aye aye, Captain."

"I want two boarding teams ready to go when we catch up to her." He paused, and added deliberately, maybe even raising his voice a little, "Each boarding team is to be issued shotguns."

Yeah, Sara thought, not without respect, the old man was really pissed. It gladdened her heart, even though she didn't believe anyone should ever be shot over fish. "Aye aye, Captain," she repeated.

"XO?" the captain said.

"Sir?"

"I want you to go with one of the boarding teams."

There was a brief, startled silence. "I want you to report to me personally every step of the way," the captain said. "Go codes one, two, three. Understood?"

"Understood, Captain," Sara said. She reached for the 1MC and her voice boomed out over speakers all over the ship. Through the aft windows she could see men and women boiling out of various hatches and swarming around the two rigid-hulled inflatables lashed to cradles on either side of the ship.

Like any capable executive officer Sara knew her crew, from EO Nathaniel McDonald, who so far as she knew never left the engine room except to eat, sleep, or depart the ship, to FS3 Sandra Chernikoff, a mess cook not a year out of boot camp and an Alaskan like herself and Eugene Razo. She knew which of three categories each member of the crew fit in, the keepers, the time-markers, and the no-hopers. She knew who was on watch and who wasn't. From memory she reeled off a list of twenty names, beginning with Ensign Ryan, their legal enforcement officer and boarding officer, and ending with PO

James Marion, a fireman, damage controlman, and boat crew member. Everyone on board had at least two jobs and probably three. She had about twelve the last time she looked, but then she was a keeper herself.

By the time she got to the armory the rest of the team had donned their orange-and-black Mustang dry suits, Kevlar vests, helmets, life jackets, helmets, and sidearms. She jerked her chin at the rack of shotguns and said to Chief Petty Officer Marvin Katelnikof, "Break out the shotguns."

He complied without comment. Katelnikof, a balding veteran with twenty-nine years in, had earned his cutterman's pin before Sara had graduated from high school. Not a lot surprised him. She accepted a shotgun and headed below to the fantail where the rest of the BTMs were mustering, followed by Katelnikof, who was their designated Russian translator on board. The two Zodiacs had already been lowered into the water with their three-man crews and were now circling back to pick up the boarding teams.

Ryan saw her coming. "You're stylin', XO. Something about Kevlar that really does it for you." He nodded at the shotguns. "The old man must really be pissed off this time."

"The *Agafia*'s over the line just south of here."

Ryan whistled low and long. "Man, they've just got to push it, don't they? You'd think they would have learned after the last time."

Sara scanned the horizon. "Yeah, where's the Russian Federal Border Service when you really need them?"

Ryan followed her eyes and stiffened. "Hey—"

"I see them," Sara said, and keyed the mike clipped to her shoulder. "Captain Lowe, XO. I'm seeing a couple of other vessels approaching our location at speed."

"We have them in sight, XO. There are three vessels, identified as the *Nikolai Bulganin,* the *Nadeshda,* and the *Professor Zaitsev.*"

"So, okay, this is new," Ryan said. He cocked an eye at Sara. "Do we go?"

"Captain, do we go?"

There was a momentary pause. The wind bit into her in spite of the dry suit, and her face was already damp with salt spray. "Go, XO," the captain said.

"Yep," Ryan said, "seriously pissed." He grinned and climbed over the side to scamper down the rope ladder and drop solidly into the small boat. The rest of the first boarding team followed. "Rrrrrraaaaamming speeeeeeeeeeed!" Ryan yelled at the coxswain in a passable *Animal House* imitation. The Zodiac roared away and the second pulled up neatly behind it and Sara led the second team down.

Petty Officer Duane Mathis hated not to be first in line for anything and roared after the first boat. The hull thudded over the top of the chop in a bone-jarring but exhilarating ride. Sara looked over at the coxswain and he was leaning forward, teeth bared as if he wanted to take a bite out of the wind. Mathis was from San Francisco, she remembered, and he'd grown up off the coast of Peru on the deck of his father's tuna boat. He and Sara had swapped a lot of lies about fishing over this patrol, although it seemed to Sara that the only difference between fishing off Peru and fishing off the Aleutian Islands was the temperature and the species of bycatch.

They stood off as Lowe goosed the *Sojourner Truth* to overtake the *Pheodora,* giving the Russian just enough sea room to slow down and no more. If you're the captain of an oceangoing vessel in the middle of the Bering Sea, ninety miles from the nearest land and that land not under the flag of your own nation, there are worse things

than having a two-hundred-and-eighty-four-foot Coast
Guard cutter bearing down on your port side with no indication of slowing down before impact, but not many.
When the distance between the two closed to two hundred yards the *Pheodora*'s skipper caved and pulled back
on the throttle. A moment later a rope ladder was tossed
over the lee side.

Sara was first on deck. The conditions of the processor
were about what she'd expected, the deck slimy with guts
and gurry, lines loose from gunnel to gunnel, and anything with a moving part so long overdue for an overhaul
that it all probably ought to have been junked. Ten feet
away the deck sported a jagged hole, which disappeared
into darkness and whose edge had yet to be cordoned off
and flagged.

Seaworthiness had two entirely different meanings on
either side of the Maritime Boundary Line. Sara revised
severely downward her estimate of how much the
Pheodora might fetch at auction. They might just possibly be able to sell her for scrap.

"XO?" her radio said.

She keyed the mike clipped to her shoulder. "Code
one," she said in a mild voice. She didn't like anything
about this situation, but as yet the boarding team had not
been threatened, not counting the imminent peril everyone stood in of breaking an ankle tripping over crap scattered across the deck.

"Code one, roger that," the captain said. "Keep me
advised."

She clicked the mike twice in reply. A man in a bulky
sweater and stained pants stepped forward. In heavily accented English he said, "Vasily Protopopov. I am master
of vessel." It came out "wessel" and behind Sara there
was a snicker, followed by the flat slap of a hand on
someone's helmet.

Ryan stepped forward. "Captain Protopopov, I am Ensign Henry Ryan of the United States Coast Guard. You have been stopped because you were fishing over the Maritime Boundary Line in American waters."

Protopopov let his eyes slide past Ryan to Sara. He gave her a long, leisurely once-over. Sara, crammed into her dry suit like chopped pork into a sausage skin, girded about with Kevlar like a medieval knight in his armor and feeling almost that seductive, felt like laughing in his face. Instead, she remained silent, keeping her expression calm and nonconfrontational. Protopopov waited just long enough to make his rudeness clear, and then shifted his attention to CPO Katelnikof, standing at Sara's elbow holding the shotgun she'd handed off to him in the Zodiac. "No gear in waters," he told Katelnikof.

Chief Katelnikof, a salty old fart and the last man to agree that women on board ship were a good thing, was already stiff with outrage at Protopopov's insolence to his executive officer. This blatant untruth did not soften his attitude. He dropped the shotgun from shoulder arms to cradle it in deceptively casual hands, the barrel now pointing at the deck between himself and the Russian captain.

Sara looked aft and saw that Protopopov was correct; the *Pheodora*'s gear had been reeled on board.

The captain's voice came over her radio. "XO? Status?"

She keyed the mike. "Code two, Captain."

The codes were the captain and the executive officer's way of assessing a boarding situation. Code one was standard operations, no threat. Code three was get us the hell of here. Sara didn't see any weapons other than their own, but it was a big ship, the crew was obviously hostile, and there were too many windows and doors looking out on the foredeck in which someone with a weapon could be stationed.

Lowe's voice was full of grim purpose when he responded. "Stand by, XO, and we'll fix that for you."

Sara clicked her mike twice in response. Ryan looked at Sara. He was the boarding team officer and the person to whom Protopopov should be addressing his remarks, but the Russian captain had good instincts for spotting a superior officer. Not to mention which, it was the first time since Ryan had rotated on board that she'd come along on a boarding. She jerked her chin and he turned to face Protopopov.

"Captain," Ryan said, "we have you, with your gear in the water, on videotape, a good mile to the east of the line. As this seems to be coming something of a habit with your vessel, I'm afraid we are left with no option but to seize your ship and your catch and to place you and your crew under arrest."

Protopopov looked at the boarding teams, both now fully assembled on the deck of his vessel. They each had nine-millimeter sidearms strapped to their waists, and half of them carried shotguns. He raised his head and opened his mouth. His eyes looked past Sara and his sullen expression lightened.

She turned to see what he was looking at, and found that while they'd been talking the three other Russian vessels had arrived on scene and were now circling the *Sojourner Truth* and the *Pheodora* about three hundred yards off.

"One boat it's a Sunday sail, two boats it's a race, three boats it's a bloody regatta," Ryan said.

Nobody laughed. Protopopov looked back at Sara with an expression that couldn't be called anything other than triumphant. "Maybe you leave now."

"I don't think so, sir," Sara said, who had been monitoring the activities on the deck of the *Sojourner Truth* out of the corner of her eye.

"Oh, yeah," Katelnikof said approvingly, following her

gaze, and Protopopov turned to look as one of his men let out a warning shout.

Lowe had closed to within a hundred yards of the *Pheodora*'s port bow without slowing down. The .50-caliber gun now mounted to starboard was manned, with a belt of ammunition already threaded into the magazine. In addition, Lowe had manned the starboardside 25-millimeter cannon, which Sara happened to know was the one that worked. The portside cannon had been waiting on parts for months. They were U.S. Navy guns, and the navy had never liked the idea of giving weaponry they'd bought and paid for to another service.

Lowe gave the Russians a good long look as the *Truth* flashed by, to cut neatly across the *Pheodora*'s bow with what felt like inches to spare.

Somebody screamed. Sara hoped it wasn't one of hers. Captain Lowe was doing the thing in style, and she had to repress a chuckle.

Ryan didn't bother repressing anything. "Flame on, Captain Lowe!"

They all staggered as the *Pheodora*'s helmsman panicked and spun the wheel and the processor lurched abruptly to starboard. Protopopov let out a stream of Russian, face going from red to white to purple. He could have been yelling at his helmsman, but then he turned on Sara and pushed right up into her face, still shouting.

"I'm so sorry, Captain," she said blandly, ignoring the spray of spittle, "I'm afraid I don't speak Russian."

"But I do," Katelnikof said to Protopopov, or so he translated for Sara when they were back on board the *Sojourner Truth*. "Don't let this broad's lack of balls fool you, Captain. Given half a chance she'll order our ship to run right over the top of this paddle wheeler of yours."

Aghast and agape, Protopopov stared at Katelnikof, whose grin was wide and not at all friendly. The Russian captain rounded on Sara again. "Your captain crazy! What you do, ram us, sink us! Russian government will not stand for this! I lodge complaint!"

The combination of speed and the show of weapons, in addition, Sara believed, to the display of extremely able seamanship, was enough to cause the other vessels to veer off and make best speed for the horizon. Besides, they all had catch quotas, which if not met might relieve the skippers of their commands.

And it wasn't like there wouldn't be another opportunity to yank the Coast Guard's tail on the Maritime Boundary Line. Job security, she thought, for all of us, and turned to Protopopov, whose face had yet to regain any semblance of normal color.

"Captain Protopopov, I relieve you of command of the *Pheodora*. Chief," she said to Katelnikof, "have Captain Protopopov identify the rest of his crew and place them under guard. Ensign," she said to Ryan, "go below and tell the working folks that they've got an all-expenses-paid trip to beautiful downtown Dutch Harbor."

An hour later they were under way, following the wake of the *Sojourner Truth* as she headed south-southwest in pursuit of the *Agafia*.

The *Pheodora*'s bridge was in a little better shape than the rest of her, but not much. A large spoked wooden wheel reinforced with tarnished brass stood at the center, ranged about with a fathometer and radar and radios and a GPS. The GPS had been trashed, but that was to be expected, the crew covering their asses. All Sara really cared about was that at an ambient temperature right around fifty-eight degrees Fahrenheit, it was warmer than the bridge of the last foreign vessel she'd had to board.

Ryan entered the bridge through the port wing hatch. "Ship's crew all secure in the galley, XO, and the workers are getting out their party clothes. I put Katelnikof on watch in the engine room. Not that the Russian engineers want to miss out on a shopping trip in Dutch Harbor, either."

Everyone laughed, a little giddy at the success of their mission. Their mood was hardly dampened when they saw the helo return and land on the *Truth,* which meant that the *Agafia* had slipped back over the line before they could arrive on the scene. Bagging the *Pheodora* was enough of a prize, and besides, they were headed back for Dutch Harbor riding on a white horse, in distinct contrast to their recent exit.

Sara couldn't keep the smile from tugging at the corners of her mouth. Looking around, she saw that same suspicion of a smile on the faces of the rest of the other two boarding teams.

It was hard sometimes for her to believe her luck, that she got to whup bad guy ass on her nation's territorial frontier. "Just another day at the office," she told Ryan, a big fat lie if there ever was one.

"We are the defenders of the homeland," Ryan said, dropping his voice to his best basso profundo.

"We are the shield of freedom!" Sara said, and the bridge exploded into laughter, in part triumphant because they were the prize crew of a seized vessel and because at heart every Coastie was part pirate, and in part relieved because no shots had been fired and everyone was going home alive.

11

HUGH COULD BARELY WALK when the Federal Express MD-11 rolled to a stop at Stevens International in Anchorage. It had taken eight hours and change en route from Tokyo, crammed into the cargo net seat the crew had hung from the fuselage. The ambience of the airplane, one enormous cavern crammed with pallets and igloos lashed down with a spaghetti-like construction of webbing and belts, was not enhanced by what seemed a preponderance of crates of chickens. Every time the airplane hit an air pocket the chickens clucked and shrieked and little feathers floated out through the cracks of the crates. Hugh would inhale one of the feathers and wake up in the middle of a sneezing fit. Why the hell anyone would air-freight chickens to America was beyond him. He would have thought there were already plenty in residence.

He was cold, too, having only the lightweight jacket he started out with in Washington three days before. Four days? Or was it five, with the delay in finding a plane going in the right direction? He'd lost track, and besides he was going back over the dateline again. Even if he was right about how long he'd been on the road, he was going to be wrong about what day it was when he got there.

This wasn't what he'd signed up for. He'd signed up for a silver Aston Martin, a Walther PPK and a vodka martini, shaken, not stirred. Not to mention Halle Berry in a bikini. Not barely endurable trips in flying warehouses. Not making end runs around a boss too motivated by politics and patronage to be effective. And most especially not duct-taping people to chairs and beating on them with claw hammers.

He stumbled down the stairs the ground crew brought to the forward door and almost ran into Frank Clifton, captain of the aircraft.

"Whoa there," Frank said, steadying him.

"Sorry, Frank," Hugh said. Frank looked cheerful and well rested. Hugh hated him. He mustered up what shreds of civility he had left and managed a smile. "I appreciate the ride."

Frank shrugged. "My pleasure. Lucky I was on my way back from Manila when you called the office."

"I know."

Hugh had inherited Frank from the previous holder of his job. Frank Clifton had flown cargo for Flying Tigers and now flew MD-11s for FedEx. Agents and case managers became very adept at finding pilots who would turn a blind eye at an extra body riding in the back of their jets. It was a useful option in intelligence gathering in that cargo jets went everywhere, including places passenger jets would never dream of landing, and it was very cost effective, usually entailing a bottle of Glenmorangie, paid for out of petty cash. Management probably knew all about it but turned a blind eye, because you never knew when helping out your government was going to translate into another federal subsidy, which couldn't hurt the golden parachute waiting for the CEO to don and bail.

The pilot regarded him quizzically. "So, what's the big emergency, buddy boy?" He reflected. "Well, not that a ride in last class on a commercial liner is much better these days."

"I can't say," Hugh said. "Not yet, anyway. It's important though, Frank. I can't tell you how much I appreciate it." He managed another smile. "I gotta go."

"Need a ride?"

Hugh blinked at him, and then around at the spread-out, much-added-to package-sorting warehouse, the huge hangar built to annual MD-11s, the seven—he counted—other MD-11s lined up in a proud row on the tarmac outside. It was dark, with stars and a hint of pale green aurora on the northern horizon. The cold seared the insides of his nostrils and he hunched his shoulders inside his sport jacket and tried not to let his teeth chatter. January in Alaska. He'd forgotten. "What time is it, anyway?"

Frank consulted an enormous silver watch the size of a horse's hoof, bristling with accessory rings and function knobs. It looked like it could jam the Internet all by itself. "Five thirty-seven."

"What day is it here?"

Frank looked at him with a sapient eye. "January ninth. Do you need a ride or not? I've got my truck in the lot."

Hugh forced his tired mind to think. "Let me make a phone call first, okay?" He fumbled for his cell phone.

"Sure, but no point in making it in the cold." Frank led the way to a door leading into a small room in the main office building. It was furnished with some shabby couches and a couple of beat-up coffee tables. A counter held a sink and a coffeepot and a miniature refrigerator, and copies of *Northern Pilot* and *Aviation Week* and *Penthouse* littered every available surface. It was warm, that was the main thing, and the warmth made Hugh realize just how cold he had been. His hands shook as he punched in an autodial number on his cell phone, and it was only by clenching his teeth together that he kept them from chattering.

The number answered on the third ring. A warm contralto voice said drowsily, "Hello?"

"Lilah? It's Hugh."

"Hugh? What are you— What time is it?" There were rustling sounds. "Hugh Rincon, it's not even six A.M.!"

"I know, I'm sorry. Is Kyle there?"

"Who is it, honey?" he heard Kyle's voice say.

"It's Hugh," she told him.

"Hugh?" Kyle said into the phone. "Where the hell are you? And what the hell are you doing calling at the crack of dawn?" Kyle's voice sharpened. "What's wrong? Sara? Your folks?"

"No, nothing like that. I have to talk to you, Kyle, right away."

"Are you in Anchorage?"

"Yes. I'll meet you at your office."

"For crissake, just come to the house."

"No," Hugh said. "The office. I'm grabbing a ride, I'll meet you there."

"Hugh—"

"Fifteen minutes." Hugh hung up, and followed Frank outside to a brand-new Dodge Ram Power Wagon. Frank was believer in conspicuous consumption. The truck seemed to ride at least ten feet above the ground. Hugh struggled in, muttered, "FBI headquarters, Sixth and A," and passed out before the truck had warmed up enough for Frank to judge it safe to be put into drive.

Hugh had spent the hours prior to departure from Tokyo on the phone with the director in Langley, who stubbornly refused to connect the dots, the same dots

Hugh had spent the last two months painstakingly tracing in a trail that led from the bombing in Pattaya Beach, the sighting of Fang and Noortman there, to Peter the Wolf in Odessa, to Harvey Mott's report, to Hugh's shakedown of Noortman in Hong Kong, who in his terror had confirmed much of this continuing story and who had added a whole new chapter that Hugh had utterly failed to sell to his boss. At this point Hugh was frantic to find a true believer.

"If it was Egypt, Hugh, my boy, or Iran," the director had said in benevolent tones, "why, that kind of rumor I could see, that I could generate interest in."

In the White House, Hugh correctly deduced, but by then he was angry enough to be indiscreet. "Sir, this isn't a rumor. We have confirmed reports of Korean terrorists training in al-Qaida camps—"

"Do you have proof of al-Qaida involvement in this particular operation?" the director said sharply.

Hugh set his teeth. "No, sir."

The director lost interest. "Hugh, I think it's time for you to come home. Let us debrief you, get all the facts laid out on the table—"

"With respect, sir," Hugh had said, "there isn't time. According to my informant, their plan is already in motion. We have to act. We must act. Now."

There was a momentary silence. The director was probably surprised that the worm had finally turned. "Hugh, my boy," he had said slowly, "I understand your concerns, and I appreciate the hard work you've put into this operation, but like I said, you come on home now. I'm not even going to slap your wrist for hightailing it out of here without permission. I tell you what, we'll put some people on it, some good people, we'll investigate these reports and track this celium of yours down."

"Cesium, sir," Hugh said, biting off the words. "Cesium-137. I've got a lead on its whereabouts and I want to pursue that lead. Sir."

The director's voice cooled. "You said you were in Tokyo, did you not? There is a Northwest flight out of Narita that'll put you into Dulles at eight-oh-five tomorrow evening." There was a forced chuckle. "Seems odd to think of flying almost seventeen hours and getting in the same day you leave, don't it?" He became very brisk. "I'll have a ticket waiting for you at the counter, Hugh. We'll see you in the shop tomorrow. Good night, my boy."

"Yes, sir," Hugh said, hung up, and started calling all the pilots listed on his cell phone directory. His fifth try produced Frank, who himself happened to be on the ground in Manila, loading a shipment of semiconductors just prior to taking off for Tokyo to pick up a shipment of Sony digital cameras, en route to Memphis with a stop in Anchorage for refueling and crew change, a piece of luck second only to being able to pick up Noortman in the restaurant. Well. Maybe third, after recruiting Arlene.

Arlene, to whom he had said before going through Hong Kong security to the gate to board his plane, "This never happened. You were never here. Write no reports, no memos, submit travel expenses only by hand and only to me. If I'm fired before you make it into the office, you might get stuck with them."

She shrugged. "I was there. I heard him talk. You had to do this."

He nodded, grateful that here at least was one person he didn't have to convince of anything. "I'll handle the charge for the Hong Kong ticket on your credit card. Leave. Now."

She had nodded, asking no questions, and the last he'd seen of her was the bottle-green back of her blazer as she left the terminal. Watching the sliding electric door whisk out of her way, he thought that he was going to have to find some way to show his appreciation of her professionalism. Always supposing his own head wasn't served up on a platter when he got back to Langley.

Frank's MD-11 wouldn't be in for hours, so he hunted up a cybercafe that served coffee and checked his e-mail, hoping Peter would have been sighted, Fang apprehended, the two Koreans identified, anything he could take to the director as proof. There was nothing. Nor had Sara replied to the e-mail he had sent from D.C. before he left. When his cell phone rang and it was Frank, wanting to know where the hell he was, he'd been genuinely surprised at the passage of time.

"Hugh," Frank said.

"Huh?"

"Wake up." Frank shook his arm. "We're here."

Hugh blinked blearily through the windshield and saw the immense brown brick shoebox squatting ten feet away. A figure stood on the corner, huddled in a parka. It stepped forward into range of the streetlight and Hugh saw Kyle's face peering out from the wolf ruff around the hood. "Thanks, Frank," he said, opening the door and stepping gingerly onto the ice.

"You're gonna tell me what this was all about someday, right?" Frank said.

"If I can," Hugh said, and shut the truck's door firmly behind him. Frank demonstrated his displeasure by kicking up a little snow when he pulled out of the parking lot, but Hugh wasn't paying attention.

"Hugh," Kyle said, pulling Hugh into a bear hug and whacking him on the back hard enough to make him slip and almost fall. Icy parking lots. Something else he didn't miss about home. "What the hell's going on?" Hugh's teeth had begun to chatter again and Kyle said, "Never mind. Come on, let's get in out of the cold."

KYLE CHASE'S OFFICE WAS on the third floor, a square box with a desk, a chair, and a couple of bookshelves. Every horizontal space was piled high with paperwork, magazines, and books. Kyle removed a stack of newspapers and a box of nine-millimeter ammunition from what was revealed as a second chair. "Sit down before you fall down." He busied himself at a coffeepot on a table.

He was almost as tall as Hugh and had almost as much hair, although his was black. His eyes were blue and his smile was quick and wicked. He was almost as smart as he thought he was, and he, like Sara and Hugh, was a rabid overachiever, which meant he was a rising star with the FBI. He'd had to ask to be posted to Alaska, but he'd always wanted to come home, and in spite of much headshaking on the part of his superiors, who freely prophesied that he was killing his career, he had prevailed. "There must have been something in the water in Seldovia," Hugh said.

"Huh?"

"Never mind. Thinking out loud."

The coffee finished brewing and Kyle poured two mugfuls, not neglecting creamer and a huge hit of sugar for Hugh. "Terrible Trio," Hugh said, raising his mug in the traditional toast.

Kyle smiled. "Terrible Trio," he said and clinked mugs with Hugh. He sat down behind his desk.

Hugh drank. Strong enough to melt the bowl off a spoon and sweet enough to send him into a diabetic coma, the coffee had a reviving effect. "Is Lilah as beautiful as ever?"

"You know she is, you just saw her in October."

"Kids good?"

"As good as the little monsters ever are," replied their loving father. "Come on, Hugh. You look like hell. What's going on? Are you sure Sara is okay?"

"She's fine," Hugh said. "So far as I know."

"Oh. Ah. Well. What's going on, then? These aren't my usual office hours. It's gotta be good to get me in here this early. Or a friend," he added pointedly.

"The FBI still regard Alaska as one of four states on a short list where the threat of domestic terrorism is regarded as real?"

Kyle stared at him, puzzled. "Are you awake yet? You know we do, along with Montana, Wyoming, and Idaho. It's why our manpower's been so beefed up here over the last five years."

Hugh had had a long flight during which he had marshaled his arguments and worked out a way to phrase them that would make his case without tempting Kyle to have him committed. "Have you considered the possibility of an attack from an international source?"

Kyle set his mug down with a thud. "What the hell's going on, Hugh?" His eyes narrowed. "Does the CIA have information to that effect? And if it does, why haven't we been notified?"

"Let me talk it through," Hugh said.

Kyle looked at him for a long moment. Hugh Rincon was tall and blond and brown-eyed without being in the least bit pretty. His ease of manner belied his intellect, both of which were obvious without being offensive. He was, in short, the kind of man other men liked and all women loved. He always had been, Kyle thought ruefully. Kyle was lucky he'd seen Lilah first. Not that Hugh had ever given anyone but Sara a second look.

Across the desk Hugh shook off his fatigue and turned

a mental switch. He spoke as if he were giving this briefing for the first time, a little tentatively, as if Kyle was the first focus group for this particular presentation. His speech was deliberate without being pedantic, but even if he had turned into the world's worst teacher his subject would have guaranteed Kyle's interest. "Given Alaska's strategic location on the Pacific Rim, and given the great circle route reality of international commerce, I don't think it's unrealistic that intelligence agencies in Alaska hold a watching brief for terrorist traffic coming in the opposite direction from Asia."

Kyle thought. "What would be the target if, as you suggest, we did have terrorist traffic coming at us from Asia?"

"In Alaska, the first target we think of is, of course, the terminal in Valdez," Hugh said. "Fourteen percent of the nation's annual supply of oil travels through that port in very large crude carriers."

"Given the regularity and efficiency of USAF patrols—"

"Understood. I consider that threat remote. However, speaking of the air force, there are two large military bases in the state with nuclear weapons on site. They're attractive targets, and they have the added advantage of being perceived as too far off the national radar to worry about."

"Location, location, location," Kyle said, expecting at least a smile. He didn't get one.

"As for targets beyond Alaska, try every shipping port, oil refinery, and military base on the West Coast of the U.S. All they'd have to do is put a bomb on a VLCC and sail it into any harbor with a refinery from Bremerton to San Diego. Very big boom."

Kyle relaxed a little. "Is that realistic?"

"You tell me, Kyle," Hugh said, his voice hard. "Was Oklahoma City realistic? Was 9/11 realistic? No, they won't try that exact MO again, but who knows what else they've got up their sleeves? We have information that bin Ladin has his own personal fleet of oceangoing vessels. Some sources number it at as high as twenty vessels total. Where are they? Where are they going? Who, and, even more importantly, what are they bringing with them? You know the story of Container Bob, right?"

Kyle shook his head.

"The Italians stumbled across an Egyptian-born Canadian named Amid Farid Rizk inside a container en route from Port Said to Rotterdam, changing ships in Gioia Tauro. He never would have been caught if he hadn't decided to drill more holes for air and the Italian police hadn't heard him. The container came equipped with all the modern conveniences, including a heater, a toilet, and a bed. Not to mention the satellite phone, the laptop, and the Canadian A and P certificate."

"Jesus," Kyle said, shaken in spite of himself. "He was an airplane mechanic?"

"You bet. We checked. He did the work. The certificate was valid."

"So it was a test run?"

Hugh shrugged. "We don't know. The container's final destination was listed as Halifax, Nova Scotia."

"What did this Rizk say?"

"He didn't say anything. He got himself a smart lawyer who got him bail. He was in the wind by November."

"What was his lawyer's name?" Kyle said. "Just in case I ever decide to rob a bank in Italy."

"That's not the point, Kyle."

"What is the point then, Hugh?" Kyle said, mimicking his tone.

"My point is, they've been practicing traveling in container ships," Hugh said.

"Okay," Kyle said, putting his mug down and placing

both hands flat on his desk. "What the hell's this about, Hugh? You hitch a ride from Tokyo on a cargo jet, you get me out of bed to come down here, and so far all I'm getting is a lecture on terrorism. A lecture I've already heard."

Hugh held up a hand. "Bear with me, okay, Kyle? Please?"

Kyle took a deep breath, exhaled. "All right. Go ahead."

"I don't know about you, and I admit, maybe it has something to do with where I was born and where a lot of people I love still live, but I've never been as concerned over terrorists in the Middle East as I have been terrorists in Asia."

"Like North Korea," Kyle said. "It's why you took your master's in Asian studies. I know all this, Hugh."

"What do you know about North Korea?"

Hugh hadn't meant it to sound like a challenge, but Kyle responded as if it were. "Since the end of World War II, the Korean peninsula has been split into two, with the north under Chinese domination and the south under Western, uh, influence. South Korea has a stable government, a booming economy, and a well-armed and well-trained military. North Korea? North Korea is starving to death, mostly because instead of figuring out how to feed their people they've concentrated fifty years of gross national product on the development of long-range missiles and research into weapons, including chemical, biological, and, yes, nuclear."

"Not bad," Hugh said, complimentary, and Kyle gave a curt nod. "They know how to do it well enough that they've been exporting their expertise overseas, most recently to Iran. I've been to the Korean DMZ, Kyle, and it's not a pretty sight. Every now and then North and South shoot at each other across the DMZ, air to air, ship to ship, whatever's handy. The North has missiles in place targeting the South's nuclear power plants. Instant dirty bomb."

"Didn't our going into Iraq tone down their rhetoric a little?"

Hugh's short laugh was without humor. "They figure the only way to keep us from doing the same to them is to keep building bigger and better and more weapons. And they've been force-fed hatred of Americans with their mother's milk for going on sixty years now."

"I've read the reports, Hugh. I am the agent in charge of the Joint Terrorism Task Force in Alaska."

"Yeah, well, I just read a news release from the Korean Central News Agency which said, in part, and I'm quoting verbatim here, that 'the U.S. is restless with its ambition to conquer the world.'"

Kyle had to smile. "Funny. I don't feel all that ambitious."

Hugh shook his head. "Not so funny. That peninsula is a pile of kindling just waiting for a spark, and the first people who are going to have to respond to the fire are right now sitting up over there on Government Hill, warming up their F-15s."

"Okay," Kyle said, "they're pissed and they're motivated. What does that have to do with terrorism? Is Kim Jong Il sponsoring state terrorism? What are we looking at here, another Lockerbie? Another *Cole*? Another 9/11?"

Hugh drank the rest of his now tepid coffee and set the cup carefully on Kyle's desk. "I think the men responsible for the Pattaya Beach bombing in October are planning to launch a Scud missile with a cesium-137 payload at a target somewhere on the western coast of North America. Do you know what cesium-137 is?"

Kyle's voice failed him. He shook his head.

Hugh told him.

"Jesus Christ," Kyle said, stunned. "Hugh, are you sure?"

He met Kyle's eyes and said firmly, "I'm sure, Kyle."

"Then I don't get it." He aimed an exaggerated look over Hugh's shoulder. "Where are the marines? Why aren't you out at Elmendorf briefing the pilots so they can take these guys out? Why come to me?"

"Do you know anyone at Kulis?"

"The Air National Guard base? Sure. Why?"

"Do you know where Sara's ship is?"

Kyle's expression changed. "Hugh."

"I know she's on the *Sojourner Truth*. I know the *Sojourner Truth*'s on patrol in the Bering Sea."

"It was," Kyle said.

Hugh looked at him.

"The *Sojourner Truth* interdicted a Russian processor fishing on our side of the Maritime Boundary Line. The Coasties boarded them, arrested the crew, confiscated the vessel, and are now on their way with it into Dutch Harbor to turn it over to the authorities."

"You sound like you're reading a press release."

"I am. Actually"—Kyle looked at the clock on the wall—"they've probably been and gone by now. I read all about it on District Seventeen's Web site yesterday. Wanna see?"

"No time." But for the first time that morning Hugh couldn't stop a grin. "That's my Sara."

"Ride 'em, cowgirl," Kyle said, and sobered. "Seriously, Hugh, what are you going to do now?"

"I can't get my boss off the dime," Hugh said, his smile fading, too. "I've got to find that damn freighter before I take another run at him. When I do—"

"If you do. There's the hell of a lot of water to look in, Hugh, and boats don't exactly leave tracks."

"It was scheduled to leave Petropavlovsk on the seventh—what day is it again?"

"The ninth. Was your source on the departure date reliable?"

Hugh thought of Noortman curled into a fetal position on his living room floor, his knee swollen up to the size of a basketball. "I don't know. He would have said anything to make us stop."

"Stop what? Hugh?"

"Can you check to see if Sara's ship is in Dutch Harbor yet, and if not, where it is?"

Kyle gave Hugh a long look. "Sure. I can do that."

"And then could you call your buddy at Kulis, see if they've got anything going in that direction, and ask if I can bum a ride?"

Kyle shook his head and reached for the phone. "Sure. I can do that, too." He began to punch in a number and paused. "You know, Hugh, when I suggested you figure out a way to spend more time with Sara, I wasn't suggesting professional suicide as a means of making that happen."

Hugh looked back without smiling. "Where are Lilah and the kids?"

"At home. Lilah'll just be getting them ready for—" Kyle stopped. "Yeah. I see what you mean."

He hunched over the phone with a will. Hugh slid down to rest his head against the back of his chair and enjoyed the first slackening of tension in what felt like days.

12

january 9
anchorage

KYLE WAITED UNTIL THE Hercules C-130 was in the air before he drove back to his office. He hung up his parka and stewed around a while before calling his wife.

"Where's Hugh?" she said when she heard his voice.

"Back on the road," Kyle said. "Listen, Lilah, I want you to take Eli and Gloria down to Seldovia for the weekend."

There was a brief silence. "Kyle. It's Monday."

"Oh. Yeah. Of course. Well, then take the week."

"I've got work, Kyle, as you well know."

Lilah worked for the FBI, too. "Take some leave," he said. "If I have to I'll pull strings."

"The kids have school."

"I'll call their teachers and tell them they'll be back in a bit."

Another silence. "Kyle. What's going on?"

"I want you to take the kids to Seldovia, Lilah. Stay with the folks. You know they'd love to have them."

"Kyle. We were there for a week over Christmas, if you recall, and I got the distinct impression that that was about six days too long for your father. Why this sudden urge to get me out of town? You got a girlfriend or something?" She paused. "Has this got anything to do with Hugh showing up in the middle of the night?"

"No," he said, "nothing at all. Where on earth did you get that idea?"

"That response is so totally feeble I'm not even going to comment on it."

"Lilah." Kyle rested his forehead in the palm of his hand. "Just take the kids to Seldovia. Rent a bed-and-breakfast, I don't care. Just go. Today."

When she spoke again her voice was softer. "You're scaring me, Kyle."

"Good," he said.

The seconds ticked off while she made up her mind. "I'll take them to Seward," she said finally. "Is that far enough away?"

Seward was a hundred miles down the road, with the Kenai Mountains between it and Anchorage. "Yes. That should be far enough."

"I'll call the Edgewater. At this time of year we could probably rent the whole hotel for fifty bucks a night."

"That sounds good," he said, trying not to show his relief.

"Kyle?"

"What?"

"Come with us."

"I've got something I've got to do here first."

He hung up and swiveled to look out the window. It was a pity he wasn't really seeing anything, because the window had a spectacular view of Denali and Foraker on the northern horizon. The day was clear and cold and icily bright for the measly five or so hours the sun was willing to poke its head up over the horizon. They'd actually had snow this year before December and it was piled in four-foot berms between which traffic negotiated streets that had gone overnight from four lanes to two. If the weather didn't suffer a meltdown in the interim, there ought to be plenty of snow for the dogsled races.

He loved this time of year, that fleeting time before the tourists came back and you could get a table at Simon's without an hour's wait. He was happy to be back in Alaska, too, a duty assignment he'd been hoping for since he'd joined the Bureau. Unlike the traitorous Hugh and Sara, Kyle had stuck loyally to the West Coast, graduating from the University of Washington with a degree in criminal justice and then going to work for the Internal Revenue Service. Truth to tell, in spite of the grief he received from pretty much everyone when he admitted to his employer's identity, he'd gotten kind of a bang out of the work. He loved catching righteous citizens—and they were always righteous—who insisted indignantly that the law didn't apply to them. In his own small way, he felt he was contributing to the reduction of the deficit, although the current administration in Washington was doing its enthusiastic best to keep that goal well out of his or anybody else's reach.

He'd signed up to take Russian at a community college, because by then the Wall was long down and he'd been headed for home from the moment he graduated from college. The borders were opening up between Alaska and Siberia and there was a future there for a Russian-speaking FBI agent.

In Russian 101 he met Lilah, fresh out of school with a degree in accounting—large, dark eyes, hair a downpour of heavy black, a body by Venus. He was sunk at first glance. After class he followed her into the parking lot and wouldn't let her leave until she gave him her

phone number. When he walked her to her door at the
end of their first date he knew she had a brain and a
sense of humor to go with the looks. By Russian 201
they were engaged, and by Russian 301 they were married, and before starting on children they applied together to the FBI. Both had been accepted immediately.
The Russian had helped, and it had also helped when
they both requested assignment to Anchorage, as Kyle
had known it would. Lilah was from Snoqualmie in
Washington State and no stranger to snow and ice, although she didn't much care for the four and a half hours
of daylight Anchorage was reduced to in winter. But then
who did?

Her picture smiled up at him from his desk, with Eli in
her lap and Gloria leaning against her shoulder. Yes, he
had one beautiful family.

His thoughts turned naturally to Hugh and Sara, also
part of his family. Not, at present, quite so beautiful. Odd,
he thought now, how they'd all wound up in law enforcement. But perhaps not so odd, when he remembered the
first time an Alaska state trooper had come to Seldovia, a
tall man with a deep voice and an unshakable sense of authority. There had been a stabbing death in a community
where if you weren't related by blood you were related by
marriage to everyone there. The town had been in a tur-
moil, which might very well have escalated into a lynch-
ing if the trooper hadn't flown in from Ninilchik to
investigate. It took his calming presence half a day to
bring people to their senses, and at the end of it he removed the perpetrator to Homer to be bound over for
trial. There was chaos, and then the trooper came, and
there was order. It had been a powerful example to three
awestruck little ten-year-olds.

Kyle straightened in his chair. His childhood buddy
Hugh Rincon was not an alarmist. If Hugh thought there

was a terrorist threat from the Far East presenting itself to a western American port sometime in the near future, then his buddy Kyle was going to take it seriously. All three of them, he and Hugh and Sara, too, had family in Alaska.

He called the local Coast Guard member of his task force. "Joe? Kyle. I'm headed out of the office. Can I drop by?"

He shrugged into his coat on the way out. "I'm going down to the port. I'll be back after lunch," he told the receptionist. One of the joys of being the boss was, so long as your case file didn't back up, nobody looked over your shoulder.

Eve's eyes followed him all the way to the elevator. Inside, he turned and winked at her. She blushed. She was just a kid, barely twenty years old, fresh out of Charter College with an associate degree in computers. He was well aware that she had a slight crush on him. He worried all the way down to the garage that he should have told her to get out of town, too.

Joe's office was eleven blocks down the street from Kyle's, in a handsome building erected right where Anchorage began a short slide into Knik Arm. "You know you're toast when the next big one hits," Kyle said.

Joe Brenner shook his hand warmly. "Yeah, but I'll have a great view on the way down." Behind him the Knik was beginning to fill up with bergs of ice, created by the freezing temperatures and broken by the forty-foot rise and fall of the tide. A containership was nosing into the bergs on the far side of the Knik, its hull crusted with sea spray. It was riding right down on the Plimsoll line.

Kyle thought of Hugh and wondered what the ship was carrying in its hold.

He turned. Joe Brenner was a tall, trim, broad-shouldered, square-jawed man in Coast Guard blue, with brown hair, blue eyes, and a charming manner. He was a weather forecaster on a local television station. He was also a commander in the Coast Guard Reserve who had been called up after 9/11. He still made the occasional 10:00 P.M. newscast, and he was something of a local heartthrob, because for some inexplicable reason best known only to the great television audience weather forecasters got all the action.

"Lately," he said to Kyle with an engaging grin, "the worst part of this job has been chasing people who watch me on the news away from the gate."

"Any potential there?"

Joe shook his head. "Nah," he said, a little sadly. "All jailbait."

"Shame."

"Yeah."

They communed together in silence over this grievous misfortune.

Kyle jerked his head at the window. "I see the CSX *Anchorage* is on its way in."

"Yeah," Joe said, and got to his feet to stand next to Kyle. "Riding low in the water."

"I was noticing. What're they carrying?"

Joe cocked an eyebrow. "What's up?"

Kyle shrugged. "Curious."

Joe didn't believe him. "Well, you'd have to ask the port about that."

"Okay. Wanna go for a ride?"

"Down to the port?"

"Yeah?"

"You sure you want to do that?"

Kyle's brow creased. "Why wouldn't I?"

Joe grinned at some secret joke. "Upon your own head be it."

The Port of Anchorage was a three-story building painted beige with red trim, accented with oversized porthole-style windows. The manager was a large young man with the pink clear skin of a baby's bottom and fine flyaway blond hair. Greg Wladislaw loved his job and he was a born cheerleader, anxious, even eager, to share every bit of this most wonderful job with anyone who didn't move fast and far enough out of range first. He was devastated not to have an answer for Kyle as to the contents of the containership docking behind him. "We don't have the manifests here, you understand. That'll be over at Horizon with their agent. I can call, if you like. Or take you over and introduce you."

Kyle said, "Can you tell me about traffic in and out of the port of Anchorage? When and what kind?"

Indeed Wladislaw could. "We get in two domestic ships a week, one Horizon on Sunday and one Tote on Tuesday. We've just started getting a third carrier in." He dropped his voice, as if he were imparting a state secret to a select, trusted few. "Some are foreign carriers."

If he was expecting expressions of awe and amazement he was disappointed. "Really?" Kyle said. "How often?"

"Once a week, out of Asia."

"Asia?" Kyle said. "What ports?"

"Hong Kong—well, China now, I guess—Japan, Taiwan, Korea, Singapore."

"Mmm," Kyle said. "That it?"

Wladislaw was shocked at the very suggestion. "Oh no, we have petroleum tankers coming in and out, too."

"Any ships come in from Russia?"

Wladislaw made a face. "What do they have that we want to buy?"

"Point taken. How often do the petroleum tankers come in?"

"One tanker a month," Wladislaw said proudly.

It wasn't exactly Long Beach, Kyle thought, and felt relieved. Not enough traffic to hide something the size of a freighter in. Maybe Hugh was wrong. He looked out the window at the dock, which appeared to stretch from the Knik River bridge to Turnagain Arm. The three men watched as three C-130s came spiraling in from the north to touch down at Elmendorf Air Force Base's runway, which ended on the edge of the bluff immediately above the port. A subsequent roar of engines indicated a takeoff immediately following. Aircrews doing touch-and-goes, to keep their skills sharp.

"Man, I love those big old Hercs," Joe said. "Been flying for fifty years. No place they can't get into or out of. Ever cop a ride in one?"

Kyle nodded. "I got to go out to Savoonga with the Alaska Air National Guard. A fun trip. Noisy, though."

"Yeah, I pack earplugs."

"I'll remember that for next time. So," Kyle said, turning to Greg, "you only get one ship in at a time?"

"Oh, no!" Wladislaw said, clearly appalled at the suggestion. He hustled Kyle and Joe to the outer office to where an aerial photograph the size of a tablecloth dominated one wall. It showed the port of Anchorage on a sunny summer day and every inch of the dock of the port used up by four ships moored bow to stern along it. "Two containerships and two petroleum tankers, all on the same day," Wladislaw said proudly.

"Must have been a busy day."

Wladislaw nodded vigorously. "You bet. You should come down on a ship day, Special Agent Chase. It's a real zoo. An organized zoo," he hastened to add.

"It's Kyle, Greg, and I'll take you up on that. Next week, maybe."

Wladislaw beamed. "Anything else I can help you with?"

"What kinds of goods move through here?"

Wladislaw spread his hands expansively. "What kinds don't would be an easier question to answer." He smiled widely at Kyle, and Kyle had to resist the temptation to scratch Wladislaw behind the ears. "The port of Anchorage supplies ninety percent of the population of Alaska. What do you drive?"

Startled to be asked a question instead of being answered, Kyle had to think. "Ah, Subaru Legacy."

Wladislaw nodded approvingly. "Family man, am I right? But with style."

Behind Wladislaw, Joe rolled his eyes. It wasn't the first time.

"Well, that Subaru came in on one of those ships. So did the gas to power it. So did the parts and oil your dealer uses to service it. Got snow tires?"

"Yup," Kyle said. Wladislaw was so delighted with his game that Kyle didn't have the heart to shut him down. "All came through this port, did it?"

Wladislaw beamed at him the way a teacher smiled at a promising pupil. "Yes, it did. The raisins in your oatmeal, the oatmeal, the bowl you eat it out of, and the spoon you eat it with." Wladislaw patted the aerial photograph proudly. "All through the port of Anchorage. Apples to zinc, straight from the port to your pantry shelves."

Kyle looked toward the windows, at the ice choking the narrow neck of Knik Arm between Anchorage and Point MacKenzie. "Has the port ever been shut down?"

Wladislaw was affronted at the very idea. "The port of Anchorage has never been closed to cargo. Ever."

"However—" Joe said.

Wladislaw seemed to wilt a little, and cast Joe a look

that could only be described as reproachful. "Well, yes, now and then when the ice is thick, it has been closed, but only to single-hulled petroleum vessels."

"We issue ice rules of the road every year," Joe told Kyle.

Kyle nodded thoughtfully. "Lot of silt washes down the Arm from the Knik Glacier annually."

Eager to redeem himself in the FBI's eyes, Wladislaw said promptly, "We dredge a million cubic yards per year out of the Knik. We maintain a depth of minus thirty-five feet at mean low tide."

"The dredge only works in the summertime, of course," Joe said.

"May to October," Wladislaw said.

Kyle nodded again. "Any other traffic?"

"Bulk cement ships, from China or Korea, also May through October. And, of course, a lot of ships make their maiden voyages to Anchorage, to see how the new ship handles in our weather and tides. We had two big cruise ships last summer, and a fresh-off-the-ways petroleum tanker. Double-hulled, too!"

"Quite the operation," Kyle said, congratulatory. "Thanks, Greg. You've been a lot of help."

Back in the car, Kyle said, "What's the port got in the way of security, Joe?"

Joe started the car and let it idle, turning up the heater. "Right now, nothing. Next April, the new MSST will be in place and operational."

Kyle thought back. "The Marine Safety and Security Team."

"Got it in one. A one-hundred man unit trained and equipped to handle everything from explosives to drug and migrant interdiction. It'll have dive teams, K-9 teams, and six boats."

Kyle nodded. "This is the team you told us about at the last JTTF meeting."

"Yeah," Joe said.

"But not deployed until April."

"Okay, Kyle, what's going on? You knew most of this stuff before."

"A refresher course never hurts."

Joe raised a skeptical eyebrow.

"I got a heads-up about possible terrorist activity, maybe involving marine shipping," Kyle said.

"And you think Anchorage might be a target?"

The disbelief in his voice was plain to read. "You never have?"

Joe shrugged. "I heard what your buddy Hugh said last October, same as everyone else, Kyle, but come on. Anchorage?"

"You got family in Alaska, Joe?"

"No," Joe said. "I'm divorced, no kids, parents live in Michigan along with about a billion other relatives. All of whom are among the reasons why I moved to Alaska."

"I do have family here," Kyle said. "And in Seldovia, and a lot of friends in Anchorage."

"I get that, Kyle, but it's not like we wouldn't notice if someone sailed a destroyer up the inlet and parked it at the dock."

"It doesn't have to be a warship; all it has to be is a cargo ship with the wrong cargo on board. Bombs aren't as big as they used to be. Have you watched the news from Iraq lately?"

Joe wasn't convinced. "Still," he said.

Many Alaskans shared this odd sense of invulnerability. Partly it was an inferiority complex, in that most Americans, informed by weather maps on the television news, thought Alaska was a small island off the coast of southern California. Partly it was location, twenty-seven hundred miles northwest of and an hour behind Seattle, a place where the polls were still open when the loser in a presidential election was giving his concession speech. Ninety percent of it was owned by the federal government in the form of national forests and parks and wildlife refuges. It was also a bank of raw materials, timber, fish, and minerals upon which the nation could draw when needed and when such a draw was justified by the current price of the commodity. There were only six hundred thousand people in the state and it returned only three electoral votes. As a result Alaskans were defensive and pugnacious in their attitude toward the rest of the nation. "We don't give a damn how they do it Outside," a local bumper sticker said.

But they did. They were acutely aware of their unimportance in the national scheme of things, and Joe was no different than any other Alaskan. It made it difficult for Kyle to mount a convincing argument that a terrorist could consider Alaska a target worthy of his attentions.

Joe looked at his watch. "If that's all, I've got to be somewhere."

And Joe, evidently, remained unconvinced. Kyle, carrying the image of Lilah and the kids headed down the Seward Highway at the back of his mind, yielded to Joe's skepticism, at least for the moment. "Blonde, brunette, or redhead?"

Joe grinned. "Want me to ask her if she's got a friend?"

"I'll have you know I'm a happily married man."

Joe held his hands up, palms out. "Just asking. You never felt the urge?"

Kyle thought of Eve and said virtuously, "Never."

"Yeah," Joe said, "right."

13

HUGH HELD ON TO the back of the pilot's seat, peering through the portside window at lower Kachemak Bay passing beneath their left wing. "I was born in Seldovia," he said, raising his voice to be heard over the droning of the engines.

"That a fact," the pilot said incuriously.

Nobody else in the five-person flight crew seemed interested, either, so Hugh retreated to the padded bench that ran across the rear of the flight deck. From there he caught only the merest flash of white glacial rivers between ragged tips of mountains that formed the southeastern edge of the bay he had once called home. That was home to them all.

They'd been only children, he, Kyle, and Sara, one of the many reasons they had banded together almost from birth and by far the least important. Their fathers were fishermen, their mothers a housewife, the city librarian, and a nurse, respectively. Their fathers had fished king crab in the heyday of king crab, from the late sixties,

when Lowell Wakefield's at first idiotic and then vision-
ary idea of creating a market for a brand-new gourmet
shellfish came to fruition. All three men, owners and operators of their own crabbers, had done very well indeed,
right up until the crash of the king crab stocks in the
Bering Sea in the early eighties, and by then they'd made
their pile. They were sorry, of course, for the failure of the
local canneries around Kachemak Bay, exacerbated and
accelerated by the urban renewal following the 1964
Great Alaskan Earthquake. Hugh knew for a fact that the
city library would have been out of business were it not
for the generous financial support of his father, but those
who no longer have to worry about the rent money tend to
tune out the woes of their neighbors.

That was something else that set Hugh, Sara, and Kyle
apart, and the proximate cause of friction between the
three of them and their classmates, the children of those
less—fortunate? hardworking? adroit in their political af-
filiations? pick one—than their parents had been. School
in Seldovia was not joy unconfined. Hugh remembered
Sara's tenth birthday party. The sight of Sara, struggling
to hold back tears, surrounded by balloons and games and
little paper bags full of candies and toys for prizes for
guests who never came was one of the more vivid memories of that time.

When his father didn't have him out on the boat beating ice, anyway. Hugh hated everything about fishing, the
endless hours, the numbing cold, the constant heaving of
the deck. He suffered from chronic seasickness, which
didn't endear him to his father. No one had ever been
happier than Hugh when the king crab stocks crashed at
pretty much the very moment he graduated from high
school; it meant he wasn't going to have to carry on the
family business at the helm of the *Mae R*. He went to college instead, in search of a warmer, drier job.

His gift for languages had brought him to his present employment. He'd been recruited right out of Harvard, received his master's in Russian studies from Georgetown and his doctorate in Asian studies from Princeton while on the job. His mother lost no opportunity to brag about his admission to Harvard, but she bored everyone first in Seldovia and then in Wailea over her son's graduation from Princeton.

He'd never felt all that Ivy League. He'd spent his childhood in Seldovia chafing beneath the need to get out and see with his own eyes that the rest of the world was really there. He had wanted an education that would get him a job that had him traveling all over that world.

His face stretched into a grim smile. Be careful what you wish for.

They landed in Dutch Harbor two hours after the *Sojourner Truth* departed the dock. Hugh swore a lot as the flight crew waited him out placidly. When he ran out of breath he turned to the pilot. "Anything you need in St. Paul?"

The pilot regarded him for a moment with a meditative expression. "No, but they may need something from Dutch."

"Like today's paper," the copilot chimed in. He didn't care where Hugh was going so long as it got him more hours in his logbook.

Hugh looked at the pilot, who was not immune to the siren song of more hours, either. He looked from Hugh to the copilot and said, "Let's top off the tanks."

january 10
east of agattu, in the aleutian islands

THE INSIDE OF THE container smelled like a prison sewer. In spite of the deliberately reduced diet, both chemical toilets were ready to overflow. The floor was slippery with vomit, piss, and shit, and last night Jones had given the order for the stove to be disconnected for fear that the open flame might actually ignite the air. Pirates, mercenaries, and terrorists alike had been reduced to a state of speechless misery.

The cold air whistling in through the cracks and the air holes and the flapping canvas roof was the only thing that made the journey endurable. Chen Ming, Fang's second in command and suffering from the cold even more than his boss, stayed in his hammock, cocooned inside his sleeping bag with only his nose exposed. Jones was not forthcoming with information, but with the degree of roll they were experiencing Chen was sure they were on the deck of their freighter, which meant they were probably on an older vessel, possibly a tramp freighter.

He wasn't sure if it was the fourth day or the fifth day of the voyage when Jones pulled out the satellite phone and dialed a number. Chen watched through the forest of swaying hammocks as Jones spoke in Korean, a language Chen recognized but did not speak himself.

He watched Jones listen, speak a few more words, and hang up. He wondered why Smith and Jones hadn't just brought walkie-talkies, which would have been cheaper and just as effective on five hundred fifty feet of ship, but Jones stowed the phone and raised his voice to speak to the men. "It is time. Arm yourselves."

Almost before he finished speaking men began to roll out of hammocks and drop to the floor, indifferent to the muck they stepped in. Elbows were thrown in the rush to get to their gear but no one took it personally. They were all professionals, this wasn't their first or even their tenth op, and there was the added bonus that to go to work they had first to get out of the container.

Chen was interested in seeing how Jones was going to accomplish that, and was impressed in spite of himself at Jones's combination of imagination and finesse. He used four very small amounts of plastic explosive slapped to the four corners of the doors, with a remote detonator triggered while the men crouched behind the cargo lashed between them and the doors. The resulting explosions were four loud pops barely distinguishable from each other and completely drowned out by the noise of the ship's engine and the rush and plunge of water against the hull. All four hinges were destroyed and the two doors, still locked and sealed, fell outward as one unit, the top edges landing on the next container over. The doors separated a little down the middle, twisting, but they had to kick the bottom half of the left door free before they could climb out and shinny down the two containers stacked below them to the deck.

It was tricky because the ship was experiencing a roll of about five degrees. The prevailing wind appeared to be coming out of the southeast, Chen guessed at around twenty-five to thirty knots, and it was cold enough that ice was beginning to form on the outsides of the forty-foot containers stacked three deep on the deck. He felt a sudden desire to get to the bridge immediately for a look at the barometer.

But this was Jones's show; Chen was just the hired help. He called up the specs of the vessel in his head. She was an aging catcher-processor three hundred forty feet long, with a crew of a hundred twenty-five. They'd smuggled themselves on board in an empty container, one of a dozen that the ship's crew was confidently expecting to fill with filets of Bering Sea pollock and Pacific cod.

Fifteen men going up against a hundred twenty-five might seem like bad odds, unless the fifteen were armed as well as Smith and Jones's were. Chen checked the magazine of his AK-104, the smaller, lighter, faster version of that classic assault rifle that won the Vietnam War, and, as always, felt reassured. Thirty rounds in the hands of someone who knew where to put them were always capable of calming hysterical crowds.

"Let's go," Jones said, and they filed out behind him into a dark, dank hold that smelled of salt air, fish, and rust.

january 10
anchorage

"IT'S YOUR WIFE ON line one."

"Thanks, Eve." Kyle picked up the phone. "Hey, baby."

"Hey. Just wanted to check in."

"You all settled?"

"We've got rooms on the top floor overlooking the bay for one quarter the summer rate. One has a small kitchen, so we don't have to eat out unless we want to."

"How are the kids?"

"A little restless. I took them to the SeaLife Center today. There were a bunch of kids there from the local school, and I talked their teacher into taking Gloria and Eli along on the tour."

"Lilah?"

"How much longer are we going to have to stay down here, Kyle?"

"A few days," Kyle said.

"When are you coming down?"

He took a deep breath. "I'm not coming down, Lilah."

"But you said—"

"I know what I said."

"Kyle—"

"I can't, Lilah. I have to stay here. I'm the head of the task force. If Hugh's right, if something's going to happen, I have to be here to work it."

There was another silence. When she spoke again her anger was obvious. "When this is over, you and I are going to have a conversation."

He winced. "I know."

IN SEWARD, LILAH HUNG up without saying goodbye and stood for a moment, staring unseeingly out at the wind-whipped surface of Resurrection Bay. Behind her, Gloria was reading *Green Eggs and Ham* to Eli, hitting hard on the last word in each line so her little brother would get that it was written in rhyme. He was making those deep, rich chuckles that only seem to come from five-year-olds.

If it hadn't been for Gloria and Eli, Lilah would still be in Anchorage. She'd be at work, maybe involved in whatever it was that had Kyle so spooked. Here there was nothing to do but tick down one interminable hour after another.

"The hell with it." She found the phone book, looked up a number, and dialed.

"Kenai Fjord Tours."

"Hi. Do you guys do any boat rides at this time of year?"

14

january 10
bering sea, maritime boundary line
on board the *sunrise warrior*

A RE WE THERE YET?" Vivienne Kincaid said.

Dylan Doyle grabbed for a handhold when the *Sunrise Warrior* heeled to port as they ascended the weather side of the swell. "We are there, Vivienne," he said with a faint hint of County Cork in his accent, "but be damned if I know where there is."

"Do my ears deceive me? You've finally found a stretch of water that has the North Sea beat?"

Doyle gave a snort of laughter. "It might be that I'm wishing I was on my way to Foinaven." The ship rolled over to starboard and skidded down the opposite side of the swell into the trough. Heaving green seas gave way only to dense ice fog in every direction. Vivienne was hovering over the radar, attention fixed on targets.

"They're icebergs," a new voice said at her shoulder.

She looked around to see that Kevin had arrived on the bridge.

"I don't think so," she said.

"It's ice, and we're drifting into it."

"There are two echoes with the same course and doing the same eleven knots. Of course they are ships. Not to mention which, the last reports have the ice pack stuck at fifty-nine degrees."

Kevin's lips tightened. Doyle grinned at him, which didn't help.

Footsteps sounded and Ernie Hart and Darryl Hickey tumbled into the room. Jack Lestenkof, Concetta Dalilak, and Evelyn Caudle were right behind them. They were dressed in orange jumpsuits, hard hats, and their Deep Sea Defender vests. "We got 'em?" Jack said. "Vivienne? We got 'em?"

Vivienne looked at Doyle. "Full steam ahead."

Everyone whooped except Kevin, although he looked less sullen than he had a moment before. Doyle worked the controls, and the engines responded with an eager roar. They closed to within half a mile of the closest echo, and the outline of another ship materialized out of the fog.

"And what to our wondering eyes should appear," Vivienne said. She was tempted to stick her tongue out at Kevin, but resisted.

"Hello, *Marinochka,*" Doyle said.

"Oh, shit," someone else said.

In one of those rapid Arctic shifts the weather had decided enough with the fog and the snow and the ceiling was rising rapidly, all the better to see the scene before them. Everything was still green and gray, sky, water, everything except for the rich red of the blood draining from the carcass of the little narwhal tangled in the long net the catcher-processor was at present winching in.

"Son of a bitch."

Vivienne reached for the mike and said in Russian, "Fishing vessel *Marinochka,* fishing vessel *Marinochka,* this is the MV *Sunrise Warrior,* campaign vessel of the environmental organization Greenpeace. We are here to protest your taking of illegal bycatch in protected waters. Please haul in your gear and leave this area immediately."

They got a lot of static in reply.

"Gee, maybe they don't want to talk to us."

"Ya think?"

Into the mike Vivienne repeated, "Fishing vessel *Marinochka,* fishing vessel *Marinochka,* this is the MV *Sunrise Warrior,* campaign vessel for the environmental organization Greenpeace. Please leave this sanctuary immediately. If you leave now, we will leave with you. If you choose to continue your activities, we will use any and all means to prevent you from continuing to fish. We are a nonviolent organization and we will do nothing to put your crews and vessels at risk. I repeat, we are a nonviolent organization, but we will use all peaceful means at our disposal to prevent you from taking any more illegal bycatch."

They waited for a reply and didn't get one.

"Vivienne?" Jack Nuyalan said tensely.

"Launch," Vivienne said, and Jack was out of the bridge before the word was all the way out of Vivienne's mouth.

"Vivienne?" Ernie said.

"Launch, launch, launch!" Vivienne said, watching the stern of the catcher. Sure enough, water boiled up as the catcher kicked it in gear.

Vivienne couldn't stand it. She headed for the door.

"Wait a minute, where are you going?" Kevin shouted.

Doyle laughed. Vivienne followed Ernie's crew to the starboard boat deck where they were scampering down a rope ladder to the inflatable, heaving and tossing on the waves below. Vivienne tumbled in after them and Ernie gunned the engine. He yanked hard on the wheel, jerking the bow around in an eyeballer of a course heading that would have them crossing the catcher-processor's bow with maybe an inch and a quarter to spare.

The dead whale was half up the chute, but Jack's crew didn't let that stop them. As they approached, the *Marinochka*'s crew opened up with water hoses. Concetta and Evelyn responded by holding up clear Plexiglas riot shields, one on either side of Jack. The force of the water from the hoses caused the shields to waver but Jack held grimly to his course.

"Those riot shields were a good idea!" Ernie shouted.

"Yeah!" Vivienne shouted back, and then they were on the *Marinochka* and Vivienne lost sight of the other inflatable.

"Oh man oh man oh man," Evelyn said, eye to the shutter of his camera. Evelyn was British and notoriously hard to impress, but not today. "This is beautiful," he breathed as the shutter clicked rapidly through a roll of film.

Vivienne knew that Neil was on the bridge wing getting it all on videotape as well. "Hoo-yah!" Concetta, the ex-marine, shouted, and then immediately cursed when the inflatable came into range of the water hoses. Vivienne and Concetta got their shields up but not before the water had knocked Evelyn to his knees, and they were all soaked through.

"Is your camera all right?" Vivienne shouted.

He looked at her, dazed and still on his ass in the bottom of the boat. She hauled him up and grabbed the camera. The shutter didn't respond when she pressed the button.

"It's okay!" he shouted. "It's waterproof!" He tucked it inside his coat and pulled out another. No wonder he looked so lumpy.

Ernie, in an attempt to avoid the water hoses, took the inflatable beneath the bow of the *Marinochka* with inches to spare, and an unexpectedly large swell raised it nose to nose with one of the men handling the hoses. He gaped at them. Vivienne smiled and extended a hand. "Hey," she said in her best Joey Tribbiani imitation, "how you doing?"

He stared at the hand, openmouthed, and then the swell dropped them down again, and Ernie hit the throttles, laughing out loud.

Jack's crew managed to hook his craft on the line that was pulling in the gear and his inflatable was hauled up the slipway right along with the net. They were hit with all four water hoses at once. Even the riot shields were no use, and Jack let go and they slid back into the water.

It went on like that for the next two and a half hours, until it started to get dark. "Let's pack it in," Vivienne said, and they returned to the *Sunrise Warrior* and a hero's welcome.

A hot shower and dry clothes later, Vivienne was on the phone to Amsterdam. "Well done," Benjamin Cavo told her.

"Thanks. We got some terrific film. Neil is editing it right now. We'll upload it and get it out to you pronto."

"Good. We've got an interview set up for you on CNN."

"CNN? They're actually paying attention?"

"Looks like."

"Let's hope no one takes a shot at the president today."

"Yeah, that would cut into our airtime," Ben said.

There was a knock at the door, and at her call Doyle stepped inside. "What's up?"

Vivienne said goodbye and hung up. "Ben's pleased."

"He'll be even happier when he sees the video."

Vivienne's grin was tired but satisfied. "Neil get it all?"

"Oh yeah," he said with a matching grin. "Miles of it, on the main camera and the backup. He's already started editing it into spots."

In spite of his protestations of devotion to the seas east of Iceland, Doyle was loving every minute of this. Since signing on board a tramp steamer as a common seaman when he was seventeen, he had worked his way up to a master mariner's license and had captained container-ships, LNG carriers, and cruise ships over the navigable waters of all the seven seas. He'd been studying for his marine pilot's license for south-central Alaska when the *Exxon Valdez* went hard aground on Bligh Reef.

It wasn't that he'd never seen an oil spill before, he'd told Vivienne. In 1978, his fourteenth year at sea, he'd been a mate on a freighter carrying Seville oranges to Portsmouth when the steering mechanism failed on the *Amoco Cadiz* in stormy weather and she ran onto the Portsall Rocks. Sixty-eight point seven million gallons of Arabian light and Iranian light crude oil spilled across two hundred miles of coastline, fouling the beaches of seventy-six Breton communities. The sight had sickened him.

By contrast, the *Exxon Valdez* had spilled a mere eleven million gallons, but it had spread four times as far, across much of what had previously been a pristine marine wildlife habitat. And after thirty years at sea, maybe he'd just had enough of slipshod seamanship, lousy ship management, and an international maritime attitude of "out of sight, out of mind." He'd left the marine pilot's program and flown to Amsterdam, where he offered his services to Greenpeace. Now sixty-three, he'd been master on a dozen campaigns, including a protest to disrupt the arrival of construction barges at Prudhoe Bay and prior visits to the fishing grounds on the Bering Sea. He had more sea sense that any other ten sailors Vivienne knew. Grudgingly, Ben Cavo had gone along with her insistence that Doyle be master on this campaign, not without some serious hinting in the way of payback, the form of which could be left to her imagination. Vivienne hinted back a convincing enthusiasm for the idea without being so rash as to make any specific promises, and Doyle had been on the bridge to greet her when she flew out to join the ship in San Diego.

"Food?" Doyle said now.

"Deal," she said, and followed him to the galley a deck down. Two long tables with matching benches were bolted to the floor at one end of the room. At the other end was a serving line of steam tables with a mini salad bar at the end. Today lunch was kielbasa and sauerkraut. Feet braced against the pitch and roll of the ship, Vivienne loaded her plate. Doyle assembled a salad of massive proportions and followed her to the table.

He looked around at the otherwise empty galley. "Is everyone else seasick?"

Vivienne was watching the cook, Nils Johnson, a young redheaded man whose face was so pale she could count his individual freckles. He gave a stifled moan, staggered over to a trash can, dropped to his knees, puked, puked again, got up, blew his nose on a paper towel, washed his hands in the galley sink, and went back to work. "I think so." She turned back to her meal and tucked in with an enjoyment that was not lacking an element of smugness. "You ever get seasick?"

"Not yet."

She smiled. "After, what, forty-six years at sea, chances are you won't."

He waved a loaded fork at her. "Don't tempt the fates, Vivienne. There's a sea out there with everyone's name on it."

When they were done, she carried the dirty dishes to the pass-through to hand to Nils, who was still pale but no longer sweating. The first fifteen minutes after you threw up were a grace period between bouts of nausea, she knew, which was one of the reasons she was smug about not being seasick now. She brought back two cups of coffee, heavy on the cream for her and heavy on the sugar for him, and they wedged themselves between table and bulkhead so they wouldn't keep sliding up and down the benches.

"CNN?" Doyle said.

"Ben says they're interested. It's about time. The Bering Sea fishery makes up half of the United States' fish production, mostly pollock. There are smaller fisheries, including pacific cod and snow crab. The industry is worth over a billion dollars annually."

Doyle grunted into his coffee cup. "What's the bad news?"

"Everything is down, species across the board, pollock, fur seals, sea lions, sea otters. King crab used to be big, but the stocks crashed in the early eighties and they have yet to come back."

"There was king crab on the menu in that restaurant in Seattle."

Vivienne gave him a look. "Just because there are hardly any left doesn't mean they don't let the fishermen go after what little there are. Ever hear of the North Atlantic cod?"

"What North Atlantic cod?"

"Exactly. The Bering has an abbreviated king crab season in January, about two weeks, I think, limited to area 517 only, and limited to a catch of a few hundred thousand pounds."

"Still too much, if the species is that close to the edge."

"No argument here. If I had my druthers, the government would buy out all the fishermen and close the area to fishing for the next hundred years, give it time to recover."

"Like they did with the cod fishery?"

"Yeah, but there they waited until it was too late, until the Atlantic cod was gone before they did anything about it." She could hear her voice rising. "Sorry."

"Never liked anybody the less for their having a temper, Vivienne." He winked. "Been known to beller a bit myself, now. Might be why I'm here, same as you. What else?"

"Bristol Bay, on the eastern edge of the Bering, used to be the world's largest salmon fishery."

"And now?"

"It started failing in the mid-nineties."

"Not a lot of good news in the Bering Sea. What do the scientists say?"

She shrugged. "They say what they always say. They use the annual catch numbers to refute charges of over-fishing. They say it's too early to attribute any of these changes to global warming. They don't know which trends are cyclic and which are long-term. They don't have enough data to separate and quantify the human effects from what may be natural variability."

"They don't know a hell of a lot," Doyle said, and shook his head. "In 1900 there were around a billion, a billion and a half people on the planet. Today, there's over six billion. All of us wearing clothes, driving cars, eating our heads off. Seems pretty cause and effect to me, but then that's just this poor ignorant sailor talking." He brooded for a moment. "I sailed up around the coast of Norway one summer, all the way from Oslo to Murmansk. It was a beautiful sail, great weather, gorgeous scenery." His grin flashed. "A lovely young bit of a thing for deck crew. Wasn't old enough to call the Beatles by name, but could she cook." His grin faded. "We didn't see a single whale. Or a seal, or a sea lion. Damn few fish. We did see a cow about a week into the trip, who had slipped her leash to browse on seaweed on the shore. A few seagulls." He shook his head. "It was eerie."

"We've already lost so much," she said, and sighed. "They're ripping up the bottom of the North Pacific Ocean, Doyle. Sometimes I think . . ."

"What?"

She spread her hands. "That we're bailing with a sieve."

He pretended shock. "Heresy. Calumny. Sacrilege!"

She smiled, but it was a tired smile. " 'O Lord, your sea is so vast, and my boat is so small.' "

"Quit stealing my lines. How many ships up here on their side of the line nowadays?"

"Last report I got said sixteen."

"How long do they stay?"

"Until they break down and have to go into port for repairs. Supply boats bring in food and water and change out crews."

He looked at the porthole, through which they could currently see a lot of frothing dark green water. A moment later the ship heeled in the opposite direction and the porthole was dark again. "I'm not seeing a calming in the weather anytime soon, Vivienne."

She knew he was thinking about the inflatables out on those seas. He was the master of the vessel. He was responsible for all the people on board. Campaign or no, they wouldn't get into the water unless or until he said they could. "The more we're in their face, the more time they waste dealing with us. The more time they waste on us, the less time they spend fishing. The less time they spend fishing, it's just that much less sea bottom they're ripping up."

"And it goes without saying that heavy seas make for good film at eleven."

He was just snide enough to make her smile. "That it does."

"So what's our next target?"

She pulled a list from her shirt pocket and consulted it. "The *Agafia*. Panamanian-owned, Niue-flagged, Russian-leased. A killing machine. A three-hundred-and-forty-foot killing machine."

15

C APTAIN ON THE BRIDGE."
     Captain Lowe climbed up into his chair. "Report."

"We've got the fishing vessel *Lee Side* off our starboard bow, sir. She's a hundred-and-eighty-foot longliner working p-cod." Sara nodded at Ops, who was talking on the radio. "Their first mate just called and said their skipper has gone berserk."

"Berserk?" the captain said. "Berserk how?"

"They say he has armed himself and is chasing the crew around, threatening to shoot them."

The captain digested this in silence.

"The crew is asking us to board and take the captain into custody," Sara said.

"With what is their captain armed?" Captain Lowe said.

"They say an automatic pistol, sir," Ops said.

"Has he fired it?"

"The mate says not yet, sir," Ops said, and broke off when an excited voice came on the air.

"Coast Guard, Coast Guard, he's shooting at us, I repeat, he's shooting at us!"

Everyone peered through the windows as the *Lee Side* vanished into the bottom of a swell and then materialized again at the top of another.

"He's not going to hit anything in these seas," the captain said, not noticeably excited at the prospect one way or another.

"We've got a monster of a low blowing in from the southeast," Sara said, clinging to a hatch handle. "It's only going to get worse, sir."

The captain nodded. "Prepare to launch a boarding team. I want Ensign Ryan to lead it."

"Aye aye, sir," Sara said. She nodded at the chief, and he made the pipe.

Five minutes later the VHF radio came to life again. This time it was a different voice, much calmer. "U.S. Coast Guard cutter, U.S. Coast Guard cutter, this is the fishing vessel *Terra Dawn,* mayday, mayday, mayday."

Ops keyed the mike. "Fishing vessel *Terra Dawn,* this is cutter *Sojourner Truth,* go ahead."

"Coast Guard, we are taking water and we're down by the stern."

"*Terra Dawn,* cutter *Sojourner Truth,* copy that, you're taking water and going down by the stern. Give us your lat and long."

The *Terra Dawn*'s skipper read out the lat and long numbers in a clear, calm voice, and Sara went to the radar console and looked over Tommy Penn's shoulder. "Got him, Tommy?"

"Got him, XO," Penn said, rolling the cursor across the screen to a green X off the south shore of St. George Island.

"Set a course," the captain said, "all ahead full."

"All ahead full, aye," the helmsman said.

"*Terra Dawn,* cutter *Sojourner Truth,* we are en route, I say again, we are en route."

"Yeah, Coast Guard, you're not going to get here in time. I'm ordering the crew into survival suits and launching the life rafts."

Everyone looked at the almost black horizon. "Anyone else out there close enough to get to them before they go in?"

Tommy scrolled back and forth on the radar screen. "No, Captain, it looks like everyone else is up here with us."

Tommy was right; everywhere she looked, Sara could see the lights of at least six other vessels appearing and disappearing as they and the *Sojourner Truth* wallowed through the heavy seas. The *Lee Side* was beginning to fall perceptibly aft as all four engines came on line and thrust the *Sojourner Truth* forward through the waves breaking across her bow.

"Must have been hot on the cod," the chief said in a low voice.

Sara nodded. "Hard to walk away from that kind of money, no matter if you are staring down the throat of a hurricane." She should know. Her father had risked ship and crew too many times to count in pursuit of the almighty king crab. The only difference between him and the skipper of the *Terra Dawn* was he had been lucky as well as smart.

The aviators arrived on the bridge, as usual looking ready to argue their way into the air. As usual the captain heard them out with a taciturn expression. "I see no need to launch, gentlemen, especially not in these seas. The *Terra Dawn*'s captain seems to have things well in hand. The crew is in survival suits, the captain is launching the life rafts. We have a fix on their position. They should be safe enough until we get there."

Lieutenants Laird and Sams looked frustrated.

"Coast Guard, this is *Terra Dawn*," their skipper said on the radio, sounding as if he were trying to stifle a yawn. "Our deck is awash. She's going down. We are abandoning ship."

"Gosh, he's real excited, isn't he," Chief Edelen said to Sara in a low voice.

Sara nodded. She'd been wondering what the *Terra Dawn*'s skipper had been smoking herself. The handheld crackled into life. "Boarding team ready to launch, Captain."

"Thank you, XO. Let's give them a lee, Chief."

"Aye aye, Captain. Helm, come to course heading one-eight-zero."

"One-eight-zero, aye."

The cutter took the change of course with attitude, rolling heavily into the trough of a swell, heeling to starboard, and then rolling to port down the opposite side. She nosed through the wind and steadied.

"XO?" Even over the handheld Ryan's voice betrayed his youth and excitement. Sara couldn't blame him, she could only envy him.

"Ensign, your orders are to disarm and detain the captain and remain on board the *Lee Side* until we return. Understood?"

"Understood, XO," Ryan said.

"What arms are you carrying?"

"Sidearms and shotguns, XO."

"Good. Don't shoot if you don't have to, but don't get shot, either."

"Understood, XO," Ryan repeated, much more soberly this time.

Sara looked at the captain. He got out of his chair and walked to the hatch leading onto the port wing and stepped into the wind. "Launch when ready," Sara said into the mike.

"Aye aye, XO, launching," Ryan said, and Sara followed the captain out onto the wing. They stood in silence because to speak would have necessitated screaming above the wind, and they held on like grim death to the railing because otherwise the *Sojourner Truth* would have tossed them into the inflatable casting off below. The coxswain hit the throttle—all coxswains were speed demons; Sara thought it must be in the job description—and the small boat powered up and in spite of the heavy seas fell smoothly off the side of the ship and into a curving course toward the *Lee Side.*

"Who's the coxswain?" the captain said.

"PO Mathis, sir," Sara said.

The captain watched the small boat maneuver up a swell and down its backside and tackle the next without hesitation. The wind paused long enough for them to hear the sound of the engine throttling up and back and up again. "Nicely done," the captain said.

"Yes, sir," Sara said in complete agreement. The *Sojourner Truth* was lucky in its boat handlers. Coxswain Duane Mathis was as good as the chief in that respect. She watched the small boat labor up another wave. That was one hell of a boat ride she was missing out on.

The captain returned to the bridge, Sara following. "Resume course and speed, Chief."

"Helm, resume course and speed," Chief Edelen said.

"Resuming course and speed, aye."

Inside, every available pair of binoculars was focused on the small boat as it approached the *Lee Side,* once more retreating astern. Everyone swayed shoulder to shoulder with the heave and fall of the deck. Sara, straining her eyes like everyone else, saw the orange blur against the dark hull start to move off. The radio blared into life. "*Sojourner Truth,* this is the boarding team. Boarding accomplished safely, all members on board."

"Understood, boarding team." Sara resisted the urge to ask questions, like where was the captain of the *Lee Side* and had he shot any of her BTMs yet.

The VHF chose this moment to erupt. "U.S. Coast Guard, U.S. Coast Guard, this is the fishing vessel *Chugiak Rose,* come in, Coast Guard, Coast Guard, come in."

This skipper sounded considerably more excited than had the skipper of the *Terra Dawn,* and Ops replied in his most soothing voice, "*Chugiak Rose,* cutter *Sojourner Truth,* reading you five-by, go up to two-two."

The skipper either didn't hear Ops' request or ignored him. "Coast Guard, *Chugiak Rose,* I've got an injured crewman who needs an immediate emergency medevac, I say again, I've got an injured crewman who needs an immediate emergency medevac."

The aviators, standing in glum silence at the captain's right hand, brightened.

"I don't fucking believe this," someone said.

"Belay that!" the captain barked.

The aviators looked at him, mute with longing.

"*Chugiak Rose,* cutter *Sojourner Truth,* what is the nature of the injury, I say again, what is the nature of the injury?"

"His right arm is hanging by a one-inch strip of skin."

"Oh Christ," someone said, and this time the captain let it slide.

"I've got a tourniquet around his upper arm but he's lost a lot of blood. He's unconscious and I think he's in shock. Can you help us?"

"*Chugiak Rose,* Coast Guard, give us your lat and long," Ops said. He had to ask for them again when the skipper's voice stumbled so badly over the numbers the first time no one could understand what he was saying.

"Find them for us, Tommy," Sara said.

"Aye aye, XO," Tommy said, and bent over the radar

screen. As usual, Tommy was so calm Sara had to quell the impulse to take her pulse to see if she was still breathing.

"Here they are," Tommy said, straightening up so everyone crowded around could see the screen. Everyone moved when the captain came to take a look. The *Chugiak Rose* was three boats away in the opposite direction.

Sara looked at the captain. "Flight ops, Captain?"

He pressed his lips together, looked out the windows at the seas, and gave a reluctant nod. The aviators faces lit up like it was Christmas, and they vacated the bridge at speed. The captain nodded at Ops.

"*Chugiak Rose,* Coast Guard cutter *Sojourner Truth,* we are preparing to launch our helicopter to come to your aid. We will lower a basket for you to load your crewman into. Do you understand?"

"I understand, *Sojourner,* you are sending your helicopter to hoist off my crewman. Please get here as quick as you can."

"Understood, *Chugiak Rose.* Tell me about your ship, length, masts, wires."

Ensign Bob Ostlund at Helo Control piped flight ops over the loudspeaker and everyone's hats came off.

"Boarding team to *Sojourner Truth.*"

"Go ahead, boarding team," Sara said into the handheld.

"Yeah, XO, we've got the situation here contained."

"Good to know. Everybody okay?"

"Yeah, pretty much." Ryan sounded very casual, almost too much so, like he'd been smoking the same stuff the skipper of the *Terra Dawn* had. Sara looked at the captain and raised an eyebrow. He shook his head once, very slightly.

"Roger that, boarding team, we just got a SAR case off the third vessel northeast of you, personnel injury. How do you want to handle things there?"

"*Sojourner Truth,* boarding team, yeah, we noticed the change of course. The mate here is capable of taking the vessel back to Dutch. They say they'll take the captain with them, under restraint."

"Roger that, boarding team, stand by one." Sara clicked off the mike and looked at the captain.

"We'll launch the helo first, then pick up the boarding team," Lowe said.

"Aye aye, sir," Sara said, and relayed this information to Ryan.

"Aye aye, XO, standing by."

"Stay sharp, we'll be operating on the fly. A boat went down on the south side of St. George and their crew is in the water in life rafts."

A burst of static was the answer. Sara thought it was probably just as well. She looked up at the video monitor and saw that the hangar had been rolled back and the deck crew was in the process of a heavy weather traverse. It was too rough to just roll it out. Every deck officer's nightmare was that they'd lose the helo over the side, so they'd move the helo a foot, detach the forward two tie-downs, move it out another foot, reattach the forward tie-downs, detach the aft tie-downs, move it, reattach the aft tie-downs, and start the process all over again.

They were also taking spray over the starboard side. "Can you nose her a little more into the wind, Chief?"

"Can do, XO," Mark said. "Helm, bring her around to one-two-five."

"One-two-five, aye."

The *Sojourner Truth,* great ride that she was, responded instantly to the new course, water from both propellers hitting the rudder full force, bow pulling to port, slicing neatly through the heavy seas. With the bow taking the brunt of the southeast gale, the deck immediately aft of the hangar had a little more shelter. It helped, but it was still going to take another thirty minutes to get the helo ready for launch.

There was another potential problem, Sara thought, watching the salt spray hit the foredeck. She turned her head to look at the status board, where Tommy was marking their new course and speed. Barometric pressure was 99.2 and falling. She looked out on deck.

The chief followed her gaze. "We making ice?"

"Not yet," Sara said.

A half hour later the aviators were buttoned into the helo, the captain gave the go, and they were up and off a few minutes later. The *Sojourner Truth* resumed her former course, all ahead full for the south shore of St. George. "How long before we get there, Tommy? Sara said.

Tom's eyes went out of focus as she calculated. "It's about a hundred miles to the location of the sinking, we're doing"—she glanced up at the Transas screen—"fifteen knots." She looked at Sara. "A little under six hours, XO."

"Thanks," Sara said, and went to stand next to the captain's chair, feet spread to ride out the plunging motion of the ship. No one was taking a step without holding on to or leaning up against something.

He looked at her. "All assholes and elbows today, eh, XO?"

She was slightly shocked at the use of profanity, but recovered enough to say reproachfully, "I thought that was an aviator's expression, sir, unbecoming a sailor."

The corners of his mouth quirked. She saw it, and dared to smile. "I just hope we don't get something else thrown at us today, XO."

Ostlund touched his headset, listened, and spoke into the mike around his neck. "Captain, the helo has their man and is on its way to the St. Paul clinic."

Everyone raised binoculars. The hull of the *Chugiak*

Rose was by now the barest line appearing and reappearing on a violent green horizon, but the bright orange of the helicopter showed briefly as it sped toward the island, which also kept appearing and reappearing in the mist and the sleet. It was getting dark, too.

"Lieutenant Sams says the guy's in a bad way. He's lost a lot of blood."

"Best speed for the clinic," the captain said, "all they've got."

"Aye aye, sir. Lieutenant Sams wants to know if they should refuel when they get to the island and then go look for the *Terra Dawn*'s crew."

The captain looked again at the southeastern horizon. It looked not just dark, Sara thought, but black with ill-tempered weather. "Tell them yes. Tell them to take a run right after they deliver the injured man to the clinic, see if they can get some idea of what direction the rafts are drifting."

Probably onshore, Sara thought, as the wind was blowing from the southeast. It would depend on how far to the west off the coast of St. George they had foundered, though.

"After which they are to return to base, refuel again, and stand by. We'll recover them when the weather eases up."

"Aye aye, sir."

They came abeam of the *Lee Side,* the inflatable bobbing between them, and pulled the bow around enough to give the small boat as much shelter as could be found in seas like these. Shortly afterward Hank Ryan was on the bridge, making his report to the captain. The ensign was not pleased. "They could have handled it themselves, sir. There were five of them and one of him."

"He had a weapon, they said."

"Yes, sir, but not a nine-millimeter automatic."

"What was it, then?"

"A twenty-two pistol that hadn't been cleaned in

twenty years. If he'd tried to fire, it would have blown up in his hand. Always assuming he'd thought to load it first."

"I thought that they said he was firing at them."

Ryan shook his head. "They were mistaken, sir."

"We sent ten men and a small boat in twelve-foot seas to go to the rescue of a ship's crew held hostage at the point of an old, unloaded twenty-two pistol?"

"Yes, sir."

There was a long, thoughtful silence on the bridge, which lasted through a complete swing of the pendulum, all the way to port, all the way to starboard.

"Maybe we could bill them," Sara said.

Nobody laughed, but then Sara hadn't been joking.

The door to the bridge opened and closed, and a seaman brought a slip of paper to Ops. He read it, and read it again. Sara, watching him, caught his eye. He held out the slip of paper. She read it. She, too, read it twice. She returned it to Ops and took an unobtrusive step back, she hoped far enough out of range.

Ops gave her a look of burning reproach, waited for the tilt of the deck to be right, and then stepped up to take Sara's place next to the captain's chair. "Captain, we've just received a message from District."

The captain swiveled to give Ops a quizzical look. "Do not tell me what I don't want to hear, Ops."

"Sorry, sir. District says a Herc on the last patrol found a fishing vessel over the line. They want us back up there."

Captain Lowe was not a man given to public invective, but Sara, standing a little behind him, did notice his ears begin to redden. He slid to the deck and said curtly, "I'll be in my cabin."

"Aye aye, sir," she said smartly.

The door closed behind him.

"Cap'n below," Tommy said.

Ops looked at Sara. "Think he can talk them out of it?"

"Whoever talked District out of anything?" If Sara hated anything about the Coast Guard, it was that operational decisions were made on shore. The job was difficult enough without someone looking over your shoulder from Juneau.

It didn't help to know that the fishing vessel in question would be long gone by the time they got there. It wasn't like they wouldn't have seen the Herc and known what that meant.

Ops said tentatively, "He could always just say no."

"He could," Sara said, and left it at that.

Lowe wouldn't, and they both knew it. "Get me a weather report for the Maritime Boundary Line," she told Ops, and followed the captain below.

16

•

BY A MIRACLE THEY had picked up every single
crew member of the *Terra Dawn*, close enough to St.
George that the small boats were able to ferry them
in and drop them off in St. George's harbor. "It was one
hell of a ride in, though," Ryan told Sara.

It was the first time in the twelve months he'd been assigned to the *Sojourner Truth* that Sara had seen the
young ensign look tired. "Hit the sack," she told him.
"You can write your report tomorrow. We're underway
for the line. Holiday routine until we get there."

"Aye aye, XO." He gave her a tired smile and stumbled below.

They plowed northwestward for the rest of the night.
No aids-to-navigation malfunctions were reported, no
fishermen fell overboard, and no skippers went apeshit,
which marginally mollified the tone of the e-mails coming at them from District, and, more important, let the
crew catch up on their sleep. FSO Kyla Aman worked a
heroic fourteen-hour shift in the galley, producing,

among other various and succulent things, peanut butter chocolate chip cookies, Rice Krispy treats frosted with a melted mixture of chocolate and butterscotch chips, and strawberry shortcake, dedicating mess cooks to carry trays of said bounty up to the bridge, the wardroom, and the engine room as well as putting out loaded trays in the crew's mess. It was amazing how the aroma of baked goods lightened the crew's mood.

They were coming up fast on the line, the seas having smoothed out between the last outgoing storm and the next one incoming, which, Ops had assured her with far too much insouciance, was breathing right down their necks. She made the mistake of asking him what the next storm looked like, and he replied, one eye on the door, "Well, XO, the last one they called a hurricane."

"And this one?"

"Well, actually, this one they're calling a hurricane, too."

"Get away from me, Ops."

"Getting away from you immediately, ma'am."

But for now the seas had smoothed out to a moderate six feet and the *Sojourner Truth* was taking the swells easily. The horizon was lightening, and if Sara was not delirious, she thought she might even have seen a patch of blue, high up and far away, true, but there nevertheless.

They arrived on station after lunch. "Captain on the bridge," Tommy said.

"XO," Lowe said, climbing into his chair. "What's our status?"

"We're on the MBL at fifty-nine lat, almost dead on a hundred eighty degrees long, sir. We have traffic on the radar, fifteen processors, cruising the Russian side. None on our side, and none on visual."

"Sir?" Tommy said from the radar screen.

"Go ahead, Tommy," the captain said.

"We've got someone over the line."

The captain swiveled around in his chair. "Say again?"

"We've got a ship over the line, and I mean way over the line, sir." She manipulated the cursor ball and read down the column of numbers on the lower-left-hand side of the screen. "About two and a half miles over, sir, and not looking like she's going to turn around anytime soon."

Lowe looked at Sara. "They have to know we're here."

She shook her head. "Just our turn in the barrel, sir, I guess."

"XO?" Tommy said.

"What?"

"There's another ship out there, too. It's closing on the first one."

Sara's eyes met the captain's for a pregnant moment.

"Plot us a course to intercept," Lowe said, the words barked. "Give me an ETA. Ops, get on the sat phone to District."

Ops took the sat phone and retired to the deck aft of the wheelhouse in good order.

"XO, when we come up on them, I want you on the conn."

"Aye aye, Captain," Sara replied very correctly.

Ops came back into the bridge and presented himself to the captain, very nearly going into a brace. "I'm sorry, Captain, the sat phone is not connecting today."

The captain vaulted out of his chair and said curtly, "I'll try to raise District on e-mail."

"Aye aye, sir." She waited for the door to close behind him. "Captain's below." She pretended not to hear when someone gave a low whistle.

She walked over to stand behind Tommy at the radar.

"Where are they, Tommy?" Tommy pointed. Sara looked up to the horizon. They were headed south by southwest, and they and the blips on the screen were now both well and truly inside the Doughnut Hole.

The Doughnut Hole was a roughly triangular area in the center of the Bering Sea, far enough away from the United States and Russian coastlines to form a no-man's-ocean outside of any nation's jurisdiction. It had been so overfished during the last century that it was now closed by international treaty to allow the native marine species, especially pollock, to repopulate. What the fishing vessel the *Sojourner Truth* was now in pursuit of thought they could pull out of the Doughnut Hole was a question only they could answer. Sara had a feeling that Captain Lowe, who had been tried pretty far on this patrol, was determined to have an answer.

An hour later one of the lookouts posted above called down a sighting. Out came the binoculars.

Sara braced her legs against the swell and peered forward. The rise and fall of the waves intermittently obscured the stern, but not for so long they couldn't make out the name.

"I don't fucking believe this," Mark Edelen said.

"No gear in the water, though, ma'am," Tommy said, eyes glued to binoculars.

"I'll be with the captain, Chief," Sara said.

The door to the captain's cabin was closed. Sara rapped on it hard enough to make her knuckles sting. "It's the XO, Captain."

"Enter." She opened the door and she stepped inside. "Close it, XO."

She closed the door without comment. The captain was sitting at his desk, in front of his computer. He didn't look happy, and Sara didn't imagine that what she was about to tell him would make him any happier. "Captain—"

He jerked a thumb at the monitor. "Make ready to go to flight quarters, XO."

"—the fishing vessel has been— What?"

"Go to flight quarters," he said. "Make ready to bring our helo back on board."

"Helo? I thought our helo was in St. Paul."

"So did I."

"Captain," Sara said, and found herself momentarily and uncharacteristically at a loss for words. She tried again. "Captain, St. Paul is over three hundred nautical miles from here. They can't make it that far on their fuel tanks."

"Not without a good southeasterly," he agreed. "They refueled midway."

She thought quickly, and remembered the cutter they had passed the day before going in the opposite direction. "The *Alex Haley*?"

He nodded.

"They did, what, a hot refueling?"

"They did an in-flight refueling," the captain said, "a little over the midway point."

Sara wondered for how much longer Lieutenants Sams and Laird were going to be members in good standing of the United States Coast Guard. "Sir, far be it from me to leap to the defense of an aviator, but this just doesn't sound like something either Lieutenant Sams or Lieutenant Laird would do. They're both pretty cautious."

"Not all that cautious, it would seem," the captain said with dangerous calm.

"They're going to be dragging by the time they get here," Sara said, appalled at the notion of bringing the helo back on board with exhausted aviators at the controls.

"Yes," the captain said, but he didn't fool Sara. He was almost vibrating with worry. And rage.

All she could think to say was "Why?"

"Apparently they've got a VIP on board."

She gave up trying to maintain any semblance of cool and said, "Who absolutely positively has to get here overnight."

"That's right."

"Who? And for god's sake, why?"

"They won't say. They say the VIP will explain upon arrival."

Sara tried to think of a reason so important to put a helo on the nose of forty-five-knot winds and fly three hundred miles, and failed. "Are they going to make it?"

"They've got something of a tailwind, so I'm told. That hurricane of NOAA's is giving them a little push in our direction."

"I just bet it is," Sara said.

"And then the e-mail went out again before I could ask District what the—what they're up to," Captain Lowe said, gesturing toward the computer. "But not before I got us a letter of no objection."

By which was meant, District was leaving the method of pursuit and interdiction of the fishing vessel they'd caught in the Doughnut Hole up to the discretion of the captain of the *Sojourner Truth*.

She opened her mouth and he waved her to silence. "I know, XO, we say we don't shoot anybody over fish. But I'm tired of these guys stepping all over us. I want to throw a little scare into them. Let's send them home with a story to tell about how crossing the line into U.S. territory is, to paraphrase that known felon, Martha Stewart, not a good thing."

"You can shoot at these guys with my great good will, Captain," she said cordially. "You can sink them and I might be so upset I'd have to make myself another cappuccino."

He looked taken aback. "I beg your pardon, XO?"

She met his eyes. "It's the *Agafia*, sir."

17

january 12
the maritime boundary line
on board the uscg cutter *sojourner truth*

CAPTAIN LOWE RETURNED TO the bridge, Sara on his heels. "Flight quarters," he said.

Everyone stared.

"Flight quarters," he repeated.

"We're bringing our helo back on board," Sara said when nobody moved.

Everyone stopped staring at the captain and started staring at her.

"Flight quarters," she said patiently.

"But, XO, the *Agafia,*" Ops said. He even pointed at the outline of the ship nearing a threateningly black horizon that also seemed to be moving, only toward them instead of away. "We're half a mile off and they're still way inside the exclusion zone."

"Flight quarters, Ops," the captain said in a deceptively gentle voice. He even smiled.

"Aye aye, sir," Ops said.

Hats were whipped off smartly and the news was

piped to the crew. Shortly thereafter phones began to ring as various members of the deck crew called the bridge to see if they were serious. Assured that the bridge was, they began to assemble aft, not without a lot of nonverbal communication that indicated a certain lack of faith in the sanity of the entire command structure of the U.S. Coast Guard. Shortly thereafter the hangar was retracted, and as if that was the signal, the radio sparked into life, signaling the approach of the helo.

"Tallyho!" Mark Edelen said, pointing, and they all looked east to see a bright orange speck against the now black clouds boiling up out of the south.

"Put our nose on the seagull's ass, Chief," Sara said.

"Aye aye, XO," Chief Edelen said. "Helm, zero-seven-zero, all ahead full."

"Zero-seven-zero, all ahead, aye, Chief."

"XO," the captain said.

"Sir?"

"Get aft. I want that VIP standing in my cabin talking fast thirty seconds after they hit the deck."

"Aye aye, Captain," Sara said.

She hit the portside hatch at not quite a run, registering by the wind on her cheek that the temperature had risen a couple of degrees since she'd last taken the air on deck, and slid down the ladder with her elbows on the railings.

"Hey, XO, you're out on deck without your float coat," said Seaman Rosenberg as she trotted past. She wanted to flip him off but it didn't suit either her rank or his.

She hit the main deck and fetched up behind a cowling. The helo was running up on the stern about a hundred feet up. They throttled it way back and approached the hangar deck on tiptoe, nose down, tail up. The closer they got, the smaller the deck looked to Sara. The swell was increasing in height, pushed up by the approaching storm, and the stern bobbed and weaved like Muhammad Ali. Float like a butterfly and sting like a bee.

The helo made it over the taffrail and hovered over the hangar deck. It was ten feet from touchdown when the ship slammed down into the sea and the deck slid out from beneath it. The superstructure of the ship stopped shielding the helo from the wind and a good forty-knotter caught her upside the head. Whoever was driving wisely decided that discretion was the better part of valor and hit the throttle, roaring off to port, circling around, and coming up again on the stern.

Sara crouched down behind the cowling, the force of the wind threatening to pull her hair out by the roots, and worked at reswallowing her heart. The LSO was crouched against the exterior of the hangar. "You okay?" he yelled, or she supposed he did. She saw his lips moving, but she couldn't hear him over the wind, the all ahead full the *Sojourner Truth* had going on. She gave him a thumb's-up, and then they both heard the second approach of the helo and he duck-walked forward to stand in front of the hangar and guide them in.

She could hardly bear to watch, but this time they plunked her down right in the gold, in the exact center of the circle painted on the hangar deck. Sara scuttled around the hangar, dragging her knuckles like an ape, and yelled in Ostlund's ear, "They've got a passenger the captain wants to see pronto."

He nodded and followed the rest of his deck crew forward, hunched over so the rotor wouldn't take their heads off. He reached the helo and slapped the side. She could see Sams, in the left seat, crack his door. Ostlund yelled at him. Sams nodded. The LSO walked around the front of the helo and disappeared. Through the windscreen Sara could see the helo's aft door slide open and someone step to the deck.

Ostlund came scrambling back around the helo on a heading for Sara, followed by someone tall bundled into a Mustang suit and a watch cap pulled low over his brow.

"This here's our XO, she'll take you to the captain."

"Thanks." The man unbuckled his helmet and turned to Sara.

Her jaw dropped.

"Hi, Sara," Hugh said. "I need to talk to your commanding officer. Now."

The ship heeled suddenly and hard to port, and everyone staggered to regain their balance. There were shouts and curses from the hangar deck as the deck crew hung on to the helo's tie-downs. With a great sense of foreboding Sara looked around to see that the next storm had indeed come upon them. Blowing snow needled into her exposed skin. The seas were rising, and the wind howled around the ship like a hungry wolf.

"Follow me," she said to Hugh, and then had to yell it again so he could hear her over the sound and fury of the storm.

"ALL RIGHT," LOWE SAID.

They were in the wardroom. Lowe sat at the head of the table facing Hugh, who stood opposite him at the table's foot in front of a dry board which was covered with an outline of names, dates, and places. On the captain's left were Sara, Ops, and the Engineer Officer, a tall, pencil-thin young man who could barely find his way to the bridge but who could disassemble a Caterpillar generator and put it back together again blindfolded. On the captain's right were Ensign Ostlund, Ensign Ryan, and Chief Mark Edelen.

"You want us to believe that a North Korean terrorist—no, two—have built themselves a backpack bomb filled with radioactive material, loaded it into a mobile missile launcher, which they have then smuggled on board an oceangoing vessel, and are currently attempting to sail it into these waters, for the purposes of aiming the weapon at a target in Alaska, which you have been told by a less than reliable source to be one of the military bases, Elmendorf or Eielson. Why not Valdez, by the way? The oil terminal ought to go up with a bang big enough to keep any terrorist happy."

Hugh met the captain's sarcasm with the same stoicism he had displayed for the last hour. He held a black marker, the cap of which he repeatedly clicked on and clicked off. Click, click. "First of all, sir—" Hugh was respectful but firm. "A backpack bomb is generally held to be nuclear, and, uh, well, in a backpack. I don't think that is the case here."

"Really? What is it, then?"

The ship rolled over a swell and Hugh took a quick step to keep his balance. "It's a dirty bomb. Instead of a weapon of mass destruction, it's called a weapon of mass disruption."

Sara, watching the captain out of the corner of her eye, saw him take a deep breath, and wondered what room on board she could convert to a brig when the captain finally lost his temper and ordered her to throw Hugh into it. "What's the difference between the two?"

"What's most important to a terrorist is that the weapon of mass disruption is a lot cheaper to make."

"More bang for your buck, eh?" the captain said.

Hugh didn't make the mistake of smiling at this almost genial query. "Partly, sir. There is also the fact that fissile, that is, weapons-grade uranium and plutonium are much more closely controlled and monitored than radioactive matériel."

"Like cesium."

"Like cesium-137, yes, sir. Cesium-137 is an isotope used in medical procedures like radiotherapy. It's relatively easy to get, and much cheaper to buy in bulk than weapons-grade uranium."

"Or plutonium."

"Yes, sir."

The ship rolled. Hugh hung on to the edge of the dry-board, waiting for the ship to regain the vertical.

"What's it look like?"

"Talcum powder."

"Handy," the captain said. "You could hide it in an Old Spice bottle."

"Yes, sir."

"But you don't think they're hiding it. You think they're about to use it."

"Yes, sir." Click, click.

"Based on nothing but a lot of circumstantial evidence."

"A lot of what I do is connect the dots, sir."

The captain didn't rush to contradict him, but Sara knew he would be marginally impressed by this frank admission.

"But if you connect these dots"—Hugh pointed at the dry board—"you'll see that in this case there is enough circumstantial evidence to warrant concern. The intelligence accumulated about North Koreans trained by al-Qaida in Afghanistan. Recovery of blueprints for such a bomb from the al-Qaida caves. The report of the sale of enough cesium-137 to build such a bomb. Much more than necessary, actually, my informant said that—"

"How much is enough?"

"Less than two ounces, sir."

Sara, watching the captain because she didn't want to look at Hugh, saw him trying to hide his shock. "How is it detonated?"

"A couple of pounds of dynamite will get the job done."

The officers exchanged glances. "You are talking about a piece of ordnance that could fit into a shoebox."

Hugh thought about it. "Not much bigger than that, sir, no. Easily loaded into the warhead of a missile."

"A missile that can be launched by a mobile missile launcher."

"Yes, sir."

"Like from a ship."

"Like from a ship, sir, yes," Hugh said.

Ryan cleared his throat. "If I may, Captain?" The captain nodded. "Mr. Rincon, you're going to need a pretty heavy ship to carry a missile launcher, and an even heavier one to launch it without sinking the ship that is carrying it. The force of the thrust generated by the fuel upon liftoff would crack the spine of your average freighter."

"I don't think they care if they sink their ship, Mr. Ryan. I think they only care about delivering the weapon and wreaking as much death and destruction as they possibly can. These aren't soldiers we're talking about here; these are terrorists."

"Do they have a missile launcher, Mr. Rincon?"

"They bought one, Captain. At the same time and through the same dealer as the cesium-137."

The phone rang. Sara answered it. "Wardroom."

"XO, I—"

"Is the ship sinking?"

"Uh, no, but—"

"Then not now, Tommy." Sara hung up.

"As I said before, sir," Hugh said respectfully, displaying a heretofore unknown—at least to Sara—talent for soothing the savage breast of command, "terrorists don't think in terms of big bangs. They think in terms of numbers of people killed, and of television footage broadcast worldwide of those people in body bags laid out in rows. The more rows the better. A weapon of the sort I have just described will destroy Elmendorf, and a city the size of Anchorage along with it." Click, click.

"Okay, that's another thing, excuse me, Captain," Ryan said. "What's the range of a mobile missile launcher? Because Elmendorf is twelve hundred miles from the Maritime Boundary Line."

"The range of your standard Scud is three hundred kilometers," Hugh said.

Ops got that faraway look in his eyes he always got when he was carrying the one. "That's less than two hundred miles."

Ryan looked at the captain, and the tension around the table relaxed.

"I think that's the whole point of loading the weapon onto a commercial vessel," Hugh said. He was speaking slowly and deliberately, displaying no impatience. "There's hundreds, thousands of them in and out of port cities every day. We can't look at them all or we'd bring global commerce to a halt." Click, click.

"What kind of a commercial vessel?" the captain said.

"Initially I thought a freighter. A Scud would fit very neatly into a forty-foot container. All they'd have to do is make sure it was loaded on top."

"Could it be controlled by remote?"

Ryan stirred. "Logistically, sir, given the distances involved, they'd have to launch it themselves."

The captain looked back at Hugh. "You said initially you thought a freighter. Has something changed your mind?"

"A source in Hong Kong tells us I was right about the container but wrong about the ship. It's a fishing vessel, a catcher-processor, one big enough to load empty containers on board, which they then fill with product. Only two won't be empty."

"One for the weapon, one for the terrorists."

"Yes, sir." Click, click.

The captain's head turned toward Ops. "Ops?"

"Still no joy on the sat phone, sir," Ops said. "And our e-mail is still down."

There was no point in killing the messenger, but Sara could tell that Lowe was greatly tempted. So could Ops, who was regarding the table with a rapt look, as if by not making eye contact the captain might forget that he was present.

"There's always the VHF," Ryan said.

"With the entire Bering Sea listening in," Sara said. "Including, always supposing they exist, these terrorists."

Hugh's gaze was level and flat, his tone impersonal, without inflection. She could have been a total stranger. "They exist." Click, click.

The silence hung heavy over the room. The captain pushed back from the table and rose to his feet. "XO, with me."

Sara followed the captain from the wardroom into the pantry. The captain shut the door behind them—the door into the companionway had long since been secured, with BMOD Meridian braced against it and staring stolidly ahead, pretending to be deaf—and turned to face her. "How reliable is this guy?" he said bluntly.

"Very reliable," Sara said, and added irresistibly, "in everything except marriage." And then wished very much that she had not.

Lowe's eyes narrowed.

"He's not a nut case, Captain," she said, unconsciously straightening to attention. "We've been married for ten years. I've known him all my life. He's intelligent, very well educated, and not prone to flights of fancy. The CIA recruited him before we graduated, and however little I may like the CIA they don't recruit dummies. Most of the time he's a by-the-book kind of guy. He wouldn't have gone to such extraordinary lengths to get here if he didn't think the threat was real."

"He sure as hell convinced Sams and Laird in St. Paul. Of course, they're aviators and they'll believe anything that'll get them into the air."

"Yes, sir."

Lowe jerked his head toward the door. "You didn't sound even a little bit convinced by his argument in there, XO."

"Devil's advocate, sir," she said sturdily. "Part of my job."

Lowe looked at her for a long, long minute. He reached past her to open the door into the wardroom. They filed in and took their seats.

"All right," the captain said. "What are we looking for?"

There was a collective exhale of breath. "A fish processor slash stern trawler," Hugh said. "Three hundred forty feet long. She's leased to a Russian fishing consortium by a series of limited liability corporations. Niue flagged." He looked up to find everyone looking back at him with an enraptured gaze. "What?" he said.

Mark Edelen had to clear his throat to get the words out. "What's her name, Mr. Rincon?"

"Oh." Hugh looked down at the notes he'd spread on the table in front of him. "The *Agafia*."

TOMMY WAS A LITTLE startled when the whole horde thundered up the ladder and erupted onto the bridge. "XO?" she said.

"Where's the *Agafia,* Tommy?"

Tommy, mute, pointed at a steady green blip on the radar screen. "She's heading southwest."

Sara looked up to peer through what was now a stygian gloom. She saw no lights on the horizon. She saw no horizon. They had felt the ship begin to roll more heavily in the wardroom, and she was beginning to pitch and yaw as well. The storm was well and truly upon them, but by now it wouldn't have felt natural if it hadn't been.

"And—" Tommy said.

"Wait a minute," Sara said. "Who the hell is this?" She indicated a second blip not far from the first, both of them lying less than a half mile off.

"It's the *Sunrise Warrior,* ma'am," Tommy said reproachfully. "I tried to tell you on the phone. She hove up over the horizon just as you all went below."

Captain Lowe jumped up into his chair. "Get them on the horn."

"Belay that," Sara said. She stepped to the captain's side and lowered her voice. "Forgive me, Captain, but are you thinking of ordering them from the area?"

"That was my plan, yes," the captain said. "The last thing we need right now is a bunch of idealistic civilians getting in our way. I want them long gone before whatever goes down out here goes down. You have a problem with that, XO?"

Sara refused to be intimidated by the implied menace. "Firstly, sir, I don't think they'll take to being ordered. They don't, as a rule, if you recall."

They both remembered last August and the whole whaling debacle. "No," he said, "they don't, do they. Secondly?"

"Secondly—" Sara hesitated.

"Spit it out, XO."

"Well, sir, I was thinking that we might be able to use them."

"Use them how?"

"It's a big ocean, captain. If Hugh—if Mr. Rincon is right and there are terrorists on board the *Agafia,* and if they do have a weapon they are preparing to launch, we might be able to use another ship. The *Sojourner Truth* and the *Sunrise Warrior* are both faster than the *Agafia.*"

Lowe snorted. "That's a stretch. What's her top speed, five, six knots? A baby stroller is faster than she is."

"Yes, sir. For another thing, I'll bet both of us are more seaworthy than she is, too. You remember what the *Pheodora* was like when we boarded her."

"If the *Agafia*'s in that bad shape we can run her down on our own."

"Still, sir, it wouldn't hurt to have another ship standing by. Just in case. And . . ." Sara paused. She hadn't wanted to draw this card, but there wasn't a whole lot of choice left to her. Besides, in this she knew she was right. "I know the international campaigner she's got on board."

"The international campaigner?"

"The ship is here on what they call a campaign. It was someone's idea, and that someone, once they sell the idea to Greenpeace headquarters in Amsterdam, usually heads up the campaign when it goes into action. I know the point person on board."

"How?"

Sara looked at the overhead. "I arrested her once."

The captain stared at her, disbelieving what she had just said. "You what?"

"I worked one year at Prudhoe Bay, sir, when the freight barges were coming in. Greenpeace was getting in the way with inflatables. Vivienne Kincaid was ramrodding that campaign with a crew of six. I was with the detachment that arrested them."

"And because of this history you think she's going to help us?"

"She's not an unreasonable person, sir, and she's an American. I think when it comes down to it she'll chose country over cause."

The captain's voice was cold and hard. "I don't like the prospect of trusting the fate of the crew—not to mention an entire city—to a fanatic, XO."

"No, sir. But they're what we've got." She could have said more, but she knew when to shut up, and did so.

He brooded for a moment, and then raised his voice. "What's it doing out there in the way of weather?"

"Barometer still dropping, sir," Tommy said. "Temperature in the low twenties. Rain, snow, freezing spray. Winds out of the southeast at forty-five knots. Seas eighteen to twenty feet. Forecast is for fifty-five knots before midnight."

The captain looked at Sara. "We'll never be able to launch a small boat in this."

"No, sir."

"Are we still on an intercept course for the *Agafia*?" he asked Tommy.

"Of course, sir," Tommy said, a little hurt.

"How long?"

"We're closing to half a mile now, sir. I don't think she's making much headway in the storm."

"Probably ran into it on purpose, trying to hide," he said.

The deck rolled and Sara took a quick step to regain her balance. Hugh lost his balance and crashed into the bulkhead. PO Barnette, on the conn, stood rooted to the deck, hands clasped in the small of his back, staring straight ahead.

The captain made up his mind. "Let's make the storm work for us for a change. Bosun, pipe the aviators to my cabin. XO, Mr. Rincon, with me. Chief, you have the conn."

"Aye aye, sir."

"WITH ALL DUE RESPECT, sir," Lieutenant Sams said, and halted, at a loss for words. He didn't say, "You gotta be kidding me," but the words were on his face for anyone to read.

Captain Lowe was not unsympathetic. "I know it's a lot to ask. Can you do it?"

Sams's eyes were red-rimmed. He ran his fingers up into his thinning hairline and scrubbed vigorously at his scalp. "There's a question of fatigue here, Captain. We were in the air for—" He stopped, obviously trying to add up the hours.

"A long time," Laird said.

Sams nodded. "A long time."

"The question is, can you do it," Lowe said.

"The question is, can I even get off the ship," Sams said. "I'm sorry, sir. I beg your pardon for raising my voice. It's been a long day." He glared at Hugh, who looked back without apology.

There was a knock at the door. "Come," Lowe said.

It was Ops. "Still no response from the *Agafia,* Captain. Either their radio's down or they're ignoring us. And e-mail is still down."

"Just as well," the captain said with a hard look at Hugh. "District isn't going to believe this anyway."

"Look, Captain," Sams said, "we're coming up hard on her stern, right? We're going to be close enough that we don't have to put the bird in the air. We can just put a boat in the water."

"I don't believe this," Sara said. "An aviator thinking up reasons not to fly. A thing unheard of in memory of man."

They all smiled, except for Hugh. It lightened the tension, just a little, maybe just enough.

"Ah hell," Sams said, shaking his head, "this'll be one for round the bar."

"Yeah," said Laird, "and I never said I wanted to live forever anyway. Let's take a look at the pitch and roll."

They went back up to the bridge. They were close enough now to be able to see the *Agafia*'s lights, diffused through the blowing snow and fog into an enormous halo off their port bow. There was a smaller glow illuminating the fog and snow to starboard, indicating the position of the *Sunrise Warrior.* The lights were bobbing up and down with the motion of the sea, no more so than the cutter. Sara took two quick steps to grab hold of a pipe to steady her footing.

Ops got on the VHF again. "Fishing vessel *Agafia,* fishing vessel *Agafia,* this is the United States Coast Guard cutter *Sojourner Truth,* please respond, I say again, please respond."

The result was a weighty silence. Ops repeated the hail. Same response. Ops looked at Lowe and raised one shoulder. Lowe climbed up into his chair. "XO."

Sara presented herself. "Sir."

He nodded at Hugh, standing silently to one side. When Lowe spoke, he was at his most formal, which could be extremely intimidating and which immediately straightened the spines of everyone within hearing. "Regardless of the reliability of the intel provided by Mr. Rincon of the CIA"—his voice was even and pleasant but no one on the bridge was left in any doubt as to the captain's opinion of Hugh's employer—"the *Agafia* has already crossed the Maritime Boundary Line, trespassing multiple times on the territorial waters of the United States. We have in hand a letter of no objection from District. We can board and seize her at our discretion."

"Agreed, sir."

"However. We are looking down the maw of a nine-sixty-millibar low, heavy seas, and freezing spray. These are not ideal conditions for a boarding." A wintry smile broke through. "I'm not even going to ask for a GAR assessment on launching the helo."

This actually raised a chuckle around the bridge, which did nothing to lessen the level of tense expectation. "We're good to go, Captain," Sams said, and next to him, Laird echoed his assent.

"No, you're not," the captain said, "but if Mr. Rincon's information is correct, we don't have a lot of choice here. Therefore, I—"

"Captain?" Tommy said, her puzzled expression reflected in the green back lighting of the radar screen.

"Tommy—"

"Captain, the *Agafia*. She's come about."

"What?" Lowe pulled upright. "Come about? You mean she's coming at us? Why would she—"

They all looked up to see lights bearing down on them out of the fog. The next thing Sara knew she had been hit by a couple of hundred pounds of hurtling male that knocked her across the deck from next to the captain's chair to up against the starboard hatch, which fortunately was closed or they would both have tumbled out onto the starboard wing of the bridge.

She lay there, stunned into immobility, staring up at Hugh. She opened her mouth to ask him what the hell he thought he was doing and at that moment four of the forward bridge windows blew in with a sound like a thunderbolt, only ten times as loud. There were loud thumps and crashes as high-velocity metal projectiles stitched a line across the bridge five feet high.

Glass broke, metal housing splintered, flesh was shredded, and the bridge was filled with screams, curses, the angry howl of the wind and the bitter force of the blowing snow.

18

january 12
maritime boundary line
on board the uscg cutter *sojourner truth*

SARA HAULED HERSELF TO her feet with numb hands reaching for anything left intact. "Captain," she said, groping her way forward, trying to find some footing in the debris on the deck, fighting the roll of the ship's hull. The sleet driving through the shattered windows seemed to penetrate every pore.

She heard a moan. Someone swore. This time she yelled. "Captain!"

Her outstretched hand touched an arm. It was dangling down the side of the captain's chair. The ship jerked, off course because the helmsman was no longer at his post, and the motion caused the body attached to the arm to fall to the floor. She had to jump out of the way to avoid being knocked over.

She got her eyes open against the wind enough to see that Captain Lowe was dead, his torso severed almost in two by a large gaping wound, a bloody mass of torn tissue and splintered bones. The motion of the ship caused his body to roll onto his back. His eyes stared in surprise at the ceiling.

Sara looked around and slowly the rest of the bridge came into focus. Tommy was clutching a shoulder, a dark liquid seeping from between her fingers, her other hand clutching the radar console to pull herself erect. The helmsman, Razo, had been thrown from his chair and lay facedown on the floor, unmoving. His head looked misshapen. Ops was bleeding from his right temple and Sara could hear him swearing. "Ops?"

"I got hit by some glass, XO, I'm okay!"

Everyone was yelling to be heard over the wind roaring in the broken windows. It didn't help when general quarters sounded and alarms whooped up and down the length of the ship. "Chief? Chief!"

A hand came up to grasp the controls console and Mark Edelen pulled himself to his feet. His face was bruised and his right eye was swelling shut, but the rest of him was mercifully intact. "Find out if our controls still work and put our ass to the storm!"

"Aye aye, XO!" He stumbled over bodies and binoculars and broken glass to the helm. A few minutes later the gale roaring through the bridge had eased.

"Sara!" Hugh said, voice fighting the sound of the wind. "You're bleeding!"

She looked down and saw with some surprise that he was right. No wonder her left arm felt so numb. She touched her reddened sleeve and found a three-inch splinter of metal run completely through the flesh. It didn't hurt yet, but it would.

She raised her head and saw them all gaping at her.

"XO," the chief said, taking a step forward and being thrown back by the movement of the ship.

"Are you okay, XO?" Tommy said.

"I'm fine." She looked around and raised her voice. "How is everyone else?"

There were more wounds from flying glass and debris. Due to the chest-high sills of the windows, most of those wounds were to the upper torso, shoulders, arms, and heads. The captain and the helmsman had both been seated, the helmsman behind the captain and to his left. They were the only fatalities on the bridge.

"Tommy?"

Tommy had to shout to be heard. "XO!"

"Does the pipe still work?"

"I don't know, XO!"

"Try it! Pipe damage control to the bridge at once! And Doc!"

Tommy was shaken but still capable of thought and action. "Doc and damage control, aye aye, XO!"

"Sams! Laird!" Sara lurched across the bridge, staggering from one handhold to the next, slipping and sliding in blood and glass. "Sams!"

"We're here, XO!" Both had facial wounds from glass cuts but were otherwise unhurt.

The pipe worked. Tommy must have cranked the volume knob all the way over to the right because her voice blasted out all over the ship, loud and high but amazingly calm. "Damage control, Doc Jewell, report to the bridge immediately, damage control and Doc Jewell, to the bridge at once."

Sara continued to move around the bridge, trying to assess the damage. The Transas hanging from the bulkhead in front of the window before the captain's chair was gone, nothing left but shreds of circuit board and wire, but the one over the plot table was still there, to all appearances intact and still working. The radar console was still blinking out contacts, too, but then it was located almost directly behind the captain's chair, which had taken the brunt of the attack.

People began to tumble onto the bridge. The captain's and the helmsman's bodies were removed. Doc Jewell bandaged everyone who didn't move out of his way first. He winced when he came to Sara's splinter, and it hurt like hell when he extracted it, but she refused anything stronger than aspirin. He looked as if he wanted to insist.

Sara cut him off curtly. "Not now, Doc." She flexed her arm beneath the bandage. Everything still worked, even if it felt like she'd been seared with a red-hot branding iron. "Anyone hurt anywhere except on the bridge?"

"No, ma'am."

"Very well." She pulled her fleece back on. Damage control had unearthed some Plexiglas from somewhere and cut rough squares to fit over the gaping holes where the windows had once been, riveting them in place with power drills. The ravenous howl of the wind was reduced to a distant snarl of disappointment at being balked of its prey. Hugh had found a broom and was sweeping debris into someone's cap and chucking it out the port hatch, which was still latched open. Tommy was standing at the chart table, staring at the captain's chair with a set face. She looked at Sara. "If he hadn't been sitting there—"

"Belay that, Tommy," Sara said. "PO Barnette, you have the helm."

Tommy's face stiffened. "PO Barnette has the helm, aye aye, XO," she said, and there was a chorus of ayes.

"Aye aye, XO." Barnette took Razo's place at the small brace wheel.

"Tommy, you have the conn."

"BM2 Penn has the conn," Barnette said. He had a deep voice and it seemed to boom off the Plexiglas.

Tommy looked at him, swallowed, and pulled her way around the console to stand in an imitation of Barnette's brace. "I have the conn, XO."

"Doc, canvass the ship for any casualties. I want a report ASAP. Chief?" This to Chief Lindsey Moran, the head of damage control on board, who stood waiting, power driver at the ready. "Report."

"They only hit the bridge, XO. There has been no other damage reported."

"Make sure of that yourself, Chief, and then report back to me."

"Aye aye, XO."

"Mr. Rincon, follow me. Chief Edelen, pipe all the officers to the wardroom, and then join us."

THEY STOOD INSTEAD OF sitting, mostly because Sara refused to take the captain's chair and no one else would sit down while she was still standing. "Talk to me, Lieutenant."

"I was watching the roll indicator before we got hit," Sams said. "It's showing at least seven degrees, and sometimes more."

"Which means?"

"We can do it, if we pick our moment." Sams looked at Laird. "Maybe you should stay behind."

"What!"

Sams looked at Sara. "Maybe you'll need a spare pilot, if we don't make it."

"It's a moot point, since we only have one helo," Sara said. She looked at Ryan. "Put together a team. I want them armed. Anything you can find on this ship that will shoot, stab, or explode on contact, you make sure every member of your team has two of each."

"Aye aye, XO."

She looked at Sams. "How many can you take?"

"Well, maybe a few less than before you loaded them down with an armory," Sams said.

Several of them smiled, but Sara was too focused on the

task at hand and too close to what had happened on the bridge for anything remotely resembling humor. "How many?"

Sams's shoulders straightened at the snap in her voice. "Six boarding team members total, XO."

Sara looked at Ryan. "Can you get the job done with six?"

He started to go with bravado, saw her expression, and ratcheted it down. "Depends on how many people they've got on board and how well armed they are."

She looked at Hugh.

"I don't know," he said. "I know about the two brothers. Noortman told me that the brothers told Fang he couldn't bring all of his usual crew, that they were hiring some help of their own. Could be ten. Could be twenty, could be fifty. I just don't know."

She nodded and looked at Ryan. "Who is your best man on the cannon?"

"Sullivan," he said without hesitation.

"Have him report to me immediately. And then start putting your team together. Remember, the goal is to commandeer the ship, disable the launcher, and get her into the nearest port."

"Aye aye, XO." Ryan vanished.

"But if we have to, we sink the son of a bitch, and I'm not saying that's a bad second-best." She looked at Ostlund. "Ensign, start prepping for helo launch. I imagine you'll have to do another traverse."

Ostlund shrugged. "Not like we haven't had a lot of practice lately, XO. I think we've got it down."

"Good. Go." She looked at Sams. "Anything?"

He thought, and shook his head.

"We won't be able to bring you back on board the *Sojourner Truth,* not in this soup," she said.

"I know, XO."

"So once the boarding team is on board, you haul ass for Cape Navarin."

He gave a curt nod.

"Good. Go."

The aviators left.

"Chief," Sara said to Edelen, "I want you on the conn."

"All due respect, XO, I want you on the conn."

She gave a half laugh. "Go on up to the bridge. I'm right behind you."

"Where's Cape Navarin?" Hugh said.

"About a hundred miles northwest of where we are now. It's the nearest land."

He thought about it. "In Russia."

"Yes."

"That going to be a problem?"

"The fact that they'll be out of fuel before they get there is a bigger one."

BACK ON THE BRIDGE she looked at the radar screen. The *Agafia* was still there, still not making enough speed to pull out of range, but enough to keep her tantalizingly out of reach. It was almost as if she were playing tag with them, which made no sense to Sara. Perhaps all terrorists were by definition mad.

The *Sunrise Warrior* was lagging about midway between the other two ships. Sara looked up and out the new Plexiglas windows. She thought she could make out lights off their port bow. She noticed something else, too. "Are we making ice?" she said.

"We are, XO."

Sara swore, a round and mighty oath. "Assemble a crew to chip ice, Chief," she said, snapping out the words.

"Aye aye, XO," Chief Edelen said, moving with alacrity.

Sara told Tommy, "I need to be able to talk to the *Sunrise Warrior.*"

"The VHF is down, XO, like almost everything else. Whatever they hit us with took out all our communications, except for handhelds."

"I know. How's your Morse, Tommy?"

"My Morse?" The bosun's mate looked dubious. "It's okay, XO. It's not great, but I can make myself understood."

"Good." To the chief, finishing up his pipe for the ice-chipping team, Sara said, "Get me in close enough for them to see our signal."

He hung up the mike. "Aye aye, XO."

on board the *sunrise warrior*

"IS THAT MORSE CODE?" Vivienne said.

"It is, Vivienne, now hush up so I can read it."

They all waited with varying degrees of impatience. No one had been very happy with pursuing the processor into the storm. For one thing, it made for horrible photography, and Greenpeace was all about film at eleven.

Doyle lowered the binoculars.

"Well?" Vivienne said. "What'd they say?"

"They said those explosions we heard was the *Agafia* firing on them," Doyle said.

There were exclamations of disbelief all around.

"Come on, Doyle," Vivienne said. "A fishing vessel fired on a Coast Guard cutter?"

"That's what they're saying," Doyle said. "And that's not all they're saying, Vivienne. They want a favor."

Vivienne stared at him. "The U.S. Coast Guard wants a favor from Greenpeace?"

"Not exactly," Doyle said. "They want a favor from you."

◆ ◆ ◆

THE FLIGHT CREW HAD finished their second heavy-weather traverse in three days on the hangar deck, although this one had been a lot dicier due to the steadily increasing layer of ice that was forming on every surface above water. A crew had already been detailed to the bow with clubs, where the ice was accumulating faster than they could beat it off.

Sams called the bridge. "We're good to go, XO."

Sara was standing next to Seaman Royce Lee Cornell, North Carolina–born, a year out of boot camp and barely qualified on the helm. She could hardly see his black face in the dim light of the bridge. "Hold her steady, Seaman."

"Holding her steady, aye, XO." Just turned twenty, Seaman Cornell had the maturity of a petty officer with twenty years in. Mark Edelen had recommended he replace Razo, and it spoke well for Cornell that he was on the bridge before he'd been called to duty.

Sara looked at the indicators hanging from the overhead. Bubbles of air in twin curving plastic tubes full of water, the bubbles rolled back and forth and pitched backward and forward with the motion of the ship, indicating degrees of pitch and roll with a gauge printed beneath. As Sara watched, the roll went to seven, and the pitch went to nine. She swore under her breath. "Let her fall off the wind a little, Seaman."

"Aye aye, XO," Cornell said. His hands moved on the small brass wheel. A minute passed, two, and then the *Sojourner Truth* hit a patch of what felt like relative calm.

"Launch," Sara said.

On the monitor they saw the rotors increase to a blur and the body of the helo begin to lift. Sara made it to the port wing of the bridge in time to see them appear, and then Sams really goosed it. The helo shot past the bridge in a bright orange blur fifty feet off the deck.

Sara stared after them, until recalled to where she was by the wind and the cold and the snow and the fog and the ice and, oh, the hell with it. She went back inside.

"Will she do it, Sara?" Hugh said.

"Who? Oh. The *Sunrise Warrior*? Yes."

He was silent. "What?" she said.

"I guess what I meant was, will the rest of them let, what's her name, Kincaid, do it?"

"Yes," Sara said firmly, "they will." She couldn't stand still. She paced back and forth in front of the controls console and around it several times, not an easy thing to do on a packed bridge in twenty-foot seas, until Chief Edelen said, in a very respectful voice, "Why don't you have a seat, XO?"

She stared at him. He gestured at the captain's chair. The back was ripped up but someone had cleaned off the blood and guts and bone.

"No," she said, a little more strongly than she ought to have. Hugh, standing next to Tommy over the radar screen, looked up. She recovered, and managed a smile. "Thank you, Chief. But no."

After that, she stood in front of one of the intact forward windows, staring through the fug on the other side of it, praying for the sun to rise.

uscg helo 6527

HARRY SAMS HAD SEVENTEEN years on helos, first with the U.S. Navy and then with the U.S. Coast Guard. He was fond of quoting that old aviation aphorism, "There are old pilots and there are bold pilots, but there are no old, bold pilots." He didn't hold with that other old aviation aphorism, "Any landing you walk away from is a good landing," either. He not only wanted to bring home his people alive and well, he wanted his craft intact and ready to fly again.

Which was why he was wondering, with the very little portion of his brain allowed to do anything so entirely frivolous, why it was that he was speeding twenty-five feet above twenty-foot swells at a hundred fifty-seven knots with a cargo hold full of Coasties armed to the teeth toward a blip on a radar screen that had already proved itself to be rather better armed than the average Bering Sea catcher-processor.

And then the *Agafia*'s lights loomed up out of the driving snow and fog, and there was no time to think of anything but the job at hand.

The processor was pitching and rolling and yawing worse than the *Sojourner Truth,* which meant it would be noisy on board with the creak and groan of the ship, the slipping and sliding and rolling of everything not lashed down, and the whip and slap of the ocean.

"Target in sight," he said into the mike, and heard Ryan reply, "Target in sight, àye." Next to him Laird moved like an automaton, hands in constant motion, senses reaching out to listen to the bird, to what she was saying, how she was handling a tailwind of forty-five knots and gusts of over fifty.

"I'm not making any test runs," Sams said. "We don't have enough fuel for that. One shot is all we get. Everybody ready?"

"Ready, Lieutenant," Ryan said.

"Ready, Lieutenant," Airman Cho said.

"Okay," Sams said. "It's all going to happen very, very fast, so be ready." He took another look as the *Agafia*'s stern came into view, and added, "And she's making ice as fast as the *Sojourner Truth,* so watch your asses, Ryan."

"Watching our asses, aye aye, sir."

Sams banked rapidly to slide up her hull, slowing speed as they approached the bow. The only even reasonably empty space was a triangular section forward of the mast and boom, framed by the two massive anchors and the bow itself. He estimated a bare twenty square feet, if that. The good news was that the six containers stacked on the fore-deck hid the helo from the windows on the *Agafia*'s bridge.

"Lieutenant?" Laird was looking at him.

Sams shook himself back into the present. "Are we good to go?"

Cho had the line hooked to the hoist. The helo came around the bow and Sams popped up on a rapid flare, vir-tually halting the helo in midair, letting it hang there like it was painted on the fog. Cho dropped the line and out of the corner of his eye Sams saw it hit the deck. A second later a man in a Mustang suit was sliding down it. He grabbed the end, belayed it around a stanchion, and five more men, bristling with weapons, hurtled down in rapid succession. Cho disconnected the line at the hoist and let it fall and Sams let the helo fall forward.

He stood off far enough to grab some fog for cover but not too far to be out of range of the boarding team's ra-dios. He made a wide circuit of the ship and was re-warded when Ryan's voice came over the air. "All down safely, Lieutenant. See you back in Kodiak. You did say the beer was on you, right?"

"In your dreams, Ryan. Good hunting. And watch your back!"

Laird brought up Cape Navarin on the GPS and set a course, and as he did so the *Sojourner Truth* loomed up out of the mist looking like the wrath of God. She was even throwing a few thunderbolts by way of the portside 25-millimeter cannon.

The shells crossed the *Agafia*'s bow with inches to spare and were immediately followed by a voice on a loudspeaker turned up high enough to be heard on the moon, never mind over the storm. "Fishing vessel *Agafia,* this is the United States Coast Guard cutter *Sojourner Truth.* Heave to and prepare to be boarded. I say again, heave to and prepare to be boarded."

And the guns on both sides opened up and Sams pointed the helo's nose at three-five-zero and hit the gas.

on board the *agafia*

THE MEN ON BOARD the *Agafia* were demoralized and panicking, especially the mercenaries. They had shot at the American ship and then proceeded to lead it farther south, as Jones had instructed. The storm was hitting them hard, tossing the ship around like a Ping-Pong ball in a bathtub full of Jell-O. It never stopped, everyone was getting slammed into bulkheads, hatch handles, and other crewmen.

Fang's men were more disciplined and had the advantage of time served at sea, but they, too, were growing increasingly alarmed. Someone had come at them out of the snow and the sleet and the hail and had begun shooting. Windows had shattered; men had been hit and were screaming in fear and pain. At first Chen thought the ship's crew must have broken loose and were trying to retake the ship, and then he remembered that Jones had put them all over the side.

And then a blue-hulled ship with a rainbow on the bow materialized on their starboard side on what looked like a course to ram them amidships. Even Jones yelled at that. Chen spun the wheel into a blur, only to find that way blocked by the *Sojourner Truth.* All three ships were pitching and tossing violently, adding to the feeling of an uncontrollable and imminent doom.

During those precious minutes when the bridge crew of

the *Agafia* was preoccupied with finding some sea room in twenty-foot seas, Ryan's men were working their way aft, picking off the enemy one at a time. Later, his report would state that most of these fell overboard into the Bering Sea. Hank Ryan had helped carry Captain Lowe's body below. He still had the captain's blood on his uniform and he was not inclined to show mercy, especially when he didn't know what his team was facing in the way of opposition on board the *Agafia*. He knew that they had at least one big gun, and that was all he needed to know.

The first man they took out was the mercenary who had run aft to man the Browning machine gun newly bolted to the *Agafia*'s deck. Ryan disarmed the weapon by pulling the bolt securing it to its stand and letting it follow its gunner over the side.

They were on the bridge fifteen minutes later without a scratch on any of them. One Asian guy was screaming something at them in his native tongue, which no one understood or even tried to very hard. From the way the other four surviving crew looked at him, he was the boss.

Ryan almost shot him down where he stood before he remembered that command might actually want to talk to the boss, so he said, "Secure them all below somewhere and mount a guard. If they so much as sneeze, shoot 'em. The rest of you, let's start looking for Mr. Rincon's missile launcher."

An hour later, they had inspected the *Agafia* bow to stern, containers hold, engine room, galley, and staterooms, and they still hadn't found it.

uscg helo 6527

ICE WAS BUILDING UP on the rescue hoist. No one in the aircraft said anything about it because what was the point, but the silence was getting a little strained.

Laird pointed at the radar screen. Sams nodded without leaning over to look. The radar was degrading because ice was building on the nose of the aircraft, too.

They'd left the *Agafia* with forty-five minutes of fuel remaining in their tanks. They'd been in the air forty-seven minutes. Sams avoided looking at the fuel gauge, concentrating instead on the horizon, a dark gray, featureless expanse. He'd put some altitude between the helo and the deck so he'd have some choices when the time came.

When it did, it came fast, and it looked like a tall iceberg, so he didn't see it at first. Laird shouted and pointed, and there it was, a steep cliff footed with a narrow strip of beach. He eyeballed it. It ought to be wide enough for the fifty-one foot rotor.

It had to be.

One engine died, and they made the beach.

The other died, and they started to fall.

After that, they started to spin.

19

SARA WAS ICILY CALM. "I believed you, I backed your story with the captain. Now he's dead and there is no missile launcher on the ship we just boarded at gunpoint."

Hugh was standing on the bridge, his hands dangling at his sides. "I don't understand it," he said.

"That makes you and a ship full of Coasties who don't understand it," she said.

There was a rumble of agreement which she stilled with a glare.

"Noortman gave me the port, he gave me the ship, he gave me everything." Hugh stopped suddenly, brows furrowing.

Sara waited. When he didn't say anything else, she said, "Yeah, well, your thumbnail-pulling skills must not be quite up to CIA par because it looks like he lied through his teeth."

Hugh met her eyes and the words dried up in her mouth. She'd never seen that expression on Hugh's face.

"They were running with their lights on," he said.

"Who was?"

"The *Agafia*. They were running with their lights on."

"So?" she said. "It's kind of, oh, I don't know, the law?"

"Why? If they wanted to run from you, why run with their lights on? Why make it easier to follow them?"

"I can find a boil on the ass of a wildebeest in Africa with our radar," Sara said. "I don't need running lights."

"Still, it helped you find them," Hugh said. "And what about Noortman?"

"What about your unimpeachable source?"

"They didn't kill him," Hugh said. "They may have killed Peter, but they didn't try to kill Noortman."

"And Peter is?" Sara said.

"The arms dealer in Odessa who brokered their deal with the North Korean for the cesium and the North Korean missile launcher. Why? Why try to kill him and not kill Noortman?"

Sara said, a little impatiently, "Peter was a danger to them, Noortman wasn't?"

"That's not it," Hugh said. "Or not all of it."

The *Agafia* was riding their stern, under the command of Ensign Ryan and the prize crew. The *Sunrise Warrior*, after the spectacular maneuver that had so ably distracted the attention of the *Agafia*'s hijackers long enough for Ryan's team to board and take control of the ship, was keeping pace off their starboard side. "Greenpeace is signaling us, XO," the chief said.

"Tommy?"

Tommy's lips moved as the light blinked. " 'I am now in possession of one Get Out of Jail Free card. Agreed?' " At Sara's look, Tommy said, "I'm just reading here, XO."

Sara gave a grudging nod. "Send 'Agreed.' "

" 'We're heading back up to the line to continue our work. Good luck with yours, *Sojourner Truth*.' "

"Once a crusader, always a crusader," Chief Edelen said. "That was pretty slick back there. I wonder who their master is?"

"I don't know, and I don't want to know. Let's forget we ever saw them."

"Forget who, XO?"

The *Sunrise Warrior* altered course and was almost immediately swallowed by the storm.

"Maybe they didn't mean to kill him," Hugh said. "Peter," he said when Sara looked momentarily blank. "In Odessa. Maybe we were just supposed to think that they tried. The bomb went off in the middle of the night, long after everyone had gone home."

Hugh was beginning to shiver. He was soaking wet from standing out on the bridge wing, trying to follow what was going on on the other ship. Sara made a sound of disgust. "Follow me," she said, and led him to her cabin. She muscled him into a chair. "You," she said to the first person she saw, "towels, lots of them, and find him some dry clothes."

The towels came immediately; the clothes took a little longer. Halfway out of his shirt, Hugh said, "They didn't want us to find out what weapons they had bought. But they didn't mind if we knew what the target was."

She was still angry, but she was listening. The *Agafia* had been commandeered by pirates, those pirates had fired on the *Sojourner Truth* with a machine gun that appeared to have been freshly mounted specifically for the purpose, and Sara knew there had to be more of a reason for that than that the *Sojourner Truth* had caught them with their nets in American waters. Especially since she hadn't.

Besides, where was the *Agafia*'s crew? A three-hundred-and-forty-foot catcher-processor, between ship's crew and fish handlers, could have upward of a hundred people on board. There was a cold feeling in her gut. "What did the survivors say about the processor's crew?"

Hugh, as the only Korean-speaking person on board, had tried to talk to the pirates via Ryan's handheld. "Nothing. Same thing they said about everything. They're not talking."

Sara smiled, and he shivered again. "Maybe when it calms down enough to bring them over here, you will find them a little more forthcoming face-to-face."

"Maybe."

Someone had actually found a pair of pants that would cover Hugh's long legs. He stood up to pull them on. He paused. "They had to know we'd catch on."

"Who? Who knew? And zip up your pants."

For the first time since he'd come on board he looked at her as Sara, his wife, instead of the executive officer of the *Sojourner Truth*. "Making you nervous, babe?"

Her brows snapped together. "Knock it off. This isn't the time or the place."

"You're right, it isn't." He stepped into sneakers that were only half a size too small and sat down again to tie them, returning to his line of thought as he did so. "The terrorists knew we'd catch on."

"What?" Sara was a little bewildered at the rapid change of topic.

"It is next to impossible to keep a secret in that world," Hugh said. "There is always somebody standing around with his ears wide open who is going to sell what he hears to the highest bidder. They knew that."

"So?"

"So," he said, eyes bright with realization, "they set up a dummy to distract us."

Sara caught on. "You mean they *wanted* us to catch the *Agafia*?"

"Sure," he said. "Why else choose a ship that has that high a profile with the U.S. Coast Guard? What did you call it, a High Interest Vessel? You'd already chased it back across the line on this patrol, and multiple times before."

He snapped his fingers and pointed at her. "And that's why they shot at us! They didn't mean to sink us, or even hurt us that badly."

"Of course not," Sara said acidly. "I myself never mean to kill people I shoot at."

Unheeding, he said, "What they wanted was to get and keep our attention for a nice long time. It was just their bad luck that their strafing us took out our communications. They wanted us to yell for help, Sara. They wanted everything we've got in the Bering, hell, in the North Pacific Ocean to come chasing after them."

She already knew the answer, but he waited so expectantly for her to ask the question. "Why?"

"So that the ship with the weapon on it could slip through." He finished tying his shoes and sat back in the chair. "Noortman, you little shit," he said, sounding almost admiring. "And after all we meant to each other."

He looked up and saw Sara's startled gaze, and laughed out loud. "It's a long story. Don't worry, I survived, virtue intact." He leaned forward, his elbows on his knees. "Sara, has anything odd happened out here lately?"

"Odd? You mean, other than my ship coming under fire, my captain being killed, and me sending a boarding team to commandeer said ship in a helo with an aircrew of three I may have sent to their death? No. Nothing out of the ordinary. Nothing we don't run into every day out here, and twice on Sundays."

"Before this," he said patiently. "Have you heard anything over the air, seen anything that didn't quite fit?" He lifted his shoulders and spread his hands. "Maybe ship traffic where it shouldn't be?"

Before the words were all the way out of his mouth she was on her feet and headed up the ladder outside her stateroom, Hugh dogging her heels.

"XO," Ops said. He and all five of his techs were jammed inside the comm room, looking like they wished they had hammers in their hands instead of tiny little screwdrivers and alligator clips. All the equipment had its faces off, revealing a colorful mass of wire and dials and digital readouts and computer boards. Mostly it looked like a mess. A nonfunctioning mess.

"Anything yet?" Sara said without hope.

Ops shook his head. "We caught a stray bullet back here and it must have ricocheted around somehow." He displayed a misshapen piece of metal that looked entirely too small to have caused this much damage. "We don't even know what it hit yet, that's why we're looking at everything. They took out our satellite dish. They must have nicked the antenna array, too. And I can't send anyone up there in this weather to fix it. Even if we had the parts."

"Understood," she said. "How long before someone comes looking for us?"

"In this weather?" He shook his head. "The Hercs will be patrolling, but we aren't exactly keeping to the last route we filed with District before the e-mail went out, and right after that the comm got shot out. And we're the only cutter in the Bering Sea at present. The *Alex Haley*'ll be back in Kodiak by now. They'll be looking for us, though."

She nodded. "District hasn't heard from us in a while, and they've probably got red flags up all over the place. Ops, you remember that freighter we saw up on the line? The one we all figured was lost?"

He blinked behind his glasses. "Yes," he said, although it was obvious that he was remembering the incident as if it had happened years ago instead of days ago.

Sara didn't blame him. If she'd had the luxury she would have felt like that herself. "What was its name, do you remember?"

He thought. "*Star of Wonder? Star of Night?*"

"That's star of wonder, star of light, Ops," Sparks said.

Ops snapped his fingers. "The *Star of Bali.* Sorry, XO, I must be a little out of it."

"What was it's last port of call?"

"Petropavlovsk."

Sara looked at Hugh.

"Petropavlovsk," he said, "was where Noortman's partner, Fang, and his employers planned to board the ship Noortman found for them. It was also where the *Agafia* was sent for repairs and maintenance in November."

The silence was heavy and long. At the end of it Sara said, "You think there were two ships."

He nodded. "And one was a decoy."

"The *Agafia.*"

"Yes, whose activities were designed to draw your attention away from the *Star of Bali.* Where was the *Star of Bali* headed?" he said to Ops.

"Seward."

Hugh looked at Sara. "Seward's only a hundred miles from Anchorage and that's road miles, not as the crow flies. The range on the mobile missile launcher Peter sold them is—"

"Two hundred miles, I remember," Sara said. "Which means they don't have to get to the dock to launch."

He hadn't thought of that, but she was right. The terrorists could launch as soon as they were within range, which meant while they were still well out at sea.

"We've got to find them, Sara. Now."

20

january 14
bering sea

WHEN DID WE PASS her?"

"On the eighth, XO."

"Six days. Damn, damn, damn."

"What?" Hugh said.

"She's slow but she's not that slow," Sara said.

Hugh and Sara and Ops and Tommy and the chief were hunched over the chart table, staring at the Transas screen as Sara right-clicked and dragged and dropped them all the way up the Aleutian Chain and back down again.

"You said they wouldn't want to draw attention, right, Hugh?" Sara said. "My vote is for Unimak Pass. It's like the intersection of Main Street and First Avenue for the North Pacific maritime freight fleet. All the freighters on the great circle route between Asia and North America run for the lee of the Aleutian Islands. Most of them transit Unimak Pass. If the *Star of Bali* is trying to maintain a low profile, that's the way she'd go."

Hugh looked for flaws in her argument and found none. "Then that's the way we should go."

"Yes, well, XO, there's another problem."

"Of course there is," Sara said. "Serve it up, Ops."

"We got weather coming straight at us."

Sara sighed. "Ops, I though you said we had a problem." The ship lurched but everyone was already hanging on to something. "It's just another storm."

Ops shook his head. "This one's worse, XO. The last Bering Sea offshore forecast we got before our comm got shot to hell was for sixteen hundred yesterday. Today we're looking at a thirty-knot wind, eighteen-foot seas, rain and snow and freezing spray."

"And?"

"Tonight the wind will be south to southeast, forty to forty-five knots, seas eighteen to twenty-one feet. And did I mention the rain and snow and freezing spray?"

Sara looked at him.

He spread his hands. "Sorry, Captain."

There was a strained silence on the bridge, broken only by the faint whistling of wind as it forced its way between Plexiglas and bulkhead.

"The captain's dead, Ops," Sara said.

"Cap—XO—ma'am, I—"

"And I don't accept your apology for the weather. There is absolutely no excuse for it, and I'll expect you to do better in the future."

There were a few smiles, lightening the tension. "Besides," Sara said, "there's no choice here. We've got to go after the *Star of Bali,* and we've got to go now."

"Try out the old girl's sea legs," the chief said.

Sara gave him an approving smile, which brought an answering grin, both witnessed by Hugh. There was a degree of intimacy there that raised his hackles.

"Tommy," Sara said, unheeding, "plot us a course for Unimak Pass, best speed."

"Aye aye, XO."

They stood away from the plot table to let Tommy crunch numbers on the computer.

"It's almost six hundred miles and she's got a six-day start on us, XO," Chief Edelen said. He looked at Hugh. "And this gentleman has already proved to us that he's just guessing here."

Hugh met the chief's eyes, saw how they shifted to Sara's oblivious face, looked back at the chief, identified the expression there all too easily, and couldn't find it in himself to kick a man while he was down. "That's right, I am. But I'm thinking the *Agafia* offered herself up as bait for a reason. She fired on us, don't forget."

"Not likely," the chief said with some sarcasm. "XO, why not just commandeer us the first freighter or tanker we see? They'll have all the sat comm we need."

Sara hooked a thumb at the storm. "Always supposing we find one in this slop, all we've got for ship-to-ship communications are the handhelds and the emergency radios from the life rafts. What's the range, line of sight?"

He was silent.

"Right," she said, "so we launch and row over. Probably won't lose more than half the boarding team."

"Then let's make a run for Dutch Harbor and yell for help from there."

"We could do that," Sara said. "And the *Star of Bali* could get close enough to shore to launch her weapon."

"If she has a weapon."

"If she does," Sara said.

There was a heavy silence. Hugh broke it. "I'm starving. When's chow?"

She glanced up at the digital clock on the wall, forgetting that it had been shattered in the strafing. Ops followed her gaze and looked at his watch. "Lunch should be served in the wardroom shortly, XO."

Sara felt suddenly and unutterably tired. "Can you find your own way there?" she said to Hugh.

"Sure, but what about you?"

"I'm not hungry."

He followed her out the door and down the ladder. They both heard "Captain's below" but neither chose to acknowledge it. "You should eat, Sara."

When she didn't answer, he said to her back, "They're looking to you to lead them into battle and to get them home after. Hungry has never been your best mood. Eat."

That expressive back stiffened, relaxed again, and her shoulders slumped a little. "All right."

Again she deflected hints that she should sit at the head of the table, in the captain's chair. Hugh sat next to her. Seaman Wooster began serving steak and potatoes. FSO Aman was pumping up everyone's red blood cells. Sara was pretty sure the day's menu had called for macaroni and cheese.

Hugh piled her plate high and she ate. She even thought it was pretty good, although later on she couldn't for the life of her remember what she had put into her mouth. Hugh seemed pleased, and afterward he let her go to bed, which was all she wanted. She fell into her bunk fully clothed and sank into a deep, dark, dreamless sleep.

Hugh stood in the doorway and watched the face of his dream girl, the cap she hadn't bothered to remove a little awry, mouth slightly open, maybe even drooling a little into her pillow. He stepped inside her stateroom long enough to ease her shoes from her feet and to cover her with her sleeping bag. Why the sleeping bag? he wondered, and then remembered how much she hated to make the bed.

It was a very utilitarian shoebox of a room, desk and shelves on one side, two bunks on the other, but he would have known it was Sara's room on sight. She had always had the ability to transform any living space into something uniquely her own, from her room when she was a kid in Seldovia, to the tent on the hill in back of her house the three of them had shared as a secret hideaway, to her dorm room in college, to the skanky—Kyle was right about that—apartments that had been all they could afford when they were together, and now here. Her clothes were neatly folded, there was a poster of Jimmy Buffett on one wall, and her walkaround coffee mug was a giveaway from the Kodiak public radio station.

And the top bunk was, of course, filled with books. Books to do with the sea and sailors, naturally. Hugh was pretty certain that Sara owned a copy of every sea story ever written. She kept a fair representation on board, he saw now, one of the Hornblowers, one of the Aubrey-Maturins, a history of the Coast Guard, a biography of Frank Worsley, Walter Lord's *A Night to Remember,* a book on knot tying, and a collection of sea shanties. Between *How to Build a Wooden Boat* and a one-volume collection of biographies of woman pirates he found *Blue Latitudes* by Tony Horwitz. He pulled it down and thumbed through it, to find that she had done her usual thorough job of reading, with massive amounts of underlining, highlighting, dog-earing, and marginal notations.

"XO? Oh. Excuse me, Mr. Rincon."

Hugh replaced the book and stepped into the passageway, closing Sara's door firmly behind him. "Yes?" he said to Ops.

Ops looked uncertain. "I need to speak to the XO about something."

"Listen, Ops— What is your name anyway? No one has called you anything but Ops in my hearing since I came on board."

Diverted, Ops smiled. "Yeah, Coastie custom. We call each other by our job title instead of our name. Ops. XO. Supply. EO. Like that. Probably due to the continuous rotation of crew. Easier than learning everyone's names."

"So what is your name?"

"Oh. Clifford Skulstad. Cliff."

Hugh stuck out a hand. "Pleased to meet you, Cliff. I'm Hugh Rincon."

Ops took Hugh's hand and felt himself being steered firmly away from the XO's cabin. He looked back over his shoulder at her door and said, "But I have to talk to the XO about—"

"Tell me something, Cliff," Hugh said. "Who's third in command on board the *Sojourner Truth*?"

Ops looked startled. "Uh, I am."

"I thought so. Your commanding officer needs some sleep if she's going to be worth a shit when we catch up to the *Star of Bali*. Why don't you see if you can't handle any problems that come up over the next six or eight hours?"

Ops looked horrified. "What if there is an emergency?"

"If there is an emergency," Hugh said gravely, "I think she would expect you to wake her up. However," he added, "just for today, why don't you set the gold standard for emergencies a little higher than usual?"

He smiled again when he said it, but Ops had the uncanny feeling he was speaking not to a pleasant man with an engaging manner, but a very alert Doberman with very sharp teeth. "Good idea," he said. "I'll just take care of any problems myself."

"Excellent," Hugh said. "Here's your first. Where do I sleep?"

january 14
the bering sea
on board the *star of bali*

SOME ROMANTIC WITH A severe case of myopia had named her the *Star of Bali*. Five hundred fifty feet in length, steel hull, single screw, best speed in ideal circumstances eleven knots. In less than ideal circumstances she could probably make seven or eight, and in a storm such as this Fang hoped she would have enough power to keep her stern to the storm. Built in Italy in 1973, she was old for a cargo ship and the reason she was a tramp steamer now. At her age it was all she was fit for, that or hauling molasses, traditionally the last job of the elderly cargo vessel before she was retired to the scrap yard.

Ten miles short of Unimak Pass, something went wrong with the engine. Their best speed was cut in half, with a nasty front squeezing through the narrow gap between Unimak Island and the Krenitzin Islands at fifty knots an hour, pushing them relentlessly back in the direction from which they had come.

They knew this because Smith was watching their progress on a handheld GPS. Before that, he'd been talking a lot on the satellite phone. Then calls had suddenly ceased. He gave no explanation as to why, but he looked cold with fury.

Fang was just cold.

He looked around the container in the half-light provided by the gas lanterns. Most of the men looked numb with discomfort. They'd stopped playing mah-jongg when the ship began pitching so heavily that the tiles would no longer stay on the board. Mostly they just stayed in their hammocks now, rolling out only to pee. Fang had to force them to eat.

They were well trained and disciplined and they had been ready to hold out until the time came. Now the schedule was delayed and they would have to remain in their hammocks for however long it took the ship's crew to fix the problem and get the ship back on course. Fang didn't like some of the looks he was getting, and halfway to seasick himself he didn't like the extra effort he had to put into keeping them in line. It didn't help when they could listen in on the crew's shouted conversations on deck. They were speaking Tagalog, of which none of Fang's men knew more than a few words, but it wasn't hard to identify the trace of panic.

The draft through the soft top was constant and bitter cold. Ice was forming on the insides of the container and the outsides of their sleeping bags. The irregular thudding sounds they heard from the deck, thuds followed by crunches and splintering cracks, was outside their experience and therefore more cause for alarm. It had started two days before, had continued almost without stop, and was interfering with everyone's sleep. Because of the continual activity on deck, they hadn't been able to reconnoiter to discover what the sounds were.

The problem was that when something went wrong here there was nowhere to go and no one to ask for help, even if they could have without fear of immediate arrest and imprisonment. If they had been in Singapore Strait there were a hundred little bays and inlets and islands they could hide in, living off the coastal fishermen in their tiny villages until the problem was fixed.

Fang wanted to go back to those tiny villages, to the Malacca Strait, to the South China Sea. He wanted to seek out that plump little woman upon whom he would father many sons, he wanted that snug little house in a Shanghai suburb. He had decided on a house instead of an apartment because it was his intention to take up gardening, exotic flowers in incandescent colors to brighten the view as he looked through the windows. And his children—he would father only sons, naturally, but a tiny daughter would not be unwelcome, someone he could spoil, because of course his sons would be raised to be hardworking and self-sufficient, just like their father.

Something intruded on this rosy picture of his future life. For a moment he couldn't identify it, and then his head jerked up. The dull rumble of the freighter's engine had changed. It was running very roughly, missing beats, almost clacking out its distress.

Smith noticed. "What is it?"

Fang held up his hand, palm out. "Can't you hear it?"

"Hear what?"

At that moment the freighter's engine coughed, spluttered, and died.

january 14
on board the *sojourner truth*

"YOU SHOULDN'T HAVE LET me sleep so long, Ops," Sara said.

"No, ma'am," Ops said, not looking at Hugh.

Truth was, Sara felt immeasurably more alert after four unbroken hours of sleep. She'd been wakened by the pipe telling the crew that dinner was being served in the galley and had been made very aware that it was well past time to pee. She staggered down the hall to the head, and when she got up again, she looked down and saw that blood had dried all down the front of her uniform. Captain Lowe's blood.

The deck lurched beneath her feet and she thought she was going to throw up. Instead she went back to her room for clean clothes and returned to the head, where she took a long, hot shower, bracing herself against the rolling of the ship so she could stay beneath the showerhead. At least the terrorists hadn't taken out the hot-water heater.

Half an hour later, wearing clean clothes, she felt like a new woman. "Did I miss dinner?" she said, surveying the empty serving dishes on the wardroom dining table, the half-empty dining plates before each officer. Looked like country-fried steak. Her mouth watered.

"Wooster!"

Wooster's pale face peered out of the wardroom pantry. "Yes, sir?"

"The XO needs food," Ops said. "Go down to the crew's mess and go through the serving line for her, will you? A little of everything."

"Coming right up, sir." Wooster vanished.

"Ops," she said, "you're sitting in my chair."

He met her eyes and said evenly, "No, ma'am. I'm not."

The only empty chair was the captain's chair at the head of the table. Her eyes traveled around the table and she saw nothing on any face but expectation, acceptance, and approval.

She swallowed hard and sat down, and was instantly aware of the feeling of relief emanating from the other officers. The U.S. Coast Guard was the closest thing the U.S. military had to an egalitarian service, but when all was said and done, Hugh was right. They wanted to be led. With that expectation came the added burden of the appearance of leadership.

"You would have woke me up if communications had come back on line," she said to Ops, "so I'm guessing it hasn't."

He shook his head. "No, ma'am. We finally got Sparks up the mast to the communications array. The sat dish is literally in pieces; it's going to have to be replaced. The antennas—you'd think they'd been aiming straight for them, because they're wrecked, too. We managed to raise a fishing vessel south of St. George on the VHF, but we lost 'em again before we could yell for help. And," he said, looking at Hugh, "someone made the suggestion that it might not be wise to broadcast our location over a channel everyone in the Bering Sea stands by on."

Which would very probably include the *Star of Bali.* "Good point. How are the wounded?"

"Maintaining. Doc's shot them full of antibiotics and antiinflammatories and I forget what else, and he says they should hold until we get to port. Well." He looked at her. "Depending."

"Depending," she said, nodding. She didn't ask about the helo because there was no way they could have received word. She wondered if the aviators had been able to raise anyone on their radios before they reached Cape Navarin. If they had reached Cape Navarin. "What about damage to the ship other than the fatal injuries to communications?"

"The portside small boat got torn up. We're patching it up."

"EO?"

Nate McDonald pushed his glasses up his nose and blinked owlishly at Sara. "The generators and the engines are good for another thousand miles, if we need them, ma'am. Nothing came anywhere near them."

Lucky for the pirates, Sara thought, because if anything had happened to the engines or the EO's best beloved Caterpillar generators, the EO would have swum to the *Agafia* under his own steam and slit all their throats. Which reminded her. "How is Ryan holding up?"

"He said fine, until the *Agafia* dropped out of range of the handhelds."

"No working radios on board the *Agafia,* I suppose."

"They were all destroyed when she was taken."

"Pretty thorough, our pirates."

"Yes, ma'am."

She turned back to McDonald. "How are we on fuel?"

"We've got enough to get us to Melbourne and back, Captain."

"Just get us to Seward, EO."

"Yes, ma'am."

Wooster came through the door with a plate so over-loaded it was dripping sausage gravy all around the edge. He set it down hastily in front of her, and produced flatware and a handful of napkins. "Be careful, ma'am, it's hot."

"Thanks, Wooster."

He beamed. "Yes, ma'am."

"Thanks, Wooster," Ops said. "Dismissed, and close the door behind you, please."

"Aye aye, sir."

Wooster left the room, the door closing gently behind him.

"Where are we?" Sara said, tucking in.

"Thirty miles west of Unimak," Ops said.

"We made good time, and against the wind, too," Sara said. "Well done, EO. Given even a little luck, we just might catch them."

"We're about due for some luck," Ops said.

"Hear, hear."

"What do we do if we do catch them, ma'am?" This from Ensign Ostlund, a serious young man who would go on to flight school in June, if they all survived. A dedicated planner, Ostlund never made a move without knowing what was going to happen next.

"I don't know," Sara said. "Let's discuss that, shall we?" She gestured with her fork. "To recap. Mr. Rincon seems to think they're carrying a mobile missile launcher on board, armed with a chemical warhead. How certain are we that this is the case, Mr. Rincon?"

Hugh, seated at the foot of the table, said, "I'd give my right hand if I could show you statements from witnesses to the bomb being built and loaded on board. It's a gut thing, Captain, based on circumstantial evidence and eye-witness accounts." Before the chief could say anything he added, "Which are not always reliable, I admit, but taken all together, plus the attack by the *Agafia,* I find pretty convincing. That attack was a deliberate feint, designed to draw attention away from the *Star of Bali* and their real mission."

Sara looked around the table and didn't see a lot of skepticism, which surprised her. After the boarding of the *Agafia* and the big zero they had found there, she had expected to have to lean on her officers to listen to Hugh ever again. So far as she could tell, they weren't even thinking about how Hugh Rincon and Sara Lange were husband and wife, and that in and of itself was a minor miracle. It was amazing how being shot at cleared your head of extraneous detail.

"Since our gunnery officer is on detached duty at present, Mr. Rincon, tell us about Scud missiles in general, and anything you know about this one in particular."

He stood up, swayed a little with the motion of the ship, and went to the dry board. "The original Scud, the R-17, was based on the V-2 rocket built by German scientists and captured by the Russian army at the end of World War II. It's simple, reliable, and easily mass-produced. They call it the AK-47 of the missile world. Even the Russians don't know how many they built, and nobody knows how many were built by others ripping off the original design. The original Scud and subsequent models are known to have been exported to Afghanistan, Hungary, Romania, Vietnam, Egypt, Iran, Iraq—" He stopped. "Actually, it'd probably take less time to list the countries the Russians haven't sold Scuds to.

"Specifically, a Scud's purpose is to bombard enemy positions, staging areas, and cities, anywhere the enemy is grouped together into a big enough target. The Scud isn't exactly a precision instrument, but then, with a maximum seventy-kiloton nuclear warhead, it doesn't have to be."

"We're not talking about a nuclear warhead in this case, however, Mr. Rincon."

"No. I believe this Scud is equipped with a quantity of cesium-137, a radioactive isotope used in radiology for medical and industrial purposes. Packed into the warhead with some dynamite, upon detonation it will disperse and cause a widespread epidemic of radiation poisoning. It's got a half-life of thirty years. Yes, it will kill you. Eventually."

"How much did these terrorists of yours buy, Mr. Rincon?"

"Fifty kilos."

Ops carried the one and blurted out, "Jesus Christ! That's like a hundred and ten pounds!"

"Yes. Which leaves room in the warhead for eighteen hundred pounds of dynamite."

"There are two hundred and forty thousand people in Anchorage," Sara said into the stunned silence. "Also Elmendorf Air Force Base, and Fort Richardson. Also the port of Anchorage, through which is shipped most of what the state of Alaska eats, wears, and drives, which would include Eielson Air Force Base outside Fairbanks and our own base in Kodiak."

She let that sink in, and deliberately met Chief Mark Edelen's frowning gaze. "I believe Mr. Rincon is right in his assessment of this situation. I believe that the *Star of Bali* is carrying a group of terrorists armed with a Scud missile armed with a WMD, and that their target is Anchorage."

Ostlund stirred. "The master told us that their next port of call is Seward, Alaska."

"Which is less than a hundred air miles from Anchorage. Mr. Rincon says the Scud's range is just under two hundred miles. All they have to do is put it into the air over Anchorage and light it off."

"Captain," Chief Edelen said respectfully but firmly, "I

still say we should head for Dutch Harbor. These people on board the *Agafia* almost took out our entire bridge crew. They did take out all our comm systems. I doubt that the ones on board the *Star of Bali* will be less well armed. We don't help their prospective target by getting ourselves killed."

"Noted, Chief. Anybody else got anything to add?"

Ostlund looked around the table. "XO?"

"Yes?"

"Are we the only ones who know?"

Sara looked at Hugh. He raised his shoulders and spread his hands. "Yes, Ensign. I believe we are."

Ostlund swallowed hard. "Then we have to stop them."

Sara took a deep breath, let it out. "Agreed."

The chief stirred, opened his mouth, and closed it again.

"All right," she said, pushing back from the table and getting to her feet. They followed suit. "I want every ounce of speed you can get out of the engines, EO. Ops, keep working on getting us some way to talk to shore over a secure line. I would just love to be able to call up an F-15 out of Elmendorf and paint a target on these guys. Failing that, Mr. Ostlund, we're minus our helo and our law enforcement officer, not to mention our gunnery officer. We're going to need a plan if we decide to board her. You up for that?"

"You bet I am, ma'am."

"Then get on it. Dismissed, gentlemen. Suppo? Hold up a minute."

Warrant officer George Kale said, "Ma'am."

"Give us a minute, will you, Mr. Rincon?" Sara said.

He nodded and left, closing the door behind him.

"What have you done with the captain, and Seaman Razo?"

He shifted uncomfortably. Pappy Kale didn't talk a lot.

"We cleaned out one of the freezers. Put them in there in plastic bags."

She nodded. "How's the crew doing?"

The supply officer, perhaps because of his habitual silence, heard more from and about the crew than the rest of the officers put together. He met her eyes steadily. "They're okay, ma'am. They're pretty shook up, but they're behind you. They know what happened to the captain and Seaman Razo, they want these guys, and they're ready to do whatever it takes to make that happen. You can count on them, ma'am."

january 15
seward

"HI," LILAH SAID.

"Hey," Kyle said. "I was just going to call. How are the kids?"

"Ask them yourself." Lilah put first Gloria and then Eli on the phone with their father. They told him all about the sea otter they had seen out the window of their hotel room every morning.

"How are you, babe?" Kyle said when Lilah got back on the phone.

"Bored. Lonely. Horny."

He laughed. "I miss you, too."

"I'm waiting for the but."

Kyle took a deep breath, let it out. "Sara's cutter is missing." His wife said nothing. "Lilah?"

"How can a two-hundred-and-eighty-four-foot Coast Guard cutter go missing?"

"It's been out of communications with District for over a full day now."

"Did it sink?"

"They don't know."

They listened to each other think for a while. "Does Sara's missing cutter have anything to do with why we're here instead of there?" Kyle took longer to answer this time. "Kyle?"

"I don't know for sure," Kyle said. "But I'm afraid so. Hugh—"

"Hugh's here?"

"No. He's not here." Kyle lent a slight emphasis to the last word.

"Oh," Lilah said on a note of discovery. "Oh no, Kyle, no."

"Yeah," Kyle said. "Stay there for a few more days, okay, honey?"

"We'll stay here," Lilah said.

She hung up and stared out the window at Resurrection Bay, a deep fjord walled in by steep, snow-covered mountains. She was not blind to the beauty, but she couldn't help but wonder what lay buried beneath its wind-whipped surface.

She very much hoped that Kyle's two best friends weren't.

The phone rang and she snatched it up, hoping it was her reprieve from purgatory. "Kyle?"

No, instead it was a preternaturally perky young woman who chirped brightly, "No, ma'am, this is Kenai Fjords Tours. Is this Mrs. Lilah Chase?"

"It is," Lilah said, voice dull with disappointment.

"We're calling to confirm your Resurrection Bay excursion, one adult, two children, departing at noon on January nineteenth."

Four interminable days from now. "Yes, that is correct."

"You'll want to check in at our office down in the marina half an hour prior to departure. A hot lunch will be included with your tour."

"Yes, I know. We've sailed with you before." Twice in

the past week, she thought. Stuck here much longer and they'd have to start repeating cruises.

"That's fine, then, ma'am, thank you so much, and we'll look forward to seeing you on the nineteenth."

She replaced the receiver and fought a sudden and irrational upwelling of tears. "Come on, kids, let's hit the beach."

21

january 19
gulf of alaska
on board the *star of bali*

THEY WERE UNDER WAY again. From overheard conversations they deduced that the fuel filters on the freighter's one engine had clogged up, leaving them adrift for almost forty-eight hours. Fang bore a grudging respect for Smith, who had maintained his own calm and order among the men during that time.

But in truth there had been little danger of the *Star of Bali*'s crew calling anyone for help. In the schedule-driven world of maritime shipping all that mattered was getting the goods to market on time. The last thing any shipowner wanted was a boarding by the U.S. Coast Guard, which would cause significant delay and who knew how many citations for safety and security violations requiring expensive legal action later on. The hired hands that captained most oceangoing vessels nowadays were well aware of this, and they would do everything in their power to avoid the official attention of authorities on shore.

Fang listened to the engine, which it seemed to him was still running a little rougher than it had before it quit.

It was running, however, which was preferable to the alternative. The two days adrift had not been enjoyable, with the ship at the mercy of the heavy seas.

Fang turned his head to see that Smith was watching the digital readout on his GPS. Everyone else was watching him.

"How long?" Fang said, voicing the thought that was on everyone's mind.

"Soon now."

Fang looked around at the men, swinging in hammocks, huddled in sleeping bags. They'd run out of fuel for the stove and the lanterns the night before. This morning they'd eaten dry noodles for breakfast. Everyone looked as cold as he felt. He wondered how well everyone would be moving when Smith finally set the plan in motion. Although one benefit of the cold was that the smell was much less noticeable.

He wondered, not for the first time, what they were doing here, and rued, perhaps for the last time, the greed that had led him to this place.

Smith said something. Fang stared at him, uncomprehending.

"One hour," Smith repeated.

"One hour till what?"

"We take the ship," Smith said, and held up the GPS. Fang took it and squinted at it. "Here," Smith said, and pushed a button which lit up the display. "When we hit fifty-nine degrees forty minutes north latitude, we take the ship. If we wait any longer, they'll call for the pilot."

"Pilot?" one of Smith's men said.

"Every ship needs a pilot to get them into port. Someone who knows the local waters." To Fang he said, "Tell your men to get ready."

Fang was still squinting at the GPS. Fifty-nine degrees thirty minutes latitude, one hundred forty-nine degrees and thirty minutes longitude. He tried to imagine the nearest port to that location and came up with Anchorage, Alaska. What the hell were they doing here?

"Get ready," Smith said, more sharply this time, holding his hand out.

Fang gave him the GPS and went to get his men suited up.

gulf of alaska
on board the *sojourner truth*

"BEST SPEED CAN'T BE more than twelve knots, XO," Ostlund said. "She's only got one engine. We've got six knots on her." The *Sojourner Truth*'s top speed was eighteen knots.

"We've lost her," Chief Edelen said.

Sara ignored him. "What's our location, Tommy?"

"South-southwest of Rugged Island, XO."

"Mr. Rincon?"

Hugh was leaning over Tommy's shoulder, staring intently at the readout on the Transas. "Pan up a little, Tommy, would you? Thanks." He pointed. "Right here. What's that?"

Tommy pointed and clicked. "Caine's Head."

"What are those, feet or meters?"

"Feet."

"So the point's a little under seven hundred feet high, and the mountain in back of it?"

"Fifteen hundred."

Hugh stood up and looked at Sara. "They'll want a straight shot right up the valley. My guess is they'll light it off when they've cleared this point."

"Caine's Head?"

Hugh nodded.

"EO?" Sara said.

"We're peddling as fast as we can, XO."

"Vessel in sight!"

PO Barnette's shout caused a surge toward the windows.

It was indeed the *Star of Bali,* gaining on the southern end of Rugged Island.

"Yeah," Sara said, binoculars trained on the ship, "that's our baby all right. Well done, everyone."

"I think she's got engine problems, XO," Barnette said, eyes still glued to his binoculars. "She's barely making way."

"Mr. Ostlund, assemble your team."

"Aye aye, Captain."

When Hugh started to follow him Sara, said, "Hold up, Mr. Rincon. Anything from the *Agafia,* anyone?"

"No, ma'am," Ops said.

"Pull one of the emergency VHF radios from the lifeboats and start trying to raise her."

"Those radios only have a reach of two miles, ma'am."

"I know, Ops, but she'll be on our tail, and I want to know as soon as she's within reach."

"Yes, ma'am."

"All right, let's tell the troops what's going on." Sara caught a down swell to port and was at the microphone in two steps. "Attention all hands, attention all hands, this is Lieutenant Commander Lange," she said, wincing a little as her voice boomed back at her from the speaker. Tommy reached quickly for the volume knob and Sara thanked her with a nod. She only hoped that the pipe wasn't reaching across the water to the *Star of Bali.*

"Yesterday I told you what we've been doing and why. We are going into action again against a bunch of suspected terrorists who present a serious threat to the nation. They must be stopped and they must be stopped now, before they get any closer to their target. I don't have to remind you that there are two hundred and sixty thousand people living in and around that target. Our communications are still out, so we have no way of alerting anyone on shore to the threat. We can't risk letting them out of our sight, so it's up to us."

She paused to take a breath. "This is going to be tricky and dangerous. To be on the safe side, I want every one of you with a survival suit in arm's reach. Chief Saunders is standing by in the portside equipment locker ready to issue them. Proceed there directly following this pipe and then report to your duty station."

She wanted to be able to say something inspirational but all that came to mind was lame words about duty, honor, and country. She remembered the blood all over the bridge after the attack, the limp bodies of Captain Lowe and Seaman Razo as they were carried from the bridge. Captain Lowe would have been much better at this than she was.

It never occurred to her that Captain Lowe had had twenty years on her, during none of which had he faced a situation like this one, so he probably wouldn't have known what to say, either.

Sara said, "The sea is vast and our ship is small, but never doubt that we will prevail. That is all."

She hung up the mike and looked at Hugh, who was standing in front of the open portside hatch. She jerked her head, and he nodded. "I'll be right back, Chief," she told Mark Edelen, and left the bridge, Hugh following behind.

SHE LED THE WAY to her stateroom and closed the door. He raised an eyebrow. "Won't people talk?"

"Shut up," she said, and walked into his arms.

They held each other as the precious seconds ticked by. She pressed her face against his heart and heard its steady reassuring beat even through the Mustang suit. He might have kissed her hair, she couldn't tell, but she felt his arms tight around her, to where it started the wound on her arm aching again. She didn't move.

Ostlund's voice sounded on the pipe. "Boarding party, assemble aft, I say again, boarding party, assemble aft immediately."

His grip loosened. She looked up. "I love you, Rincon."

The corner of his mouth quirked up. "Same goes, Lange."

On the way back to the bridge she blundered into Chief Katelnikof. If he saw the tears in her eyes, he was tactful enough not to say so.

THE FOG AND SLEET dissolved so suddenly it startled everyone on the bridge, especially when Rugged Island thrust up out of the heaving gray seas like a fifteen-hundred foot claymore in the hand of a vengeful ocean god. On this monolith of cracked granite, stunted evergreens clung to microscopic crevices all the way to the top, where a sharp-toothed peak gnawed at the belly of the gray skies.

"I've never seen anything more beautiful in my life," Tommy said fervently, and no one contradicted her. Chief Edelen miracled them up a course that gave the small boat a lee to port and at the same time kept their starboard side to the *Star of Bali,* in case anyone on the other ship looked in their direction. So far their luck was holding, because it didn't appear that anyone had. They lowered the inflatable and loaded the crew the way they always did. It helped that the seas had dropped five feet overnight, but the boarding team was still taking one hell of a pounding.

Sara watched them labor up a wave and disappear into a trough. She looked up at the sky. They'd planned the boarding for this hour specifically, that hour between darkness and dawn when the light played tricks on the mind and at least for a few moments no one could be absolutely sure of what they were seeing.

"I wanted to go with them," Chief Edelen said from beside her.

"So did I," she said, and went to stand in front of the captain's chair. She still couldn't bring herself to sit in it. She wanted to pace but it would drive everyone crazy, so she refrained.

She couldn't help following along in the inflatable in her imagination. Were they shipping water? Had they come up on the freighter yet? What if someone saw the grapnel come up over the taffrail and hook on? What if the stern was too high for climbing and Hugh couldn't get up and over? It wasn't like he was a field agent; he was an analyst. He wasn't trained in boarding hostile vessels in the open ocean from a small boat that wouldn't stay still underfoot.

What if the *Star of Bali* had had icing problems, too? What if the hook wouldn't hold? What if the motion of the ship caused Hugh to lose his grip and he fell in?

What if the freighter sank? Would the Scud go off underwater? If it did, what kind of damage would it do? How long before they would know?

Was Hugh seasick yet?

on board the *star of bali*

THEY WERE OUT OF the container and on deck. It was daybreak, and the sky was going from a dour black to a sullen gray. They were rolling hard enough to ship occasional water over the sides, which led Fang to believe that the engine had yet to regain full power, because it was obvious that either the storm had run its course or they had gained shelter in the lee of whatever land they were approaching. The spray was freezing on contact into a pearlescent sheen over every exposed surface, a sight that frightened Fang right down to his marrow. He nudged Smith in the small of the back and pointed at the ice. "Let's go!"

Smith looked at the ice and appeared to understand, because he moved out.

They were careful, but there wasn't much need for it. The first crewman they encountered went down without a sound, blood bubbling out of his mouth and chest from Fang's knife. The second crewman, one of the junior officers if the markings on his shirt were correct, backed away with his hands upraised, but he, too, went down.

Fang motioned to Soo to heave the bodies overboard and followed Smith. They swarmed up the outside ladders to the bridge to surprise the officer on watch with his feet up on the instrument panel, admiring the proportions of this month's *Playboy* Playmate. They burst in and he looked up, gaping. He reached for what later proved to be a radio, and Fang shot him. He spun out of the chair and fell on the floor, his eyes wide and surprised beneath the bullet hole in his forehead.

"No," the helmsman said, backing away, "no, no." He tripped and fell and Fang's bullet caught his arm on the way down. "No, no," he said as he tried to scrabble out of the way. Fang shot him again, this time in the chest. He tried to speak and couldn't.

Fang wedged a foot beneath his body and flipped him over for a swift search of his pockets. He found a wad of cash inside a wallet otherwise filled with pictures of a young Filipino woman and several toothy children of various ages. The officer was wearing a very nice watch. Fang took that, too. When he was done, he hauled the helmsman out of the bridge and onto the catwalk. "No, no," the man said faintly, as Fang tipped him into the sea. The officer's body followed.

The rest of the crew were either in their bunks or at breakfast in the mess and were easily cowed into submission by the automatic weapons the pirates held. The captain, surprised in the shower, was inclined to put up a fight and was clubbed into unconsciousness with a rifle butt, after which he followed the officer on the bridge over the side. It silenced the rest of the crew, as if they imagined that keeping quiet would save their lives. It didn't.

Fang took over the bridge, sending Liet, his second in command and his best engineer, to the engine room. A while later a phone rang on the bridge. It was Liet, reporting that while all the moving parts were at a stage that could only be described as geriatric they were, in fact, still moving and it looked as if they would continue to do so. Liet, a Thai with almost uncanny intuitions about the internal combustion engine, was completely to be trusted, and Fang breathed a sigh of relief.

His relief was tempered by the southeastern horizon, which was looking very black. The horizon was backed up by the barometer, which was dropping like a rock.

"The AIS," Smith said, and Fang found it and disabled it.

"Steer this course," Smith said, handing him a piece of paper.

Fang looked at it and raised his eyebrows. "North?" he said. He looked up and peered at the horizon. "That's right into that bay." He realized something else. "Hey. Where's Jones? Where are the rest of the men?"

"Steer that course," Smith said. "Watch him," he said to one of his men.

"What for?" Fang said. "And where's the rest of my men?"

Smith left without answering. The man remaining behind kept his rifle pointed in Fang's general direction.

Fang stood at the wheel for a few moments, getting the feel of the ship. The pitch seemed to him to be heavier than it ought to have been, given the height of the waves. He looked out on deck, over the rows of neatly stacked and lashed containers. The gray dawn revealed the topless container they had ridden in, and Smith and his men pulling back the canvas top of the container next to it.

He looked around for Catalino, one of his own men who had also remained behind. "Find me a cargo manifest."

Catalino, an Abu Sayyaf guerrilla from the southern Philippines who in a shockingly procapitalist gesture had abandoned the fight for freedom for the acquisition of personal wealth without a backward look when Fang recruited him, was back in less than ten minutes with a clipboard and some new blood spatters down the front of his jacket.

The manifest showed the containers to be filled with drilling equipment bound for the port of Seward, Alaska, and a hold full of Chinese steel bound for Seattle. Fang put the manifest down and looked out the window again. He had a sinking feeling that the container Smith was busy with didn't have drilling equipment inside it.

He headed for the door to the ladder down and was stopped by Smith's man.

"Let me by," Fang said angrily.

The man watched him out of expressionless eyes, said nothing, and didn't move.

Fang headed for the starboard door and the mercenary was there before him. This time the mercenary deigned to speak. "No," he said.

Fang had set his rifle next to the wheel, and he eyed it now, wondering if he could get to it, click off the safety, aim, and fire before the mercenary shot him.

"No," said the mercenary, who was evidently also a mind reader.

"What the hell is going on here?" Fang said. "What's in that container?"

The mercenary said, "No." He motioned again with the rifle. Fang looked at Catalino.

Smith's man fired. Catalino's weapon clattered to the floor and a second later Catalino's body followed it.

Smith's man motioned with the rifle again, and this time Fang returned to the helm.

22

january 19

IN THE INFLATABLE, HUGH was too terrified to be seasick. The walls of water surrounding the small boat were so high he could barely see the sky, and the boarding team was so packed in and so bristling with weapons that even if he was sick he wouldn't have been able to do anything but puke down the front of his Mustang suit. The coxswain was a square-shouldered young man with a large flat brown mole on his left cheek. He had his teeth bared in what looked more like a snarl than a grin, and his hands on the controls were quick and deft.

Hugh had insisted on going with the boarding team. "I speak Korean," he had said. Since he was the only person on board who did, it had been impossible to gainsay him, and Sara was the first to back him up. She knew what he was thinking because she was thinking the same thing. No way was he letting whatever it was on board the *Star of Bali* any closer to a populated landmass, especially his populated landmass.

Suddenly the stern of the freighter was looming above them, water smacking against the hull and rebounding to spray them all. Ostlund slapped Ensign Reese's helmet. "Go!"

Ensign Reese, the best arm on the ship in Ops' opinion, stood up and braced himself against the steering column. Everyone ducked as he swung a rope with a grapnel on it around his head, once, twice, three times, and let fly.

It missed. He reeled it back in as the coxswain, cursing under his breath, coaxed the small boat back beneath the stern. Another wave smacked the stern of the freighter and rained down on their hapless heads.

Again, Reese started the windup, once, twice, three times, and it flew up, up, and over the stern, and Seaman Lewis grabbed him around the waist as he hauled on the line as hard as he could. Seaman Lewis was six feet four inches tall and weighed two hundred and fifty pounds and he had been selected for this mission for just that reason. If Hugh was not mistaken he was wearing Seaman Lewis's pants.

"On belay," Lewis bellowed.

"Feels solid!" Reese yelled. The coxswain turned the small boat off the stern of the freighter, just enough to keep the line taut, or as taut as possible in these heaving seas.

Seaman Delgado, the size of a monkey and just as agile, stepped up to the rope. He was five-one and wouldn't tell anyone what he weighed, but he had been observed in the gym bench-pressing one-fifty. He wore no pack and carried only a sidearm.

"Go!" Ostlund shouted, and Delgado went up the rope hand over hand without pause and vanished over the stern. A second later the grapnel came hurtling down, splashing into the water next to the small boat, to be reeled in briskly by Ensign Reese.

The coxswain took that as a sign and opened up the throttle to maneuver the small boat around to the freighter's starboard side. He dropped off the stern a little, where they endeavored not to be squashed by the freighter's rise and fall, and waited.

Hugh noticed a sheen of white across Ostlund's shoulders, and reached out to touch it. Ice. He looked around and noticed that the small boat was adding a layer of ice with every wave they took. He started beating on the sides with his fists, and everyone else woke up from their frozen stupor and started beating. It got rid of most of the ice so long as they kept beating, and it warmed them up a little, too.

"There!" Ostlund said, after what seemed hours and was probably only minutes. Hugh followed his pointing finger and saw a rope ladder rattle down the hull of the freighter. The coxswain goosed the engine until they were alongside, and kept them alongside until Ensign Reese managed to snag it. Hugh looked up and saw Delgado grinning down at them from the gunnel, and his mind numbly remembered the briefing. This would be the pilot's ladder, the ladder the ship would let down to board the local marine pilot when the ship got close enough to port to need one.

Ostlund was first up.

"Mr. Rincon?" Ensign Reese said.

It was a very small ladder, and the hull of the freighter seemed impossibly high.

"Mr. Rincon?" Ensign Reese said again.

In some small part of his mind that was still functioning Hugh knew he was holding up the line and endangering the mission. He grabbed the side of the inflatable and rose shakily to his feet, losing his balance immediately and pitching forward. He flung up his hands to catch himself and by sheer luck fell into the ladder.

The sea fell away from beneath the inflatable and he was left clinging to the ladder. His feet scrabbled automatically for the narrow slats of wood that formed the steps. The hull of the freighter rolled away from him and he found himself lying facedown against it, his knuckles caught between the rope of the ladder and the metal of the hull.

"Go!" Reese shouted. "Go now!"

His feet fumbled for the rungs and he gained a few shaky steps before the hull of the freighter rolled back and he found himself swinging wildly away from the hull, the ladder twisting and twirling. He looked down and saw faces turned up to him. When the ship rolled back he slammed hard against the hull.

"Ouch," he clearly heard someone say.

"Climb, goddammit, Mr. Rincon! Climb! Climb now!"

Reese's urgency got through, and Hugh unclenched one hand for the next rung, and the next, fighting the heave of the sea and the roll of the freighter and the shove of the wind and the sting of the spray. About halfway up he lost all contact with his feet, and his hands were bloodied and painful from rubbing against the hull. It felt like an hour later when a hand grasped the back of his Mustang suit and began to pull. "It's okay, Mr. Rincon, I've got you," Ostlund's voice said, and the next thing he knew he was sitting on the deck and dry-heaving between his legs. Nothing had ever felt as good to him as the solid deck of the *Star of Bali* beneath his ass.

When he recovered enough to look around, the coxswain was climbing over the gunnel. He staggered to his feet in time to see the inflatable fall off the hull of the freighter. The line fastening the small boat to the bottom of the rope ladder pulled taut, twisting the ladder into a helix.

This had been much discussed in the planning session. "Mr. Ryan said they had fifteen people on board the *Agafia*. We have to assume there are at least that many on board the *Star of Bali*," Sara had said. "We can fit ten of you, plus Mr. Rincon, into the small boat without swamping her. We will need every gun we've got. Everyone boards. They can leave the small boat tied off to the ship." An escape hatch, in case things went sour, was what she was thinking.

On board the freighter, Delgado closed the door behind the coxswain and slammed down the hatch handle. He donned his pack and shouldered his shotgun. "This way," he said, and they followed him single file through bundled pallets of rebar and angle iron stacked as high as the hold.

They came to a hatch. Ostlund put his ear to it for a moment. "Can't hear a goddamn thing," he said cheerfully, and cranked it open. Delgado slithered through, gave an all-clear, and motioned the rest of them inside. Hugh was last in, and he closed the hatch behind him. Ostlund tied a strip of red cloth to the hatch handle. "Hansel and Gretel," he told them, "only better than bread crumbs."

They went through a series of corridors without seeing a soul. "Where the hell is everyone?" Lewis said in a hoarse whisper. "This is getting creepy."

Hugh didn't say what he was thinking. He was thinking the crew of this ship was dead, every last one of them, the same way the crew on the *Agafia* was dead. He touched the nine-millimeter Smith & Wesson in the holster strapped to his side. It comforted him.

They went through an exterior hatch and began to climb the outside stairs to the bridge. The fresh air was welcome to them all, but especially to Hugh, in whom fear was beginning to be superseded by nausea. He was almost wishing he were back in the small boat. He thought of Sara. He'd seen her standing on the bridge wing, watching as they pulled away from the cutter. Don't worry, babe, he thought, I'll be back. Me and Arnold Schwarzenegger.

Which was probably why he was the one to stumble into the first man they'd seen since they boarded. He came around a corner the rest of the team had just passed, with Hugh bringing up the rear. He had earphones on and walkman in one hand, the other hand snapping to the beat.

He was also armed. When he saw Hugh, he drew and fired in one smooth motion. The shot went wide and he was smothered by a pile of furious, frightened Coasties before he could get off a second. When they got up, he was out cold, possibly for good.

The shot had been heard. They heard cries from the deck below and footsteps from above and quickened their pace, the stairs clanging beneath their feet. A shot ricocheted off the bulkhead near Hugh's head, followed by the sound of another shot from the deck. A third shot, this one from above, made them all duck. Delgado, who seemed to have the instincts of a cat, didn't flinch but trotted directly to another hatch, which led to an inside stairwell. He pointed up. "Bridge."

"Weapons," Ostlund said briskly. He looked as if he might not so secretly be enjoying himself. Hugh, still nauseated, wanted to shoot either Ostlund or himself. "Okay, Delgado, take Segal and Chernikoff and locate the engine room." Segal and Chernikoff were the EO's choice for this insertion. "Segal, Chernikoff, disable any secondary controls. If you find the hydraulics controlling the rudder, cut it or break it. Once we're in command we can always take her in tow. What we want is control."

"Aye aye, Ensign." Delgado and the two engineer's mates disappeared through a hatch.

"Okay," Ostlund said, "let's go," and then a surprised look crossed his face. He looked down at the blood welling from his thigh and said, "Oh, shit."

The crack of single bullets alternated with the explosion of shotgun rounds. It didn't sound at all like it did in the movies. Hugh reached for his sidearm and then was hit in the back with a large club and felt himself falling forward, ever so slowly, ever so gently, onto a big black bed, oh, so soft.

Sara, he thought.

"Delgado!" Ostlund yelled into the handheld, right into Hugh's ear from where he had fallen next to Hugh.

"Sir!" Delgado responded over the radio. "Segal and Chernikoff are both down! I am pinned down!"

"Understood, Delgado, I am sending assistance!" Ostlund pressed his hands against his thigh and looked at the men still standing. "Reese! Take two men and go get them!"

"Aye aye, sir!"

The next shot sounded like a cannon, like the last trump, like Armageddon. The ship, already trembling from the pounding it was taking from the seas and the violent change of command, shuddered.

Okay, not sounding at all good for our side, Hugh thought. As for himself, he was tired, and he thought he'd take a little nap.

on board the *sojourner truth*

A GREAT SPOUT OF water went up off their port bow.

"What the hell was that!"

Mark Edelen, looking through binoculars, said calmly, "A bunker buster."

"A what?" Sara said.

He elaborated, sounding like a firearms manual. "A shoulder-launched assault weapon firing rounds with explosive loads."

Another puff of smoke from the bridge of the *Star of Bali,* another trail of darker smoke, and this time the marksman didn't miss. The shell impacted aft of the bridge. The deck shuddered and everyone turned to see that the starboard cannon was gone.

"Yes," Sara said, speaking over the ringing in her ears, "I see. Let's fall off a little, shall we, Chief?" She looked down at where Edelen was crouched against the console.

"Jesus," the chief said. He straightened. "I mean, aye aye, XO. Helm, all ahead one quarter."

"All ahead one quarter, aye," Seaman Cornell responded with a sangfroid to match Sara's own.

Sara looked at Ops. "What's the word from Ostlund?"

"Ostlund's down. Delgado got to the boat and is picking up the ones who went over the side."

"Who didn't?" Sara said sharply. "Who isn't with them?"

"Lewis. Segal. Chernikoff." He looked away. "Mr. Rincon."

Sara's face went gray. Ops seemed to recede into the distance. She brought him back into focus with great difficulty. He looked worried as he watched her. "Are they sure?" she said, the words coming from a great distance.

"Ostlund saw him go down, XO," Ops said. "I'm—I'm sorry."

There was a dreadful silence on the bridge that seemed to go on forever.

When Sara spoke again her voice was hoarse. "Did they find the missile?"

Ops swallowed. "No, XO. Delgado says the *Star of Bali* had too many men and they were too well armed. Our guys were driven back. Most of them went over the side. Like I said, Delgado is picking them up in the small boat."

Another dreadful silence.

"Chief," Sara said.

"XO?" Edelen said.

She said in a distant voice, "If you wanted to disable a ship, and you didn't think your twenty-five-millimeter cannon would do the job, especially if the only working one had just been destroyed, what would you do next?"

He actually paled. "XO, I—"

"Where would we want to hit her, Chief? Where would it do the most good?"

He swallowed audibly, and said, calmly enough, "She's probably a five-hatch ship. Somewhere between the second and third hatches."

"My thoughts exactly," Sara said.

"What?" Ops said.

"Hitting them at a ninety-degree angle would be best, XO, but we'll still lose the bow."

She nodded, almost dreamily. "I figured. The collision bulkhead should hold her, though." She went to the plot station and looked at the Transas. "Pan in, Tommy, would you, please?"

Tommy, looking a little gray herself, zoomed in.

"Yeah," Sara said, and pointed at the screen. She looked around and found everyone frozen in place. "Huddle up," she said. "Now."

There was a scramble of feet as everyone except Cornell on the helm stumbled across the heaving deck to peer over Tommy's shoulder and follow Sara's pointing finger.

"They're headed straight up Resurrection Bay," Sara said. "I'm guessing we decided to board them at just about the same time the terrorists took control of the ship. And why not?" she asked herself. "Why wouldn't they just ride it in until they absolutely had to have the ship under their control? Makes perfect sense. It's what I'd do myself."

"XO?"

"Never mind. They're going up the inside." She traced the *Star of Bali*'s route up Resurrection Bay. "We'll go up the outside." She traced the *Sojourner Truth*'s route up Eldorado Narrows.

"That's awful skinny, XO," the chief said.

"We'll never catch them, Captain," Ops said.

"We've got six knots on them, and they think they've disabled us. Even if they were looking for us, they'll be watching for us to come back at them from behind, not from the side. Hugh said—" Her breath caught, and she swallowed painfully and went on. "Mr. Rincon said that they probably wouldn't fire the missile until they cleared Caine's Head, and that it would take an hour for the firing sequence to be activated. The pilot boat will come out, and when they don't take him on board, it will probably be the first time the people on shore know something's wrong. By then it'll be too late."

She saw her second in command's anguished expression and said with a thin smile, "Don't worry, Ops. I don't plan on sinking us. I don't even have to sink them, although I admit it would be a nice bonus."

There were nods all around. She looked at Mark Edelen. "Yes, Chief?"

He swallowed. "Permission to speak freely, XO."

"Granted, Chief," Sara said, almost pleasantly.

The chief squared his shoulders and spoke directly. "How personal is this?"

"It's personal as hell, Chief," she said, still in that eerily friendly tone of voice. "They killed my husband. I want them dead." Another shot from the assault weapon whistled toward them and went long, poking entirely too large a hole in the wave about to crash over the stern. In some distant part of her mind Sara noticed that they now had a following sea. She wondered how much this would increase their speed. Of course, it would also increase the freighter's speed. "However, the missile they're getting ready to fire trumps my need for revenge. We have to stop them, people. I don't want them getting any closer to the mainland. I don't want to turn my back on them for an instant. There are two hundred and forty thousand people a hundred miles from here who don't know they're counting on us. I'd like to keep it that way."

She didn't wait for a reply. "Chief, fall off to starboard. Let them think they've chased us off." They hunched over the Transas again. "Okay, Tommy, what's your best guess for intercept?"

Tommy punched in some numbers. "If we want to surprise them, right here."

"We do. How long?"

"About an hour."

Sara looked over her shoulder at the receding stern of the freighter. "Man, that's just cutting it too damn close." She turned back. "Lay in a course. Chief, we slow down over long enough to pick up the crew."

"What about the inflatable?"

"Leave it, we don't have time. Ops, break out the machine guns. Order the gunners to lay down a covering fire to suppress the hell out of that bastard with the rocket launcher when we catch up to them."

"Aye aye, XO." Ops took the portside hatch at a run.

She slipped and slid across the deck and grabbed the microphone. "Attention all hands, attention all hands, this is XO Lange." She paused. She really didn't know what to say this time. She only hoped she didn't start a mutiny. She struggled to sound as calm as possible, as if one heard this kind of order everyday on board a U.S. Coast Guard cutter. "You've got about an hour to prepare for collision, I say again, one hour to prepare for collision. Batten everything down and keep one hand on those survival suits. I say again, all hands, prepare for collision."

on board the *star of bali*

HUGH WOKE UP TO the feeling of someone pushing a red-hot poker through his lower left back. He groaned, partly in pain, partly in humiliation. He'd been shot in the ass. He could hear Kyle laughing. "Shut up, Kyle," he muttered.

"Hello," someone said in Korean.

With a tremendous effort, he turned his head and pried his eyes open to see a pair of combat boots in front of his face. He groaned again.

"Yes, you have been shot," the voice said. "I'm sorry about that."

"Me, too," Hugh said, surprised that he still had the ability to speak.

"I have noticed that there is no blood, so I assume you are wearing body armor." One of the shoes nudged him. "Get up."

Sweating, straining, Hugh pulled himself to his knees, where he threw up on the combat boots.

"Very amusing," the voice said. "Stand up."

He pulled himself the rest of the way to his feet, and stood, swaying, partly from the motion of the ship, partly because little stars were flying around his head and chirping. Or was that little birds twinkling?

He was on deck. They must have dragged him there. That would explain why every bone and muscle in his body ached.

The deck beneath his feet jarred and twisted and his hand slipped and let go of whatever it had been holding on to. Hands caught him and set him ungently back on his feet but not before he'd caught a face full of spray. He blinked around at the circle of hostile faces.

"Careful," the voice said, revealing itself to be a young Asian man with sallow skin and expressionless dark eyes. Not Kyle, then. "We wouldn't want you falling overboard."

He held a pistol in his hand that Hugh recognized. He looked down and though his head swam at the movement he could see that his holster was empty.

"Who are you?" the man said.

Hugh licked his lips. "Could I have some water?"

The man nodded at someone behind Hugh. A bottle of Evian appeared. Hugh almost laughed but he was afraid it might hurt. He unscrewed the cap and drank thirstily.

"Who are you?"

"Who are you?" Hugh said.

The man gave a little bow. "Ja Yong-bae." Almost as an afterthought he brought the pistol up and hit Hugh in the face with it.

Hugh went down again, and was caught again by the same rough hands and dumped back on his feet.

"Who are you?" the man repeated.

A head appeared over the side of the container and said something to Ja that Hugh didn't catch over the sounds of wind and sea. "Don't stop!" Ja shouted.

He turned back to Hugh. "You came from a U.S. Coast Guard ship. I must assume that you have captured the *Agafia*. Where is my brother?"

One brother per boat. "He is a prisoner, along with those of his men who survived."

"You lie," Ja Yong-bae said. "He would rather die than live in captivity. As would I."

"Why are you doing this?" Hugh said.

The man gave a very European shrug. "I would have thought it was obvious."

"It isn't. Please explain it to me." Hugh was only half paying attention to their conversation. He didn't know what Sara was going to try next, but he knew Sara and he knew something was coming and that it would be big and bad. Sara didn't do redundant. And she would be operating on the assumption that he was dead, so she would not be constrained by fear for his safety, and she would be highly motivated for revenge. Hugh wanted off the *Star of Bali,* and he wanted off now. If Ja offered him the chance to jump overboard he'd take it and thank him.

Ja considered. "Why not? There is time, and you have come so far."

He had Hugh hoisted up over the side of the container. There wasn't a lot of room inside because it was mostly filled with the missile and its launcher. Men hunched over the controls.

"Why do this?" Hugh said. It had bought him time before and he liked to go with what worked. "Who do you work for?"

"Myself."

"You trained with al-Qaida in Afghanistan."

Ja raised an eyebrow. "You're remarkably well informed for a member of the United States Coast Guard."

What the hell. "I work for the CIA."

Ja's eyebrows raised. "Do you," he said after a moment. Then, amazingly, he smiled. "It took you long enough to catch up with me. Didn't I leave enough clues?"

With a groaning of gears, the head of the missile began to rise.

on board the *sojourner truth*

"WE'RE JUST COMING UP on the northern point of the island, Captain."

"Are they in sight yet?"

Everyone on the bridge strained to look. "No."

Sara hoisted herself into the captain's chair to see if height would give her an advantage. The dark green seas were whipped into whitecaps by the winds howling up out of the southwest, but the swell was way down, and what was left of it was pushing them north.

It would also be pushing the *Star of Bali* north.

"Let's kill the lights," she said.

Ops nodded. The ship's lights went out, inside and out. Sara got down and walked out onto the starboard wing and looked back. Even their running lights were out. They were as indistinguishable from the dark green water as a two-hundred-and-eighty-four-foot white hull with an orange stripe down both sides and a big white square retractable helo hangar could be. She wondered where Laird and Sams were, if they were alive and safe.

Probably not, because if they had been they would have been able to yell for help, and if they had been able to yell for help there would have been no need for the task in hand. She hoped yet again that she was doing the right thing. She hoped she wouldn't lose any more of her crew.

Sara had heard all the clichés about command, but she had never understood until now the definition of the word "lonely." She turned and saw Mark Edelen looking at her, and thought she saw condemnation in his eyes.

She squared her shoulders and went back inside, this time climbing into the captain's chair without thinking about it.

They were coming up Eldorado Narrows all ahead full, as fast as the EO could push all four generators. Fox Island, a series of three mountain pillars connected by two ridges, was passing by on their left. The ridges were high enough that they couldn't see the *Star of Bali*, presumably passing up the outside of the island as the *Sojourner Truth* was passing up the inside. Which meant that the ridge concealed the *Sojourner Truth* from the *Star of Bali* as well.

Cape Resurrection, on their right, had been succeeded by a series of sheer cliffs contorting themselves into a sinuous convolution of coastline that was mostly bare rock dropping into eighteen, twenty-nine, thirty-seven fathoms of water. Ahead, a narrow spit thrust out from Fox Island to the northeast, a rude gesture of land thickly crusted with trees, most of them dead and bare of limb. An old fishing boat was tossed up among them, its wooden sides as gray as the dead tree trunks.

"Getting kind of skinny through here, XO," the chief said.

Sara looked at him. He was sweating. "Maintain course and speed," she said.

The *Sojourner Truth* seemed to have been swallowed alive by the encompassing walls of land. The sky looked very narrow above, and the throb of the engines echoed back at them. Sara saw a group of sea lions hauled out on a rock dive back as the cutter passed by. In the next moment the cutter's wake rolled over their rock in a cold green wave.

She knew what the chief was feeling. She was feeling it herself. The channel was three hundred yards wide from land to land and only two hundred of that was navigable due to shoals and rocks and reefs protruding from the shore on either side. They were an hour away from low tide, and the *Sojourner Truth* was making the better part of eighteen and a half knots.

Sara was glad the chief was scared. It would keep him sharp.

Everyone on the bridge seemed to hold their breath as the cutter flashed between spit and headland, and then they were through.

Sara let out the breath she didn't know she'd been holding. "Well done, Chief, helm."

Mark pulled off his cap and wiped his forehead on his forearm. His hair was soaked. He saw Sara watching and resettled the cap on his head. "Helm, steer three-zero-zero."

"Steering three-zero-zero, aye."

The bow of the *Sojourner Truth* swung to port and the northern point of Fox Island.

on board the *kenai fjords*

"NOW HERE'S SOMETHING YOU don't see everyday, ladies and gentlemen." The fifty-foot cruise ship slowed down until it was almost dead in the water as the passengers lined up on the port rail. "We've got two pods of orcas, also known as killer whales, in sight. The one closest to us is a resident pod. The one farther off is a transient pod."

"Mom, look!"

"I see, honey." Lilah blew her nose and tucked her hands back into her pockets, leaning against the rail to steady herself against the roll of the boat.

The captain's mellow voice continued over the loud-speaker. "The residents reside right here in Resurrection Bay. The transients, the ones farther off, they travel all over Prince William Sound. The resident orcas eat fish. The transient orcas eat everything, including sea mammals like sea otters and sea lions. The two pods speak different languages, and they don't interbreed."

Eli tugged at her hand. "Mom! Boat! Big boat!"

Lilah looked up and saw a freighter pass them en route to the dock in Seward. Men were at work in one of the containers stacked on deck. She squinted at the name on the bow. The *Star of Bali*. Such a pretty name for such an ugly ship.

"If you'll look up on the cliff above us, you'll see a couple of bald eagles—"

on board the *star of bali*

"IT'S VERY SIMPLE, REALLY," Ja said, watching the nose of the missile point toward the sky. "My nation is in serious need of an invasion. Your government used the bombings in New York and your capital to launch a war in the Middle East. If I detonate this weapon"—he patted the undercarriage of the Scud—"in an area with a military presence responsible for protecting most of the North Pacific Ocean, your nation will take this as an act of war. Especially when they learn that North Korea is behind the attack. Which they will, as your people discover the evidence I have left behind."

Ja smiled at Hugh. "And you have thirty-seven thousand very conveniently placed soldiers just over the border, ready to lead the charge. I imagine it won't take long."

"Why do this?" Hugh said. "Why not take it into the heart of Kim Jong Il's palace in Pyongyang and blow him to bits? He's your problem, not us."

"We will need help in rebuilding," Ja said.

"You certainly will," Hugh said, "and we're just the folks to do it. Look how well we're doing in Iraq."

Ja continued to regard him with a tranquil expression. "When did you find me out?"

Hugh saw no reason not to tell him. The longer they spent talking, the longer Hugh stayed alive. "Last October I got word of your meeting with Fang and Noortman. I've been tracking you since then."

Ja gave him an approving smile. One of the men said something to him. "Fire when ready," he said almost casually.

"No!" Hugh said, and stumbled forward to do something, anything.

"Help me," Ja said to one of the men, and they took Hugh by the hands and feet and tossed him out of the container. Hugh landed hard and awkwardly. He heard something crack, and he didn't think it was anything he'd landed on.

Over the wind and the waves he could hear men shouting. Over the shouting he could hear the engine of the missile ignite. "No!" he shouted, and grabbed something to haul himself to his feet.

He was on the starboard side of the *Star of Bali* and was the first on board the freighter to see the *Sojourner Truth* bearing down at flank speed, cutting through the green swells like a juggernaut.

He couldn't be sure, but he thought he heard screaming over the ship's loudspeaker in what he thought was Mandarin. "We surrender! U.S. Coast Guard, U.S. Coast Guard, we surrender! I am a citizen of Hong Kong! I demand asylum! Take me with you!"

Now there was screaming and swearing from the container. A man appeared in front of him with a very large weapon he didn't recognize, but then he'd never been much of a one for firearms. The man raised the weapon to his shoulder.

"No," Hugh said, this time to more purpose, and threw himself at the man. This yo-yo was not going to get any free shots at Sara. They crashed to the deck in a horrible tangle.

But Sara had provided for that, too, as he heard the distant chatter of an automatic weapon and heavy thuds began sounding in the containers all around him. The man beneath him tried to club him with the stock of his weapon but it was too long to maneuver between them. Hugh, trying to pull away before the two ships hit, was helped when whoever was at the wheel—Fang? It would explain the Mandarin—yanked at the rudder in an attempt to get out of the cutter's way. The deck listed to starboard and Hugh let gravity do the rest, breaking into a stumbling run between the containers toward the port side of the ship.

He was knocked off his feet when three thousand tons of Coast Guard cutter crashed into the *Star of Bali*. It was louder than any 747 he'd ever heard on takeoff. It shook like the biggest earthquake he'd ever been in.

Time seemed to proceed in slow motion. The ship shuddered. Metal tore and screeched and groaned. A man fell from above, and then another. The man with the weapon had chased Hugh to the port rail. He lost his balance and his back hit the railing. Momentum flipped him over the side.

He let go of the weapon in a frantic attempt to grab something to halt his fall. What he grabbed was the front of Hugh's Mustang suit, pulling Hugh halfway over the railing.

Hugh tried to fight free, but the various beatings he'd taken in the last hour were catching up with him. He was overcome by a wave of dizziness and followed the man over the side.

23

MOM!" GLORIA POINTED. NEXT to her Eli watched, his eyes wide, his hand clutching hers.

"I saw, honey," Lilah said, pale.

They'd all seen, an almost front-row seat, a U.S. Coast Guard cutter, apparently deliberately, ram a freighter in the middle of Resurrection Bay. The boat was listing to port as everyone on board leaned against the port rail and stared, most of them with their mouths open.

"There are people going into the water," Lilah said, and turned to wave frantically at the bridge where the skipper stood with his mouth open. "There are people going into the water! We have to pick them up!"

on board the *sojourner truth*

"BULL'S-EYE, CAPTAIN," OPS CALLED out, "dead amidships."

There was no cheering on board the bridge of the *Sojourner Truth*. They could clearly see the nose of the missile pointing skyward from the container. They could also see the smoke from the fuel pouring out of the opposite end of the container.

"We weren't in time!" Mark Edelen shouted.

There was a groan. "No," someone said. "This isn't happening."

All they could do now was watch.

The momentum of the freighter continued forward, dragging the cutter down the freighter's starboard hull. The skin of the other ship punctured and peeled back.

"There goes another compartment," someone said.

"And another."

The force of the strike had pushed the freighter's starboard side down. "She's shipping water," the chief said.

"That missile is launching!" Ops shouted.

Sara, hands clenched on the arms of her chair, watched with dread.

And then the weight of all the water that had been pouring into the gaping wound in the freighter's side began to move. The *Star of Bali* began to roll to the left, slowly at first, through vertical and then heavily to port. The containers on deck began to break loose and fall off. The one with the missile in it clung stubbornly to its fastenings.

"Helm amidships, emergency full astern!" Sara shouted.

"Helm amidships, emergency full astern, aye," Cornell said imperturbably. The engines of the *Sojourner Truth* paused for a moment and then started again, grumbling at first, then opening into a full-throttle roar.

Sara leaped from her chair and ran out onto the starboard wing. The freighter's natural stability was trying to regain the vertical. The weight of the water she had shipped through the holes torn in her side wouldn't allow it, pushing her over on her starboard side again. The weight of the steel in her hold increased the speed and violence of the roll.

The missile launched, with the *Star of Bali* starboard side down, the momentum of the roll giving impetus to the launch, like a kid throwing a rock with a sling.

"Come on," the chief muttered behind her. "Come on."

"Oh my God," Tommy said steadily and clearly, "I am heartily sorry for having offended Thee, and I detest all my sins—"

Sara rounded on Ops with such a ferocious expression that he backed up a step. "It's got an internal gyroscope, right? It can correct its own course?"

Ops was pale. "If it gains enough height—"

The contrail of the exhaust seemed to twist and turn on itself.

"—because I dread the loss of heaven—"

Sara raised the binoculars she had thought to snatch on her way outside. The mountains behind the missile loomed large. Were they large enough? "Thumb Cove," she said. "Thumb Cove, how high are the mountains in back of it?" Too late to go check, too late—

For agonizing seconds the missile looked as if it would clear the landmass. Sara tried to think what it could hit, and how she could warn them. Valdez, and the oil terminal? Cordova? Would it go inland? Or could it still self-correct its course in midair? If it did, did it have enough fuel to still make Elmendorf and Anchorage? Would it fall short? If it did, where would it fall?

"—and the pains of hell—"

Then it hit, the very tip of the tallest mountain in its way. The jagged corner of the peak crumbled like a too-dry Christmas cookie. A huge fireball flared and vanished, followed by an even huger cloud of snow. Avalanche, Sara thought, and then realized she'd said the word out loud.

"Glacier," Ops said, and backed up to lean against the bulkhead next to the hatch. "There's a bunch of glaciers in back of Thumb Cove."

"But most of all," Tommy said, "because I thought you weren't watching. I was wrong. Thanks, God."

The sound of the impact reached them then, a thunderbolt that echoed across Resurrection Bay. Lilah and Gloria and Eli heard it on board the *Kenai Fjords.* A crew of fishermen heard it on board the *Moira P.,* trolling for white kings off the Iron Door. The prisoners at Spring Creek Correctional Facility heard it, and in Seward it brought people out of their homes and offices to look south and wonder. The deafening blast rolled up Resurrection Bay in a mighty wave that crashed against the bowl of mountains and triggered massive avalanches of snow. Birds launched themselves into the air, crying in alarm, and every otter, seal, and sea lion sought shelter beneath the surface of the water.

"Captain!" Ops shouted, pointing. "The freighter!"

The bridge crew turned as one to look.

The thrust of the missile's propulsion system had put the *Star of Bali* down by the stern, her taffrail awash.

"What's happening, captain?" Tommy said, coming out on the wing to watch.

"She's got two million gallons of water sloshing around inside her, pushing her back and forth," Sara said quietly.

The chief looked almost sorrowful. "She's got all that steel in her hold, too. And with all the boxes broken off she doesn't have any weight left on deck, so no help there."

Some of the containers that had broken off were floating away, some were crashing against the sides of the freighter. The *Sojourner Truth* was pulling away at her maximum speed in reverse, a lofty four knots.

Not quick enough not to watch the *Star of Bali* slide backward into the sea, though, her engine pushing the hull around in a semicircle. The bow slipped beneath the water with a resigned sigh.

They watched, mesmerized, as air bubbled up. The remaining containers broke off and bobbed up to the surface one and two and three at a time. Life rafts self-inflated and exploded twenty feet in the air, smacking down again.

"There are people in the water, XO," Ops said, looking through binoculars.

"They're alive?" Sara said. "How could they still be alive after this long in the water?"

The lieutenant looked at her. "It's only been ninety seconds, Captain."

Sara looked at the clock. He was right.

"Damage control, report," she said into the handheld.

"Damage control reporting, Captain!" Chief Moran yelled over the handheld with the sound of rushing water in the background. "The bow's all torn up! The portside bow is buckled all the way back to the collision bulkhead! We'll shore it up, slow down the flooding, but she won't last long, especially in heavy seas!"

"Understood," Sara said. "Carry on."

"Aye aye, Captain!"

She went back into the bridge and got on the pipe. "All hands, all hands, this is the XO. Brace for collision, I say again, brace for collision. We have sustained serious damage to the bow and we're going to put her ashore so we can keep our feet dry. This is the last time, folks, I promise. Grab hold and hang on, it won't be long."

She went back out on the starboard bridge wing. They were proceeding in reverse back down Resurrection Bay and into the cove formed by the middle and northern peaks on Fox Island. There was a good beach there, made of nice, solid gravel with a steep incline that Sara hoped would serve to adequately ground the *Sojourner Truth* and keep her from sinking altogether.

The cutter was shuddering, as if with disbelief at this outrage perpetrated against her. Sara rested her hands lightly on the railing. It was folly to anthropomorphize wood and steel, but she heard herself whispering anyway, "I'm sorry. I'm so sorry."

She was facing aft, in the direction the ship was traveling. The northeastern point of the island began to curve around the ship in a granite embrace. The beach was rapidly approaching. "Tommy?"

Tommy's voice came over the loudspeaker. "All hands, brace for impact, I say again, brace for—"

Sara grabbed the railing, braced her feet, and held on.

The propellers hit first. Sara was knocked off her feet by the vibration. The keel hit next in a grinding, shrieking protest of steel over rock.

In her mind's eye Sara followed the action in the engine room as the EO pulled all the stops and ordered his crew out in case of fire or flood or both. She pulled herself upright. "Tommy, let go the anchors!"

There was no corresponding reply. "Tommy! Let go the anchors!"

Tommy's head poked out of the hatch. "Uh, we can try, Captain. But . . ."

Sara met Tommy's apologetic expression and realized that when she ordered the *Sojourner Truth* to ram the *Star of Bali* the anchors had probably been pushed into the emergency bulkhead along with the bow. She staggered forward and looked out over the bow to see the deck crew clinging to cleats and stanchions. The *Sojourner Truth*'s hull settled.

And then there was silence.

The chief picked himself up off the deck, looking white and shaken. "I don't ever want to have to do that again, Captain."

"Me, either," Sara said, trying to smile, and then turned away quickly, before he could see the tears in her eyes.

• • •

MUSTANG SUIT OR NOT, Hugh was already numb with cold when the life raft exploded out of the water not a foot from his head. Floating on his back, he watched it shoot into the sky, where it seemed to hover for a moment or two. It fell back into the water with a mighty smack.

It took a moment to realize that salvation was at hand. When that moment came, he paddled clumsily over to the raft and began a laborious ascent over its side. Every muscle screamed as he hoisted himself up with the aid of the rope threaded around the raft's gunnel. As he was somersaulting inside he saw with mild surprise that another man was climbing over the opposite side of the raft.

They tumbled in together and lay on their backs, staring at the sky and gasping like stranded fish. Hugh raised his head and looked at the other man. He looked familiar. It took a while—everything seemed to be moving in slow motion—but eventually he figured out why. "Why, hello there, Mr. Fang," he said, and then had to repeat it in Mandarin.

Fang's face twisted. Hugh tensed instinctively. If Fang had had a weapon, he would have killed Hugh on the spot. Instead, he doubled over and began coughing up seawater.

Hugh relaxed again and lay where he was, wondering somewhat dreamily if perhaps he should search the raft for some way to restrain the pirate. He didn't want to move, though. He was just starting to warm up.

A shadow came up beside them and belatedly he became aware of the sound of an engine. Something hit the side of the raft.

"Hey," someone shouted, "grab the line!"

He looked up to see a row of faces peering down at him from the side of a small cruise ship.

He blinked at one of them. "Lilah?"

• • •

A FISHING BOAT SKIPPERED by a crusty old fart
was the first to arrive off the *Sojourner Truth's* bow. He'd
never seen anything like it in all his born days, nosiree-
bob. Oh, it was a woman commander? That went a long
way toward explaining things. Our tax dollars at work.
Sure, he'd let someone board to use the radio. The deck
crew jury-rigged a bosun's chair and Ops slid down in it
to the fishing boat and disappeared into the old fart's
cabin.

After the first flurry of orders, Sara subsided into her
chair on the bridge and watched numbly as the crew went
about the tasks of making the ship as secure as possible
and to alert command to their present location. Any
minute now she expected to see a fleet of aircraft coming
over the horizon like the leading edge of an invading
army. She ought to go below, inspect the damage, check
on the injured.

Hugh was gone. No matter how many times she repeated the words she could not quite believe them. Hugh
was gone, and she was alone. No more shared suffering
through required parental visits home to Seldovia. No
more fights over who had to move where when one of
them got transferred. No more quickies in hotel rooms.

No more Hugh. How could she still be breathing? How
could she still be here, when he was not?

She became aware of the tears running down her face
and of Mark Edelen standing nearby, looking helpless
and not a little frightened. "XO—"

"Let her alone." Tommy's voice was almost unrecognizable, rough and loud. "Just let her alone, Chief."

So they did, leaving her bent over in the captain's
chair, tears dripping off her chin and into her lap. After a
while she stopped seeing them as they moved around her,
stopped hearing their voices when they spoke.

Sometime later she felt a tap on her shoulder. She looked up to see Ops standing in front of her with a concerned look on his face. His mouth moved, but she couldn't make out the words. She shook her head tiredly and put up her palm to fend him off.

He wouldn't go. She knew a tiny spark of anger, immediately quenched by grief.

"Come with me, ma'am," he said, and put a hand beneath her elbow to assist her out of the chair.

"What—" she started to say.

"Please come with me, ma'am," he said with unaccustomed firmness, and such was her state of mind that it was easier to follow him off the bridge and down the outside stairs to the main deck.

He led her to the bow. There were a half dozen small boats clustered around them by now, fishing boats and a couple of skiffs. A small cruise ship had a line to what was left of the cutter's bow, its foredeck all but obscured by a crowd of paying passengers gaping at a sight that for sure hadn't been on the itinerary.

Ops said something.

Sara could not make it out. "What?"

Ops took her firmly by the shoulders and turned her in the direction of the cruise ship. He pointed over her shoulder so that she had no choice but to follow the direction of his finger.

She couldn't see what Ops thought was so important. There must have been fifty people on board the little cruise ship. Who went for a boat ride for fun in January?

And then she saw his face staring up at her, wet hair matted on his brow, eyes intent on hers, a smile of such joy breaking across his face.

The next thing she knew she was balanced on the gunnel and reaching for the rope mooring the cruise ship to the *Sojourner Truth*. She grabbed the line with both hands without a thought to seeing if it was on belay and launched herself from the cutter, swinging into space over the water.

There were alarmed shouts from both ships. She ignored them, wrapping her ankles around the line and going down hand over hand so fast that later she found rope burns on her palms.

She hit the deck of the little cruise ship and before she had regained her balance she was in his arms.

EPILOGUE

march
washington, d.c.

EVERYONE WAS THERE, FROM the secretary of state to all of the Joint Chiefs, even though no one was ever going to be allowed to admit to attending.

"How many killed?" said the representative from the Senate Armed Services Committee.

They looked at the Coast Guard captain, a nondescript man of middle age with a carefully cultivated air of dullness. "Seven killed. Thirteen wounded. Those are just our own casualties, you understand. There are ninety-seven crew members on the *Agafia* and eighteen on the *Star of Bali* yet to be accounted for."

"Who is handling the interrogation of the surviving terrorists?"

The FBI agent said, "That's us, sir. It's slow going but we're getting some good stuff from the hired hands. I think we'll have a pretty solid report for you soon."

"What about the missile?"

"The wreckage has been recovered."

"And the payload?"

"The payload was dispersed upon impact and detonation."

"Dispersed where?" This question came a little more sharply.

The FBI agent looked at the Coast Guard captain, who looked at the mad scientist on his right. His hair looked more Donald Trump than Albert Einstein and he wasn't really mad, but when your job was primarily providing worst-case scenarios it helped if the people to whom you were delivering them thought so. "Impact was about twelve miles south of Seward, in Spoon Glacier, at an elevation of about twelve hundred feet. There was a steady onshore wind of fifteen to twenty knots. The cesium-137 was dispersed across the northern half of Resurrection Bay. We estimate that the fallout would disperse most heavily on the maximum security prison on the east side of the bay, but that the wind was blowing strongly enough that some of it would have reached the town. However, not in such quantities as to prove an immediate hazard to the health of anyone living there."

For those who were listening for it, the stress on the word "immediate" was readily apparent. No one commented on it, though.

"So that's good news, then," the president's man said. "Nothing that can't be explained as a conventional missile. No reason to tell anyone otherwise." He looked around the table for opposition to this eminently sensible viewpoint and of course found none.

The mad scientist made a noncommital noise. His report had gone in days before, and the president's man knew full well that it would be years before the effects of the fallout would be known. The cesium had dispersed over a wide area covered with snow and ice that would melt into streams and rivers and flow eventually to the bay and the sound. In the meantime, the Centers for Disease Control would maintain a quiet watch through local clinics to monitor the health of the community, in particular the incidence of cancer.

"Very well," the president's man said with satisfaction, "our line will be that a terrorist attempt to attack the homeland was unsuccessful due to the diligence of our own counterterrorism forces, who had the operation under continuous surveillance from the moment of its inception. When the terrorists were discovered, they fired off the missile prematurely in the hope of doing random damage. Due to the vigilance and skill of the United States Coast Guard"—he inclined his head toward the Coast Guard captain—"no such damage was suffered." He shrugged. "There was no serious threat to the public at any time." He cocked an eyebrow. No one contradicted him, but the Air Force general was displaying less enthusiasm than he liked to see. "General? Something you wanted to share with the rest of the group?"

The Air Force general raised his head. "Why Anchorage? There are half a dozen ports on the West Coast with military bases to target and far more people to kill, and therefore that much bigger a message to send. Why Anchorage?"

"We weren't looking for them to attack Anchorage for precisely those reasons," the man from the CIA said. "I think it's fair to say they took that into account in their planning of the attack." He shrugged. "And besides. It's Anchorage. What's more, it's Alaska. Most Americans think Alaska floats off the southwest coast of California, right next to Hawaii, with occasional appearances on the Discovery Channel."

There was a rich chuckle all around at this witticism. When it died down, the man from the White House looked at the man from the CIA. "And the motivation behind this attack?"

The agent shook his head. "Not what you would have expected, sir, not at all. For one thing, the Ja brothers seem to have acted independently."

There was instant and vocal skepticism, and the CIA agent had to raise his voice to be heard. "That's what Ja Bae-ho is claiming, sir, and so far his story hangs together."

"They were al-Qaida trained," said the army general. "Bin Laden's got his own fleet of ships. Didn't you say you couldn't trace the owner of this freighter?"

The CIA man met the general's contemptuous look with a bland expression. "Ja Bae-ho makes a very convincing case that this was a personal mission, General."

"Then where did they get the money to finance this operation?"

"We don't know yet, sir. We have some leads, which we are tracing now, and—"

The general glared. "Yeah, well, I know, and I don't need to trace any so-called leads and neither does anyone else in this room with half a brain." His tone made it clear that he was excluding the CIA's man from that number.

"Ladies, gentlemen," the representative from the White House said, and everyone shut up. "This was too close. We must take steps to see that it never happens again."

"Sir—" the Coast Guard representative said.

"Stir up your service, Captain. Come up with some recommendations for the defense of the coastline and our ports that we can put into effect immediately. What almost happened here is deeply disturbing to every thinking member of this committee. Thank you all for coming."

The audience was at an end. The crowd dispersed. The representative from the White House lingered to talk to the Coast Guard captain who had given the briefing. The captain concentrated on gathering up the handouts, perhaps two of which had been looked at by the attendees.

"Imagine," the man from the White House said, chewing reflectively on the earpiece of his reading glasses, "they almost pulled it off, they almost sailed that puppy right into an American port and set off a dirty bomb that if detonated would have taken out nearly three hundred thousand people and rendered a strategic air force base and an entire city uninhabitable for years to come."

The captain closed his briefcase.

"This is going to happen again, isn't it, Captain."

It wasn't really a question, but the Coast Guard captain answered it anyway. "Yes, sir, it is."

CAPTAIN LOWE WAS BURIED with full military honors in his hometown of Valentine, Nebraska, his wife, son, and two daughters present. His wife was presented with the flag that had draped his coffin and she accepted it, dry-eyed, as her daughters wept quietly and her son stared straight ahead with a stony face.

HELMSMAN EUGENE RAZO WAS buried with much more fanfare and ten times the family members present in his hometown of Kodiak. His fiancée's family hosted a memorial potlatch that is still remembered for its cornucopia of food and the amount and quality of the gifts given those who attended. His parents started a scholarship fund in his name at the University of Alaska, and the response was such that they were able to fund a full ride for one student the very first year. Five years later his fiancée married Hank Ryan, by then a lieutenant commander, who had kept in touch.

THE BODIES OF THE Coasties who were killed on board the *Star of Bali* were never recovered. Their families were told that their sons and daughters had died in the performance of their duty.

THE FORMAL THANKS OF the United States was offered to Greenpeace's headquarters in Amsterdam for the assistance their ship, the *Sunrise Warrior,* had rendered the *Sojourner Truth* and the nation in the taking of the *Agafia.* The *Sunrise Warrior* was ordered to the nearest port, Dutch Harbor, and Vivienne Kincaid and Dylan Doyle were summarily fired. A new campaign manager and ship's master were flown to Dutch and sailed back to the Maritime Boundary Line, where they stayed for another month, harassing Russian fish processors and making life hell for the Coast Guard cutter assigned to patrol there.

LIEUTENANTS SAMS AND LAIRD and Airman Cho crashed their helo on the shore of Cape Navarin, where they were rescued by a Siberian Yupik Eskimo on a snow machine and taken to his village. They were there for a week before they were found by the Russian authorities, and Lieutenant Sams later became famous for his vivid descriptions of the tastes of fermented seal and dried whale blubber. Upon their return, Airman Steven Cho resigned from the Coast Guard and entered a Trappist monastery in California.

THE PIRATES AND MERCENARIES were arrested and taken into custody in Seward by a planeload of FBI agents led by Kyle Chase. Ja Bae-ho was removed to an undisclosed location, probably Guantánamo, and under the new Homeland Security Act application of individual rights was being held indefinitely without bail or representation. His uncle died later that year, but he never knew it.

• • •

THE BODIES OF TERRORISTS, mercenaries, and ship's crew floated ashore in Resurrection Bay for months following the incident. Ja Yong-Bae's body was not among them.

The younger Noortman's leg healed, although he would walk with a slight limp for the rest of his life. He remained in Hong Kong doing contract work for various organizations, some legal, some not. A year after the events recorded here he was recruited by a Russian mafia don who wanted to expand his empire into maritime shipping. He never did track down the true owners of the *Agafia*.

PETER WOLF NEVER RETURNED to Odessa. There was a Pedro Lobo who surfaced in Rio de Janeiro a year later. He was joined by a ravishing young Russian woman who lavished affection on him and then disappeared with a substantial portion of his more liquid assets, including a handful of uncut diamonds from the wall safe, the combination of which he had been so unwise as to give her. He took it well. "At least she left me enough to live on," he said, and was soon seen in the clubs with another, even more ravishing girl from the Philippines.

No evidence was ever found to connect the Ja brothers to the bombing of his office.

WHEN LAST HEARD FROM, Arlene Harte was in Anaktuvuk Pass, Alaska, writing a column about the annual migration of the Western Arctic caribou herd. Knight-Ridder has made an offer for a syndicated column, and she is considering it.

IN MAY ENSIGN HANK Ryan was promoted to lieutenant and given command of a one-hundred-ten-footer out of Pensacola, Florida. Ensign Robert Ostlund took early retirement with a medical disability. Ensign Reese was promoted to lieutenant, junior grade. Seamen Delgado and Lewis were promoted to petty officers. Chief Mark Edelen put in for retirement and invested in a marina in Corpus Christi.

FIVE YEARS LATER, LILAH Chase was diagnosed with a virulent case of pancreatic cancer. She died two weeks later, in great pain. Shortly thereafter Eli Chase was diagnosed with leukemia. He survived.

july
washington, d.c.

"IT REALLY IS OVAL," Sara said, looking around her.

"Ye-ees," the flunky said. "The president will be right with you, Commander, Admiral."

"Thank you," Sara said politely. She seemed incapable of being anything but these days. She limped forward with the aid of a cane. It turned out she had cracked her right fibula when the *Sojourner Truth* went aground on Fox Island, and in the press of business hadn't noticed. It was taking a tiresomely long time to heal.

Admiral Elwood "Woodie" Long, commandant of the U.S. Coast Guard and no fool, gave her a penetrating look and held his peace.

Sure enough, a few minutes later the president walked in and exchanged handshakes and backslaps with Admiral Long, who then introduced Sara. Sara accepted the president's hand and stared at the face usually seen at the top of the hour on CNN and pretended to listen to his words of praise with a pleasant, attentive expression.

She became aware of silence and realized that the

president had stopped speaking. "Thank you very much, sir," she said gravely, and looked at the admiral, waiting for the signal to go.

"I mean it, Commander," the president said, who seemed like a nice man, only very insistent on getting and keeping her attention. He smiled. "I heard you backed your cutter onto the beach. Is that true?"

"Yes, sir," she said, still polite. "We lost the bow when we rammed the freighter. It was the only way."

His smile widened. "An inspired solution." He sighed, his smile fading. "I wish we could acknowledge your heroism, Commander, and that of your crew, but we feel at the present time that it would be most unwise to allow this story to be told. Later, perhaps, when the country is less unsettled . . ."

"I quite understand, sir," Sara said, looking at the admiral again.

"Anything we can do, Commander," the president said, "say the word."

Sara smiled her bright, shiny smile and took the offer for what it was, a politeness, a courtesy, meaningless.

And then, halfway through the door, she turned. "Mr. President?"

He looked up from his desk, around which more flunkies had begun to gather like moths to a flame. "Yes, Commander?"

"There is something you could do for me."

The admiral put his hand on Sara's elbow. She shook it off.

The president missed these cues and smiled at them both. He really would like to do something for her. Yes, a nice man. "What's that, Commander?"

"Fire your CIA director," Sara said. "He's too dumb to live."

• • •

IN THE CAR THE admiral said heavily, "You just kissed your two-eighty goodbye, Commander."

"Yes, sir," Sara said.

"I'll do what I can, but . . ."

"Yes, sir."

august
london

THE BRITISH AIRWAYS 747 taxied up to the gate at Heathrow, and passengers, weary from five hours of sitting with their knees jammed up against the seatback in front of them, began to disembark, stumbling a little from sheer exhaustion.

Sara went through immigration, where the officer raised his eyebrows when he saw her Coast Guard identification. "A sailor, are you?" he said as he stamped her passport and handed it back to her.

"I was," she said.

She got her luggage and walked unmolested through customs. At the arrivals gate, she paused, looking around. She had been told that she would be met.

"Hi, Sara."

She turned. "Hugh." She felt a glad rush, and put her face up to be kissed. He looked like she felt, older and by some indefinable measure less idealistic, as if he had lost his innocence.

He, too, was leaning on a cane. "Look," he said, holding it up. "Matching outfits."

"I thought you were in D.C. lobbying for a transfer to the U.S. embassy in London," she said. "What are you doing here?"

"I'm meeting my wife. I told your office I'd pick you

up." He looked at her epaulets and whistled. "A full commander now, I see. Congratulations."

"Thanks."

"I've got a taxi. I bribed a security guard to let it wait for us out front. This way." He gestured with his cane. "So," he said, "the nation's representative to the International Maritime Organization. That's pretty impressive."

"I wanted a ship," she said.

"You always want a ship, Sara," he said, holding the door.

The sun was shining outside, warm on their faces.

"Here," he said, stopping by a black London taxi. The driver got out and helped stow her bags.

"This is going to cost a fortune," she said.

"That's okay. I've got plenty of money," he said.

She looked at him. "Since when?"

"Since I quit and cashed out my retirement."

They climbed into the cab and settled in behind their luggage. "Where to, mates?" the driver said looking in the rearview mirror, and Hugh gave him an address. "Righto," the driver said happily, and they pulled into traffic.

All Sara could think to say was, "Why, Hugh? It was your dream job."

"Not much point in working for them if they won't listen to me. Because, as you know, I'm always right."

Another ghost of a smile. Encouraged, he said ruefully, "Besides, I wasn't getting all kinds of encouragement to hang around. The director seemed suddenly to have taken a dislike to me. I can't understand it myself, but there it is."

"What are you going to do?"

He smiled at her. "I'll think of something." He changed the subject. "Is it true that you told the president to shove it?"

She was honestly shocked. "No! Where did you hear that?"

"The O'Reilly Factor."

She relaxed. "Oh. Well. Consider the source."

"Also the *New York Times,* the *Washington Post,* the *Chicago Tribune,* the—"

She waved a hand. "Okay. Okay. I may have said a little something."

He nodded, as if she had confirmed something he already knew. "And," he said softly, "it cost you your ship." He looked at her. "Defending me."

She looked out at the passing fields, at the airplanes above lining up for final approach into Heathrow. "Where are we going?"

This time he let her change the subject. "I've found a flat in Kensington."

"That was quick."

"I sublet it from a Brit, a diplomatic type who got transferred to South Africa. It's not very big, but it's got all the modern conveniences, and it's a short bus ride from your office."

Sheep and cows and horses flashed by, their noses buried in the lush green grass. She rolled down the window and breathed deeply of the aromas of manure and airplane exhaust. No salt tang to the air here.

At least she was on an island. She would never be far away from the sea.

"About the flat," Hugh said.

She turned to meet his eyes. "What about it?"

"I was thinking," he said, "that we could share it."

ACKNOWLEDGMENTS

I COULD NOT HAVE WRITTEN this novel without the sixteen days I spent on patrol on the United States Coast Guard medium endurance cutter *Alex Haley* in the Bering Sea in February 2004. My entirely inadequate thanks to Commander Craig Barkley Lloyd and his superb crew for putting up with my colossal ignorance and my million questions. It was an honor, a privilege, and a joy to be on board.

Going above and beyond the call, Commander Lloyd and CPO Marshalena Delaney fact-checked the manuscript. Aviator Lieutenant Dan Leary helped me get the vertical insertion right after I horrified both him and Commander Lloyd with the suggestion of a controlled crash. Any errors which remain, by accident or design, are mine alone.

My infinite gratitude goes to my editor, Kelley Ragland, who took this manuscript out to the woodshed and beat all the errors in chronology and character out of it. A good editor's price is far above rubies.

My thanks also to my agent, Rich Henshaw, who kept insisting I write a thriller. Now that I have, maybe he'll leave me alone.

I first read about modern pirates in Richard Halliburton's *The Royal Road to Romance,* and much later in John McPhee's *Looking for a Ship.* William Langewiesche's "Anarchy at Sea" in the September 2003 *At-*

lantic Monthly was an invaluable overview of what is happening on the world's oceans today, as was his book, *The Outlaw Sea*.

Peter Landesman's "Arms and the Man" in the August 17, 2003, *New York Times* was an excellent introduction to the international arms trade. Especially helpful on the subject of North and South Korea were Jonathan Kandell's "Korea: A House Divided" in the July 2003 *Smithsonian* magazine and Philip Gourevitch's "Alone in the Dark" in the September 8, 2003, *New Yorker* magazine.

Kieran Mulvaney's *The Whaling Season* is a matter-of-fact first-person account of the Greenpeace fight to end commercial whaling, and Kieran was kind enough to answer more of my questions. Special Agent Eric Gonzales of the Federal Bureau of Investigation helped me understand much about the FBI's antiterrorism efforts, both foreign and domestic. Robert R. Kresge (CIA, retired) provided insight into the workings of the Central Intelligence Agency.

Researcher Sherry Merryman helped get me started on all of the above. Thanks to Chris Carlson and Jo Carlson for naming the *Sunrise Warrior*. Jim Kemper, world's greatest meteorologist, conjured me up yet another magnificent and terrifying Aleutian storm. USCG Commander Robert Forgit briefed me on USCG operations in Anchorage and introduced me to Port of Anchorage operations manager Stuart Greydanus, who gave me the dollar-and-a-quarter tour, after which I repaid them by doing my best to blow it up, fortunately only in fiction. Chief Engineer Bruce Sherman toured me over the CSX *Anchorage* twice, which he may not be pleased to know helped my pirates no end.

Special thanks go to librarian Nancy Clark, who found me the perfect ordnance, and to marine pilot Don Ryan, whose help with the bang-bang part of the kiss-kiss-bang-bang ending was inspired and invaluable. It is safe to say that I wouldn't have been as successful at nearly destroying Elmendorf and Anchorage without them.

Turn the page for a preview of

THE DEEPER SLEEP

The exciting new novel by DANA STABENOW—available in hardcover from St. Martin's Minotaur

Sec. 11.41.100. Murder in the First Degree.

(a) A person commits the crime of murder in the first degree if

(1) with intent to cause the death of another person, the person

(A) causes the death of any person . . .

—Alaska statutes

S HE'D HAD TO SPELL the word *weary* in a spelling bee in grade school. She'd spelled it correctly, but she'd never really understood what it meant, until now. It sounded like what it meant—there was a word for that, too, but she couldn't remember it—and she was weary, weary from the marrow of her bones out. If he would just let her sleep one night all the way through, if he would just let the old bruises heal before he gave her new ones, if she could just have one single moment in the day to think, to rest, to be.

At first his roughness had been exciting, from the very first time when his hands shackled her wrists over her head, his knees forcing hers wide, the foreign invasion so shocking, his eyes narrowed and intent, and then the rush of feeling that spread out and up in a searing flush that seemed to melt down to the base of her brain. He enjoyed making her body rise to his; she could see it in the triumph in his face. In those early days—how many months was it now?—when she had said no, he had always been able to seduce her into a yes, always.

Now he didn't even seem to hear the no.

She wondered when Ekaterina would come out to visit again. In spite of the old woman's obvious disapproval of her marriage, of her husband, which always provoked retaliation after she left, her visits offered a respite. He couldn't hit her when Ekaterina was there.

She'd been coming out more often lately. Maybe she'd come tomorrow.

Next to her the bed heaved and feet hit the floor. She lay unmoving, willing herself to disappear beneath the covers.

Maybe Ekaterina would come today.

He stripped them back. "You aren't asleep. Get up and get down to the creek."

When she didn't move as fast as he thought she ought to, he kicked her off the bed.

She thumped onto the floor and scrambled to her feet and scurried to the door. She reached for her parka.

"You don't need that," he said, handing her a bucket. "Get going. I want my coffee."

She slid into boots barefoot and opened the door of the cabin. She gasped when the bitter February air hit her lungs, and shivered in her nightgown.

A hard hand shoved her off the step. "Get a move on, you lazy bitch!"

She stumbled down the path to the creek. It was frozen over. She took the axe leaning against a nearby spruce and chopped a hole. She squatted over it, dipping the bucket into the clear, cold water beneath.

A sound made her look up, but she wasn't quick enough. Something hit the back of her head. In the seconds she had left, she felt a starburst of pain, and knew only an astonished relief that it was finally over. It was with gratitude that she fell forward into a welcoming black eternity.

A quick hand moved the bucket out of the way so that her head dropped through the hole she had chopped in the ice.

The soft splash when her face hit the water was the gentlest kiss she ever received.

ONE

January
Niniltna

THIS IS JUST WRONG, on so many levels, Jim thought.

For one thing, he was freezing his butt off. Even if the front of him was plenty warm.

For another, his boss might legitimately qualify his current activity as a colossal waste of Jim's time, not to mention the taxpayer's dollar. Crime had yet to be committed anywhere near or about his person.

If you didn't count the one he was about to commit if Kate kept rubbing up against him like that.

Her head was a very nice fit beneath his chin, even if her hair did tickle. She shifted again, and when he spoke, his voice was a little hoarse. "Are you sure you didn't get me out here under false pretenses, Shugak?"

He heard the smile in her voice when she replied, felt the warmth of her breath on his throat. "Well, since it seems crime is the only thing that makes my company tolerable to you, I figured I'd find some."

He disregarded what she said for what she meant. "I'm not afraid of you."

She stirred and tilted her head back to meet his eyes. "I make you want to run away like a little girl."

"You do not." It sounded weak, even to him.

She leaned back against him, warm and firm from chest to knee, and dropped her voice to a whisper roughened by the scar that bisected her throat. "Say it again. And make me believe it."

He could have told her to step away. He could have pushed her away. He did not do either of those things, and the sound of the truck coming down the trail was the only thing that saved him.

And, sadly, Jim wasn't one bit happy when Kate's focus shifted, too.

It was an elderly blue Ford pickup minus tailgate and rear bumper, its passenger-side window replaced with an interwoven layer of duct tape, the body rusting out from the tires up. The engine, however, maintained a steady, confident rumble that indicated more beneath the peeling hood than met the eye.

The homeowner had dutifully cleared the requisite thirty feet of defensible space around her house in case of forest fires, which in this era of dramatic climatic change were inclined to hit interior Alaska early and often each spring. This and the winter's meager snowfall made it easy for the pickup to crunch through the thin layer of snow on the driveway and pull around to the back of the house, where half a dozen fifty-five-gallon drums rested in an upside-down pyramid on a solidly constructed two-by-four stand, connected to each other so that the fuel from the top drums ran down into the lower drums, with the bottom drum connected to the furnace in the house by an insulated length of copper tubing.

Kate and Jim had positioned themselves in a convenient stand of alders at the edge of the clearing, so they had a clear view of Willard Shugak as he got out of his truck, disconnected the copper tubing, connected a hose to the spigot, and began to siphon off the fuel in the drums on the stand to the black barrel tank in the back of his pickup.

Kate swore beneath her breath. Jim kept his arms around her so she'd shut up and stay put. When he judged that enough fuel had been transferred from the drums to the truck's tank to merit, at the $3.41 per gallon for diesel fuel he had last seen on an Ahtna pump, the definition of theft as provided for in the Alaska statutes, specifically 11.46.100, he said, "Shall we?" and turned her loose.

Willard looked up when they emerged from the alders. When he saw Kate, he went white and then red and then white again. "Oh shit," he said, his voice an insubstantial adolescent squeal that sounded odd coming out of the mouth of a forty-year-old man.

"At least," Kate said, boiling forward.

Willard Shugak was all of six feet tall, but he dodged around Jim, keeping the trooper between him and Kate. His voice went high enough to wake up bats. "No, Kate, wait, I—"

"You moron," Kate said, forgetting for the moment that Willard was almost exactly that, "what if Auntie Balasha came home to a cold house, her pipes all froze up?"

She reached for him and Willard backpedaled, stumbling and almost losing his balance, both hands up, palms out, in a placating gesture totally lost on its intended recipient. Jim watched, delaying official law enforcement action, mostly because he was enjoying the show.

"I wasn't going to take it all, honest I wasn't."

"You're not even out of oil," Kate said, cutting back around Jim and catching the cuff of Willard's jacket. "I went out to Howie's place this morning and checked. You were going to sell it, weren't you, Willard?"

Willard yanked his arm free and darted back around Jim. "I would have paid Auntie back, honest I would!"

"Sure you would, you little weasel. Howie put you up to this because you were behind on the rent?" Kate feinted a move, Willard dodged back out of the way, and the Darth Vader action figure peeping out of his shirt pocket fell out and vanished into the churned-up snow.

Willard let out a cry of dismay. "Anakin!" He lumbered forward, his hands pawing wildly at the snow. Kate took advantage of his distraction and grabbed a handful of Willard's dirty blond hair to haul him upright.

"Ow! Kate! That hurts! Jim! Help!"

Jim had less than a second to revel in the sight of a man the size of Willard terrified by a woman the size of Kate before Mutt burst out of the undergrowth, mistook the attempted homicide for a game and romped around the three of them, barking madly while trying to catch the first available hem in her teeth.

At this point Jim, tired of feeling like base in a game of kick-the-can, grabbed Kate and Willard by the scruffs of their necks and held them apart as far as his arms would stretch. If he'd been an inch shorter, he wouldn't have been able to pull it off with near as much aplomb. "All right, you two, knock it off."

Kate kicked out with her right foot in reply, which would have connected in a meaningful way with Jim's left knee had he not moved it smartly out of range just in time. It threw him off balance, though, and Kate wriggled free and was on Willard before Jim could recover. She had Willard flat on the ground, her hands at Willard's throat and a knee in Willard's balls. Mutt divined that this was not a game after all and added her two cents' worth with snaps and snarls that came entirely too close to Willard's left ear for anyone's comfort. Willard was bawling, eyes squeezed shut, mouth wide open, face wet with a river of tears, shoulders shaking with big sloppy sobs. "I confess, I confess! Jesus, Jim, couldja please just arrest me? Please?"

"Oh, for God's sake." Kate let him go in disgust and rose to her feet, brushing snow from her pants. "Get up, you big baby. I didn't hurt you."

His eyes rolled toward Mutt, whose head was sunk beneath her shoulder blades, her impressive canines bared in a manner that could only be described as distinctly unfriendly. It was a sight made even scarier by the bloodstains and the ptarmigan feathers adhering to her muzzle, remnants of the lunch she had just finished in the next spruce copse over.

Kate made an impatient sound. "Mutt," she said.

"Graar," Mutt said to Willard, conveying a wealth of meaning in one syllable, and trotted more or less obediently to Kate's side, where she received a compensatory scratch behind her ears in lieu of bloodshed, always Mutt's preference.

Jim stretched out a hand to haul Willard to his feet for what they both sincerely hoped was the last time. Willard gulped down a sob, smeared tears and snot across his face with his shirtsleeve, and said in a plaintive voice, "Couldja guys help me find Anakin before we go to jail? Please?"

THE STATE TROOPER BUILDING in Niniltna was so new, it squeaked. In a rare decision of foresight and wisdom, the state had built it on a five-acre lot next to the Niniltna Native Association building, whose authority rolled downhill to embrace the post and whose chairman, Billy Mike, was known to Park rats as a law-and-order kind of guy. The post was a solid structure, an unthreateningly bland beige square divided into fourths, a front office, Jim's office, an interview room, and the jail, two cells big enough for a bunk and a toilet each.

Willard, Anakin tucked safely back in his shirt pocket, scooted inside and turned to watch closely as Jim locked the cell door behind him. He wrapped his meaty hands around the bars and gave them a shake. The door trembled but held. He appeared reassured, and looked at Jim, his dark brown eyes still wide. They were set far apart, giving him a fey, elfin look. It was a look seen all too often in Bush Alaska. "Kate's crazy, Jim," he said.

"Tell me about it," Jim said.

"Yeah, I heard you got a thing going with her." Willard's expression approached something like awe. "Man. You must have some kinda death wish."

"Ain't got no thing," Jim said, and he might have closed the door to the cells a little more firmly than absolutely necessary.

Kate was pacing his office, fuming. Mutt had wedged herself into a corner, her tail tucked safely behind her and her front paws as far back as she could get them.

Kate rounded on Jim as he came in. "You're going to throw the book at him this time, Chopin."

Jim sat behind his desk, shoulders very square and correct. He turned on his computer and clicked on the icon that brought up the right form. "I'm going to charge him with theft in the third degree—"

He waited out the expected eruption and continued unhurriedly. "Theft in the third degree if the value of property is between fifty and five hundred dollars. Even at third degree I'm pushing the envelope here. I know Mac Devlin's charging three seventy-five a gallon for fuel oil, but I doubt if Willard was able to pump fifty gallons before you mugged him."

Kate called Willard's legitimacy into serious question and then started in on his friends.

Again, Jim waited her out. He was prepared to be patient, for two reasons. One, there was no Alaska statute for Crimes Against Auntie, which was what Kate really wanted Willard charged with. Two, it had never done anyone a bit of good to try to match Kate Shugak in either volume or vituperation. The wisest course—he winced when she kicked one of the visitors' chairs across the room—was to wait her out.

The arm of the chair thudded into the wall. Kate glared at the resulting chip in the brand-new Sheetrock as if it were to blame. Into the gift of silence Jim said, "You know she won't press charges."

"She can decide that for herself when she gets back," Kate said with a snap.

Mutt decided that a mediating influence was called for and, albeit with some trepidation, positioned herself between the two combatants. She followed the conversation with her head, her tail wagging vigorously, as if this display of goodwill would put out the fire blazing up between her personal human and Mutt's favorite man.

"You know she won't, Kate," Jim said. "She'll shake her head and look like her heart is broken, and I'll feel like six different kinds of slime for delivering the bad news. Then she'll make me a cup of tea, and she won't forget I like honey in it, and then she'll sit down across from me and reminisce about how she babysat Willard's dad when he was little, and got a great set of pink-and-purple towels at Willard's paternal grandmother's potlatch, pink and purple, her favorite colors, and she's still

using them, they're such good-quality towels, and what a
lousy boat Willard crewed on last summer and how Alvin
Kvasnikof never does pay off his crews at anything like
what they're worth, and then she'll remember that bad
girl Priscilla Ollestad, who broke Willard's heart when
she married Cliff Moonin, and then—"

He could hear the rising exasperation in his voice and
broke off. "She won't press charges."

Kate fetched the chair she had kicked across the room
and sat down in it. She folded her arms and scowled.
"And it's only a class-A misdemeanor."

"That's all it is," he said. "And if all of that doesn't
work, she'll say it was all her fault anyway because she
couldn't get her daughter to stop drinking while she was
carrying Willard."

Gloom settled in heavily over the room. Mutt's tail
slowed. Comfort was needed. Jim was the love of her life,
in spite of that human male thing he had going on, but
Kate had time served. She laid her chin on Kate's knee
and blinked up at her with a sympathetic expression, or as
much sympathy as predatory yellow eyes could exude.

The phone rang, and it was a toss-up as to which of the
three was more relieved. "Yeah?" Jim said into the receiver. His face hardened. "Thanks."

"What?"

He put the phone down. "Jury's come back, but it's so
late, Singh is delaying hearing the verdict until the morning." He hesitated, but she'd been helpful to the investigation, with a history of Deem's past offenses. Plus she was
related to the victim somehow. She usually was. "I'll fly
to Ahtna tomorrow morning. Wanna come?"

"Are you kidding?"

"Hey?" Willard's mournful howl was muffled by the
intervening walls but perfectly understandable. "Um, I
hate to bother you guys, but Anakin and me, we're kinda

hungry?" A pause. "Maybe we could have a coupla those cookies I saw next to the coffeepot on the way in? And maybe we could have some coffee with them? Maybe with cream? And a couple three sugars? Anakin really likes his coffee sweet."

Jim closed his eyes and shook his head. "Willard Shugak could smell the filling on an Oreo cookie at a hundred yards." He got up, and Kate followed him to the outer office.

"Maggie, I'm outta here, and I won't be in tomorrow until late. Get Laurel to bring Willard some dinner, would you, please? He'll be staying with us for a few days."

Kate growled, mostly for show, and because she knew Willard was listening.

"Protective custody," Jim said.

Maggie gave Kate a wary look. "Got it, boss."

AS JIM TURNED THE Blazer around to head back to Kate's homestead, she said, "What's your prediction? On the verdict?"

The road was mostly bare, frozen gravel. "I heart global warming," Jim said, and eased up the Blazer to a steady forty miles an hour. "I stopped guessing jury verdicts after my first case, Kate."

"What happened on your first case?"

"First case that came to trial, I should have said." A bull moose sauntered out from the undergrowth and paused in the middle of the road, looking around with a distracted air, as if he were trying to remember where he had mislaid his rack. Jim tapped the brakes and flicked the headlights on bright and back again. The moose blinked at them bemusedly and then galumphed back into the undergrowth, embarrassed by his naked head.

Jim stepped cautiously on the gas, goosing her back up to speed. The Blazer rattled over the gravel base, and he had to raise his voice to be heard. "Perp and his best buddy pick up the victim on the road, try to get him to perform oral sex on them. When he won't, they shoot him nine times with a twenty-two. And then cut his throat just to be sure. Tossed the body in the city dump and hot-wired the dozer to run it over him a few times to mash him into the garbage.

"Vic was missing for four days before anyone noticed it, but amazingly enough, we had a witness who saw him get into the perp's truck, and at lineup could ID the driver and the passenger." He shrugged. "Eyewitnesses, you know . . ."

"Yeah. I know." In five and a half years as an investigator for the Anchorage district attorney's office, Kate knew that you could have five witnesses to a crime and come up with five different descriptions of the perp.

"But we found blood and hair matching the vic in the truck's cab."

"Excellent. And the gun?"

"No such luck, and of course the perp and his best bud denied everything. And then we caught a break: a bear rooting around in the dump uncovered what was left of the body when some guy was pitching out his old dishwasher. Plus, the best bud's girlfriend was mightily pissed off that we were suspecting her bright angel of anything as heinous as murder. It was all the perp's fault, she said, why were we even looking at his best bud, as the best bud got out of the car after the perp picked up the vic."

Kate silence was eloquent.

"Yeah, I know," Jim said, "nobody ever said jails are filled with smart people, and why should anybody they hang out with be any smarter? I—persuaded—the best bud to turn state's evidence."

"Excellent," Kate said again.

"Yeah."

"But."

"But." Jim sighed. "He wasn't real convincing, and he had a rap sheet it took a whole ream of paper to print out. Jury didn't believe a word he said. Hell, I didn't believe a word he said, and I knew it was all true. Well. Mostly true."

"And the perp?"

"The perp says he was out of town at the time. Real sincere on the stand, as I recall, young and clean-cut and all his family in the courtroom, including his Miss Alaska fiancée."

"Please tell me you're kidding."

"I would if I could. She spent the whole trial trying to hold hands with him over the divider."

"What happened?"

"The third time the judge told her to stop holding hands with the defendant, he raised his voice, and she burst into tears. You should have seen the jury, you'd have thought he'd just shot their pet cat."

"Not guilty?"

"Not guilty." He sighed. "The case was mostly circumstantial anyway. As I recall it, Brendan—"

"Brendan McCord was prosecuting?"

"Yeah. One of his first cases. He was good, even fresh out of law school. Brendan said a member of the jury came up to him after the verdict and scolded him for harassing that nice young man and putting his fiancée through such a terrible ordeal."

Kate had also seen the inside of her share of courtrooms, and she had very few illusions left about the wheels of justice. "What happened to the perp?"

Jim brightened a little. "Six months later, he accompanied his fiancée to the Miss America pageant in Dallas and shot a cabdriver during a robbery. He is currently enjoying the hospitality of the state of Texas at Huntsville.

One of four hundred and ten on death row, last time I checked."

Kate wondered what had happened to the fiancée and the perp's family. She always wondered what happened to the rest of the victims. It was one of the reasons she'd left the DA's office.

"So," Jim said, "I don't predict verdicts. The game is rigged, all right, but in this case the house doesn't win often enough. It's discouraging enough without letting your hopes ride on it, too."

What little snow had fallen that winter had melted off in a four-day chinook that was the lump of coal in the Park's stocking the week of Christmas. At five thirty in the afternoon, it had already been dark for an hour and a half and with nothing to reflect what light there was, anything beyond the reach of the Blazer's headlights looked like a black hole. The good news was that the road was drivable at all. It wasn't maintained in winter and normally became a snow machine track from October to May, but not this year.

Kate peered up at the sky. "Lights'll be out tonight, I bet."

"Yeah." He didn't bother looking at the stars; he was watching for the next moose. "Ever thought about getting a telescope?"

"Binoculars work."

"Yeah." He was silent for a moment. "In high school my junior class drove to Tucson and visited the planetarium at the University of Arizona. They had it pointed right at the Orion nebula. It was amazing, like this star had exploded and smeared right across the sky."

She checked the exterior temperature readout. Thirteen below. The red digital three changed to a four as she watched. "Couldn't stay out very long to look, it'd be too cold."

"That's why God invented Carhartts."

She laughed, a low husk of sound that transported him instantly back to the moments in the clearing that afternoon, waiting without enthusiasm for Willard to show.